FINALLY FOREVER

NADIA LEE

To Yuka Yamamoto.
Thank you for your friendship and love.

1

NICHOLAS

"You're the biggest asshole in the world!"

I raise an eyebrow. Alicia's sharp accusation was expected, but the accompanying theatrics are over-the-top, even for her. Her impressive chest heaves in the low-cut green dress she bought with my money. Maybe she wants me to feel bad about turning her down, but all I can think is that she needs to see her colorist. Dark roots clash with her over-bleached platinum hair. And the fake lash over her left eye isn't well glued. Every time she blinks, it droops a little. *She can't feel that?*

Well-heeled diners in designer clothes start turning discreetly to catch the drama. A woman in a mauve dress drops her napkin and takes a quick look at our table as she retrieves it. These people might be wealthy enough to eat at a glitzy restaurant with a menu that doesn't have prices, but they aren't impervious to the thrill of witnessing a juicy scene. And Alicia's shrill tone promises just that.

"It isn't that much money," she adds in a slightly calmer voice. She knows I hate drama.

The disappointment from the people around us is palpable. They were hoping she'd throw the '98 Lafitte at me. But that'd be a terrible move. I'm steady and reasonable as long as I'm not pushed too far. But when I've had enough, I explode. Most people never see it because my threshold is high. Not even my brothers, except for that one time in high school.

"I'm not throwing money at some whim of yours," I say calmly.

"It's a *business*."

"With no plans or financial projections."

"It's going to be profitable, Nicholas. I'm giving you an opportunity to invest early. It's only two million dollars. Not that much money. Practically pocket change."

That's rich, coming from a girl who maxed out seven credit cards. The only reason she hasn't declared bankruptcy is that her hedge fund manager daddy is paying off the balances. "In that case, just scoop it up from between your couch cushions."

She leans forward. "Your new car is worth half a million."

"Exactly. I don't even spend two million on a car for *me*, and I'm not spending that kind of money on your 'business.' I'm not your piggy bank."

"I'll pay it back."

"A sloth will finish a marathon before you can make enough to repay the interest-free loan you're asking for."

"Why do you have to be so greedy?" she demands. "I've been counting on your support!"

"Because it's my money, not yours, and I'm not your father." My phone buzzes. I glance at the screen, which flashes a text from my stepsister.

—Georgia: Hey, are you in town? If so, can you come to Eat Pray Drink now?

—Me: What's that?

—Georgia: A bar. It's Molly's birthday, and she's a little drunk. And nobody can drive her home.

Molly. Georgia's best friend and fellow UC Irvine student, who just turned twenty-one today. Everyone she's out with is probably pickled in alcohol, including my stepsister.

—Georgia: I'm also in no condition to drive, so I'm going to walk over to Jerry's. But Molly probably wants to head home. You remember where our apartment is?

—Me: Of course. I helped you move.

Mainly because I wanted to spend some time with Molly. Otherwise I would've just hired a crew to help Georgia.

–Georgia: If you can't, I'll ask somebody else. Maybe Dan. I think he said he wasn't going to drink that much.

Dan, huh? Does she honestly think I'm going to trust a tipsy college kid with Molly?

–Me: I'll be there. Tell Molly to hang tight.

–Georgia: Thanks. I knew I could count on you.

More like I told her not to screw around with her or Molly's safety. Although those two didn't enter my life until three years ago, I take their wellbeing seriously. Georgia because she's my stepsister, and Molly... Well, because she's just special. The smile on her face when we first met struck me like Cupid's proverbial arrow, and I haven't been able to fully shake it off even though I know she's too young. I'm eight years older, and we don't have a lot in common.

But something about her keeps pulling me in. Hard to put my finger on it, but she makes me feel like I can just...breathe easy and be myself.

"Have you been listening to anything I said?" Alicia demands. The flush on her face is blotchy and unbecoming.

"I already told you no." I catch our waiter's eye and hand him the valet parking ticket. He disappears.

Alicia doesn't pay attention to what I'm doing with the waiter. To her, the restaurant staff is of no importance. Actually, most people seem to be beneath her notice unless they're rich or well connected. I probably shouldn't have gone out with her, even if she does make decent arm candy. But I was trying to forget my attraction to Molly, and the best course seemed to be to look for somebody who was nothing like her. A woman my age, with some fancy high-society gloss and...stuff.

And now here I am with this melodramatic banshee, who's shouting, "I said if you're going to be so cheap about it, at least take me to your father's birthday party!"

More eyes turn in our direction.

"No." I say it coolly but have to hide an inward shudder. As a rule, I avoid taking dates to Dad's birthday parties. They're *always* embarrassing, although he calls them "fun," and of course everyone in his circle agrees. You don't disagree with Ted Lasker, the Hollywood god who's produced nothing but mega-hit movies in his decades-long career. Even I admit his filmography is impressive. I drop a few hundred-dollar bills on the table. "I need to go."

"What? You can't do that!"

I get up.

"If you walk out, we're done!" She slaps the table hard enough to make the silverware rattle.

"Okay." I start moving away.

"*What?* Nicholas! No, wait!" Her chair scrapes the floor with a screech as she jumps to her feet.

But I get out before she does—my strides are longer, I have a head start and she's in wobbly heels.

The valet and I exchange cash and fob. I climb into my Aston Martin.

"You can't leave me here! I'm your girlfriend!" Alicia screams.

Girlfriend? Is she kidding? I lower the window on the passenger side about two inches. "I thought we were done. You broke up with me just now, remember?" Then I head down I-5 toward Irvine.

Eat Pray Drink is near the campus, and looks like a typical college bar. Garish lights, lots of neon writing on reflective black surfaces promising cheap booze and even cheaper food.

I park and climb out. A few girls are walking by. One says, "Wow." Some guys stare openly at the car, but I ignore them and roll my tight shoulders. There's a full moon in the night sky, unusually round and bright.

Pretty. The sight of it helps calm my annoyance from dinner. The moon shines the same way, no matter where you are...or how you feel. It isn't overly bright and flashy like the sun, either. It has a sort of understated steadiness that I find comforting.

Eat Pray Drink is packed tighter than a box of doughnuts. I'm overdressed in my Armani suit and Gucci loafers. The interior's dimly lit, and terrible songs boom in the air. The lyrics are more cuss words than not. Her friends should've taken Molly to someplace classier. At least with better alcohol that would be worth a hangover.

I finally spot Molly and Georgia in the back. My stepsister's eyes are slits, and she purses her mouth as some guy next to her says something.

Molly's next to Georgia, nursing a beer. From the way her body is swaying, I know she's had a few.

I walk up and put a hand on Molly's shoulder. "Hey."

She turns to me. "Hey, Nicholas." She slurs the greeting and gives me a wonderful bright smile. But her green eyes are positively glassy. "I'm twenty-one now!"

"Yes, I know. I sent you a happy birthday text this morning, remember?" I also sent her what Georgia calls "book money" so that I don't appear like a "weird guy with too much money." Georgia is *great* for my ego.

"Oh yeah, you did." Molly giggles. "Are you here to buy me a drink?"

"Yeah...not sure that would be a good idea. I'm actually here to take you home."

Georgia turns her head. "Oh hey, you're here."

"Yes." My eyes slide to the guy next to her.

"This is Jerry," Georgia says. "Jerry, my stepbrother Nicholas."

Jerry looks athletic, like a large tennis jock. I nod in acknowledgment and approval. At least she has somebody to walk with. I don't care what college administrators say about the safety of the area. I'm not letting my stepsister become a statistic. "Make sure she gets home safely, okay?"

He gives me one of those Hawaiian salutes, thumb and pinky extended from his fist, and waggles it. "You know it, step-bro."

I turn to Molly. "Let's take you home now."

"You're going to drive me back?" she says.

"Yep. I'm your personal chauffeur tonight." I help her up.

"Oh, goodie." She wobbles a little and then collapses against me. Her curves crush against my side, and my mouth dries. She's slightly sweaty and smells like alcohol. But she fits perfectly against me, and her softness says she's not a kid.

She's only twenty-one. I'm almost thirty. I have no business feeling these hot zings through my body. Georgia would've never asked me to take her best friend home if she knew the kind of unholy thoughts going through my mind.

As I escort her out of the bar, she slurs, "Good night!" to a bunch of people along the way. Many of them have to have hugs and confused farewells before she leaves. They probably came here to celebrate her birthday, but are too drunk now to remember.

Finally, we exit the bar. The night air couldn't feel sweeter. Molly sways along, her sweet little body pressed against me. Silently reciting the Lord's Prayer—which doesn't do much to distract me—I help her climb into the car, then get behind the wheel. She blinks a little.

"This is a real nice car," she says with awe, sliding her fingertips along the leather seat and dashboard. "Aren't you worried I might puke?"

"Feel that bad?" Concern roughens my voice. "You need a doctor or something?"

She giggles. "No. I'm fine."

We'll see. I should keep an eye on her. I'll never forget the group stomach-pumping incident back in college when a bunch of juniors overdrank. I start the engine.

"Do you know where I live?"

Sigh. "Yes. I helped Georgia move, remember?" I also carried tons of boxes for Molly because she was moving alone. For some reason, her father is never available to help. She was apologetic at first, then thanked me profusely. She made me and Georgia a quick chicken and veggie stir-fry for dinner. I couldn't remember the last time somebody cooked for me. And it was the best meal I'd had in forever. Something about Molly's home cooking will beat a Michelin three-star restaurant every time.

She yawns and stretches. "I thought maybe you forgot."

I remember everything about you. Memories accumulate. Each one is different, but they all make me smile with affection.

She makes a small noise deep in her throat and closes her eyes.

"Let me know if you aren't feeling well," I say as I maneuver the car gently through the traffic.

"Don't worry. Not gonna throw up in your car. Can't afford to clean it."

"I don't care about the car. I'm worried about you."

She looks like she's fallen asleep. "Thought I'd feel different when I was twenty-one, but it's pretty much the same," she murmurs.

"Yeah? What did you expect to feel?"

"More... I dunno. Adult? With some clear idea about how to get what I want?"

"What do you want?" Maybe I'll get it for her.

She grows silent again. "Wish Mom were here."

Confusion and sympathy fleet through me—Molly's mom passed away when she was just a kid.

"But she's gone, so..." She sighs. "I wish I could have someone who loves me the way I am," she mumbles, more to herself than me.

"Everyone loves you the way you are." I hate the resignation in her voice. Molly's normally bright, and she would never drop her guard long enough to show me a glimpse of her vulnerability if she were sober.

"Really?" Her tone says, *No way.*

"Uh-huh."

"It's so weird. Aren't you supposed to be cynical?"

"Me? Why?"

"Because you're rich? Don't people ask you for money and stuff? So you're naturally, like, 'Oh my God, I hate people.'"

I think back on the unpleasant dinner with Alicia. Then I look at Molly, who's holding on to the seatbelt like it's keeping her upright. I think about how flustered she was when I gave her a modest garnet anklet on her birthday three years ago. *Too expensive. Not something she could possibly accept.* "Well, sometimes. But not everyone is awful."

"You know what? It's totally okay for you to be rich," she says, trying to sound wise despite the drunkenness.

"Why? You like my money, too?" I smile.

She lets out a gasp. "No! I'd never be that shallow. I like you for your body."

Heat flares inside me, but then she lets out a drunken giggle, dousing the fire.

"Actually, I like your eyes." She twists a little to see me better. "They're really kind." Her soft voice is earnest. "You have a way of making people feel special just by gazing at them."

She tilts her head and peers at me as the city lights flash by. But she's the one who has the gift to make someone special. She looks at me like I'm perfect just for being myself, not for my money or my father.

She's never asked me for anything, and she never expects anything. If I lost all my money, she'd still treat me the same.

She gives me a pretty smile that makes my heart shiver, then leans back against the seat, closing her eyes.

She doesn't wake up until I take her into her apartment.

WHEN I CALL to check on her the next day, she groans with a vicious hangover but doesn't remember any of our conversation.

"You were so nice to drive me home, though," she says hoarsely. "You're the best, Nicholas. Just like your mom."

Something between shock and denial wells in my stomach. Mom is the one person I've done my best *not* to emulate. "Molly, my mother and I have nothing in common."

"Nonsense." She lets out a soft moan. "I have to go lie down before my head falls off. Thanks again."

2

MOLLY

−4 YEARS, 11 months and 23 days later

"ALL I WANT for my birthday is a hot, sexy, grumpy single dad, who hires me to be a nanny to his adorable little girl, then falls in love with me and asks me to marry him and have his baby." I glare at my virtually empty iced americano cup, an unjust state of affairs when I'm not feeling the happy effects of the caffeine yet. *Okay, out of coffee so soon?* I reach for the potato chips. I like this little deli near my work—the small, round wooden tables, matching chairs and colorful butterfly windchimes hanging from the ceiling. But they need to sell bigger coffees.

At least they're generous with the potato chips and pickles. Try to find the silver lining. It's depressing to note I'm about to be a year older when I haven't accomplished anything yet. Actually, forget accomplishments. I'd be thrilled if I just found some meaning and purpose to my life.

I should know what it is by now. I'm going to be twenty-six next week! Surely I wasn't put into this beautiful world just to be an accountant to an overly tanned, megalomaniacal creep and have transient, unfulfilling relationships.

"Grumpy single dad, huh? Is that a book you just read or something you want to read? And if it's the former, tell me the title, because I want to read it." Georgia grins, then bites into her BLT. We met as two bookworms in junior high who overcame our embarrassed awkwardness once we started to blabber about our love of *The Hunger Games* and *Twilight*. Over the years she's gotten taller and slimmer, and her dark brown hair curls adorably around her pretty face with its wide brown eyes and nose-bridge freckles. Meanwhile, I've grown taller and softly rounded, and my brown hair is as long and straight as uncooked spaghetti. But our love of reading and support for each other remain the same.

She's visiting this part of town to have lunch with me because she knows I hate having birthdays, and she considers it her duty as my best friend to cheer me up.

"Neither," I say, then exhale slowly. "It's what I wish *my* life could be." At least I'd have some noble higher purpose. Taking care of a young child is a serious but wonderful responsibility.

Georgia chuckles. "Don't we all? And Mr. Grumpy Single Dad is going to have the body of Apollo and the dick of an elephant on Viagra." She sighs, fluttering her eyelashes.

I snort. She's crazy in love with her boyfriend, and the faraway look she gets when she talks about him is genuine. "Never mind. I guess it is kind of a cliché."

"You love clichés. You call them 'comfort reads,' and everyone loves your comfort-read posts."

"Yeah..." I sigh. Even thinking about my popular Bookstagram account doesn't improve my mood. "But you know things like that don't happen in real life. Too trope-y, whereas real life is more normal. I'll settle for a contractor who hires me to be his accountant so I can help him make sense of his expanding empire."

Georgia laughs. "What the hell kind of romance is that? It sounds as dry as"—she looks around, seeking inspiration—"drywall."

"The realistic kind."

"Girl, nobody's going to be excited about working for a contractor who wants you to keep track of his taxes. Not even you could sell it to your followers. By the way, is this contractor hot? You didn't say."

"Probably. I haven't decided." My tone is light to hide how glum I feel. God, I'm dying to do something about my shitty life, except I don't know what to do. I feel stuck at the moment.

"Make him hot. And add some fun to it."

"Fine." I wave my pickle spear around like a magic wand. "He's hot."

"How hot?"

Nicholas hot. The answer almost pops out of my mouth, but I contain it. Nicholas is Georgia's stepbrother. Just thinking of him makes my heart do triple twists, but I know better than to show it. He's too sophisticated and cool—the Hope Diamond of men. And he's super nice to me, but only because I'm Georgia's best friend. If he knew I've been harboring this crazy crush on him, he'd probably get weirded out and pull away.

Since I see him once a month at the animal shelter where I volunteer, I don't want to make things awkward. He's like a beautiful special-edition hardback of your favorite book that you display in a case while your reading copy gets used and worn.

"Very," I say instead in my most innocent tone.

Georgia squints. "And what else? A hot contractor hiring you to be his accountant isn't doing it for me."

I tap the edge of my empty coffee cup, trying to think of some trope that will satisfy my bestie. "He decides to fake-date his new accountant?"

"Why can't he just fake-date you from the beginning, rather than hiring you first?"

"Because *that* way I'd have a valid reason to quit my job."

"Ohhh… Job hunting not going well?"

I nod, trying not to feel too dejected. "I've sent résumés to several places, but nothing. I'm beginning to wonder if there's something wrong with my qualifications or something." This lack of new-job progress is another reason I feel stuck.

"Nothing's wrong with your qualifications. Or you," Georgia says, picking up on my unspoken sense of inadequacy. "It's just a sign from the universe that you should open the indie bookstore you've always dreamed of."

"One in five U.S. businesses fail within the first year." That's me. All sunshine and positivity.

"You could be the four in five that don't."

"*And* almost half fail after five years."

"So be the other half. Right?"

Georgia is always confident that things are going to work out. But then, if anything happens, she has her dad to catch her. Me? I'd consider myself lucky if mine merely let me go splat. He wouldn't just let me fall; he'd berate me on my way down. Part of me is envious of her amazing relationship with her father. On the other hand, she had no part in her mother's death, so...

A sharp pain pierces my heart, and I hold my breath for a moment to recover.

You were only six.

But I could've been more patient. Acted better. My therapist back then told me it wasn't really my fault, and I nodded because I couldn't think of words to express how I didn't believe her.

"What's wrong?" Georgia's voice is soft with concern.

I paste on a smile. The lingering grief from my mother's untimely death isn't something I want to bring up. "Nothing. I was just thinking you're too optimistic."

"Somebody's gotta cheer you on. Oh, wait." Her eyes light up. "Is that why you're dreaming of fake-dating a successful contractor? So he can invest in your bookstore?"

"No. I wouldn't want a boyfriend to invest in my business, especially when there's such a big chance of failure."

"Come on. Why date a rich guy if you can't raid his bank account?"

I almost choke. "Because that's *mercenary*? Besides, mixing relationships and money is messy." I know that from personal experience. "Trying to make things work with another person is hard enough without muddying everything up with money."

"Did something happen between you and Owen?" Georgia asks, as perceptive as usual.

"Well..."

"What's wrong? I thought you were getting along great. I mean, he said he loved you..."

"I know." We started living together three months ago because he not only told me he loved me, he said he wanted to come home to me. It was *sooo* romantic—and a great dating milestone. It sounded like he was looking forward to more. Maybe even marriage.

Just the image of us in love, growing old together, made me smile with happiness.

I just didn't expect his "I love you" to be the peak of our relationship. But reality set in eventually. Georgia warned me that living with someone isn't easy—she's had three live-in boyfriends—but I didn't anticipate it to be this challenging.

"He won't leave me alone."

"So he's...what? Too frisky?" Georgia says. "It's better than what you had with Shawn."

My ex told me I had a negative effect on his libido when he had trouble rising to the occasion. He said my ridiculous expectations about men and relationships made things hard—although "things" clearly didn't include his penis. He claimed it wasn't fair that I wanted him to be like my book boyfriends when he never expected me to be like the women in his favorite porn. Then he looked at my waistline meaningfully.

That was the last time he got to look at me.

"Not really." I still can't decide exactly what to do about my relationship with Owen. I feel like it should be salvageable somehow, but I don't know how. And there's an uncomfortable knot in my belly about our relationship that continues to grow bigger as time goes by. Whenever Owen says, "Love you, babe," it shrinks a little, but then it goes back to expanding.

"Things are more complicated with Owen than Shawn," I say finally.

Georgia's eyes are glowing murderously. She knows about Shawn's shitty comments toward the end that made me break up with him. "What did Owen do?"

"It isn't, like, *one thing*. More a combination of stuff. Sometimes I want to talk to him about if we're on the same page about what we want—and where we see our relationship going. I think I got a little overcome when he told me he loved me, and moved in with him too quickly." None of my previous boyfriends had ever said the words, and they were just *wonderful* to hear, especially a day after my dad told me nobody would ever love me the way I was. I even cried a little.

"Have you tried talking to him?" Georgia says.

"Sure. Lots of times. But whenever I do, he says he has a deadline for paying publications. And he's like, 'You understand I have to do this right now, don't you, babe?' What else can I do, except nod considerately and go away?"

"How about after he's done?"

"I've tried, but... He just wants to close his eyes and drink his beer. He says nothing else really matters because he loves me and that's what's important." As sweet as it was to hear those words, my vague sense of perplexity didn't really go away. But I shut up because it seemed wrong to argue with a guy telling me he loves me when not even my own father tells me that.

"Maybe you should write down what's bothering you and make an appointment to talk to him. Dad does that with Nikki sometimes because she's so busy," Georgia says.

"Yeah. And your stepmom is easily distracted." We sit on that for a few moments. "But that isn't all that's bothering me. Every time I try to read, he interrupts me. When he knows I'm making posts and reels for my account, he wants to discuss the bills."

"The *bills*?"

"Yeah. He wants to rehash how we should split the utilities, even though we agreed on fifty-fifty before I moved in."

Red suffuses her cheeks. "Does he think you should pay more?"

"No, worse. He just wants to argue about the split for a few minutes, then agree that fifty-fifty is fair after all. But by then, I'm so emotionally frazzled, I can't focus on reading or making posts or anything."

"What a dickhead."

"When I told him it wasn't cool for him to interrupt me like that, he said—and I quote—'It's not a paying gig, just some silly book stuff. So who cares?'"

She bristles. "Did you kick his ass?"

"I've tried to talk to him about his behavior, but he just kisses me and says, 'Love you, babe.'"

"Oh my God. That's so passive-aggressive."

"Maybe he doesn't realize what he's doing is making me feel disrespected in our relationship."

"Is he jealous that his account has sixty-three thousand followers, while you have over a hundred thousand?" Georgia asks.

"That's silly. We aren't in competition. We don't even talk about the same things." Owen is a food and restaurant critic, so his account is all about the best spots to eat in SoCal.

"Maybe you should make puking sounds in the background while he's recording videos for his account." A vindictive gleam glints in my bestie's blue eyes.

"I might, if he pushes me much more. I just wish he'd quit saying my reading is making me have 'unrealistic expectations' that he doesn't feel he can meet. It'd be better if he just didn't say a word about my books and kept it to himself."

"What else does he say?" She can tell there's more.

I sigh. "Last week, I was reading *Big Beautiful*, and he said, 'No billionaire with a six-pack wants to be seen with a fat chick.'"

Georgia gasps. "Oh my God, I want to stab him!"

"Gotta admit, I thought about it. Or hitting him with a frying pan for being so insensitive." I shake my head. "He wasn't like that before. Or maybe we just didn't spend enough time together until I moved in." It's one of my biggest regrets about the whole thing with Owen. I wished I'd been more cautious—ensured that I was one hundred percent certain before moving in—rather than getting swept up in the moment when he said he loved me.

"Buyer's remorse doesn't kick in until after you've bought," she says, totally on Team Molly.

"I told him the title referred to the hero's package, not the size of the main female character, while giving him *that look*." It was unfair of me —Owen isn't small. But I was too upset to care. "He didn't speak to me for three days, and I got so much reading and other stuff done. And that bothers me. Being ignored by my boyfriend for three days shouldn't have felt..." I trail off, struggling to find the right word.

"Good...?" Georgia prompts.

"Good. Yeah." I feel awful that it's really the only suitable word. It's painful to realize that the first guy who told me he loved me is someone I'm struggling to live with. *What's wrong with me?* Or is it him? Owen seemed fine before. Or is it us as a couple?

"Girl." Georgia makes a face. "You need to get rid of Owen. And your shitty job. You need a life makeover."

I laugh. "A life makeover?"

"Hey, it's a thing. There's a podcast about it. Here." She taps her phone and texts me a link. "You should check it out. It'll give you some clarity. I listen to these ladies all the time. There's even a life makeover retreat in Seattle. Wanna come?"

"Uh... I'll take a look, but no guarantees." Part of me says I need to start looking for a new apartment, especially if Owen and I can't have a serious discussion about our relationship. We can't continue like this. I wish our issues were something we could fix—because love conquers all. But real lives aren't romance novels with a third-act breakup.

"I'm so sorry, girl. Hopefully, your birthday gets better, and you run into a hot billionaire who needs you more than you need him and treats you like the queen that you are."

I laugh. "Yeah. So do I." I smile to hide my wistfulness over how my life is off the rails even though I'm almost twenty-six and feel like I should have it all figured out by now.

3

NICHOLAS

I LOOK around the ballroom at the Ritz for a final check before my mother, the star of tonight's event, arrives. She asked for a particularly lavish birthday party with all her friends, acquaintances and the other mothers of my six half-brothers. So I invited them, but not my brothers themselves because she wanted Dad present, and they can't stand him. I try to avoid Dad as much as possible as well. Nothing embarrasses the man. Thank God secondhand humiliation isn't fatal. Otherwise, my life would've been over before I became a teenager.

Mom will be thrilled when she walks in. Four hundred balloons and teddy bears fill the space, just like she wanted, and exactly one thousand red roses are arranged in beautiful clusters everywhere. She asked for a quartet to start the party, then a DJ to get the crowd going and dancing, so that's been arranged. She couldn't decide between a buffet or a sit-down dinner, so I got both—a seven-course sit-down dinner with a dessert buffet. Plus a chocolate fountain in the center because she said she had to have one.

It took four weeks to pull it together, but the result is stunning. Not even Athena—Grant's super-critical mother—or Rachel—Griffin's hyper-melodramatic mother—will be able to find fault with the arrangements.

The only thing I need to get the party started is Mom.

I check the time. She's ten minutes late, which is to be expected. Mom isn't known for being punctual. That virtue belongs to her husband Paul. Although I could call him my "stepfather," it's never felt right. Mom didn't marry him until I was twenty-six, well past the time I needed a father figure in my life. The man is also perceptive and wise enough not to expect me to play his son.

"Just where is she?" Athena's words are clipped, and she looks at me like it's my fault her time is being wasted. A lanky strawberry blonde, she has a stratospheric IQ and gets bored easily. She believes most people are too dumb to associate with. She only deigned to come to the party because she's decided I have a sufficient number of brain cells to meet her standards, and she finds Mom likable and funny.

"Maybe she couldn't find a date," Rachel says, tossing her long golden hair over a delicate shoulder in a typically practiced gesture—she never does anything without knowing the exact effect it will have on her audience. She's in a white Grecian dress that shows off her lithe body and legs. She makes sure to stand with her hips canted just so, her chin tilted at the perfect angle. She's a former model who every woman wanted to be and every man wanted to marry, and she knows how to pose to showcase her assets.

"She's married, Rachel," Athena points out stiffly. Her tone says it's taking all her patience not to call Rachel an idiot.

"So? She might want some variety. And there's something about youthful men that just makes you feel *young.*" Rachel leans closer to her date, who's probably in his mid-twenties. He has an exceptionally pretty face, with deep-set blue eyes, a rosy mouth and a slim, wiry body that could pass for a dancer's, except he doesn't have the grace. Rachel likes her men young, malleable and photogenic. She doesn't care to be seen with men who don't enhance her.

My brother Griffin was relieved she found a date for the party. Rachel likes to have him act as her backup when she has boy-toy issues, but Griffin is too devoted to his wife and triplets to spend his free time catering to his mother's vanity.

"It's incredibly unprofessional to be late to your own party," comes Jeremiah's voice from behind me. She's one of the mothers—and one of the nastiest legal sharks in the country. I'm not too surprised that she showed up. Even though she doesn't bother with much that doesn't involve billable hours, she is quite fond of my mom. Calls her the life of the party.

Jeremiah is in a conservative navy jumpsuit more fitting for a courtroom than a party, and a huge diamond hangs from her slim neck. Her hair is dyed the shade of fresh blood.

"You look like your hair committed hara-kiri." Athena's voice is smooth, but it isn't enough to hide the naked blade underneath.

Here we go, I think with a silent, resigned sigh. Athena might be a genius, but she's also predictable in her dislike of Jeremiah. They're probably both too smart and too stubborn to get along. Athena hates people who argue with her, and Jeremiah hasn't seen an argument she didn't want to rip apart.

"It's goat's blood. What do you think? I thought if you invited me over it would match your home décor." Jeremiah smiles that shark smile. Athena at one point dated some unhinged moron who thought he could cast a love spell on her by spattering her home with fresh goat blood. She's still embarrassed and upset about the incident, since Jeremiah calls it proof that "the great Athena Grant isn't infallible." That man's lucky the police arrested him and threw him in jail. Otherwise, Athena would've found a way to rip him into little pieces and feed them to rabid dogs.

She slowly turns red. It's the kind of red you get before you scream, "Fuck you," and launch yourself at the other person. I begin to move away from the mothers before they ask me to take sides.

Where the hell is Mom?

Even Dad, who likes to make a late entrance, has arrived. Dark-haired with a square jaw, he stands tall and grins smugly at the world like he's God's gift to humanity. But then, why not? He's been consistently successful throughout a career in an unbelievably competitive field. People worship him, fawn over him and credit him for launching—or in some cases rebooting—their careers. Even studio executives kiss his feet for the oodles of profit he brings in.

Joey, his assistant with a forehead the size of a basketball court and hair the color of a shriveled California navel orange, is following him.

His chest is puffed out, his shoulders pushed back. The smile on his face is more than a little arrogant—he knows he's gatekeeper to the all-important Ted Lasker. Of course, that shit-eating grin changes to one of subservience as soon as his eyes meet Dad's.

"Hello, Nicholas." Rick Gordon, the mayor of our beautiful city, grips my hand. "When is Nikki going to be here?" His cornflower-blue eyes grow soulful as he speaks of my mother, and his face falls a little like a basset hound's. His lank brown hair adds to the effect.

The man's married—happily so, according to the people in charge of managing his pristine political image. But Rick doesn't bother to hide the unrequited crush he has on my mother. Or maybe he doesn't know he's wearing his heart on his sleeve. If Mom ever got tired of Paul and divorced him, Rick would dump his wife on the spot to pursue her.

Of course, he'd have to fight a lot of other guys for her attention. She has a particular gift for making men feel great about themselves.

"Hopefully soon. Let me check." I smile politely, then step away and pull out my phone. I scowl at the missed text.

–Marissa: Hey, I heard you bought LA Food Digest. Can you make me the CFO? I'd be fabulous in the position. I'm looking for a new career, and I feel like you're the person I can count on to help out.

Marissa is someone I escorted to a social function a couple of months ago, and the woman is woefully unqualified for the CFO position. The only numerical skill she has is an ability to count by twos —and that only to tally up the number of shoes in her closet. She spent the entire time we were out talking about her collection—and which ones she likes to wear to bed. The conversation could've been bottled as a form of chemical castration. I couldn't care less about her shoes or her plastic tits or the cloying perfume that gave me a low-grade headache.

We haven't spoken since then, and I don't understand why she thinks she can just contact me for a job. *Count on me, indeed.* I block her number, then type up a text for my mother.

–Me: When are you going to arrive? Everyone's already here, including Jeremiah.

Mom specifically said she wanted to hang out with Jeremiah. Otherwise, I would've tried to avoid having her at the same event as

Athena. I glance in their direction. They're still speaking, their smiles wider and brighter, showing lots of shiny, bleached teeth.

The text goes unread. That's unusual. Did she forget to charge her phone?

I wait two more beats, then text Paul.

—Me: When are you and Mom going to get here?

—Paul: Get where?

What the hell? He knows about the party. He was present when Mom and I talked about it, and he's a reliable kind of guy, unless he's suddenly developed a cocaine habit.

—Me: Her birthday party at the Ritz.

Three dots appear, then disappear.

Finally a text from Mom arrives.

—Mom: Enjoy the party, love! I'm about to board my flight to Madrid.

Madrid?

—Me: What are you talking about? Everyone is here! You asked for this party!

—Mom: Did I? Michelle said my calendar was empty, so I thought I didn't have anything to do. But don't worry, I won't be alone. Paul and Georgia are coming with me!

She has to be kidding. Mom's assistant Michelle is in her twenties, but a comatose donkey would be more organized. As much as I dislike Joey, I wish I could clone him and give him to Mom. He'd never let her forget an event.

—Mom: I'm so sorry. I'm sure the party is fabulous. I already feel incredibly blessed to have you in my life. You know that, don't you?

It'd be more of a blessing if she'd just *shown up*. She loves to travel, and she likes to do what she wants, when she wants, but does she have to do it *today*? After promising me she'd attend?

On the other hand, why did I ever think she'd come? She keeps her word maybe half the time. Even my being valedictorian at Brown wasn't enough. She swore she'd come to graduation, but ended up texting me the flight to the Bahamas she'd booked for me, saying it was more fun to celebrate that way.

And she threw a party so delightful, it *almost* soothed the hurt she delivered by not showing up to see me get my diploma. She always knows just how to smile and what to say to make you feel special. It's just...it's always done on *her* schedule and whim.

—Mom: They're boarding, so gotta go. But I'll bring you presents from Madrid! I'm also going to hit other European cities, so if you want anything, let me know! Love you!

She sends me a selfie of her smiling as she's walking down the skybridge. She's even winking and blowing me a kiss. The personification of *joie de vivre.*

I let out a soft sigh. "I love you too, Mom. Happy birthday," I murmur, then put away my phone.

I look at the setup, and another small sigh wells. I signal the staff. "Let's start the champagne toast."

At least all the balloons, teddy bears and flowers won't be wasted. I've made arrangements to donate them to local pediatric oncology departments. This birthday celebration was wasted, but hopefully Molly likes what I planned for hers, even if it's small and not particularly spectacular.

4

MOLLY

Owen's passed out on his belly next to me, his face pressed into the pillows. His brown hair is sticking up, making the back of his skull look like a hedgehog. He smells like stale booze. He didn't come home until well after I'd gone to bed with my trusty Kindle. He probably spent Friday night out clubbing with his friends. He says it energizes him. But the truth of the matter is he's going to spend all day today feeling miserable. I know from experience it's best to stay away from him when he's going to be crabby from a hangover. He makes the three-year-old boy I babysat in middle school look rational and calm by comparison.

I slip out of bed so he can get some extra snooze time and then shower, getting ready to go to Furry Haven. I volunteer once a month and love taking care of the animals at the shelter. It's the best feeling when we get to match them with new owners, who—hopefully—will love them to pieces and give them all the adoration they deserve.

Because every one of those animals just wants someone to love them. And in return, they give their owners unconditional loyalty and love. You literally become the center of their universe.

I pick out an old pink T-shirt with a funny quote from one of my favorite rom-coms, denim shorts and flip-flops. I'm certain Brenda's going to ask me to help wash the dogs.

I leave a short handwritten note for Owen to let him know I went to the shelter. Last month, he forgot that I had to go and acted like I'd abandoned him in his time of greatest need. His reaction was a little shocking—he'd never behaved like my volunteer work at the shelter bothered him until then. He even asked if I could quit. When I told him no, he gave me a look of absolute betrayal.

As I drive toward Furry Haven, a thought pops up.

Serial killers don't like animals.

Actually, *serial killers* practice *on animals* would be more correct. But Owen's recent attitude toward my time at Furry Haven is another thing that's bugging me. What kind of person gets jealous over some poor homeless animals? I wonder what he'd say if I asked him if we could adopt Cooper, an adorable golden retriever. Probably have a conniption fit.

Does Owen resent that I have outside interests? But I wouldn't be me if I didn't. Seriously, who is Molly Greene if she doesn't read, share her love of books on Instagram or volunteer? Without those things, I'd just be an accountant at a gym who's in a relationship with Owen. But I'm more than that. My identity can't just be my job or my boyfriend.

The uncomfortable knot in my belly grows bigger. I should force a talk with Owen, but he told me he has a deadline this coming Wednesday. Maybe after my birthday on Friday? I don't want to have an uncomfortable conversation right before my birthday, and he did say he wanted to take me out...although he didn't specify when or where.

So. Have the conversation next Saturday or Sunday. See if we can fix things. An open, honest discussion should help. It's possible we aren't communicating well about what we need from each other. Even in romance novels, couples go through crises—and make up. This is just a third-act breakup of sorts. A hiccup before the happy ending.

Furry Haven is in a pleasant part of the city, near a small park that's perfect for walking dogs. It's in a surprisingly compact square building, the white paint glaring in the California sun. The lot is mostly empty except for the cars that belong to the staff and volunteers. I don't spot one that looks like it cost a kidney, so that means Nicholas isn't here. He volunteers at the shelter too, but there are times he can't come because he's busy with work. His billion-dollar empire doesn't run itself.

Brenda's blue-green eyes light up when I walk in. "Oh thank God!" Her cropped copper hair glints under the fluorescent light as she opens her arms. A colorful Hawaiian shirt stretches over her chest, and she wraps me in a hug. "I was wondering when you'd come."

"Why? Is Cooper being difficult?"

"Along with all the others. It's like nobody wants to get washed today."

I smile. "Do they ever?"

"No, but today's extra bad." She turns around, tugging me toward the washing area. She's in denim shorts that show off well-muscled calves. She used to play soccer in high school and college.

I help her. Jessie, a high school junior who started to volunteer two months ago to beef up her extracurriculars, lets out a soft sigh. "Does this mean I get to take a short break?"

"Yes," I say with a laugh. Jessie's a good kid who loves animals—she has a poodle at home—but she's not used to washing this many dogs.

I let her take a moment to slouch on a metal folding chair and help Brenda, who seems to have unlimited stamina to deal with animals— and everything that needs to be done at the shelter. Like most shelters, Furry Haven never has enough money to do everything. Brenda wears all sorts of hats, not just managing the shelter but also handling the social media and PR.

"So were you able to find someone to do the charity auction?" I ask, toweling off Cooper, who is the last one to get washed. A charitable foundation is hosting a bachelorette auction, and unlike most such events, where the foundation decides where the money goes, the bachelorettes can decide what the funds are used for. When Brenda heard about it, she asked me if I wanted to auction off a date for the shelter.

She might as well have tased me. Put myself on a stage in front of people? And hope they like me enough to fork over their hard-earned money for a few hours of time together? I'd rather watch a horror movie and have nightmares for a month.

But then Brenda gave me her patented *sad puppy eyes*. "It's just... money's so tight. It'd mean a lot."

Noooo, don't look at me like that... "Honestly, I don't think I'd get more than a few hundred bucks."

The puppy eyes became even more sorrowful. "It would really mean a lot to the dogs. Besides, you underestimate your attractiveness, Molly."

I laughed, but it came out shaky. It's always uncomfortable when people say I'm pretty because I know it isn't true. They're either being nice, or nasty and sarcastic. I've gotten both, although thankfully the former is more common. Georgia told me I should just say, "Thanks," when people compliment on my looks, but that sounds like I'm accepting their praise as is—which is a different kind of awkward.

"If you can't find anybody, how about if I just write a check for five hundred bucks?" I finally offered. The amount wasn't something I could easily afford, but I also didn't mind since it was for a good cause. Of course, this was before I realized how incompatible Owen and I were, and I might need the money to move out.

So right now I'm praying Brenda found some other woman for the auction.

She stretches her shoulders, watching Jessie take Cooper to dry him off. "Uh-huh. An Instagram fitness influencer agreed to commit her proceeds to us." She smiles. "It's going to be great. She's fairly well known, and she's gorgeous. Should bring some attention to the shelter, too, since she offered to make some posts about Furry Haven. We need money, but some extra volunteers wouldn't hurt."

The last part is true. Although Furry Haven has been lucky to get some generous anonymous donations, Brenda is terrified that money might dry up. Before I started volunteering, the shelter had a crisis with funds when one of the donors quit sending checks. She's exceptionally frugal now, but even if she were more relaxed about finances, there isn't enough to hire a sufficient number of staff to take care of all the dogs. Basically, without volunteers, the shelter can't function.

"You might know her," Brenda continues. "Dana Mincer?"

Ugh. It's like a spoonful of lemon juice just teleported into my mouth, but I manage to maintain a neutral expression. Dana has hundreds of thousands of followers on Instagram, and she is good looking. So I should be happy she's decided to champion the shelter, even though she was mean to me in high school. If I didn't see her at the gym all the time, I might believe she'd changed since then. But Dana is still the same, just older and blonder.

I shake off my less-than-great feelings about her. These dogs aren't going to walk themselves. I start to gather the ones who haven't had a chance to go out yet. I'm so relieved I'm dealing with the happier dogs. Some of the older ones are so depressed about being abandoned, they won't even go for walks, and they break my heart. I wish I could do something to make them feel better, but the only thing would be to bring them back to their owners, and that's beyond my ability. It makes me feel so helpless and angry. Those dogs are wasting their love on the wrong people. Sometimes I wish the dogs' lives were romance novels, so I could give them all fantastic happy endings while gifting their owners with incurable gout in a bonus epilogue.

"Ooh, look!" Jessie squeaks and points out the window facing the parking lot. "It's Nicholas!"

"Wait, I thought he wasn't coming today!" another volunteer says.

"Does that matter? He's here and he's hot!"

"Shit! I should've worn something prettier!"

Wouldn't we all have?

I smooth my hair, hoping it isn't a complete mess after helping Brenda wash the dogs. And I'm not the only one.

A thrill ripples through the volunteers. I'm susceptible as well, even though I shouldn't be this shivery when I'm already in a committed relationship. But Nicholas is so gorgeous with those stunning dark gray eyes and Cupid's-bow mouth. And the body...

The breadth of his thickly muscled shoulders always makes me sigh, whether they're cased in a suit or a T-shirt—like today. His torso tapers down to a narrow waist, and as he strolls into Furry Haven, his quads flex and bulge under his shorts. Jessie isn't the only one eye-fucking him.

He's like some kind of exotic, forbidden man-fruit. Or maybe a panther lazily stalking you. How can anyone's body be that perfect? And he's one of the nicest people in the world! Given how busy he is, it's incredible he makes time to volunteer at the shelter. Just goes to show how generous and sweet he is.

He flashes a smile. "Good morning."

Female sighs go up around me. Nobody is immune to his smile—including me, even though I've seen it since I was eighteen. I'll probably never get used to its impact.

Boom boom boom boom...

I press a hand over my erratic heart, praying it will settle down. If a cardiologist were to examine me now, he'd push me into an OR for immediate surgery. Hearts can't be designed to pump this hard.

"Hi, Molly." His warm voice flows over me like a chocolate martini—sweet and potent.

"Hi." My response is more of a squeak than I'd like, and I groan inwardly. *Smooth, Molly. Very smooth. Might as well stick your tongue out and pant while you're at it.*

Nicholas's smile only widens. He probably doesn't even notice my silly reactions. Not when girls far prettier than me fawn over him.

"Ready to walk 'em?" He tilts his chin at the leashes I'm holding.

"Yeah." The dogs wag their tails faster, probably hoping he's my "safety partner," so we can get going. Although Furry Haven is in a nice area, we had an incident last month when some weirdo flashed one of the volunteers during a walk. Since then, nobody's allowed to take the dogs out without a partner. I think flashers might enjoy the chance for a twofer, but I'm not the one making the rules here.

"Awesome. Let me take a few." A couple of the younger ones bark, unable to contain their excitement.

Nicholas reaches out for the leashes. His hand brushes mine, and an electric zing shoots through my body. I bite my lip and drop my gaze to hide my reaction.

Envious gazes focus on me, but I merely smile and walk out of the shelter with Nicholas.

"I thought Matt was going to be my safety partner." I keep my tone all casual and cool as he reins in the excited dogs. Cooper in particular is overly excitable.

We walk out of the small building that houses the shelter. The dogs pant and pull on the leashes, and Nicholas tightens his grip. The man knows how to exert control, which is hot as hell. His forearm muscles flex, and I stare in absolute fascination.

"He apparently had something come up," Nicholas answers with a shrug.

"I see." I think, but am unable to add anything.

I've harbored something between an infatuation and hopeless love for him since I met him eight years ago at high school graduation. He looked at me indulgently and treated me like a kid he liked better than most because of my friendship with his stepsister, Georgia. After all, I was just finishing high school, and he'd been out of college for several years. There was nothing in common between us, and nothing about me that would draw his eye.

Besides, nothing could've made our differences clearer than his giving me a gorgeous garnet anklet on my nineteenth birthday. I was shocked and uncertain as to what to say. The jewelry seemed so expensive, and not something I could casually accept. And isn't jewelry for somebody you like romantically? Or was I reading too much into it? My head sort of went blank, and I panicked with the pressure to say something. Although I can't remember exactly what, I'm pretty sure I blabbered a bunch of nonsense and upset him. Since then, he's never given me anything except a short text and a hundred-dollar Amazon gift card for my birthdays.

And I give him a handmade card in return for his because he said that's all he wanted. He was probably just trying to be nice. After all, I can't buy him anything, not when he's a billionaire with everything he could desire at his fingertips. I'm just an accountant who lives from paycheck to paycheck. He travels all over the world—in private jets—and I don't even have my passport. He dates models with toned abs and endless legs, and I'm like... Well, let's just say the modeling agencies aren't breaking down my door. I'm just a normal girl with a soft, un-toned body and legs of average length. We couldn't be more different. Like a fish and a bird.

I can't imagine being with Nicholas. He's out of this galaxy, beyond my reach. It's like trying to do a split—except that if I overextend myself, I might just rip my heart out. Or, worse, have him pity me.

Besides, I'm loath to do anything that would make him feel awkward around me. He's too nice to say anything, but he might avoid me or quit coming to the shelter. I'm just happy to be able to spend some time with him once a month, doing good deeds for animals who need extra care and love.

We walk along the path toward the park near the shelter. It's a favorite spot for the dogs to explore.

"I heard you went to some gala for your brother. Grant, I think?" I say, oh-so casually.

"Yeah. Some sort of charity he wanted to support, and I wanted to help." Nicholas's tone is kind and patient, just like the man himself. "Speaking of which, I hear there's a charity auction Furry Haven's going to be part of. Three weeks from now, right? Are you going to be there? To auction off a date?"

"Who, me? Oh. Ha-ha. No."

He frowns. "Brenda didn't ask?"

"Well, yeah, she did." I clear my throat, wondering if that sounded arrogant, like, *of course she did—I'm hot.* "I think she asked everyone. But anyway, no. Not me."

"Why not?"

Is it me, or does he sound genuinely perplexed? Except I don't know why he would be. "Well, you know. The shelter already has somebody who's going to do the auction, and I wasn't sure if I could raise any real money."

His frown stays, and I realize he might be thinking that it was selfish of me to refuse to help raise money for the shelter. "But I, you know, offered to donate some money to the shelter if she couldn't find anyone."

His frown deepens. *What did I say?*

Finally, he lets out a small sigh. He opens his mouth like he's about to say something, but shuts up. "So. How have you been?" he asks finally.

"Great." I flash him a bright smile. *Thank God we aren't talking about the auction anymore.* I try to come up with something interesting and exciting to say about my life. Sadly, being an accountant doesn't lend itself to thrills, and I don't think my boss being overly touchy-feely or that I'm looking for a new job behind his back is the kind of topic that Nicholas will find interesting. And I doubt he wants to hear about the spicy romance novel I finished last week. Actually, it's inappropriate to talk to him about a book that's more like a collection of sex scenes strung together with a threadbare plot. It could come across like I was trying to hit on him, which I'm totally not.

"I moved in with Owen three months ago," I blurt out finally. Not because I think my boyfriend is a super exciting subject for Nicholas, but because it seems like an inoffensive topic that won't bore him to tears.

"Sounds serious." Nicholas seems...somber.

Not sure why. I try a small laugh to lighten the mood. "Yeah, I guess. He told me he loved me, so..." I smile brightly because that seems like the thing to do. "But living together isn't easy." Talk about the understatement of the century.

"Oh yeah? How come?"

"Just...different lifestyles and expectations." I shrug, like it isn't a big deal. It's one thing to dump everything on Georgia—she's my bestie. It's something else with Nicholas. Now I wish I hadn't brought Owen up at all. I should've talked about the apartment I gave up. It was perfect— the rent was reasonable, and it was in a safe area near the Get Jacked Gym where I work.

Of course, that's about as exciting as discussing how to maximize your employer's contribution to your 401(k).

My heart aches. This is another sign that Nicholas and I are totally different. I can't seem to come up with anything to talk to him about. If I were better traveled or worldlier, I could be regaling him with the dirty martini I had in London or the kind of car I bought to help fill my twelve-vehicle garage or something.

I get a ping on my phone and let out a breath with relief at the distraction. "'Scuse me for a sec." I check the screen.

–Brenda: Hey, ask Nicholas if it's okay to take some photos of him walking the dogs for our website. He's so gorgeous. The last time we posted a pic of him, we got twenty percent more donations and volunteer inquiries than usual.

Last time, the shot "of him" was in the mix because the shelter took multiple group photos to showcase what we do. This one's going to be just him and the dogs, and I don't know how he'll feel about it. Georgia said Nicholas values his privacy, and I've never seen him do an interview or any kind of social media.

—Brenda: Pick a good location—maybe that park near us?—and see if he's willing to pose with the dogs, one by one. So we can use them for the adoption page, too.

Oh, Brenda. Why don't you have me ask him for a kidney, too?

I steal a quick glance at Nicholas. He looks back, gray eyes curious.

I clear my throat. "Would it, um, be okay to take some pictures of you for the shelter? Brenda wants to put them up on the website. Probably on social media, too. But you don't have to if you don't want. It's no big deal. There are other photos." I add the last part so he doesn't feel pressured. It's a big deal for him to spend time at the shelter because he's a busy man, and I feel bad about asking him to do more than he is, even if it is for the cause. Brenda is fabulous, but sometimes she focuses so much on the shelter's mission that she forgets not everyone wants to do things her way—or with her level of dedication.

"Sure. Anything you need, Molly." He smiles.

My belly flutters, and heat infuses my cheeks. I know he means pictures, but when he talks like that while smiling at me, I feel like he's granting a wish because it's *me* who's asking.

"It might take a few minutes." My voice is a little breathless. So embarrassing. But I can't control my reaction. It's like feeling warm in the presence of the sun.

"No problem. Like I said, anything you need is yours."

5

NICHOLAS

I'm RUNNING *WAAAY* LATE for the ten o'clock brunch with my brothers. Well, technically we don't have to be there by ten because we're all busy and we understand showing up at all is a huge commitment. But still. I hate being late.

My relationship with my six brothers matters. Time is the one commodity we can't get more of, no matter how much money we have. But however busy and tired we are, we try to meet up regularly. And my brothers have been rock-solid anchors in my life.

Sadly, my parents aren't people I can rely on. Our father, the vaunted Ted Lasker, still believes he's a man in his twenties—invincible and irresistible. He doesn't practice safe sex, either, since he's confident his second vasectomy is good.

When the first one failed, he fathered us—seven boys with seven different women—in the space of four months. He was one lucky bastard to avoid getting a variety of STDs on the side as well.

It wouldn't shock me if the second one failed and we ended up with seven more infant half-brothers. But just because it wouldn't be surprising doesn't mean it wouldn't be scandalous or repulsive. Noah said he sent Dad a year's supply of condoms four years ago, but Joey sent them back, saying, "I've provided everything Ted needs," in that stiff tone of voice he uses when he feels unjustly judged.

I pull into Grant's home, a giant mansion with a massive garden and a tennis court. It's his turn to host the brunch. I spot five cars—which means I'm the last one here. Grant's wife Aspen is probably already out with Amy, Sierra and Lucie, the other wives. So far, four of my six brothers have fallen in love *and* gotten married.

Lucky bastards.

I managed the fall-in-love part, but getting married?

That, I haven't been able to do. In fact, I haven't even held her hand. And she's in love with somebody else. She flushed like a girl with a crush when she was talking about her boyfriend.

He told me he loved me.

Damn it. It was all I could do to not declare, "I fell in love with you first! Before you met that bastard." I'm sure that would have gone over well.

My heart thumps glumly, but I shove aside my morose thoughts. They don't serve any purpose. I'm here to have a good time with my brothers.

I walk into the giant foyer. Grant went overboard with the marble and crystal, but somehow the place looks homey. Must be Aspen's touch. It wasn't this welcoming before.

My brothers are in the breakfast room, grabbing food from an enormous spread Grant has had catered. The scent of strong coffee permeates the air. My brothers are coffee addicts. I prefer Earl Grey, but drink coffee when we're together.

We sport basic similar features that demonstrate we're related, even though we have different mothers. It's the dark coloring and the square jaw we got from Dad. Although my brothers don't like to think about it, we also got our height and frame from him, too. I thank my lucky stars Dad wasn't a weak-chinned, hunchbacked midget.

My brothers are casually dressed, except for Emmett, who probably has to go to the office afterward. He's a workaholic, and although he quit spending so much time at work after he married Amy, he's still ridiculously busy. Venture capital can be demanding, and Emmett tends to put more things on his plate than is wise.

"Hey, you made it!" Grant grins. "I was wondering if you could come."

"Wouldn't miss it." I grab some scrambled eggs and sausages and take the empty seat next to Noah. Huxley pours a coffee and hands it to me.

"Heard about what happened at your mom's birthday party," Grant says, his voice full of sympathy.

I give him a what-can-I-do shrug. "I kind of knew Mom wasn't going to show," I say, pretending it didn't bother me when she opted to fly to Madrid instead. When the same kind of humiliation is heaped upon you over and over again, the pain becomes dull and numbing, rather than sharp and burning. At least none of my brothers have mothers like mine. "But some local kids with cancer got some toys and balloons, so..." I shrug again.

Sebastian sighs. "She's literally treating you like an experiment pigeon."

"A what?"

"There was this experiment where pigeons were put in a cage and had to peck a button to get food. At first the pecking always produced food, so the pigeons quit pecking pretty quickly when the scientists changed the setting so food wouldn't come out anymore. Then the button gave out food every other peck, and then every third one, and when the food was cut off, the pigeons took longer to stop pecking it. But when pecking the button gave out food randomly—so sometimes they got something and sometimes they didn't—the birds just kept on pecking forever, hoping that maybe this time they'd get fed."

I exhale roughly. Sebastian is describing the relationship between me and my mom pretty well. And of course it isn't healthy or normal to have that kind of dynamic. It's just that this is how it's always been, and now we're on a train stuck on a sidetrack in toxic land.

Emmett hands me an extra piece of bacon in solidarity. He has the nicest mom out of all of us—always reliable and always puts him first— and feels terrible for me.

"What's wrong with your eyes?" Noah says.

"What?"

"They're red-rimmed."

I probably spent too much time with the dogs. Got too close. The pictures for the adoption page required that I hug them, and not even my prescription meds could save me.

"Late night," I mumble, not wanting to tell my brothers what really happened.

"Is that dog hair on you?" Sebastian says from my left. He squints at my shoulder.

"It's probably mine." Molly wasn't close enough to put her hair on me. Unfortunately.

"Your hair isn't golden." He picks it off my shirt. "And this is way too long."

Ah, shit. It must be Cooper's. The golden retriever sheds like he's going bald.

My brothers all stare at me like I've just put on a thong and jumped into a croc-infested swamp.

"What?" It comes out testy.

"*What* is you're extremely allergic to dogs and cats." Huxley sounds like a lawyer cross-examining an uncooperative witness. He should've been an attorney, rather than an ad executive. He even has the right credential—a law degree from Harvard.

"It's just one hair."

"On your shoulder? What were you doing, giving a dog a piggyback ride?" Emmett looks like he's worried about my mental health.

"It'd be easier to just stab yourself in the face with a fork if you want to be miserable," Noah says.

I take a large bite out of a sausage and chew energetically. Hopefully my brothers get the hint that I don't want to talk about it.

"Oh..." Noah stares at his phone. He's addicted to social media, and he can't help checking his phone every other minute. "Look at you, Nicholas. Are you trying to get people to adopt the dog or you?"

Shit. The photos Molly took must've already gotten on the shelter's feed.

Noah starts laughing. "Wait—it gets better. All of these shots are taken by *Molly Greene*."

"How do you know?" I demand.

"Says so right here."

Damn it.

"Lemme see," Sebastian says, an evil glint in his eyes. He's never going to let me live this down.

Emmett joins in with a grin. "Send me the link."

Oh, for fuck's sake. When did my brothers start sharing Noah's love of social media?

"Lemme screencap it first," Noah says.

"Stop." I reach for his phone.

He jumps back, quicker than the cheetahs he loves so much. "Uh-uh. Too slow! Check your phones, bros."

My phone buzzes, and there are various pings around the table. All my brothers pull out their phones to check.

"Holy *shit*..." Huxley says with a laugh. "Look at those soulful gray eyes."

"Women will adopt the dogs in a heartbeat if you come with them," Griffin says. Is it a joke? He's a grumpy bastard and sometimes it's hard to tell.

"So. Is Molly Greene the one?" Noah's tone grows sly.

Everyone turns in my direction.

"'The one'?" I keep my voice cool.

"The girl you've been pining over all these years. Why else would you look at her like, 'Take me home with you, please!'"

"Shut up!" But Noah's correct. *Fuck.* I was trying to play it unaffected, but it's impossible when Molly was giving me an encouraging smile the entire time she took the pictures.

"Stop pining and man up," Grant says decisively. "Ask her out."

Emmett nods. "Exactly."

"Like you asked Amy out?" She hated him for years because he made her redo all her work over and over again to prevent her from seeing other men.

"Well, I didn't wait eight years, that's for sure. Not even two," Emmett says.

"I'm not sure that's a lot better, manning-up-wise," Huxley says.

"Carpe Molly, dude. Who knows, she could be madly in love with you," Noah says.

Doubt that, based on how she looked when she spoke of her

boyfriend. I hate how I keep missing her in-between-boyfriend periods to make my move. But I never find out until it's too late, and by then she's with a new guy. It's like the world is conspiring against me.

"What's the problem?" Griffin says.

"She's happy with her boyfriend," I say flatly.

"So? Boyfriends can be disposed of." Noah grins. "Just hire a hooker to seduce him away from her."

I shake my head. "That's low."

"Whatever. Look, if you were in a relationship with Molly, and some hot hooker wanted to bang you—for free—would you go for it?"

"Of course not!" I'd never hurt or humiliate Molly that way.

"Exactly. And if that boyfriend is meant to be, he won't either. Although my money's on the hooker." Noah grins, all smug.

"No. He told her he's in love with her."

"His head can be in love with her, but his dick can be in love with someone else," Huxley says.

"See? Huxley likes my plan," Noah says.

"No, I was just pointing out that Nicholas doesn't have to let that other guy's 'love' get in the way. It isn't like they're married."

"Thank you, Hux. I think." I turn to Noah. "There are lines one should never cross."

Noah gives me a horrified look. "Lines exist *solely* so you can cross 'em."

"Not really," Sebastian says. "And I wouldn't cross them unless you have to *and* are dead certain you won't get caught. And the hooker idea is terrible, so don't listen to Rubicon over there. It's like some kind of shitty entrapment. Don't do it."

"Just trying to help his love life along." Noah grimaces. "Eight years is..."

A frickin' long time. But I can't erase the memory of the pretty, rosy glow in her cheeks when she told me her boyfriend loved her. I wish I could bleach my mind. "Stop. Even if she isn't dating right now, she thinks I'm like my mom." Which is another major obstacle to overcome.

Griffin and Huxley choke on their coffee. The others, thankfully, weren't drinking.

"What the... How the hell did she come to that conclusion?" Huxley manages between wheezing gasps.

"You're the most reliable one of all of us," Sebastian says.

"It doesn't matter." I shrug. "It happened."

"Oh wow..." Griffin looks at me with sheer pity.

"I didn't know it was possible for people to be steadier than you," Grant says. "What is she? An actuary?"

"An accountant," I say glumly. "Look, guys. I'm not thrilled about the situation either, but she was just really *pleased* when she talked about having moved in with her boyfriend. And her happiness matters more than my feelings for her. It'd kill me to see her miserable for any reason."

"Jesus, what a waste," Grant mutters. "She has no idea what she's giving up by judging you like that."

My brothers nod in unison.

They don't really understand. It isn't just that Molly's dating Owen right now. It's also that she's too young and innocent. She isn't like us. She wants stability, and the fact that she's convinced I'm like Mom means I'm not what she's looking for.

Since I don't want to think about those things, I turn to Sebastian. "Is the bracelet almost done?"

"Yeah. It should be delivered to your address, like we do every year." Suddenly he narrows his eyes. "Wait a minute... Is this for Molly?"

I have no choice but to nod. *Thanks, Noah.*

"Damn. I can't believe she's still saying no when you've been giving her hundreds of thousands of dollars in jewelry every year!" Sebastian bristles.

"Not everyone is dazzled by shiny objects, even if they come from Sebastian Jewelry." I don't tell him I haven't given Molly any of them since her nineteenth birthday.

Still, I've been asking Seb for a custom piece every year, hoping that one day I'll figure out a way to give them to her. Meanwhile, I've been sending her a happy birthday text and a one-hundred-dollar Amazon gift card so she can have some book money. Georgia told me the more book money the better, although anything over a hundred bucks would probably get weird.

"I know it's no big deal in your circles to drop a few thousand bucks, but you're dealing with *normal* people," my stepsister told me. "We don't do four-figure presents."

I didn't tell her I was thinking more like five or six figures. I don't want her to think I'm irredeemably weird. My stepsister often shakes her head and calls me absurd and over-the-top. *Anything but normal.*

My brothers will never understand how *not* normal we are. Hell, I probably don't fully comprehend it. But I'd give up all my money if I could be someone Molly wanted and needed. The problem is, wishes like that don't come true in the real world.

And that's the most depressing fact in the universe.

6

MOLLY

On Friday, when the UPS man shows up at Get Jacked, I sign for the package. It's my favorite author's latest release in a limited-edition hardback, special-ordered from her site. A treat to celebrate my birthday.

Anticipation zinging through my veins, I return to my tiny office, rip open the package and pull out the gorgeous tome. It even has a dust jacket. So pretty!

I flip the pages and almost squeal—she *autographed* it! Almost like she knew it was my birthday!

Swaying left and right to the happy beat in my head, I close my eyes and inhale the scent of the paper. *Aaaaah*. I love my Kindle, don't get me wrong. But there's just something so...tactilely pleasing about holding an actual *book* in my hands. The weight, the whisper of paper as I flip the pages. The smell. The whole combination.

I wrap the book in a brown paper bag so I can smuggle it into the townhouse. Owen's bound to point out that I "wasted" money on it, and I don't want an argument, especially not today, when he's taking me out to celebrate my birthday. Still, part of me is sad and slightly resentful that he judges my hobby. It's not like it hurts anybody. And I'm fine with his watching porn on his laptop when he thinks I'm not looking.

Like clockwork, a text from Nicholas arrives with a gift card.

–Nicholas: Happy birthday, Molly!

Does Nicholas care what I buy with the book money he gives me every year? Would he cut me off if he knew I was buying romance novels?

I'd be disappointed if he was biased against my hobby, even if all men harbor negative views of women reading "those silly things."

On the other hand, I can't picture him judging me. He's never said a single unkind thing to me. Then again, Owen didn't say anything nasty about my reading until I moved in with him, so...

I sigh. I'd be so disappointed if Nicholas turned out to be prejudiced against my favorite genre.

My phone pings again. I glance at the screen and grimace as acid surges in my gut. It's Dad, wishing me happy birthday as well. But his congratulations are the kind you have to brace yourself for.

–Dad: Happy birthday! What are you up to today? Any celebration plans? A party?

If I tell him I don't have any plans, he's going to insist on having dinner together. Eating with him always causes indigestion and heartburn for at least three days. Thankfully, my evening's spoken for, although sharing that puts a sick feeling in my belly.

–Me: Thanks, Dad. Owen's taking me out to Dolce.

After he turned in his article to his editor on Wednesday, Owen said he needed to eat there before the week was over and write up a review for *LA Food Digest*. He said he'd love to take me with him, so we could also celebrate my birthday on the magazine's dime. I said fine, since going out twice is too much, given the timing.

–Dad: That's a great restaurant, but is it wise to eat there? The food is rich, and their desserts are irresistible.

Naturally.

–Me: Thanks, but I think it'll be fine.

–Dad: Drink two glasses of water before you go. And have three sips before each bite. You aren't even thirty, and you're going to grow out of all the nice stuff I bought you.

My queasy feeling turns into outright nausea. Dad is constantly worried about how I look. He wants me to be as athletic and fit as he is, which is impossible. He was a football jock in high school and runs 10k races for charitable causes all the time. Meanwhile, I'm lucky to manage 1k.

He occasionally splurges on expensive dresses for me that never fit right and make me feel like an overstuffed sausage. He says I need to wear them anyway to make myself "presentable" when he shows me to his girlfriends. He has a certain reputation he needs to maintain, and a frumpy, boring daughter "doesn't contribute."

To him, image is everything. He bought a Lamborghini with Mom's life insurance money. Says it's critical that he project *success*, especially as a widowed real estate agent. I don't understand the connection between his marital status and how successful he looks, but I don't ask too many questions. They're upsetting for both of us, and I feel like I owe Dad for my role in Mom's death.

–Dad: You should wear that dress I bought you to meet Renée last month. That one probably still fits okay. It makes you look good. I saw how people admired you.

By "look good," he means *appear more like Mom*...which is somewhat possible so long as I stay still and keep my mouth shut. She passed away in a car accident when I was six, on the way back from a grocery store. She went to buy me blueberries because I begged and cajoled her for them. Dad never told me outright that it was my fault, but he's said things.

If you'd been just more patient...
If you hadn't been so demanding...
If you hadn't been so difficult...
If you hadn't been so stubborn...

He never finished the thought, but he'd get a wistful, faraway look, sniff a little and force a tight smile.

In many ways, I understand his grief. Although Mom's face is a bit hazy, I always remember her as being radiant, warm and wonderful. Just being with her made me happy. Dad filled in the blanks, describing how Mom was and telling me stories about her as I grew up. She was the captain of her high school cheerleading squad, homecoming queen and prom queen. She was slim, beautiful, cheerful and fashionable, with hair that looked like somebody had spun sunlight into a crown and a personality that attracted everyone.

"She could make a garbage bag look like a designer dress by simply putting it on," Dad said, while looking at me like I have the exact opposite effect.

No matter how hard I tried, I could never live up to what Mom was. I wasn't coordinated enough to be a cheerleader. I wasn't popular enough to be a homecoming queen or prom queen. My hair is a mousy brown, and people don't flock to me dying for a smile or a warm greeting...or any other reason, for that matter. I'm just naturally introverted, and I don't think that's going to change, no matter how much Dad wishes it weren't so.

He's sort of settled—reluctantly and resentfully—for a child who doesn't embarrass him too much to be seen with.

I look down at myself. At my chest. Hips. Thighs. I see curves. And lots of softness. This is as small as I'm going to get. I'm never going to be a size zero like Mom, regardless how much water I drink with my meals. My doctor has never expressed any concerns about my health or anything, but Dad never misses an opportunity to inform me there's something wrong with the way I am.

He carefully selects pricey clothes that are just a tad too small, the idea being that having them will light the fire Mom must've left in my heart somewhere. But for the meeting with Renée, he sent me a dress that was the right size—much to my relief. Of course, it was probably because when I met the girlfriend before Renée, I ripped a side seam while trying to sit down and had to leave in abject humiliation. Renée is gorgeous and well-to-do—exactly the kind of woman Dad loves to be seen with. He'd rather lick a porn set floor after a shoot than jeopardize his chances with her.

–Dad: Remember, you're lucky you managed to snag Owen, even though he's just a food complainer.

I sigh. "If you were just more like your mom, you could do better than Owen," Dad said when I let him know I was moving in with my boyfriend.

–Dad: Men like Owen don't want to be with a woman who can't make them shine just by standing next to them.

I don't have to read the rest of his text to know what he's going to say. But I'm in a masochistic mood.

–Dad: Women are like accessories. When they lose their luster, men don't want them anymore, just like you wouldn't want to keep earrings that didn't enhance your appearance. If you remember this, you'll be ahead of the vast majority of women out there. Doesn't matter what people claim—life is a competition. The ones who can get the best spouses and most money win.

He always says the exact same thing, word for word. Does he copy and paste it every time? I can't decide if I'm upset because he thinks so little of me, or because he's too lazy to type up something new. Probably a little of both.

–Dad: Anyway, try to not embarrass your boyfriend too much. There's a reason popular and successful men hang out with popular and beautiful women.

Dad always knows exactly where to stick his verbal knives. It's time I end this text monologue before I become too depressed to enjoy the rest of my day. It's my birthday, damn it!

–Me: Got it. I'll try to drink as much water as possible.

–Dad: Good! And while you're at it, why don't you take advantage of the free membership and work out? That'll help, too.

I exhale hard. I do *not* want to take advantage of the free gym membership. Or work out. The perk is offered because it costs the company nothing.

When I have free time, I like to curl up with a good book and some fresh coffee. Why is that so hard for Dad to accept?

–Dad: I'm only saying this because I'm your father and I love you. I want the best for you and to help you become the best version of yourself. People who tell you you're fine the way you are are lying because they don't care about you enough to tell you the harsh truth.

–Dad: I don't want you to live your life blinded by sweet-sounding lies.

No chance of that. Not when Dad tells me how things really are, and how much harder I need to strive.

I start to type up a sarcastic response, then stop as guilt presses over the resentment that's been gathering in my gut. Dad wasn't like this when Mom was around. When she died, he became more temperamental and critical.

If I hadn't begged and begged for blueberries that day, Mom wouldn't have died so senselessly. And my family would've been okay. Everyone could've been happy. Dad would've been able to spend his life with the woman he loved, and I would've been able to bask in both of their love.

Tears sting my eyes, and I blink to clear them as a painful breath shudders through me. Crying doesn't fix anything, and I'm not going to break down at work. I delete the reply I typed up, and put the phone on my desk, screen-down. Needing to leave my windowless, jail-like office, I carry the book box to dump it in the cardboard recycling bin at the end of the hall.

Windows facing the gym area dot the long corridor, and I spot a gaggle of toned women working out in the cardio section. The one in the center is Dana, my worst tormentor and bully from high school. For whatever reason, she decided I sucked and that everyone should not only know her opinion of me but agree with it. Now she's an influencer, doing sponsorship stuff with some local breweries. Thankfully, her hobby has changed from sneering and snubbing me to spending hours in the gym and taking selfies and videos for her Instagram account. Her friends do, too, much to the frustrated delight of our male trainers. I can tell it's all Zeke and James can do not to stare openly. If there wasn't a policy against dating the clients, I'm sure one of them would have made a move by now.

I pause for a moment and look at the women on the other side of the glass. Dana is a bottle blonde, and her body is as toned as my mom's was. She says something, and a few of the women laugh together. She rearranges her high ponytail and poses as one of her friends raise a phone to take a few snapshots.

She was the captain of our high school cheerleading squad. And homecoming queen. And prom queen. *And* voted the most beautiful and most popular.

The sight of her pulls a resigned sigh from me. Maybe we were switched at birth. Dad would be so proud if I could be even the tiniest bit more like Dana. He wouldn't feel the need to make apologies for my rather lackluster personality to his girlfriends, either.

And he might even not have been so upset that time he was contacted about my appendicitis. It was on a weekend during my senior year in high school. He couldn't understand why I called him—*It isn't like I can operate on you.* He had an important golf outing with people who mattered, and he was furious he'd been pulled away over something that wasn't "that critical." Surely the doctors and nurses could deal with me.

"You need to be less selfish. Consider that others have priorities that might be more important than you." Dad's tone said what I was doing to him was comparable to what I did to my mom by asking for blueberries.

My heart ached more than the appendix, and I couldn't speak through the pain. When I cried, he impatiently demanded that I be given a painkiller.

Dana finishes posing and gets on a treadmill. Soon she's running like a zebra on the African veldt with a physical grace I can't even imagine for myself.

After dumping the box in the recycling bin, I go to the breakroom to get something to drink. One of the benefits of working at a gym is that there are lots of healthy options, including flavored tea and water.

I grab a bottle of plain mineral water. Otherwise, Dad's voice will be ringing in my head the entire time I'm at the restaurant with Owen.

"There you are, pretty girl!" Jack says with a broad smile. He's my boss, and the founder of Get Jacked Gyms. In his mid-thirties, he's tall, tanned and ripped, with bleached hair that's cropped tight. He began his career as a personal trainer, worked up to Hollywood celebs and then decided he'd rather own a gym. He still has personal clients—after all, celebrities pay very well—but he spends a lot of energy on the gym business, too. Get Jacked has four locations in Los Angeles, this one being the original. "Happy birthday!"

His brown eyes linger on my chest a beat too long, but I need this job, at least for the time being. "Thanks."

I start to make as wide a circle as possible to reach the exit, but he raises a hand.

"Stay put so I can text everyone." He whips out his phone and starts tapping. "I got you a mocha cake from that bakery you like in Koreatown. We should do the candles and all that." His biceps bulge as he rubs his hands together in anticipation. He grabs my shoulder and gives it a squeeze.

I take a step back and cross my arms. *Why can't I just win the lottery?* Nothing too big. Just a couple million so I can quit my job, get away from this creep and not worry about money ever again.

There's nobody I can talk to about this gym situation. I mentioned how uncomfortable his behavior makes me to my supervisor, Elaine, but she told me I was just being too sensitive.

"Jack's just a little hands-on. You've seen him when he trains his clients, correcting their form and spotting them to make sure they don't get injured."

I have, and he places his hands on their backs and hips and so on to ensure they don't slouch or lift using bad form.

She continued, "All the trainers do this, not just him. He probably just wants to correct your posture or something because that makes a huge difference in how your back feels." Her eyes swept over me, the tip of her mouth twisting in you're-delusional-if-you-honestly-think-you're-hot-enough-for-his-notice derision.

"But he doesn't touch them when they aren't in session. And he stares at my chest. It makes me uncomfortable."

I might as well have been talking to a wall. And that was when I decided it was time to find a new job. But it's tough when most places don't pay as well as Get Jacked, and I have a lot of expenses, including my student loans. Los Angeles is a costly city.

"You can't *not* have cake on your birthday," Jack adds expectantly, his gaze fixed to my chest. "It's like a law."

The cake isn't hidden between my boobs! "Right."

Even as I nod with a fake smile and pray that my boss learns the meaning of *maintaining eye contact*, my mind says it'll be faster to just find a new job.

Jack squints at me. "Are you okay?"

Finally! "Yeah. Why?"

"You just seem a little tense."

I'm stuck here with you! Where are the others? There's free cake here! "It's been a busy week."

"I can't do anything about your workload. But tell you what!" Jack's eyes twinkle like he's Satan spotting some poor sucker whose soul he plans to steal. "Let's get a workout together. The endorphin rush will totally de-stress you!"

"I couldn't possibly impose on you like that." *Or let you put your hands all over me to "correct my form."*

"Imposition? Nah. Consider it a birthday present. Nobody gets to train with me for free but you." He winks.

God, please spare me. "Hahaha. Right. Thanks."

I can't do this anymore. I wish I'd brought my phone so I could pretend to get an urgent text and make my escape. Or at least have a blunt object in hand.

Then again, why should I break my phone? I should throw the cake at him instead.

"Hey, is this where you hid the free cake?" comes a cheerful voice.

I turn and see a black-haired guy with beautiful olive skin coming into the breakroom. Something about him seems familiar, but I can't put my finger on it. I'm certain we've never met, though. He isn't the kind of guy you'd forget easily.

He's tall, with shoulders and biceps that strain against the tight fit of our trainer uniform. Given his size, he's in the largest shirt we have. Muscles bulge in his thick thighs and calves as he walks. He isn't exactly handsome, but his features are even, and his white smile puts you at ease, like you're in the presence of the protective big brother you always wanted.

Right now, he's my hero. Jack can't be as gross when somebody's watching.

"Hey, Arturo!" Jack feigns a smile and claps his shoulder in manly greeting. But the *thwack* of flesh hitting flesh is awfully loud.

Arturo doesn't seem bothered. He looks like he could hit back just as hard, if not harder. His hands are just as big as Jack's—and veinier. "Hey, boss. So who's this pretty girl?"

Amazing how when Jack called me a pretty girl, I wanted to scratch my skin off. When Arturo says it, I just want to smile and say a friendly hello. On the other hand, anybody is better than Jack.

"Molly Greene. She's an accountant here. Back office, you know? It's her birthday."

"Yeah, I saw your text." He turns to me. "Hi. I'm Arturo. Just started today."

"Hi." I shake his hand. He has a good grip. Firm and controlled.

"If I'd known it was your birthday, I would've brought a gift or something."

"That *really* isn't necessary," I say quickly.

"That's why I got a cake!" Jack booms. "For her!"

Other trainers trickle in. Elaine walks in and smiles at Jack before raising an interested eyebrow at Arturo. He gives her a glance, nods, then looks back at me.

"Looks like everyone's here." Jack claps his hands. "Let's sing 'Happy Birthday'!"

"Actually, let's light the candles first," Arturo says. "So the birthday girl can make a wish." He smiles.

And although it feels greedy to want so much, I wish for love, happiness and respect.

7

MOLLY

DOLCE'S REPUTATION is well deserved. The place isn't super glitzy, but it's definitely elegant, with lots of dark wood and ivory tiles and marble. The lighting is low and warm, and the candle on our table burns romantically, casting a dreamy glow over my sober, showered and cleaned-up boyfriend.

Owen is a good-looking man. He has wide-set brown eyes and a thin mouth that smiles easily. He's photogenic, too, which helps with his platform and career. He has a huge following online, a lot of them women. The crisp button-down shirt looks good on his lean, wiry frame. The slacks are black and perfect for the restaurant.

I changed into a black dress *I* bought, since I refuse to put on the dress Dad got me. Besides, I'm more comfortable in clothes I've paid for. They tend to fit better, and aren't overly showy the way Dad's selections tend to be.

Owen checks his phone for the third time, then smiles at the waitress when she clears our table of the appetizer dishes and brings out a fancy salad with leafy greens and tiny fruit chunks. He taps the table once, then turns his attention to me.

"Thank you for dinner. This is lovely," I say, then struggle to decide how much of the green stuff I should choke down. I should eat at least two leaves, so it doesn't look like I'm being picky. I hate vegetables. They taste like dirt, no matter how well you wash them or what kind of dressing is poured over them.

"My pleasure." His tone is overly smooth, and his smile is more polished than the mirror in Get Jacked's yoga studio. "I figured it was perfect when I was asked to check the place out. Two birds with one stone. And the menu has everything we both like, so..." A shrug and a small smile. "It just seemed perfect to order the six-course dinner. It's supposedly the best one they have."

Is it me, or does it sound like celebrating my birthday is an afterthought to his work? I shake myself mentally. I must be more upset than I thought after Dad's texts and Jack's ogling. Owen's trying to do something nice for my birthday, even if he isn't using a penny of his own money. He didn't forget, like Shawn, although that's setting the bar pretty low. Romance novels didn't give me any unrealistic expectations.

I manage to swallow two whole leaves, but my hands start to shake when I find a few blueberries in the bowl. Ever since Mom's death, I can't eat blueberries. I don't even like looking at them. I just tell people I'm allergic because that's easier than explaining the real reason.

I place a large lettuce leaf over the berries and put down my fork. Then I down the entire glass of Cabernet to wash away the lingering taste of lettuce.

Our waitress brings me another glass.

"Your hands are shaking. You okay?" Owen says. He's always more solicitous when we're out.

"I saw blueberries in the salad. Guess they forgot to take them out."

"Oh." He clears his throat. "I forgot to tell them about your allergy."

"I told you when we started dating," I say, struggling to contain my dismay and anger.

He studies my face. "It isn't like it's fatal, right? I mean, you aren't swelling up or anything."

"That isn't the point."

"I'm sorry. I'll remember next time." Owen sighs. He hates being told when he made a mistake. "Anyway, your present." He slides a small envelope across the table.

I decide to let it go. There's nothing more we can do after he said he was sorry and promised to remember in the future.

I pick up the envelope and open it to find a Target gift card. Well. That's...unusual. I don't know what I expected, really, but we've been dating for a year now. I thought he'd give me something other than a box store gift card.

"You know, in case you want to get something," Owen adds, as though he can sense my disappointment.

"Right. Thank you." I smile, trying to look at the bright side. "It's perfect. The Target by the gym has a large book section."

He frowns. "I wasn't thinking books."

"It's a gift card," I say, trying not to sound stiff. "I can buy whatever I want, right?"

"Well, yeah. But ideally something that will be good for you."

"Reading is good for me."

"I was thinking..." He stops when our server comes over to take our salad plates. When we're alone, Owen says, "I guess I should've been more specific."

Before he can elaborate, the waitress returns with our pasta, checks to see if we need more of anything, then leaves. I wait for Owen to explain himself, but he just gestures at me with his new fork.

"Go ahead. The spaghetti is supposed to be really good."

He has that stubborn look that says he's not going to do anything until I do what he asked of me first. I don't need clarification right this moment, so why not humor him? I take a bite of the meatball and chew. It's quite good. But part of me stays a bit wary—and somewhat resentful. Whatever Owen's going to specify about the gift card can't be good. But I don't know why he gave me one if he only wants me to buy some specific thing he approves of. He should've just bought me what he really wanted me to have. That way we could've skipped this unpleasant discussion.

Or is this his way of talking about what's been bothering him? But does it have to be on my birthday?

"I just think it's best if we take a moment to breathe," he says suddenly. "You know...away from each other."

I choke on the meat. Crap! The basil tomato sauce shoots up my nostrils and burns like hell! I start coughing and snorting.

Owen jumps up and shoves his napkin up my nose while covering my mouth. *Oh my God.* Is he trying to smother me to death in front of all the well-heeled diners here?

I swat his wrist a few times and he finally pulls back. The piece of meatball that was lodged in the wrong place pops out, allowing me to pull air into my lungs.

"Are you okay?" He leans forward, peering at me.

"No!" I gasp.

He raises the napkin again. I wave him away impatiently and take two big swallows of wine. "You want to *break up*?"

He retakes his seat. "That isn't what I said. Just, you know. Take a breather."

"That totally sounds like a breakup."

"*No*," he insists. "I'm not breaking up with you on your birthday."

I blink as it slowly dawns on me. *He wants to be the good guy.* He brought me to this nice restaurant and is feeding me excellent food for a reason. He's dumping me over the entrée so I'll have dessert to console myself with.

And the restaurant review site will pay for all of it.

I've been thinking things weren't right with our relationship, but an ambush on my birthday? Especially when he's been saying, "Love you, babe," every chance he gets? I'm starting to feel annoyed at being lied to and manipulated. Pain and humiliation slide into my chest like jagged glass. He must've laughed at me behind my back for allowing him to manage me with meaningless professions of "love."

"Then why do we need a 'breather'? You've been saying you love me constantly." My voice is dry to hide the anger and hurt.

"You don't have to remind me. I'm not senile," he says tightly, obviously irritated I'm arguing. "But that was before I met Dana."

Dana? "Before or after you said, 'Love you, babe,' this morning?" I press.

He scowls. "I don't know why you're upset that I was being considerate."

"*Considerate?*"

"Obviously I can't say, 'I don't find you attractive anymore, babe,' when I'm trying to be nice to you. I was telling you what you wanted to hear."

His final statement slaps me into utter silence. It's one thing to realize he's been lying and manipulating me, but another to have it confirmed so baldly. He doesn't even seem sorry. He's scowling like *I'm* the one at fault.

I wish I could freeze time and come up with the perfect comeback. I can't believe I thought we might still be able to fix our relationship because he loved me. Did he *ever* love me? Or was it just something he said to control me from the very beginning?

"Anyway, you would understand if you met her." His eyes go soft. "She's perfect. Promotes breweries and other local businesses on Instagram. You might recognize her if you saw her photos."

"Are you talking about Dana *Mincer*?"

"Yeah. You know her?" A smile splits his face, and his chest puffs out. He's obviously full of pride for Dana's fame. Suddenly, I realize with painful humiliation that he's never had that look when he talked about me. "She's just a better fit. The kind of woman I need to be seen with. You're a great girl, Molly, but you just aren't right for my personal brand." He makes a wry face and puts his hands out, palms up. *Surely you understand, don't you?* He couldn't be more eloquent.

Owen might as well stab me with his breadknife. The dull ache in my chest spreads.

You have to make men shine if you want to hang on to them.

Dad's voice rings in my head. If he finds out what just happened, the *I told you so*s will never end. If only I were hotter, had a more engaging personality, more charisma—if only I were more like Mom—Owen would never dump me. Especially on my birthday.

"I'm trying to help by letting you know sooner than later," he says. "Now you can find somebody who suits you better while there's still time. The clock's always ticking, right?" Sincerity oozes from him. He could be citing the Bible for all the grave earnestness he's projecting. "When you look back ten years from now, you'll thank me."

Thank him? More like curse him.

As I stare at his smarmy, I've-done-nothing-wrong face, I realize I let him use me for far too long because he said, "I love you." I was too emotionally invested because he was my first boyfriend to say it, and I wanted to feel loved more than I realized.

"I gave up my apartment." My voice cracks with yet-to-be-fully-processed shock. Out of all the things swirling in my head, this seems most urgent somehow. After all, I can't possibly live with an ex who dumped me because I wasn't good enough for his "personal brand."

Owen's face grows lax with faux thoughtfulness. "I'm not a complete asshole, Molly. You know me better than that."

"Do I?"

He acts affronted. "You can stay at my place until the end of the month. Give you time to look for a new apartment."

"The end of the month? Are you kidding? That barely gives me a week!"

He gives me the open hands again. "Dana wants to move in next month. I don't want to upset her."

My face heats with humiliation. As the initial horror dissipates, I'm starting to register certain things. The mild condescension in Owen's expression. The pity and contempt in his gaze, like he's been slumming all this time and now he's done screwing around with somebody who's beneath him. Confidence shines on his face. He's convinced I'm going to give in gracefully. I'm the kind of girl who knows her place, her social ranking. I'm bound to retreat meekly and spare everyone an embarrassing scene.

The knowledge throws gas on the fire burning inside me. I'll be damned if I do what he wants.

"I can't believe you." My hand wraps around my knife as I struggle with an intense desire to throw it at him. It isn't that he doesn't deserve it, but I'm afraid I'll miss and hit an innocent diner.

Alarm flares in Owen's eyes. "Molly—"

"You said you loved me and asked for a deeper commitment just three months ago. Only to do *this*?" Letting go of the knife, I hurl my napkin down on his pasta. Unfortunately, the wadded cloth immediately unfurls and the sauce doesn't hit his clothes.

He looks around as his cheeks redden. "Calm the hell down. What's wrong with you?"

"What's wrong with *me*? You want to know what's wrong with me after you dump me on my birthday?" My shaky voice attracts other diners' gazes. Actually, my whole body is trembling, but I'm not going away quietly to suit Owen. He should suffer the consequences of his actions. "You were just playing with me all this time!"

"No, I meant what I said. It's just that circumstances have changed."

"Circumstances? Your feelings are so fickle, they change every time circumstances change? You said you loved me this morning before I left for work!" My chest heaves as I raise my voice. "Did you disclose your capriciousness to your brand-enhancing Dana?"

"Stop dragging her into it," he says. "This is about you and me."

"It *was*, until *you* dragged her into it to dump me. Were you cheating on me all this time, too?"

"Of course not! I'd never do that to Dana."

Rage rocks me. "I'm not *the other woman*, Owen!" I jump to my feet and start to reach for my glass of water. Let's see if he can still play the good guy when I throw it in his face!

Owen's gaze slides away from me for a moment, to focus on something behind me. The hair on the back of my neck bristles. *Is Dana behind me?* Or—

"Hey, Molly, what are you doing here?"

Nicholas? His voice sounds like warm chocolate syrup. I drop my hand before it can grasp the glass of water.

"I thought you were celebrating your birthday today. But it doesn't look like you're having a good time...?"

I turn and almost do a double take. He's in a suit and tie, radiating power, authority and warmth as he looks at me. He's even hotter than he was on Saturday, and my heart flutters.

Owen points at Nicholas like he's an unwanted fly hovering over his meal. "Who is this?"

Oh my God, could he be any ruder? "Nicholas," I say. "Georgia's stepbrother."

Nicholas stands close enough that I can feel his body heat. My mouth dries, and I try not to focus too much on how nice it feels or how the protective angle of his body is making me feel safe.

"Why is he standing so close to you like that?" Owen demands, his voice accusatory as he glares at Nicholas. It's almost like Owen is some poor husband who just caught his wife in bed with another man.

What gives him the right to talk to me like that after telling me Dana is the one for him?

"Might want to watch your tone," Nicholas says before I can think of a sarcastic response.

"My tone?" Owen says. "You have a problem with my *tone?*"

"That's right. Nobody talks to my girl with disrespect. Not if you want to leave here under your own power."

Did Nicholas just call me *his* girl? I have no idea what the hell is going on. I'm not drunk enough to hallucinate. Maybe I'm having a dream. *Please, alarm, don't go off right now!*

Owen can dump me a hundred times, so long as it ends with Nicholas's arm around me.

"*Your* girl?" Owen says with a raised eyebrow.

"Yup. I'm claiming her, since you're obviously stupid enough to not recognize her value."

My heart booms hard and fast in my chest, and I glance at Nicholas in shock. His feelings for me are platonic, but I can almost believe he sees me as a desirable woman.

Owen sizes Nicholas up. You don't have to see him naked to know the man is built like a prizefighter. Not only that, he's taller than Owen by at least half a head.

My now-ex-boyfriend does the math and decides to snort and give me a nasty look. "I can't believe you acted all mad and shit when you've been cheating on me with this guy."

"Oh, but I haven't. I'd never do that to Nicholas!" I loop my arms around my best friend's older brother and pull him close. As predicted, he's solid, all hard muscle. Instead of stiffening or pulling back, he shifts until he's flush against my side and wraps *his* arm around *me*.

My heart beats like it's about to burst out of my chest. Shivers run through me—this isn't like me at all, but I'm too mad to behave properly. The wine I gulped down earlier isn't helping either.

Owen is staring like I've lost my mind, but it only eggs me on. "After our conversation tonight, I've decided it's time to upgrade *my* personal brand by accepting Nicholas's offer of a date. I've been declining them, since, unlike some people, I take my commitments seriously. Silly of me to think you'd do the same, but whatever. Good luck enhancing your food complainer brand with Dana!" I say, even as blood roars in my head. I've never done anything this impulsive, but I feel incredibly brave with my arms around Nicholas.

Owen flushes at the way I throw his words back at him, then nods slowly as he regains his composure. "You know what? You're right. You aren't the kind of girl who can pull off cheating. And I doubt you were entertaining an offer behind my back." The superior smirk on his face says he knows there weren't any offers. "You can still stay with me until the end of the month because I'm not the bad guy here."

Damn it. He knows I'm lying. I'm not the type of woman Nicholas would be asking out—

"That won't be necessary." Nicholas presses his lips to my temple, then gives Owen an indolently superior look. He beams at me like I'm the only woman worthy of his attention. "She's coming home with me."

8

NICHOLAS

MOLLY QUIVERS AGAINST ME. If she were just a little bit meaner, I might think she was tense with the need to kick her boyfriend's ass, but—

Actually, ex-boyfriend. Music to my ears. So much for all the "I love you" bullshit he's been feeding her. I make a mental note to thank my COO for wanting to have our business dinner at Dolce. Otherwise, I wouldn't have been able to shield Molly from this idiot's abuse.

I can't believe he had the nerve to humiliate and dump her on her birthday. He's unfit to lick the soles of her shoes. I'd spend my days thinking of ways to make her smile if she were mine.

For the first time since Molly wrapped her arms around me, Owen's confidence falters. He studies her closely. I don't need to be a mind reader to know what's going through his head. He's wondering what he might've missed. He doesn't want to make a mistake of dumping her if she has some quality that he's overlooked. He's dying to figure out what I see in her.

What an asshole.

Wanting and caring for her isn't even on his radar. The fact that she wasted time with undeserving trash like him makes me want to punch him in the nose, then hug her.

"She doesn't live with you," Owen says.

Is he high? He can't possibly expect her to go home with him. Not after the stunt he pulled. The biggest reason I didn't make a move on Molly was that she appeared content with her boyfriend, and her happiness was supremely important to me. But now that he's destroyed that, the gloves are off.

"Not until tonight. But there's no reason for her to continue slumming it at your shitty home," I say coolly. "Not when she can have an entire wing of my mansion."

He shrivels as he realizes how much more I can offer Molly. Dear God. So many men believe they're hot shit once they get a bit of fame, which he must think he possesses as an influencer of sorts. Personally, I'm blasé about fame and fortune. It's difficult to be dazzled when your father is one of the most successful Hollywood movie producers of all time.

I turn to Molly. "Ready to head out?"

Say yes.

Her wide, owlish eyes focus on me. She's so adorable I want to kiss her on the mouth, but that would probably freak her out. She's quivering like a rabbit, and I don't want to lose her.

"*So* ready." Her voice is low, but firm.

"You can't!" Owen shouts.

"Why not?" she demands. "Does Dana not want to move in with you next week?"

He shuts up, unspoken protest flashing his eyes. What did Molly ever see in this guy?

"Thought so. I'll drop by later to grab my things," she says.

"I'll throw everything out!" he seethes.

I'm not against him tossing her things because I'll be more than happy to replace everything. Hell, I'll fill her closet with luxurious things that will make her feel like a million bucks just for having them in her room.

But she stiffens. She probably has some sentimental items at his place. And the notion annoys the hell out of me. She should've never wasted time with this asshole.

"If you do that, I'm calling the police," she says. "And I'll sue your ass. Or maybe make such a ruckus that it damages your *personal brand*."

Go, Molly!

Owen turns redder as he stares at her. His face says he can't believe she has the audacity to talk like that to him.

No reason for her to waste any more energy on this loser. "You can do whatever you want if you don't mind losing some teeth." I shoot him a hard fuck-around-and-find-out smile.

His Adam's apple bobs. He gets my message. Understands it isn't a threat, but a promise. It's infuriating that he doesn't respect Molly enough to take her words seriously. He obviously dismisses people who aren't big and strong enough to turn his face into hamburger meat.

I put my hand at the small of her back. "Shall we?"

"Yes." She grabs her purse, then snatches the Target gift card from the table. "We shall."

"You're going to take my present after all this?" Owen demands.

"You said it was for me." She narrows her eyes. "I'm not giving up book money just because you're insecure. And by the way, Owen, you were right. You could never compete with my book boyfriends. You aren't big enough down there, or strong enough to last for long. And frankly, honey, you aren't that exciting."

I try not to laugh, but fail. I've never seen this sassy side of her, and I adore it.

His cheeks turn red. "I *knew* it! Your impossible expectations ruined our relationship!"

"No, it was you needing to improve your *personal brand* by dating somebody else. I'm done settling. Bet your amazingly branded Dana won't, either. So good luck, Sponge Dick."

Laughing harder, I escort her out, even as Owen splutters.

Although she got the last word, I should do something about him. I hate his smug face, his superior tone and self-satisfied smirk.

She doesn't deserve what just happened at the restaurant. How dare he hurt her on the day she should be happiest? She was glowing when she talked about him just last weekend. Even though this could be my opening, I hate to see her in pain. I don't even want to think about what other humiliation and insults he might have subjected her to if I hadn't ended my dinner and interrupted them.

Molly and I walk out into the parking lot. "Are you all right?"

"Yeah. I'm fine." Her little smile lacks its usual sparkle. "Sorry. That little scene probably wasn't really pleasant for you."

"*Me?* What about you?"

"Yeah." She lets out an awkward laugh, flushing in the dim light. "Me either."

The glimpse of shyness and embarrassment pierces my heart. She has no idea how pretty she is. How much I want to coddle and spoil her.

"Anyway, thanks for coming to my rescue and salvaging my ego. But there's no reason to put me up. You probably need your space, and I can just crash with Georgia," she says, not meeting my eyes.

Careful, Nicholas. I always thought I was a decent catch. Nobody's ever complained about me, and I've had my share of luck with girls.

But not Molly. I don't think she's uncomfortable with me, exactly, but there's an invisible line separating us. Every time I get close, she backs off, quickly putting more distance between us—like she knows I come with lots of family baggage and am too old for her.

It's frustratingly ironic that the women I don't care for want to use me, while the only woman I want has no use for me. Molly is always independent and capable.

But tonight, I wish she'd lean on me, even if she is strong enough to stand on her own.

"Georgia's out of the country," I say. "Mom just took her and Paul to Europe last week, and I'm pretty sure they won't be back for a while."

"She is? Why didn't she say something?"

"You know Mom. She just does what she wants, without any warning." How Paul accommodates all of her mood swings and whims is a mystery. But somehow he does, which is why they've been happily married for eight years. He's so good at humoring her that I initially thought he was some kind of gold digger. But no. He just really, incomprehensibly loves Mom.

"Oh. Well..." Molly shifts her weight. "I guess I have nowhere to go. I wish JJ hadn't moved to Seattle."

JJ must be one of Molly's friends. Interesting that she isn't bringing up her dad, who lives in the city. But I don't point that out. "Not nowhere. You have me."

I keep my tone casual and light. This isn't the time to reveal how her smile struck me dumb when I first saw her at Georgia's high school graduation eight years ago. Frankly, if Molly had been just a pretty girl, I probably would have lost interest. Pretty faces aren't that uncommon.

But something about her keeps pulling me back. Maybe it's the way she loves those abandoned dogs. Or the fact that she's always loyal and sweet to Georgia. Or maybe it's that she doesn't seem dazzled by my bank account or connection to the all-important Ted Lasker. When she looks at me, I'm just a guy named Nicholas who happens to be her best friend's older brother and volunteers at the animal shelter. It's incredibly liberating and flattering to be judged for the way I am, rather than what I have or who I know.

She bites her lip. "I don't know…"

"I wasn't kidding when I said you could have a wing to yourself. The place is huge—lots of bedrooms, all fully furnished. And you don't want to be on the streets because of a shitty ex. Consider it a birthday present. My home is your home."

She mulls it over. *Come on, Molly.* Haven't I proven myself to be a decent guy? Surely she doesn't suspect I'm going to do something like jump her. I want her, but I'd never do anything *she* didn't want.

Finally, she nods. "Okay. Thanks, Nicholas."

I smile in triumph and relief. I open the passenger door to my car and let her slide in, then get behind the wheel. It's a brand-new Spectre, and I'm happy I brought it out of the garage as she runs her hand along the leather interior.

"Wow. This is so nice," she says.

Her reaction reminds me of the adorable drunken admiration she expressed for my Aston Martin on the night she turned twenty-one. It's too bad she doesn't remember anything from that time.

"It's a fun car to drive." I wish we had the kind of relationship where I could buy her one and she'd just accept it. But she freaked out over an anklet. And not even a diamond anklet—one with garnets. She'd flip if I gave her a car worth over $400k.

Even though she deserves it.

She has no idea the kind of things I want to lay at her feet.

As I maneuver through the traffic, tension starts to gather in the base of my neck. My place is a huge mansion with all the amenities, but it isn't really done to my tastes or wishes. I bought it three years ago for Mom, who desperately wanted a house in Los Angeles, then spent a year having it renovated to her specifications—only to have her tell me she didn't really want to live there anymore. She'd already bought a penthouse in Denver to reside in with Paul, and she'd found a place to rent in L.A. when she wanted to spend some time in the city.

"You told me you didn't like your home. So sell it and move into the new place," she said, like that was enough to acknowledge all the work I'd put in for her.

I didn't respond, but went ahead and moved in, since my old place had never felt like home. The mansion doesn't feel much like home, either, but at least it's newer. And the pool is bigger.

I slide the car past the double gates, then speed along the driveway that winds through the huge garden and a garish plastic-gem-studded marble statue of Poseidon holding a trident. Lights at the base of the monstrosity make the thing even more hideous in the dark. It looks like something a bunch of drunk frat boys stole from Las Vegas.

Molly gapes at the mythic figure. "It's so...um..."

"Ridiculous, I know." I laugh. "It was a gag gift from my brothers for my 'housewarming' party." They knew why I ended up with this mansion, and they were sympathetic. But that didn't mean they were going to miss an opportunity to rag me. And I wouldn't expect anything less.

She turns to me. "You like it?"

"I told them I'd keep it in the garden before I realized what it was. At first, I hated it, but it's grown on me." They also wanted to ensure Mom wouldn't change her mind—again—about not wanting the mansion after I moved in. "You should see his eyes in the morning. They burn red."

She giggles. "Why would a god of the sea have burning red eyes?"

"To shoot waterproof lasers with? I don't know. But you can't really see it once you're past the driveway, so it's not too much of an eyesore if you're looking out from the house." It is, however, enough of one that Mom will never ask me to give the mansion back. "You can see the rest of the garden in the morning if you want. I have acacia and lilac."

"Ooh, they smell so good."

NADIA LEE

"Lisianthus and sweet pea, too."

"They're my favorites!" A tinge of excitement sizzles underneath her voice, making me smile. "Your garden must be amazing."

"There's a gazebo where you can see it and read or relax. There are a couple of rocking chairs and a swing."

"That sounds heavenly."

I smile at her enthusiasm. The acacia and lilac were planted at Mom's request, but the lisianthus and sweet peas—and the gazebo— were additions I made to the place after moving in. Molly mentioned how much she loved those flowers during our time at the shelter, and so I planted some. "We can rig up a hammock out there if that's more your thing."

"No," she says. "They look so relaxing in pictures, but I can never get out of one without landing on my face."

It's comical how aggravated she sounds. But good that she isn't crying over her breakup with Owen. As much as he didn't deserve her, she probably feels some pain over it. When Georgia broke up with her boyfriend—and she dumped him—she was so depressed that I had to lend her my black AmEx so she could give herself some retail therapy. "There's a trick to it," I say. "I'll show you later."

I pull into the garage and kill the engine. Before I can get around to the other side of the car, she hops out. Like it never entered her mind I might want to open the door for her.

She doesn't know how you feel about her.

I look at her standing in front of the entrance to the house, her face flushed. Her pretty green eyes are twinkling again, albeit not as brightly as before. Nerves and determination pump in my veins. I want her to know how precious she is to me, and how happy I am to share my home with her.

This could end up as a rebound. But I don't want to exercise patience, like I did after she broke up with her previous boyfriend, and miss my chance again.

I'm sick of waiting. I can take this one day at a time and convince her to give *us* a chance by indulging her, spoiling her and ruining her for other men.

"Let me show you around." I want to reach for her hand, but instead put mine on her back and usher her in.

Although I didn't initially buy and renovate the mansion for myself, it has a lot of nice features and amenities. It opens to a massive foyer with lots of natural light that pours in during the day. Pale marble covers the foyer, but oak flooring on the rest of the first level gives a warm coziness to the house. Thick rugs are thrown in the living room, while the formal dining room sports a huge table, big enough to entertain twenty. The kitchens are sizable as well; the second one was my mother's request—because apparently having two kitchens is popular, not because she actually cooks.

"Wow. I love your kitchen." Molly's gaze roams around. "Absolutely amazing." She runs her hand over the spotless stove and ovens.

I'm glad my housekeeping staff does such a good job. I should give them a bonus. "Do you cook?"

"Uh-huh. Mostly baking, but yeah." Then she notices the other kitchen. "You have *four* ovens?" She sounds like somebody just gave her a limitless credit card.

"Yeah. You can use any or all of them if you like."

"Thank you. I'm going to bake you my specialty: double chocolate chip cookies. They're to die for. Everyone at the gym comes by my office to compliment me whenever I bring them to work."

"I thought the people at Get Jacked are too worried about getting jacked to eat cookies." *Did that sound disapproving?* I hate it that they've had Molly's cookies multiple times, while I didn't even know she baked.

"Well, the back-office people don't care. And it doesn't matter to the trainers—I mean, they work out all the time, so..."

"I wasn't judging. Just jealous that I never got to have your cookies before."

"Oh." She gives me a relieved smile. "I can bake some for you every day if you want."

"Well, maybe not *every* day. I didn't bring you here to cook for me." That's not the point at all. Any pampering should flow in the opposite direction. Can't ruin her if she's working hard to spoil me. "Besides, I have people who come over to take care of things like that."

I show her the sunroom and the rest. I mention the pool and the gym, but don't take her to see them since she probably works out at Get Jacked. Although I'd prefer that she exercise with me, I do it in the morning before I go into the office. She undoubtedly doesn't want to get up that early. Besides, if she shows up in a bathing suit, I won't be swimming laps for long.

"Your home's so warm and welcoming," she says as we finish the tour of the first floor. "I thought most mansions were, like, you know, filled with expensive things. Like a showroom."

"I want a home where I can relax, and I've swapped out most of the furnishings." Mom's preference does indeed run to stuffing rooms with priceless items. I'm partial to comfort, and I love it that Molly likes my home. A castle wouldn't mean a thing if it didn't make her happy. I could live in a hut without the Internet—or modern plumbing—if it would make her content.

"I love it. It suits you," she says, her eyes shining.

"The question is, does it suit *you*?"

"Oh, absolutely."

"Good. But wait until you see the library." I'm excited about showing her my most prized room—the one I added after moving in and put the most thought and effort into. I've filled it with books she gushed over on her Instagram account.

She inhales sharply and stops in her tracks. "You have a *library*?"

"Uh-huh. Upstairs."

"We've gotta go see it! Like, *now*!" She takes my hand.

It's the first time she's done that. I freeze for a second, and my entire body is buzzing. I know it's not me but the prospect of seeing the library that's electrifying her. But that doesn't matter when her hand is wrapped around mine and she's looking up at me with excitement and anticipation shining in her beautiful eyes.

I escort her up the winding staircase as casually as possible, wishing the stairs would never end so we could hold hands like this forever. When we reach the library, she lets go—leaving me slightly bereft—and steps inside. Her hands cover her mouth as she lets out a gasp. "Oh my gosh..."

The reaction is satisfying. The architect I hired took out two walls and merged three large bedrooms into a single space for the library. The ceiling is vaulted and has skylights. When you recline in one of the armchairs, you can see the night sky through the clear glass.

Molly moves further inside. "These chairs look so comfy." Her fingertips brush the buttery leather of each seat, the soft throw blankets resting over the arms. Carelessly tossed thick rugs cover the floor. She sees an espresso machine on a stand and lets out a small squeal. "Oh my God, this is like the most perfect thing. Books *and* coffee! Yum."

I smile. I bought it because she's a heavy coffee drinker and I hoped to invite her here at some point. I could picture her curled up with a good book and fresh coffee in one of the seats with a blanket over her.

She goes over and studies the machine. "It looks new."

"It is," I say. "I haven't had a chance to use it." *I got it for you.*

"We could have coffee together and read," she says excitedly, then caution slips into her expression. "Unless you'd rather watch TV or something?"

"Reading is better."

She flashes me a smile, then studies the books on the shelves. "You have the old leather-bound encyclopedias?"

"Yeah. They don't publish them anymore, though."

"I know. Wow. I only see them in public libraries occasionally." She tilts her head and parts her mouth. "You have romance novels!"

"Yes."

"Special editions, too."

"Yeah, I buy them when they're available. But some are just regular paperbacks." Not all the authors Molly recommends on her Instagram account put out special hardbacks.

She looks surprised. "Do you read them, too?"

"Of course. I've read everything in this library." I collect romance novels because I want to read the same books Molly does. It's part of an endless desire to get to know her better, to understand what makes her happy, what makes her "swoon."

"Ooooh..." Molly goes up on her toes and stretches, trying to reach a book on the top shelf.

I admire the soft lines of her body as she extends herself. But she's not even close to getting the book. "Which one?"

"Can you grab *What He Wants* by Emma Grant, please? I started it a couple of days ago, but haven't finished it yet."

"Sure."

I take a step forward before she can move, place a hand on the bookcase to her left and lean forward, momentarily enclosing her in the space between me and the shelves. She's close enough that I can smell the floral scent of her shampoo. I raise my arm, reaching for the book she asked for. Her breath hitches—the sound is small, but we're so close. Meanwhile, her silken hair caresses the tip of my nose and chin, and the head of the erection I've had for the past twenty minutes brushes against her.

The touch is like an electric jolt. I grit my teeth to contain the low groan gathering in my chest. She just had a breakup, and I didn't mean to have my dick touch her, even through clothes. It's too fast. If I don't rein myself in, the relationship I'd love to have with Molly is going to crash and burn.

"Here." I hand her the book.

She can't quite meet my eye as she takes it. Our fingers brush—accidentally? I'm praying that it's not—that she wants to touch me as much as I want to touch her.

"Um. Thanks." She smiles. "That's so sweet of you."

"Want to see the rest of the house or your room?" Speaking is a struggle now. My throat is so dry.

"My room." She hugs the book. Either she's using it as a shield or she's going to read it all night. "It's getting late, and I should get ready for bed."

9

NICHOLAS

I GIVE MOLLY OPTIONS, but she ultimately ends up in the suite with the connecting door to mine. It's the best room in the mansion, slightly bigger than my own. This weird design isn't something I would've opted for. It was on Mom's wish list because she's convinced having separate bedrooms improves the quality of her sleep. Maybe Paul snores.

In any case, I never bothered to do anything about the connecting suites because it wasn't high on my priority list. I figured when I got married and had kids it could be used as a nursery.

The connecting door is left locked on both sides for privacy. I wish there were only one bed in this ten-bedroom mansion. Romance novels always have one bed, even at the largest and swankiest hotels. My respect for romance novelists goes up a notch; clearly, they're experts at logistics.

I go to my room, strip off my clothes and shower. My dick's hard—a condition that has persisted since I brought Molly into my home.

It isn't going to settle down anytime soon, so I grip it and give a few good pumps. Normally I don't ejaculate without thinking of some specific scenario involving Molly, but this time it shoots thick white cum with hardly any effort.

What the...?

It must be from having brushed against her in the library. My penis has never touched Molly, and I've been hyper-charged since. And the thought of her being in my house has had me on edge for hours.

I sluice off, then towel myself dry. Molly's newly single, and in my home. But I'm struggling to come up with a plan to show her what she means to me without scaring her off. My brothers have said I can be overly intense at times— apparently I'm too serious and somber. It's frustrating because I've spent years thinking of what I'd do if I had the chance, and now that I have the perfect opportunity, none of the plans seem acceptable.

Timid knocks come from the connecting door. My whole body perks up like a dog noticing his owner coming home. What does Molly need? Ideally somebody to hold her and make her feel better... Although that would be too good to be true.

I start to shrug into a bathrobe, then stop. I work out regularly to look good. Part of it is for me, but a big part is also for Molly. I always hoped I'd get my chance, and didn't want her to be disappointed.

I glance at my reflection in the mirror. Thick muscle covers my tall, wide frame, and there's not an ounce of fat. My abs are ridged—you could lose your change between the sections. I run my fingers through my damp hair, then wrap a towel around my hips and go over to see what Molly needs.

She's on the other side of the connecting door. At the sight of her, all the blood flows south. She's showered too. Unlike me, she's made use of the bathrobe hanging in her suite, and a thick towel is wrapped around her hair. Without any makeup, she looks so huggable and pretty, her cheeks rosy and her lips pink and soft. She smells like my soap—lime and myrrh. But I want her to smell like *me*.

She gazes up at me, blinking. Her gaze glides down my torso, moving over my shoulders and chest and arms...then to my abs. I feel her scrutiny like hands running over me.

Time seems to slow down as heat spreads through me. Her eyes drop further, tracing the dusting of hair on my belly that vanishes under the towel. A soft sigh drifts from her. The sound wraps around my cock like a tight fist. Knowing the attraction isn't just one way boils my blood.

Suddenly, she jerks her eyes back up.

Oh, baby, you could've done more than just look. You could've asked me to drop the towel and lick you to an orgasm, and I would've done it gladly.

Her face is scarlet. "Uh... Sorry to bother you. I didn't know you were in the shower."

"No problem. I just got done." I paste on a friendly smile, like it's totally natural to answer the door in a towel.

"Would it be okay if I did a quick load of laundry? I, um, don't have anything else to wear."

"Sure. This way." Still in the towel, I show her the second-floor laundry room. I hope she appreciates the years of work I've put into my body. "If you need anything else..."

"Yeah. Thanks." Her cheeks turn rosier. "I think I'm good. Just gonna read a little and go to bed."

My mind conjures up the image. She probably doesn't sleep in a bathrobe, so... Does this mean she's going to read in bed and then go to sleep nude? The book she asked me to grab is pretty explicit. Will it give her ideas? Turn her on? Will I be on her mind?

Molly naked in one of the beds in my house, reading a romance novel, is hotter than any porn scenario. Suddenly, my skin feels overly hot and stretched too thin. Any more tension and something's going to snap.

"Actually, could I borrow one of your T-shirts? Anything is fine. I just need something to sleep in."

I almost groan. Her in my T-shirt is *even hotter*. Makes her seem mine.

My girl. *My Molly.*

I try to speak but can't. I clear my throat to get rid of the weird lump. "Yeah. I have plenty you can take." *You can have all of them. And me, too, while you're at it.*

The first T-shirt I grab from my closet is a simple white one. The cotton's thin and cool, and it's one of my favorites. I hand it to her.

She takes it, careful not to touch my fingers. "Thanks. Good night, Nicholas," she says, then slips into her room.

An hour later, I'm lying in bed staring into the darkness. I should be sleeping, but my body's wound tight.

I keep picturing Molly in my T-shirt. She isn't wearing any underwear. Her nipples are most definitely visible through the fabric. Is she still reading? It has some great sex scenes. Is she getting turned on?

My cock grows even harder. *Fuck.*

But my dick isn't the only problem. My fingertips tingle, too. I imagine pushing one inside her to see if she's wet while she's reading.

Forget that. I'd just lick her.

I grip my dick and close my eyes, imagining her propped up on pillows stacked against the headboard. Her eyes are on the page as I climb on to the bed and slowly make my way to her. She doesn't notice—she's too engrossed in the book. But that's okay because I'm a man with a plan.

Her nipples poke against the T-shirt. They look so pretty. My mouth waters. She moves her legs restlessly. I catch a glimpse of pink flesh between her thighs. It glistens, and I know...

The book has a very long, extended oral sex scene.

Her legs twist, giving me another peek. Her clit is slightly swollen. Unable to hold back, I kiss the tender flesh at the junction of her thighs. Her breath catches before she moans softly. The scent of her is sweet, drives me crazy.

Holding the book with one hand, she uses the other to lazily play with my hair. I slip my hands under the T-shirt and slide them up to cup her breasts. She arches into my palms, and air catches in her throat. She spreads her legs wider in shameless invitation.

I oblige, running the flat of my tongue over her sweet flesh. Tasting the honey and need. Feeling her squirm, trying to get closer.

I tug gently at her nipples while I devour her. I suck her clit, roll it like a hard candy. She makes a soft sound, and I move down, fucking her pussy with my tongue.

She's dripping. I love it that my face is drenched with her juices. I'm the one making her wet. I want to be the only man to ever do this to her.

Her pelvis moves, rocking against my face. She's chasing her climax, and lust burns in my veins—

A hot stream of fluid slaps my cheek and streaks my torso and belly.

I open my eyes and finally inhale. *Fuck.* That was some orgasm. I've jerked off to the thought of Molly before, but never shot my wad this hard.

But then, I've never believed that she could be in my T-shirt or in my home.

Breathing hard, I wipe the mess on the sheet and toss it aside. I'm too heated up for any kind of cover. But the orgasm I've given myself in the darkness in my bed, alone, is unsatisfying. It leaves me craving the taste of Molly on my tongue for real.

10

MOLLY

I SLOWLY COME AWAKE and blink up at an unfamiliar ceiling. Disoriented, I rub my eyes, then stop when I feel the huge T-shirt over my body.

I'm in Nicholas's bed.

Well, not exactly *his* bed—alas—but one of the beds in his massive house.

I stare up at the ceiling again. I guess I finally fell asleep. It was difficult last night. All the nerve endings in my body were tingling. The worst was my clit, which throbbed so hard that pressing my legs together didn't do a thing to help.

Usually I would have touched myself until I got a nice, pleasant orgasm and went to sleep. I tried to refrain, since it felt like I was violating him or something by touching myself in one of his beds. I mean, I'd be annoyed if I helped some guy out and he masturbated in my home to dirty fantasies about me.

But the sheets smelled like Nicholas's laundry detergent, and that only made me more turned on, like I was surrounded by him.

Hey, if the guy who was masturbating to dirty fantasies about you was Nicholas, you wouldn't be particularly upset...

My body temperature jumped at least ten degrees at the notion.

And my fingers slipped between my legs, to my swollen and slick flesh.

The memories from the evening came flooding back. The feel of him when he wrapped his arm around me in front of Owen. His scent in the car when he drove me to his home.

And his *body* when he showed up topless...

I imagined his heavy weight pressing me down, and an orgasm shattered through me with such abrupt force that I couldn't even scream. I lay panting in the darkness, stunned that I came so easily and so hard. It's always a struggle to finish, and usually it's more like a pop. I thought orgasms that left your heart racing and you utterly breathless only happened in romance novels.

I hug the pillow and inhale the laundry soap scent. My mind drifts back to last night again—but what happened feels surreal.

I still can't believe Owen dumped me the way he did. I guess the fake-nice guys are the cruelest. If Nicholas hadn't shown up, I would've spent the night under the same roof as Owen. How awful and awkward that would have been.

Nicholas was so kind, playing along like that when he didn't have to. He also didn't pull away when I unconsciously gripped his hand in excitement about the library. I was too worked up to realize what I'd done until we were halfway up the staircase. My heart raced like it was going to gallop away, but he let me hold him like there was nothing unusual about it.

So I pretended like I didn't notice, then let go when we reached the library.

I always knew Nicholas was amazing, but seeing that stunning space and the selection of romance novels he has in there made him perfect. And when he took the book from the top shelf for me...

Oh my God. Just thinking about it makes me want to scream into a pillow. I froze when I felt his breath on my hair. And I thought I'd die when what I thought was his erection brushed against my back for a second. But now that I've had some time to reflect, I'm pretty sure it's just my pervy mind being...well, pervy.

He doesn't have any special feelings for me. He isn't attracted to me at all. He stepped up to save me from humiliation last night because he's a nice guy and has always cared for me like an honorary baby sister or something because of my friendship with Georgia. And besides, whatever I thought I felt was too big to be a penis. It was probably something else. Like maybe a phone.

Besides, the final evidence he doesn't have any feelings for me is when he answered the door in nothing but a towel. He didn't check me out, and he certainly didn't try to make a move. I was the one who ogled him like a sex-starved nympho. But his body was just too perfect to ignore. Those broad shoulders for me to grip and that wide chest I could lay my head on...or kiss. And the abs! I thought abs like that only existed in superhero movies or Photoshopped model photos. I could run my tongue along those ridges all day...

I've never seen a male body that beautiful in person. I was also wondering if his penis was as impressive as his physique. I even wished the towel would just...slip a little. Actually, just come loose altogether.

Thank God he couldn't read my mind. But my money's on him definitely noticing I was having less-than-pure thoughts—he's too observant. He's just too gentlemanly to say anything about my mental inappropriateness. He won't even hint. He'll just act like nothing's happened.

Why couldn't Nicholas be a little bit more like— No. Then he wouldn't be the Nicholas I know and like. Besides, he wouldn't have taken advantage of my emotionally weakened state. More like he'd just start avoiding me.

It's for the best that I behaved and he's a gentleman.

Although...what would he be like if he decided *not* to be a gentleman anymore...? Would he—

Stop!

I smack myself mentally, then hop out of bed. Staying put won't accomplish anything, and I need to look at some apartments. Nicholas probably wants me out of his hair as soon as possible—ideally before I lose my sanity and jump him.

After splashing my face with water and brushing my teeth with the new toothbrush and toothpaste that were laid out in the bathroom, I put on my freshly laundered underwear and head downstairs. Nicholas's T-shirt is so big, it reaches two inches above my knees.

When I get to the kitchen, I don't smell coffee. So he probably hasn't been down yet. I set the coffee machine for a couple of servings—I'm sure he's going to want some.

Something beeps. Then it comes again and I look around. *Not an alarm from one of the appliances.* I finally locate an intercom on the side of the main kitchen wall. On the screen are a group of women. *Four...maybe five?* It's hard to tell. They seem well dressed and well made-up, though. Their tops are low enough to showcase massive cleavages.

Definitely not missionaries trying to get you to enter God's Kingdom. And I don't think Nicholas's neighborhood allows for door-to-door sales.

I hit "speak" on the control. "Hello?"

"Hi. Is Nicholas home? Nikki sent us," one of the women says.

"I was sent by Ted," another one says. "He said to mention that specifically."

Nicholas's mother and father sent these women?

It presents a dilemma. I'm not sure if Nicholas is up yet, and I don't want to disturb him if he's sleeping in.

"Look, can we come in? Nikki said he's expecting us." The women shift around.

"Should I call her?" another one says. "Just in case there was a mix-up?"

I don't want them to bother Nikki, especially when she's out of the country. "No. I guess it's okay," I say, hitting a button with a key symbol on it. I'll just ask them to keep it quiet and wait until Nicholas is up.

"Thanks, doll."

Doll? I think, but the screen goes black.

Just then, Nicholas comes down the stairs. Despite dark half-circles under his eyes, he looks amazing in a pale gray T-shirt that stretches across his shoulders and chest, and shorts that cling to his narrow hips. Dark stubble shadows his square jaw.

The sight makes me want to take a picture so I can preserve the moment forever. This is Nicholas at his most casual and relaxed, something I've never seen before. He could've come down all dressed up like he normally is. The fact that he's letting me glimpse his private side makes me like him even more. I feel like I'm part of his inner circle.

He pads silently across the distance on bare feet until he reaches me. The corners of his eyes crinkle. "Morning."

I smile back, trying to hide how giddy I am. "Good morning."

"Did you sleep well?"

No. I was too turned on. You made me wet. But I swear, I'm not a nympho. I promise not to touch you inappropriately. "Yeah. You?"

He nods.

"I started coffee. For us."

His eyes light up. I knew he'd love some in the morning.

"Let me get it for you." I head to the kitchen and pour him a generous mugful. "And do you want me to make some for your guests?"

"Guests?" He frowns and checks his phone. "Weird..."

"Your mom sent them. Actually, one's from your father."

He whips around. If he were a billboard, a neon red *Oh fuck!* would be flashing. "You turned them away, right?"

"No. I—"

Chimes go off and the door opens. The women spill into the foyer. Nicholas runs toward them, placing his coffee on the counter.

I follow him out, feeling a kernel of panic. Did I let in stalkers or something?

The intercom screen didn't do the women justice. They're even prettier in person. And fashionably dressed. Closer, the air around them smells like posh perfume. They toss glossy hair—probably straightened professionally, because it's so sleek and shiny—and wave their greetings.

If I had even half their beauty and confidence, Dad would be proud.

"Hi, Nicholas," one of them says, giving him a coy look. She's the one with the biggest breasts and roundest butt. Her skintight red dress leaves nothing to the imagination. Not even her nipples are hidden. She's most definitely not wearing anything underneath.

Nicholas's eyes narrow. "Who are you?"

"I'm Candy. Ted's pick." She giggles as she places a hand over her generous and extraordinarily well-formed chest. I've never had breast envy, but I'm beginning to feel it now. "The rest are from Nikki."

"Why are my parents together?" he says, looking slightly horrified.

"Oh, they're not."

"Is it really true that you're going to pay two hundred thousand dollars for a baby?" one of them says.

What? I swing my undoubtedly wide eyes to him.

"*No!*" Nicholas shoos the women toward the door. "Out! All of you!"

The women begin to mill around, but don't make much progress toward the door. "Wait, I really need the money! And my eggs are great!"

"I have a twin if you're into that. *Identical.*" A wink.

"I'm not even into you, much less two of you," Nicholas says. "Now, *out*! Before I call the police!"

"But I want to get paid!"

"*Invoice my mother!*"

When they're finally all standing outside, he slams the door shut, then locks it loudly. The muffled sound of women complaining comes through the solid wooden door.

"Wow," I say. "That's...not what I expected when I let them in."

"It isn't what any rational human would expect." Nicholas looks pained. "Excuse me. I need to make a call."

11

NICHOLAS

THANK YOU, MOTHER. THANK YOU, FATHER.

My good mood is gone. Hell, Molly's good mood is gone.

I was so happy when I woke up and she said she'd made coffee *for us*. It was like we were a real couple enjoying a domestic morning scene.

But of course that couldn't last. Mom and Dad just *had* to send those women! What the hell were they thinking?

Actually, the real problem is that they don't think. Or when they do, it's for their own selfish reasons.

I go to the kitchen and grab my coffee. Whether the brew is my thing or not is irrelevant—Molly could make me a laxative cocktail and I'd drink it. Then I go to the living room corner farthest from the kitchen to make a call. My parents' crazy attempts to get me to impregnate a woman of their choice are going to end *now*.

A couple of rings later, my mother answers. She has a slightly breathless and girlish voice, more suited to a woman half her age. I'm certain it's fake—up to last December she sounded like a chipmunk because she'd decided that a woman sounding like she was full of helium was "fun" and "sexy."

"Nicholas! Darling! How *are* you?"

"Mom, how could—"

"Have you seen the women I sent? Are they there now? What do you think?"

"No, they—"

"Any of them do it for you? No need to consider life goals or long-term compatibility or that sort of thing. Just picture how half of you mixed with half of them would look like."

"*Mother!* I told you no."

"And *I* told *you* I want a grandchild! Emma has one and Rachel has *three*. Why can't I? I'm just as good as they are. And you are just as capable of fathering a child as Emmett and Griffin because you're—my—son!"

I pinch the bridge of my nose. We've had this argument before, but she doesn't listen. She saw baby photos from Emma and Rachel and now is convinced she simply has to have a grandbaby as well. And she'll value the baby about as much as she did the birthday party she asked me to plan before she skipped it to go to Madrid.

Mom can hurt me all she wants. She's already damaged me enough, making promises she doesn't remember to keep, but also making me feel like I'm the center of her universe when she's with me. Our relationship isn't exactly healthy, but I've accepted it for what it is because I understand she'll never change or comprehend what she's done. But I'm not letting her do the same to a child of mine.

"Mom, listen to me very, *very* carefully. I am not, I repeat, *not* going to have a baby simply to suit your whim. Clear?"

When I have a baby, it's going to be with the woman I love—Molly. I can imagine how cute the child will be with Molly's wide green eyes. Or her button nose, complete with a dusting of freckles.

Jesus. My heart beats funny. That kid's going to have me wrapped around her chubby little finger. And I won't care. I'll lay the world at her feet.

"Don't be so cruel!" Mom whines. "I'm not asking you to carry them for nine months!"

She's completely missed the point. "You want them at the moment, but once something flashier catches your attention, you won't even remember that you have a grandchild."

"Don't be absurd! I'm not that bad."

"You told me the same thing when you asked me to plan your birthday party."

As usual, she doesn't register a word she doesn't want to hear. "Besides, unlike your father, I selected your women for both IQ *and* looks, so my grandchild will be smart and beautiful. You're welcome."

Suddenly, *Dad comes online.* "Don't worry. I was able to stick one into the mix. The hottest one. Pick her. *I want a hot baby.*"

"What the hell are you doing with Mom?"

"I happen to be in Madrid too and have an hour to spare," he says.

"What does Paul think about you two?" I demand, furious my parents are plotting against me. If they didn't get along well enough to marry, they shouldn't get along well enough to come after me together.

"He knows I don't go back for second helpings." Dad sounds entirely too cheerful, like he's proud of what he just said.

Gross. But then, Dad wouldn't be Dad if he weren't gross and improper.

"The women we sent are all very discreet surrogates," Mom says. "Now stop complaining. It isn't like you're seeing anybody serious."

"You're wrong. I am!" Maybe this will make her back off. What will Molly think if random women keep popping up at my house? This is my opportunity to convince her to go out with me...and hopefully choose me on a permanent basis. It's going to be a complicated and delicate process—like one of those mating dances birds perform to attract a suitable partner.

This is why birds don't hang out with their parents once they're old enough to be on their own.

Mom snorts. "Like who? That mystery woman you're supposedly in love with? Ha!"

A delicate clearing of the throat comes from behind me. I turn and see Molly standing there. *Damn it.* How much did she hear? Mom was practically shouting.

"What was that?" Mom says. "I thought I heard something."

"It's..." The word "nothing" chokes me. Although it's the best way to shut this line of questioning down, I don't want to say Molly is nothing. She's everything. If I could have only one thing in the world, I'd clutch her to me and never let go.

Mom can scent blood in the water like a shark. "It's a woman, isn't it? Put her on speaker right now!"

"*No.*"

"Do it or I'm flying home immediately to meet her in person."

She's determined enough to do it. Fickle she may be, but when she wants something, she goes for it with the single-minded focus of a starving teenage boy reaching for a TV dinner. Sighing, I pull the phone away from my ear and put it on speaker. I mouth to Molly, *You don't have to do anything.*

Nodding, she smiles.

"Hello? Who is this? Are you the reason my son is childless?" Mom demands.

Molly blinks at the blunt question. "Uh...hi. And, um, I don't think so...?"

"Good," Mom says, obviously not recognizing Molly. Not surprising. When Mom's focused on something, she's like a runaway train. "So are you going to have his child in the next week or two? I honestly don't want to wait a month."

"I can send Joey with some stuff to help. You know he's good at that sort of thing," Dad calls out.

Oh God, not Joey. He does everything Dad asks, including sending hookers to our homes because that's what Dad decided was the proper way to get babies out of us. Thank God my parents didn't stoop quite that low this time, but I'm not risking anything. Not while I have Molly here.

"We do *not* need Joey's help." My voice is cold enough to freeze the entire Pacific.

"If she's not going to have your baby in the next two weeks, what is she?" Dad asks. "Wait, I know! She's your side piece!" He sounds as proud as a puppy that just mastered a new trick.

Molly cringes.

I should buy a weapons manufacturer. That way, I can drone-strike my father. "She's not a side piece!"

"Fine, fine," Dad says. "The main piece?"

Mom huffs. She's probably throwing her hair over her shoulder, too. "Don't be ridiculous, Ted. It's called a *girlfriend.*"

"Uh, we're really—" Molly begins.

"Oh, honey, you don't have to explain. We get it. You think you're too young to have a baby. But that isn't true. Having a baby won't ruin your body. You'll still be hot enough to be a movie star. Tell her, Ted."

"Of course! I'll cast you in my next movie! I promise!"

Molly clears her throat. "That's not—"

Mom is undeterred. "Having a baby is easier if you do it earlier rather than—"

"Goodbye, Mother. Father," I say at the same time Dad shouts, "I'll come over right now and audition her!"

Click. *There.*

My phone rings. I tap the red button, then turn off the phone when Mom and Dad begin to tag-team call me. They'll give up after about an hour, and I'll be able to turn it back on.

"Wow." Molly is slightly wide-eyed. "So she thinks I'm your *girlfriend?*"

I pause for a moment to savor the words that just came out of Molly's mouth. *Your girlfriend.* "Apparently."

"Right. Okay, well..." She clears her throat. "If you need me to, I could be your, you know. Girlfriend."

Her statement leaves me in a euphoric daze. It's like she somehow kissed me in the solar plexus.

"I mean, not like a real one, of course. But a fake one." She's speaking fast. "I mean, that's, like, the least I can do to pay you back for your kindness."

I'd prefer her to be my *real* girlfriend, but if she wants to fake it instead...

"That would be great." Fake dating wasn't one of my plans, but I can work with it. Actually, in some ways it's better because it gives us the perfect reason to stay together and for me to lavish gifts upon her the way I've always wanted. After a few weeks, we can upgrade to real dating.

"Okay." Then she hesitates for a second. "By the way, do you think she recognized me on the phone?"

"Doubt it." *Hopefully she never will.* I'm going to have to murder my own mother if she starts to harass Molly about a baby. Parental pressure isn't what she needs, especially so soon after her breakup with Owen. Besides, she's too young. She should be able to enjoy her twenties without worrying about whether she has enough diapers or if anybody's going to notice a puke stain on her chest.

Molly's shoulders slump a little.

What did I say? Should I have offered more reassurance? "She didn't call you Molly. She would have if she knew."

"Right. Yeah, no. I mean…" Molly clears her throat, then fidgets.

"What is it?" I don't want her to feel like she can't tell me what she's thinking.

"Well. If she does recognize me at some point, she probably won't be convinced we're dating. It isn't like I fit your…um…personal brand or anything." She looks away.

"My *personal brand*?" What the hell? Who filled her head with this nonsense? Better not be Georgia, or I'm going to make her pay me back for all those special editions I bought.

"Like…you know." She makes a vague gesture. "Your reputation."

Just what kind of rep does she think I have? Unlike some of my flashier brothers, I tend to keep a low public profile. Besides, managing a private equity fund that owns a bunch of companies isn't sexy, like owning a jewelry empire or venture capital firm, even though it is quite profitable.

"I don't have a reputation, and I don't have some 'personal brand' that you have to worry about." I don't care about "personal brand." I only care about her.

"Okay. As long as it'll help you get some peace…" Molly shrugs, then smiles. "I don't mind if you use me a little."

She doesn't get it. She's supposed to use me, not vice versa. I'm going to have to show her that.

"By the way, can you drive me to my—to Owen's place? I want to grab my things before he gets any ideas. He really doesn't like my books, and I don't want him doing anything to them."

Good. She's not referring to his place as *hers* anymore. "Such as…?"

"I don't know. Setting them on fire? He joked about it a few times, but now that I think about it, he might have been serious."

"What an asshole," I mutter. "Don't worry. If he does anything of the sort, I'll replace them." *And kick his ass so hard it'll end up between his ears.*

"That's sweet of you, but it wouldn't be the same. I have highlights and notations for all my favorite books. I'd hate to lose them."

Highlights and notations? Now I'm curious what she finds interesting enough to go to such trouble. And if Owen has done anything to those books, he'll pay.

Molly's like Georgia, so there will probably be hundreds of books to box. It'd be easiest to hire movers—and same-day hiring is doable if I offer enough money. But if Owen isn't around the townhouse, it'll be an opportunity to spend time with Molly. And look at the kind of things she likes—the accessories she has, the items she likes to collect, what she's loath to get rid of.

And if there's anything heavy, I can carry it for her. I make a mental note to put on a stretchy shirt before we go. Molly might not see me as real dating material at the moment, but based on the way she was looking at my body last night, her liking for my physique is real enough.

"Let me grab a truck so we can fit everything."

"Awesome." She smiles.

I turn on my phone. Thirty-seven missed calls from my parents. Shaking my head, I text my assistant Cody.

—Me: I need to help my girl move. So get a truck big enough for that, and have it delivered to my place in the next two hours.

—Cody: Boxes and tape, too?

—Me: Yes.

—Cody: Coming right up.

"While the truck's coming, let's get you fed," I say, putting a hand on her elbow to lead her to the kitchen.

"Wait... The truck isn't here?" She gestures in the general direction of the garage, her eyes wide with shock.

"No. But don't worry. A dealer will drop one off in the next couple of hours. Brand new. Full tank." Cody knows what's expected.

Molly's jaw slackens. "You just bought a truck?" I might as well have admitted that I like to use my testicles for table tennis.

"Yeah, of course."

"But—"

"How else are we going to fit everything? In my Spectre?" Her brow remains taut. "Besides, I always wanted to own a truck."

She shoots me a skeptical look. So I try to shift her focus. "Come on. We should eat breakfast before the truck gets here. I know a good place to grab some pancakes and bacon."

"But I wanted to feed you," she says.

It's a little shocking to hear. The women in my life don't volunteer to take care of me. They expect me to do the caretaking. And for Molly to say it...

She adds, "I make a pretty mean breakfast, if I do say so myself. If you have some eggs and bacon..."

"I do." I smile, flattered and happy that she wants to put in the effort for me.

"Awesome. Prepare to be wowed."

Prepare? Ever since I laid eyes on her, I've been wowed.

12

MOLLY

Nicholas probably thought I was just saying it, but I actually do make the best scrambled eggs and bacon. It's the one thing even Dad said I do better than Mom.

I whip everything up and put the plates on the counter. Nicholas raises his eyebrows. "That looks really good."

"My specialty."

I serve more coffee, and we eat. Predictably, he puts his food away in a methodical fashion. I've never seen him frazzled or at a loss. Georgia said he's the most organized person she knows, adding that she'd love to see him shaken up a little.

I didn't have a lot of appetite after seeing the parade of gorgeous women his parents picked out. But watching him enjoy my cooking makes me relax and enjoy the food, too. Plus, of course, I'm the one sharing a meal with him, not any of them.

"I'm so glad you aren't an 'eat your veggies with your breakfast to start your day right' kind of person." Nicholas sighs appreciatively as he finishes the food and sips his coffee.

"Ew. Who eats veggies for breakfast?"

"You'd be surprised."

"Your ex?" Insisting on veggies first thing is the morning is totally a valid reason to break up with someone.

"My mother." He shudders. "Baked Brussels sprouts should never be offered before noon. Or ever, really."

I lean closer. "I *hate* veggies. I choke them down because they're supposed to be good for you." And because Dad tells me all the time about how Mom ate salad to stay svelte and healthy. I suspect he said that to get me to switch to eating more salad and less protein and starch, but my palate is what it is. "If I had it my way, I'd eat nothing but meat, eggs and potatoes."

"And cheese?"

"Well, yeah, of course. Can't forget cheese."

A beatific smile breaks over his stunning face. "My kind of woman."

My breath freezes, and I stare at the bliss radiating from him. My heart pounds, screaming, *He's the one and you're stupid not to jump his bones.*

There's no meat better than this man.

My head, on the other hand, is desperately yanking on the reins to pull back.

Just imagine how embarrassing it would be if he meant "my kind of woman" platonically, and you threw yourself at him. Your pride would never recover. Remember what Dad said? Mom never had to throw herself at anybody. Men threw themselves at her.

My mouth is too dry. I gulp down the now-lukewarm coffee. I wish I could read his mind so I could know how he really feels. His actions say he doesn't see me as anything but his younger stepsister's best friend, but I'd love to know if there's a way to make him view me as a woman.

Jump him. He'll see you as a woman, all right.

Hahaha, no. Terrible idea, I tell myself. If I mess things up, he'll never look at me with a warm smile again. He'll quit coming to the shelter and do everything in his power to avoid me.

You're his "fake" girlfriend now. You can have "fake" sex with him, too.

Why the hell is my mind putting double quotation marks around fake? I meant *fake* seriously. I'm just not the kind of girl someone like Nicholas would date for real. If I'd said, "Let's date for real to stymie your parents," he would've been like, "Sorry, not that desperate."

"Let me clean up." I need to distract my one-track libido before I do something stupid. I can't imagine him wanting to date me for real, not after I saw him turn away all those gorgeous women.

"No, no, no. You cooked." Nicholas stands up. "You go rest on one of the couches, and I'll put everything in the dishwasher." He makes a shooing motion with a small grin. "Go on. Go."

"Do you know what to do?" I eye him suspiciously. "Or are you just going to leave stuff everywhere until your housekeeper comes?"

He laughs. "My housekeeper is off on weekends, and yes, I do know how to load a dishwasher. Emma—that's my half-brother Emmett's mother—taught us basic chores around the house." He comes over and grabs my plate. As he does so, his arm brushes mine. All the hair on my skin stands, my belly winding tight with sexual zing and longing.

It's all I can do to do swallow discreetly and manage a cool, careless façade. "Okay. But if you need any help..."

He waves me away. "I'll holler."

Smiling at his confident attitude, I go to the living room and settle down on one of the plush sofas. Although the morning didn't start quite the way I envisioned, it's now progressing the way I hoped—friendly and peaceful. I check my phone for missed texts or calls. I have a few, but they aren't urgent. But there are some from Georgia that I check immediately.

–Georgia: How did the date go? Dolce is supposed to be amazing. I hope Owen splurged massively on you.

–Me: Actually, Owen was there for work, so the meal was comped.

It takes only a few seconds before my bestie responds.

–Georgia: Wow. That was cheap. But at least the dessert was good? I heard the tiramisu is divine.

–Me: No idea. I left before I could finish my pasta.

–Georgia: What? What happened?

–Me: He dumped me.

–Georgia: WTF??!!!! That asshole!

Her instant fury soothes the frayed edges of my nerves. It was amazing to have Nicholas jump to my defense, but I realize I need my bestie's support too.

My phone buzzes with an incoming call. *Georgia!*

I instantly decline and text her.

–Me: No! Stop!

–Me: Don't call!

–Me: I'm at Nicholas's place right now, and I don't want to have him hear the conversation.

–Georgia: You're staying with Nicholas?

–Me: Yes. Long story. He's in the kitchen, so probably can't hear me, but it feels weird to talk about him when I can see him from where I'm sitting!

–Georgia: Okay, got it. But I'm DYING here. Text me everything. Now!

I quickly type what's happened since Owen declared his need to improve his "personal brand" by dumping me and being with Dana Mincer, and hit send.

–Georgia: What personal brand? That he's a fucking asshole??? Ugh. And Dana's just a bitch. I never liked her. I guess those two roaches will be happy together. Great that Nicholas was there for you so you could fuck with Owen's ego. So does this mean you're going to give him a chance?

–Me: Who, Nicholas? What chance? He was just being nice. I need to find a new apartment as soon as possible so I can get out of his hair.

I'm not letting Georgia get any unrealistic ideas. She has an over-the-top imagination and can be excessively romantic. It doesn't help that both Paul and Nikki encourage her. Nikki once said to Georgia, "If a man doesn't know how to make you happy, dump him. There are other fish in the ocean with more money, better brains and bigger cocks."

–Georgia: There's nice and there's nice. He's never offered to let a girl stay the night with him.

–Me: Never? Not even his ex-girlfriends?

–Georgia: Don't think so. I overheard Nikki complain to Dad about how cold-hearted and awful Nicholas can be. She thinks that's why he's having trouble getting a long-term girlfriend.

I like Nikki, but I'm beginning to think she might not know her son as well as she should. He's anything but cold-hearted and awful.

—Georgia: So it's a huge deal that he's letting you stay at his place. If he wanted to just be "nice" like you said, he could've dumped you at a hotel and offered to pay for a night or two. And he didn't object to you being his fake girlfriend, which means he wants you around.

—Me: You think so?

—Georgia: Hello? Fake Dating Rule Number One? You have to make people believe you aren't fake-dating. Which in your case means you can't immediately move out or it'll look like you dumped him.

—Me: Ha. Nobody's going to think that. They'll think he dumped me.

—Georgia: Come on, girl. You know that isn't true.

—Me: Have you seen your brother?

—Georgia: Yes. And I've seen the way he looks at you. I bet that right this minute he's thinking of a way to date you for real.

I roll my eyes with a smile. She's such a romantic.

—Me: This is my life, not a romance novel. Things like that don't happen.

—Georgia: I love you, so we're going to have to agree to disagree. While secretly acknowledging that I'm right and you're wrong, of course.

I laugh fondly. This is how my best friend and I end minor arguments because they aren't worth hard feelings. Our friendship matters more.

—Georgia: And let's suppose the world has ended and you're right after all. Why move out so quickly? The whole point of fake dating is enjoying the benefits of being somebody's fake girlfriend. So use his house and his money and everything else that comes with the fake relationship until you fake-break up. I'm rooting for you both to get what you want out of this.

All I can do is shake my head. She's probably already written a mental romance novel about me and Nicholas. But it won't hurt to let my best friend's imagination run free. She'll realize soon enough that it's totally unrealistic.

My notifications show a text from Dad earlier this morning. Looks like I missed it when the horde of women came over, and a painful knot instantly forms in my belly. Instinct says I shouldn't look at it until later, but part of me wants to just get it over with. It's also the weekend, so he's probably going to be too busy showing properties to his clients to devote much energy to telling me what a disappointment I am.

–Dad: By the way, I realized I totally forgot to send these to you. Happy belated birthday. Here's to a better and improved you as you grow a year older.

I go still for a moment, then exhale softly. It's a much kinder text than I expected, since he rarely gets in touch without something to criticize me about. I'm grateful for whatever prompted this change in him.

I click on the link to claim the e-gift he sent. A colorful certificate for six personal training sessions at Get Jacked fills the screen. My hand tightens around my phone as frustration and indignation roil through me, buzzing like angry hornets. I blink slowly, praying I didn't see the present correctly, but no such luck.

Another text pops up, covering the certificate.

–Dad: I see you just claimed the present! Good girl! And it shouldn't be hard—you're there every day. Just get there an hour early or stay an hour late. I decided to be more supportive and give you the tools to help yourself.

Resentment and anger eat at me. If this is how he wants to be supportive, I don't want it. But at the same time, a tiny kernel of guilt won't let me tell him how I really feel. It's the same guilt that's been haunting me since Mom's death.

"Are you okay?" comes Nicholas's concerned voice.

I lift my eyes and look at Nicholas, who's drying his hands on a dishtowel. His brow is furrowed, and his expression says he's ready to give me whatever I need to make myself feel better, whether that's a shoulder to cry on or someone who can rage with me.

A sense of powerlessness and embarrassment pulses in my veins. It's too humiliating to tell Nicholas about my father. Or how messy our relationship has become.

"Yeah." I manage a small smile, although I know it's not convincing.

"Is it Owen?" Nicholas demands.

I wish. I'm done with that jerk, and I can block him from my life. Dad is another matter. "No."

Nicholas's eyes shutter, and he flattens his mouth. He's unhappy I'm not being more forthcoming, but I just don't want to get into it.

"I need to change before heading to Owen's place," I say, desperate to steer things in a different direction. "So I'll see you in a few."

13

MOLLY

I GO BACK to my room, pull the T-shirt over my head and stare at the only outfit I have—the dress from yesterday. I should put it on before going out in public, but the ember of rage from last night rebels at the idea. I wore that dress to look pretty for Owen. And I don't want to wear it again.

I've been with guys who made me angry when we broke up, but Owen is the first to make me feel *unworthy*, acting like somehow being with me was damaging to him. The humiliation and rage have tainted the dress to the point that it no longer gives me joy to wear it.

Screw it. I'm not bothering with the dress. I put Nicholas's T-shirt back on. The churning in my heart eases, and I feel safer, like I have his arms around me. Sighing, I think back to his taut expression. I should apologize, but I don't know how to do that and not share what I felt.

We're fake-dating. And fake relationships don't include unloading your problems on the other person.

I study my reflection in the huge mirror in the walk-in closet. The T-shirt is long enough to be a dress. I pull the silver hoop belt off my dress and put that around my waist. *There. Much better.* I twist my hair into a messy topknot and run some lip gloss over my mouth.

I'm ready.

When I go downstairs, Nicholas is just taking a truck fob from some dealership guy. He looks like he'd love to lick Nicholas's shoes. "We do offer a custom paint option as well. Given the time constraint, of course, we couldn't do much with that aspect of the vehicle, but—"

"I'll keep it in mind," Nicholas says.

"And our detailing service is always available."

"Good to know."

"If you need anything else..."

"I'm good. Thanks." Nicholas's voice is polite. But then, he's always polite and nice. He shuts the door before the other man can offer to sell him his liver.

"Just in time," I say with a smile. The plan is to act like our tense moment never happened, at least until I can figure out how to apologize without oversharing.

He turns around, then stares. He studies me from top to bottom, running over my shoulders to breasts to hips and legs...then back up as he takes me in. Probably just shocked I'm not in proper clothes, but my heart shivers hotly anyway. Something in his eyes makes me feel like he's caressing me with his gaze. Heat flutters in my belly and suddenly I'm slightly lightheaded, like I'm not getting enough air.

I shake myself mentally before I do something embarrassing. "Too weird, even for a fake girlfriend?" I spread my arms with an overly casual smile.

His eyebrows pull together into a V. A mixture of displeasure and confusion flashes across his face.

Maybe he really doesn't want me in this shirt. Anxiety unfurls. I open and close my hands a few times to calm my nerves, to very little effect. I already sort of blew him off earlier, and I don't want to do that again. "I was thinking about changing into the dress from yesterday, but it's my breakup dress. If I wear it again, it'll definitely be weird. Like I'm still pining over him or something. Which I'm not. For sure. No way. That would totally undermine our attempt to put up a façade."

Nicholas's frown deepens as I continue to babble. Obviously, I'm not helping. *Oh my God, shut up, shut up, shut up.*

But my mouth doesn't get the memo. "And what if your mom heard that the girl you said was your girlfriend is hung up on somebody else? I wouldn't want her to think you aren't as good as Owen. Because you are. Like, way, way better than him. Like he's a donkey, and you're a horse."

The tip of his right eyebrow twitches.

Oh crap. I insulted him. "I mean, like, he's not even a donkey. More like a jackass. And you're a stallion. A sexy horse. The kind of horse I'd like to—" I put both hands over my mouth because I was about to add "sleep with," and it'd be super perverted to say "horse I'd like to sleep with."

My heart races. Heat suffuses my face until you could fry a couple of eggs on my cheeks.

A corner of his mouth quirks up. "You think I'm a sexy stallion?" His eyes sparkle.

I lower my hands. "Well, yes." I smile, relieved he either didn't catch the other stuff or chose to ignore it. "Totally."

"I like you in my shirt." Approval warms his tone. And is that appreciation in his eyes?

"Thank you." A little of my tension dissipates. I probably just overthought the situation. More coffee might help, but then we're out the door and heading to the brand-new truck.

It's so big and high off the ground. I stare, wondering how I'm going to be able to climb inside without looking ridiculous.

"Allow me." Nicholas reaches over. This close, I can smell the fresh scent of soap and shampoo over the hot male flesh. The skin at the back of my neck tingles as he opens the door and places his large hands on my waist. The heat from his palms sends delicious goosebumps spreading over my back, and the air in my lungs holds as he effortlessly lifts me up so I can get inside the truck.

"Thank you." No man has ever been able to leave me slightly dazed from just a platonic touch, and the words come out a little breathlessly.

"My pleasure." His voice brushes me like soft velvet, while his fingertips caress my hip and thigh as he arranges my shirt dress. Although he's covering me up, the gesture feels erotic, a prelude to something more. My nerve endings sing like I just came, and my face grows hot again.

Stop thinking about sex. Or orgasms. Or anything else that's going to end up embarrassing you. This is Nicholas. *He's not interested in you that way.*

He's been nothing but a complete gentleman. Look how he just ensured I was properly covered.

Nicholas drives us over to Owen's townhouse. The huge black pickup truck purrs as he confidently maneuvers through the traffic. I don't know how he can drive something this large so easily. I can't drive anything too big because I get nervous that I might ding a door or something. His competence makes my blood run hotter. I bet if we were in the caveman era, he'd be the lead hunter. The guy who caught the biggest mammoths and got the best pelts.

I need something to distract myself from obsessing about Nicholas, so I pull out my phone and scroll around on Pulse, one of the social media apps Owen and I use outside of our Instagram personas.

I see he's tagged me. Did he post about the meal from Dolce? Owen probably finished the dinner so he could write a review for the place. But no. The post isn't about the restaurant. He must've gone clubbing with Dana after Nicholas and I left, because he posted over sixty photos of him and Dana, drinking, dancing and kissing.

He wrote one short caption for all the photos: *Having the best time of my life with my new love.*

I thumb through them with the lurid, unblinking focus of somebody who can't look away from a train wreck. It's painful to see my ex having fun with my high school nemesis, not because I have any romantic feelings left for him, but because it makes my heart ache to wonder if things went wrong because of me. Is it common for a guy to say, "I love you," a lot, then wake up one day and go, "Nope, I don't love you"?

Or maybe he has always been a bad guy, and I just never recognized it—like a pathetic, gullible fool.

Frank, a mutual friend, commented last night.

I thought Molly moved in with you like two months ago or something. What happened?

Owen wasted no time disparaging me.

Actually, three months ago. Which is about how long it took before I realized how incompatible we were. Thank God I figured it out sooner rather than later. She just drags me down and won't do anything interesting other than reading some stupid porn, and I just can't be with somebody who doesn't really enhance my life in any way.

Asshole.

What did I do to deserve this kind of public judgment? He and I aren't celebrities. Our breakup should be private, but now it's out there for everyone to see, since he didn't bother to limit the post to friends only. Some strangers left snide comments, too.

Sometimes you don't know what kind of witch they are until you start living with them. Thank God you found out before you got fooled into marrying her. Imagine how much worse that'd be. *Shudder*

Women just latch on to men to fulfill their emo needs, not caring that we have needs too. Got something blunt to say about that, but don't wanna get banned.

What strangers say shouldn't matter. They don't know me. But their cruelty still digs talons into my chest, sending out ripples of pain.

Owen responded to each of them. He must've had a lot of time since he came home from clubbing. And needed reassurance that he did nothing wrong.

Totally. Some women are just a lost cause. Time to write 'em off and move on. Life's too short.

I should've thrown the meatballs in Owen's face last night.

Nicholas places a hand on my shoulder. "What's wrong?"

I don't want to tell him how pitiful I look in this breakup saga. "Just some stupid stuff on social media."

Maybe it's my glum tone that makes him disbelieve me. He stops at an intersection, plucks the phone from my hand and looks at the screen. His mouth tight, he scans the feed.

"Can I have it back?" My voice is shaky. No need for him to see more of my humiliation.

"Gimme a sec." Suddenly, he smiles, crinkling his eyes and curving his mouth into a gorgeous line that leaves my heart fluttering. He takes a quick snapshot, then taps my phone a few times.

Uncertainty and a tinge of excitement mingle inside me. I have a feeling that he's going to do something about those horrible people, just like he rose to the occasion with Owen yesterday. "What are you doing?"

"Making my position known. I guess I wasn't clear enough last night at Dolce." He gives my phone back, inclining his head in an invitation to check what he did.

Molly's new man here. I'm glad she and Owen aren't together anymore, too. Now I can indulge and spoil her the way she deserves. Some frogs never turn into princes. Easier to just skip all the kissing and grab a ready-to-date prince.

Underneath that comment is the selfie he just took. He looks amazing in the photo, and it does its job—Owen looks like a particularly malformed warthog by comparison.

I gasp, then laugh. Happiness wraps around me like a warm blanket. "Oh wow... Thank you. You didn't have to post that, though."

"Sure I did. Nobody gets to disrespect my girl that way."

My insides go gooey at the way he said "my girl." When he talks in that tone, I feel like I belong to him.

"Also, he looks like a toad in that picture where he has his face squished up against his new girlfriend's."

I know the one Nicholas means, and have to laugh. It wasn't the best shot of Owen. Why my ex put it up for public consumption is anyone's guess. He's generally more careful about the photos he posts. "And you're the ready-to-date prince."

"Yup. Only the very best for you." Nicholas winks playfully.

His good humor is infectious, and I love how easily he cheers me up. Nobody else has been able to do that, not even Georgia.

But when we pull onto Owen's street, my mood sours again at the sight of the flashy red Ferrari parked in front of my ex's garage. He wants people to assume he must have another, even more expensive, car in there, but it's actually empty. He just prefers the Ferrari to be visible so everyone can see his dick hanging out.

"You're frowning again," Nicholas says.

"Owen's home. I was hoping we wouldn't run into him." *Please, please don't let Dana be with him right now.*

"Molly." Nicholas squeezes my shoulder gently. "Remember—I've got your back."

I look into his calm gray eyes. Power radiates from him, and I suddenly realize I can get through packing up my things no matter who's at Owen's home. It's as though Nicholas has extended an invisible shield around himself and included me within its protection. "Thanks."

Nicholas kills the engine, and we walk into the place together.

Owen's house is big enough for two adults. A few beer cans sit on the oak coffee table in the living room, and there's a faint smell of the microwavable pizza he likes to have for breakfast. For a critic who specializes in gourmet restaurants, he starts his day with the most frat-boy food imaginable.

A jacket hangs carelessly over the back of the couch, with Owen sprawled under it, stubble covering his jaw. A limp white T-shirt hangs on his lanky frame, and he's in his favorite Batman boxer shorts.

Batman is his number one superhero because he's a normal human fighting crime and protecting the innocent. Now that I think about it, he probably identifies with Bruce Wayne, although he spends his nights watching movies and eating out rather than catching criminals. I never saw him do anything else in the three months we were living under the same roof.

"What are you doing here?" Owen says. His eyes are slightly bloodshot. He sits up, then looks at Nicholas standing next to me. He sizes Nicholas up again, but this time with more insolence. "And what's *he* doing here?"

"He's here to help me move."

"And why are you dressed like a ho—?"

"Ex*cuse* me?" I straighten my spine to stand as tall as possible. I hate it that I'm barely five-five. Why couldn't I be one of those gorgeous six-foot women?

He looks at Nicholas and flinches. "I was about to say *homeless person*. You're in some...T-shirt. Where did you find it? A dumpster?"

"In my closet." Nicholas's voice is like a well-sharpened blade.

Owen shuts up.

"I'm wearing it because I want everyone to know I'm with Nicholas now." I paste on a fuck-you smile.

"Oh my God, so juvenile," he says. "I should've known you were going to show up like...like that! I saw your ridiculous comment, too."

He must be talking about what Nicholas posted. His petulant gaze is directed at me with all the skepticism in the world. He can't believe it was Nicholas who posted the picture, not me. As far as he's concerned, I'm not the kind of girl who inspires that sort of strong affection and protectiveness.

"He's just doing it out of pity," Owen continues. "You aren't even that good in bed."

He adds the last part quietly, but I hear it. From the way Nicholas stiffens, he does, too.

Humiliation burns my face. Owen never complained about sex. I always let him have as much as he wanted, even though he didn't always hold me afterward like I wanted him to. He preferred to just roll over and fall asleep on his back when he was finished. It was me who turned until I could put my hand over his torso and wrap myself around him. Sometimes he'd pat my back. But now I'm beginning to suspect it was more out of reflex than some intentional effort to show appreciation or affection.

More proof that all his I-love-yous were just empty talk. He doesn't love me—he never loved me. Actually, he probably isn't capable of loving anyone but himself...and maybe the Ferrari parked outside.

Nicholas steps closer and puts an arm around my shoulders. *I've got you.* "Owen, gotta hand it to you, man. If you weren't both blind *and* stupid, I wouldn't have had the opportunity to convince this absolute gem of a woman to finally give me a chance."

Owen's jaw slackens. In his world, people don't talk to him like this.

Even though Nicholas is just saying it to spare my ego, that delicious, fluttery feeling comes back to my belly.

"And it's good to know *you're* awful in bed." Nicholas's tone is so polite and pleasant, it takes a second before the meaning sinks into my brain. "I mean, I assumed. But nice to have it confirmed."

From the belated reddening of Owen's face, it's taken him a moment to process, too.

Nicholas continues in the same dulcet voice but takes a step forward. "However, my gratitude just expired. Next time you talk to my girl with disrespect, I'm going to force-feed you a course in manners."

I gasp. I'm not into violence—the idea of people throwing punches at each other is horrible—but Nicholas vowing to protect me is hot as hell.

Owen jumps to his feet. "You wouldn't dare...!"

"Try me." Nicholas spreads his arms in invitation. "Go ahead. I'll let you throw the first punch."

My ex is shaking, but he's too scared to challenge Nicholas, who brims with such confidence that he seems untouchable.

But Owen refuses to sit back down. That would be admitting defeat. So he huffs and glares at me. "I'll give you an hour. Pack your shit, take everything and don't come back. I'm changing the locks!"

He storms out and slams the door.

Nicholas's eyes narrow. Rage burns in their depths, and I put a hand over his arm. There's no point in escalating things any further. "You weren't really going to fight Owen, were you?" My tone's half teasing, to calm Nicholas's temper.

"I'll do what's necessary to protect what's mine, Molly."

His solemn words root me to the spot. But he can't possibly mean them, even though every cell in my being says he must. He has the most amazing power to convince me everything he's saying is true. It's those grave gray eyes of his.

But we aren't really dating. I can't ever forget that and start believing that things between me and Nicholas are real. Not unless I want to have my heart absolutely shredded.

The mood is growing too heavy between us. Time to lighten it up. "Well. Whoever gets to date you for real is a lucky woman," I say airily.

The light in his eyes dims slightly.

My gut says I'm the cause, but I shake it off and paste on an extra-bright smile. "Since we have only an hour, let's get going."

14

MOLLY

IT SHOULDN'T TAKE much time to grab all my things, mainly because I didn't place all my books on shelves when I moved in with Owen.

"Most of my books are in the garage, except for a couple of boxes in the bedroom," I say, thinking we can save a lot of time. Ms. Find The Silver Lining—that's me.

"You never unpacked them?" Nicholas asks with a small, disapproving frown.

I flush as embarrassment worms its way to my heart. Although not having unpacked everything has worked out for the best, it sort of makes me look like a slob. "Owen didn't want me to take all the space. It isn't like I read all those books at once." As the words leave my lips, I register with a mixture of shock and sadness at what a pushover I've been with my ex. If the guy in a romance novel said the same, I would've tagged him "not book boyfriend material" and said some scathing things about him in a post. I was too dazzled by Owen's I-love-yous to see all the subtle ways my ex manipulated me to his benefit and convenience, and the realization shames me, although I couldn't have known his love is as lasting as a rainbow back then. I took him at face value, like a gullible fool.

"What an asshole," Nicholas mutters. "He never deserved you. You had claim to the living space as much as he did."

His support has me relaxing as I walk with him through the living room. He puts his hand at the small of my back, the feel of his palm warm and sweet through the thin shirt. Tingling sensations start from the spot where we're connected and spread. I try not to squirm. He's expecting a fake girlfriend, and reacting to every little touch isn't part of the deal. I wish I could channel one of the women who dropped by earlier in the morning. They would've known exactly how to play things cool and smooth.

I step over a couple of wadded paper napkins, a crushed beer can and a half-eaten pizza crust. A large, dirty gray sock that used to be white at some point peeks from under the couch Owen occupied earlier.

He isn't the neatest person, and he probably hasn't bothered to pick anything up since I went to work yesterday. Sometimes I had to ask, but oftentimes it was easier to just pick things up myself to avoid unpleasant arguments. They never escalated to anything major, but always generated resentment on my part that I *had* to ask, and annoyance on his part that I couldn't just let him get around to picking up after himself when he felt like it.

A half-eaten slice of blueberry pie sits on the table. His gray eyes flashing with irritation and contempt, Nicholas grabs it and tosses it before I can stop him.

"Owen was probably saving that for later," I say. But I'm secretly happy Nicholas got rid of the blueberry pie, since I don't want anything to remind me of my mother's death. The berries in my dinner last night and the pie in Owen's kitchen make me suspect he's being passive-aggressive.

Nicholas gives me a *so what?* look. "He should know you're allergic to blueberries and not have anything that could cause you problems in the house." His lip curls in distaste, and if Owen were here, Nicholas would probably ream him.

It's surprising that Nicholas remembers, though. I only mentioned it once in passing to Georgia because her boyfriend brought some blueberry tarts. When Nicholas asked if my allergy was fatal, I said no, since I didn't want anybody to forgo a treat for my sake.

"It's just some minor discomfort," I say, in case Nicholas forgot about that part. Most people love blueberries, and I don't want Nicholas to feel like he has to give them up while we fake-date.

"So? He was your boyfriend, and that's the least he could do." Nicholas shakes his head.

"Guess that's why our relationship went kaboom," I say lightly. Hearing him talk about what I deserve in a boyfriend is oddly flustering. Although I've dreamed of an ideal relationship, I've never thought about it in any specific detail because sometimes what I wished for seemed too grand.

Maybe that's why Owen saying, "I love you," was enough for me to overlook so many issues. I settled because it seemed foolish to be too picky.

Nicholas and I go to the master bedroom, which has deteriorated significantly in the last twenty-four hours. The fitted sheet is half off the mattress, and a pillow lies on the carpeted floor. Charging cords lie in a tangled ball, and a clear mug half-full of something that appears to be black coffee sits forlornly on the nightstand. I wrinkle my nose at the stale coffee and alcohol permeating the air.

"I was being kind when I said you were slumming here," Nicholas says in shock. "This is awful."

I cringe. "It wasn't this bad when I left."

"I know it's him, not you. I saw how neat your apartment was when you were in college. I love my sister, but she has the terrible habit of leaving everything where she last used it. Obviously, Owen is worse. It's disgusting you had to act like a free maid for him."

His tone says he would've treated me like a queen if we were dating. My belly flutters and my heart clenches oddly. The notion that I could be truly important to somebody is flustering, but exciting as well. Who doesn't wish they could be the center of someone's universe? At the same time, I'm afraid if someone gets to know me too well, they might realize I'm nothing special.

Shaking off the unproductive feelings, I pull out my suitcase from the closet and start throwing my things into it, while Nicholas carries the boxes of my books out of the house I no longer live in.

15

MOLLY

It didn't take much time to pack my things and load them into Nicholas's truck. Because Owen didn't want my books taking up a lot of space, I had left almost all of them in boxes in the garage.

It was like some weird serendipity. When he asked me to leave most of my babies in the garage, I was annoyed but also realized that his place didn't have enough bookshelves anyway. Getting some was on my to-do list.

We arrive at Nicholas's home, and I grab my suitcases and backpack from the truck. Nicholas gently pulls them from my hands. "I'll take these upstairs for you."

He hoists them like they weigh nothing and carries them to my room. Thankfully I made the bed and tidied up in the morning. Otherwise I would've been utterly embarrassed, especially after Nicholas saw how messy Owen's place was.

He sets the suitcases down. "Do you want your books in your room or the library?" he asks, looking at the empty floating shelves near the reading nook.

"There are too many to put in the room."

I open my mouth to add that there's no need to unpack when I'm only here temporarily, but Nicholas says, "So maybe keep your favorites here and put the rest in the library?"

"How? It's full of your books," I say, remembering all the pristine volumes sitting neatly on the shelves.

"There are a few empty shelves. And if you need more, I can get some installed or put some of my older books in storage."

"Thanks, but I wouldn't want you to go to the trouble."

"It's no trouble. This is your home, too."

"But I'm only here temporarily."

"Nonsense. We're dating."

"That doesn't necessarily imply that we're living together. Plenty of couples date but still have their own places. And I don't want to overstay my welcome."

"Molly, darling, you could never overstay your welcome. And it'll be more convincing if we're living together."

"But Georgia said you don't bring women to your place."

"Georgia talks too much. Besides, what does that have to do with anything? You're special."

I blink, unsure how to proceed. Those women were *real dates*. I'm just a fake girlfriend. My heart pirouettes like a happy ballerina, but I hold myself back. "Of course. Aren't I, like, your first fake girlfriend?"

"You're the first girlfriend of any sort that I've wanted to bring home," Nicholas says.

I'm screaming inside, but I press my lips together. This isn't the time to lose my head and start believing things that aren't being offered. I let out a soft laugh instead. "Why don't we just leave my books in your truck for the moment? Let's not waste the pretty day. We're both sweaty from the move, so how about relaxing by the pool for a while? This weather's too nice to be spent just moving stuff."

He regards me thoughtfully.

I paste on an even brighter smile. "Unless you want to do something else? I'm flexible."

He shrugs. "Hanging by the pool is fine."

"Awesome. So I'll see you there in a few?"

But as soon as he leaves, I realize my error. Hanging by the pool means putting on a bathing suit. The red-and-white retro bikini I bought is super cute, with flattering polka dots and stripes, but it isn't going to cover up the softness of my body. My mind conjures up the taut physiques of the women from this morning, and Dad's judgmental voice starts to ring in my head.

If you'd just started training with Jack when I asked you—

I shake myself. I'm thinking like I plan to compete with those women, which is ludicrous. Nicholas couldn't have been less interested in them. I doubt that my losing some padding would make any difference to him.

I should put on my brand-new bikini, get some sun and start on the rom-com advanced reader copy I've been dying to dive into. I should also take some photos featuring the enemies-to-lovers books I plan to feature this month. A few of my favorite authors sent me paperback ARCs featuring the trope. Stack the books or spread them? Or lay them out in a fan... Choices, choices.

After changing, I stick my sunglasses on top of my head, then grab the books, my phone and sunblock and head to the pool. It looks festive with thick umbrellas and thick, pale yellow towels stretched over the loungers. The sunlight reflects brilliantly off the water, a sea of little diamonds that makes me narrow my eyes. I lower my sunglasses.

A bottle of sunblock sits on one of the loungers. Nicholas is already in the pool, doing a lap, heading away from me.

I take the lounger next to his, sitting under the umbrella on the neatly spread towel, and lay the books and my phone on a square table with a faux-glass top. I start to put sunblock liberally on my pale skin and watch Nicholas swim. He's headed back now, using a superb butterfly. Georgia and I watch swimming events in the Olympics, purely to ogle over the hot bodies and strength evident in the different strokes. My favorite is the butterfly for its explosive power and grace. Nothing's sexier than a man full of confidence and competence.

Nicholas brims with both.

My God, he is fast! And the force of his kick and the sinuous way his body moves are hot—seeing the display in person leaves me breathless. The air suddenly feels warmer, although a breeze has started up.

Nicholas reaches the edge of the pool, puts his hands flat on the rough surface and pushes himself up and out in one smooth motion.

Water sluices from his wide shoulders along the well-developed pecs and sloping lats, all the way down to his ridged abs and strong thighs. I've already seen him topless, but somehow, with the light breaking over him this way, he looks even more stunning.

Despite the shade provided by the umbrella, my skin heats. He pulls off his goggles and smiles, the corners of his gray eyes crinkling.

My mouth dries, and my heart races like *I'm* the one who did the butterfly.

"Need some help?" he says.

He's barely out of breath. A drop of water falls from the hair over his forehead and drips down his nose, all the way down until it's clinging to the fullest part of his lower lip. An inexplicable urge to lick it off rolls through me. I clench my hand in reflex—

There's a *pop*, and sunblock squirts out of the bottle. The white glop lands right on my chest, and his eyes follow. My face couldn't get any hotter at my clumsy reaction—and the fact that the sunblock spewed on my cleavage looks like something out of a third-rate porn video.

"Just, haha, putting on some sunblock. I burn, you know." I spread the glob on my already protected chest, sticking my right index finger down between my breasts to get at the remaining slippery goo. As I pull it out, I realize how it must look, and my face flames. "And I was thinking I should probably put some on my back too!" I contort my arm behind myself...which makes me arch like I'm—

"Probably need more sunblock than that," Nicholas says. *Does his voice sound a little rough?*

I can't decide if I need to say something—my mind is blank, and all I can register is the timbre of his voice and another water drop that's gliding down between his pecs.

He gently takes the bottle from my hand and pours a generous white dollop on his palms. "Turn around," he says, and his velvety voice melts over my spine.

The skin on my neck tingling with heat, I present my back and pull my hair to the side. His warm palms glide over my shoulders and spine. I feel buzzed, and a shiver runs through me as though every stroke is charged. The air in my lungs grows thin, and my toes curl as heat streaks through me and pools between my legs. It's like my entire back has turned into my most sensitive erogenous zone, and I feel his touch like a lover would.

Do not *squirm!* I tense my legs and bite my lip, relieved Nicholas can't see my expression.

Something moves in my peripheral vision. A guy with hair the color of a navel orange surges to his feet from the other side of the shrubs that dot the side of the pool. With a lanky frame and extra-pale face, he doesn't look threatening, but you never know these days. When his owlish eyes lock with mine...

I shriek.

16

NICHOLAS

I PURPOSELY WANTED to be doing the butterfly instead of sitting by the pool when Molly came out. Georgia mentioned once that it was Molly's favorite, which just goes to show my girl likes only the best. The butterfly is taxing because there are only two speeds—fast and faster—and it isn't easy to do well.

The idea was for Molly to see me doing it and—hopefully—be impressed. The charge in the air changed when she showed up, and an exuberance that had nothing to do with the high I get from swimming thrummed through my veins.

Although a pair of large sunglasses hid her eyes, I could feel her checking me out when I hauled myself out of the pool. What I was doing met with her approval. Then that sunblock had to spurt out of its bottle and land on her chest. An innocent accident, of course, but also hot as hell.

I've fantasized about all kinds of sexual acts with her, one of them being marking her as mine, and there's nothing more primitive and visceral than spilling your cum on a woman. Then when she stuck a finger between her breasts, it made me think about fucking her tits.

My blood couldn't have flowed south faster, filling my cock until it hurt.

I shifted a little to hide the reaction, but an erection is impossible to conceal in bathing trunks. I took the sunblock from her and offered to put it on her back to give myself a little time to settle down.

But her bare skin is warm and smooth under my palms, and the soft scent of her shampoo is driving me crazy. Plus she smells like my soap. I want her to smell like me in other ways, too.

A window to our left shows her reflection—eyes closed, teeth digging into the plump flesh of her lip. *Is she getting turned on?* It's possible, but—

"*Ack!*"

I jerk my hands from her back, looking around for a bug that might've scared her. But no. It's worse.

It's fucking Joey.

A leaf clings to his over-gelled hair as he tries to leap over the shrubs like an action-movie hero. But the hem of his shorts gets caught by a branch, and he crashes, landing on his hands and knees. Undeterred, he rolls once to the side and hops to his feet, then points a finger at us, smugly victorious in his dirt- and grass-stained T-shirt and washed-out khaki shorts. "Ah-ha!"

"Who *is* that?" Molly whispers. "A stalker or something?"

Straightening up, I put a hand on Molly's shoulder so she'll know she's safe. "Nothing like that. Just my dad's assistant." *I'm going to murder my father. It's gotta be justifiable homicide.*

"What's he doing *here*? Why didn't he just ring the bell?"

"Because that would be too normal," I say, wishing I had the power to catapult Joey into the middle of the Pacific.

"I knew it!" he shouts in triumph.

"Knew what?" *Why didn't I get an electric fence like Noah?*

"She's a paid actress!"

"Who is?" Molly says.

"You!" Joey points his finger at her. "You damned brunette!"

What the fuck? How much coke did he snort off his latest hooker's ass?

"Come out, Charlene!" he shouts.

"How many times do I have to tell you, my new name is *Charlie*?"

comes a soft whine as a woman stumbles forward. Since she isn't totally stupid, she doesn't try to jump the shrubs like Joey. "My legs are asleep," she says, waving at Molly with a pretty but vapid smile.

She's a typical Ted Lasker type—huge breasts that are about to spill out of a tube-top dress that's a shade I've heard Dad call "vagina red," and lips so bee-stung they look like an unfortunate allergic reaction. Her pelvis is just wide enough, and her ass is unnaturally round and tight as she twists left and right to show herself off. She's currently sporting platinum hair, but who the hell knows if it's real or not? She blows kisses like a pageant queen. Joey should get her a tiara.

Time to end this nonsense. "What are you doing here?"

Joey attempts to look down at me and fails miserably. He's too short to pull it off, although that's never stopped him from trying. "I've been following you ever since you told Ted you had a girlfriend because I knew you were lying. I've been taking photographs and gathering evidence of your duplicity!"

"Congratulations on finally buying a thesaurus. Why aren't you in Madrid with Dad?" *Could Jeremiah get me off if I stuck his head into the pool? I only want to hold him down for a minute or two.*

"My passport expired, and the lazy losers couldn't renew it in time." If he were a cat, his hair would be bristling in orange outrage. How dare they not recognize how important he is? "So I'm here to run interference, including making sure you're really making a baby with this person for Ted."

Molly blinks, and I grind my teeth. God save me from my parents and this overzealous assistant.

"How can you be a real couple? You don't even hold hands!" Joey shouts.

I give him a look. "What are we? Five?"

Molly gasps. "Are you accusing us of fake-dating?"

"Yes! I've seen third-rate actors who put on a better show than you! So I brought Charlie, who is a superior candidate. Besides, Ted wants a *hot* baby. And that isn't happening with Emmett or Griffin."

Did this motherfucker just call my precious nephews and nieces ugly?

"He plans to make your child a star!" he adds, like I should drop to my knees in gratitude.

"What about *me*?" Charlie says, with a pout that's trying too hard to be cute. "I thought he was going to make *me* a star."

Joey blinks, momentarily distracted. "Your time will come, honey." He turns back to us. "Anyway, it's time for you to go, fake baby mama." He makes a shooing motion at Molly.

She stands and puts her hands on her hips. "No, Mr. Orange Hair. It's time for *you* to go with your lady friend, because Nicholas and I are most certainly dating."

His eyes drop to our unlinked hands again. That's it. I'm shoving his face under the water. *Now.*

But before I can make a move, Molly loops her arms around me and rises on her toes. She palms my cheek, angling my face toward her, then presses her mouth against mine. Her lips are soft and plump.

All of a sudden Joey seems completely unimportant. Fiery heat zings through me. Her body is flush against me, her lush breasts crushed against my chest. We hold the kiss for a moment; she starts to pull back, but I wrap an arm around her waist and dip my head, slipping my tongue between her parted lips, dying for more.

Her sweetness floods my senses until I'm dizzy with need. She shyly strokes my tongue with hers, and I swear it's the hottest thing a woman has ever done to me.

My erection is back, harder than before. Instead of retreating, she presses closer, tightening her arms on me. My heart thunders.

Yes!

"Hey, no one said it was going to be a threesome, Joey. I should get at least *two* starring roles for this. I'm not into girls."

No.

Molly's tongue quits caressing mine. *Fucking Joey.* Never good for anything. Why did he have to bring that woman?

"There is no threesome," Molly says, breaking contact. "I don't share."

An inexplicable sense of satisfaction cascades through me. I know she's saying it to convince Joey, but the proud tilt of her chin and the firmness of her tone make it sound like she means every word.

I wrap my hand around her shoulder and run my thumb along the smooth, warm skin before facing Joey. "I don't share either, and wouldn't let any woman touch what's Molly's. So if you're done making a nuisance of yourself, kindly get out of here. Before I shove you into the pool."

17

NICHOLAS

MOST PEOPLE DON'T like Mondays. But not me. It's a brand-new beginning. A chance to shake off the mental baggage from the week before.

But I can't forget the events from Saturday, no matter what.

I shower, then change into a black suit that my sister-in-law Lucie once said is particularly well cut. She's the CEO of Peery Diamonds, and her taste is impeccable. Sticking with the theme, I also put on the cuff links she gave me for my birthday.

I take pride in my appearance, but I'm taking extra care today. Women aren't the only ones who dress for the opposite sex.

As I pick out a suitable watch from my collection, my mind wanders to what happened on Saturday after Joey left with Charlie.

I was hoping that the kiss Molly initiated would make her more relaxed around me. But she only smiled and said, "Well. I think that convinced him."

She must be thinking she's living a romance novel. She seems to love fake-dating books. I didn't want to scare her off, so I nodded. "For now, but he's going to be pretty persistent. When he's set his mind on something, he goes after it until Dad calls him off."

"Oh. I guess we should do a better job of faking it, then."

"Yeah, like holding hands like five-year-olds." I laughed, reached out and took hers, reveling at the softness of her palm against my callused skin.

She laughed as well, but didn't withdraw her hand. It felt like a big step toward my goal of turning our relationship real.

I helped her set up the loungers for some book photos she wanted to take for her Instagram account. The storage shed by the pool has all sorts of stuff, including a couple of giant inflatable red orchids. We used one of them to showcase some of what she called fun romps.

"You know what I was thinking?" she said, snapping away. "Since your dad seems so skeptical, maybe it's better if I find my own place."

Fucking Dad. Fucking Joey. "You don't have to do anything because of my dad or Joey."

"But if we aren't living together, we won't have to act so much. And I'll feel better with my own space. I don't need much. Just something reasonably priced that isn't too far from work. The place I had before was perfect, but I gave it up to move in with Owen." She shakes her head.

Later that night, I texted my assistant.

—Me: Sign rental leases with all the apartments in the area around the original Get Jacked Gym that a woman in her 20s would find "decent" enough to move into. Must be reasonably priced.

—Cody: Got it.

—Me: And every time something new pops up, snap it up, too.

He didn't ask why. He knows that when I want something done, it's his job to deliver without any questions.

Given his efficiency, all the "decent" ones are likely taken by now. I'll just let Molly stay with me until a suitable apartment turns up. After all, my place is big enough to host a marathon. Molly and I can be perfectly comfortable sharing this huge space.

What about Georgia?

Damn it. Molly mentioned something about crashing with Georgia when we left Dolce. Mom's going to be in Europe for...well, however long she wants to eat European food and drink European wine. Still, I should have a few weeks to convince Molly to stay with me rather than my stepsister. Georgia has a studio apartment. It can't possibly be big enough for two adults long term. Besides, it isn't that close to the gym. The commute would be over an hour each way during rush hour.

I go downstairs. The smell of fried eggs, toasting bread and bacon greets me from the kitchen. Molly doesn't have to cook—I made it clear I didn't bring her here to do chores like that—but she seems to want to. Fresh coffee also permeates the air.

"Good morning." She beams.

Great morning. "Good morning."

"I didn't have much time, so I just fried some eggs, sunny side up." Molly's smile turns a little shy. "I hope that's okay."

"That's fine." *Anything you make is fine. Actually, forget the eggs. I want you for breakfast.*

I picture the friendly warmth in her eyes dissipating and replaced by heat. Her mouth no longer curved so prettily as I gently pull her lower lip with my teeth, then lick and taste her. I want to push her against the fridge and grind the impossibly steely length of my dick against her, make her feel what she does to me just by existing. All she has to do is breathe and I'm hard.

I'm going too fast. It's an effort to pull my mind from the mental porn set. She just broke up with Owen.

I take the proffered mug of coffee, making sure our fingertips brush. The loveliest shade of rose floods her cheeks, and I press a quick kiss to her forehead.

"What's that for?" she whispers.

"In case Joey has his face pressed against one of the windows...?"

Her eyes are rounder than the plates she laid out on the counter. "Really?"

I laugh. "I doubt he's back. But consider it practice."

"Right. We have to look convincing in front of other people."

"Right." I take a sip of the coffee, wishing it was her mouth on my lips instead.

We share breakfast at the counter. She chatters about her agenda for the week, which includes apartment hunting.

"Don't try too hard," I say. "Mi casa es tu casa."

"You're so sweet." She flushes. There's a hint of gratitude and also an unwillingness to impose, as though depending on me would make her some unbearable burden.

I want to understand why she feels that way. I've never shown any hesitation to indulge her. To be honest, her discomfort with my gestures is why I'm unable to spoil her the way I want. But again, it's too soon. I need to ease her into changing the way she views me and our relationship.

And what better way to do that than to take her out on a date she can't refuse? "By the way, there's a charity gala with a bachelorette auction coming up."

"The one you mentioned at the shelter?"

"Yeah. I'd like you to come along as my date."

Her flush deepens, and she pushes her bacon around on the plate. "I thought you already had someone in mind for that."

"No. I wouldn't—"

"But I guess it'd be weird if you went with a different woman when everyone is supposed to think we're together." She shakes her head. "Don't know why I'm having trouble with this. Pretending we're in love is a must in fake dating."

There it is again. Her insistence that we're fake-dating. Every time she says it, it feels like a rusty nail running along the inside of my stomach.

I never liked fake-dating books. Molly loves them and recommends them all the time on her book account.

"I shouldn't do anything to look like I'm on the rebound. I mean, that'd be ridiculous because you're so not rebound material. But still—"

She's babbling again. It's cute to hear her unfiltered thoughts, but I wish they came with footnotes. That way I could plan how to make her see me the way I want her to—as a man who can make her happy, no matter what.

Once she does that, I can push us onto a more solid foundation. Not all rebound relationships fizzle. Cody had a rebound relationship that turned into an engagement just last month.

Why can't Molly and I have the same?

18

MOLLY

—DAD: Did you set up an appointment to take advantage of the present I gave you?

—Dad: By the way, what's going on with you and Owen? I thought he took you out to celebrate your birthday. Why am I seeing a post about him dating Dana Mincer?

My Monday was going so great until Dad started texting me. I glare at my phone pinging away on my desk at Get Jacked. Now that it's Monday, Dad has finally seen Owen's post. I guess he missed the response Nicholas made...

—Dad: And do you know how embarrassing it is to post another guy's photo and pretend he's your new boyfriend? Everyone can tell you made it up!

...or not.

He isn't wrong about Nicholas and me not dating for real, but him putting me down makes my heart ache.

—Dad: Nothing to be done about it now, though. Just tell everyone you broke up with that guy if people ask. Make it sound like you're the one who did the dumping. That way you can salvage your pride.

—Dad: I'm doing this for you, Molly. I don't want you humiliated publicly. It's really important to maintain a certain image. You don't have the finesse or the look to just shrug it off and not have it affect you.

It's like he's using a cheese grater on my nerves. In some ways he's probably given up on my ever being like Mom, but I know he's supremely disappointed. I've seen the photos of us when she was still alive. My hair was lighter back then—almost dirty blond, and in the right light, my eyes looked bluish like Mom's. I had long limbs and a slightly crooked smile, identical to the one Mom wore in many of the pictures. But ultimately, I ended up like...well, me.

It's always felt like a punishment—because my behavior caused her to die, I wasn't allowed to grow up into the beauty she was. Or have any of the traits that made her so popular and loved—extroverted, quick-witted and fun to be around.

Intellectually, I understand it's a superstitious thing to believe. But my gut whispers that what my head knows doesn't matter, like a chain smoker who can't quit even though she knows smoking is terrible for her.

Dad isn't going to stop until I respond, so I type up something quick.

—Me: Nicholas and I are dating, so there's no reason to pretend I dumped him.

—Dad: You are?

The incredulity is palpable. I can't decide if I should laugh or cry.

—Dad: Did you discuss expectations for your relationship?

I shake my head. Dad is big on "expectations" because "otherwise you end up disappointed."

The only thing Nicholas seems to want is to take me to the charity event and let me live in his home. He probably prefers I don't have dirty thoughts about him or daydream about how we could be just because he told me things like how I'm special. We were pretty clear on the fact that we're fake-dating.

—Me: He doesn't expect anything.

—Dad: A man saying he doesn't expect anything is when you have to try harder. It means he's given up on you!

Dad's doing a great job of jacking up my blood pressure. Did he take out a life insurance policy on me so he could buy a new Lamborghini?

—Me: He can't give up on me already. We've barely started dating!

—Dad: Sounds to me like he's just playing with you until he finds something better.

—Me: He isn't that kind of person.

—Dad: Everyone wants to grab a Big Mac from time to time. For a change of pace after eating nothing but veal.

Okay, that's it. He might as well have reached through the screen and slapped me. His words make me bleed because he isn't just flinging random insults, hoping one of them sticks. He's amplifying my fears and insecurities. Things I've always wondered and worried about.

I can strive to be a better person. I can work to become better read, more informed...kinder, even. But I can't become a carbon copy of Mom. I can't be the glamorous and perfect pinnacle of female beauty. And the thing is, I know Dad isn't the only person who wants me to. Owen was the same. And my other exes, too.

In every single one of my failed relationships, I was the one who wasn't good enough. I had to change the way I looked, the way I felt, the way I lived my life, and if I didn't want to, then it was "Bye-bye, Molly. It's not me, it's you."

—Me: You know what? I know where I fit in better than you, so you don't have to harp on it all the time. I have to go to a meeting. Please don't text me again unless it's life or death.

This will get him to quit—he hates being disruptive when I have to work. He might think I don't measure up in relationship and interpersonal stuff, but he takes my career seriously enough. Probably because being an accountant is *respectable*, which means it doesn't embarrass him when he has to talk about me to other people.

I turn to my laptop to wrap up my report. I want to spend my lunch break searching for an apartment. Much as I want to devote time looking for a new job away from Jack, I also can't stay at Nicholas's place forever. He said I could live there as long as I want, but I don't want to be a total freeloader.

At twelve, a couple of knocks come from my door. "Yes?"

"Hey, it's me. Arturo." The doorknob rattles. "I think your door is stuck."

"Hold on." I get up, unlock the door and open it. He's standing in the corridor alone.

He gives me a strange look. "You lock your office?"

"Yeah. Security reasons." I'd rather not tell him I do it to make sure Jack can't just visit me whenever he feels like. Arturo might share Elaine's opinions, and I've had enough disappointment in humanity for one day. My office is tiny and lacks windows. Although I'm not one hundred percent certain Jack would do more than just stare at my breasts, I don't want to take the chance. With music pounding in the workout area, nobody would hear even if I screamed bloody murder.

Arturo glances around. "I'd go claustrophobic, bro."

"Different strokes, bro."

He clears throat. "Yeah, so... I'm not here to discuss your office or anything. Just wondering if you wanted to have lunch together. I didn't do anything special for your birthday, so my treat." He smiles.

"Oh, that's really sweet! But I brought a sandwich. So thanks, but sorry."

He shrugs, massive traps bunching on both sides of his neck. "Oh. Okay."

"Maybe next time." I feel bad about turning him down. He might be trying to make friends here, although I don't know why he didn't ask one of the other trainers. They'd be happy to hang out with him. Our trainers are generally pretty nice. Nothing like Jack or Elaine.

"Yeah, sure. How about Thursday or Friday? I'm off on Tuesdays and Wednesdays."

"Friday sounds great."

His smile widens, and a dimple appears. "Great! Friday, then."

After he's gone, I lock the door again and return to my desk to grab my PB&J. Time to look for an apartment.

My search is disappointing. *My God, what is up with the housing in Los Angeles?* The only vacancies are in dangerous areas, where if you only get mugged, you're considered lucky.

Maybe I need to be more plugged in or something. I search for a real estate agent and email a guy named Rob who has lots of glowing testimonials.

I spend the last few minutes of my lunch break sending out more résumés. Somebody's bound to need an experienced accountant, even if they suspect I might not be serious about switching jobs. Get Jacked's pay for my position is higher than average, and a lot of people thought I was lucky to get hired here. But if that's what's holding back many of these companies, they should consider the possibility that there's a reason I'm trying to leave despite the excellent monetary compensation. Whatever extra I get at Get Jacked is hazard pay for having to put up with the owner.

I toss the Saran wrap into the trash can, then pick up my phone when it pings, praying it isn't Dad again. But it's Nicholas, and my frown turns into a smile.

–Nicholas: I'm going to be late today, so don't wait up. You want anything in particular for dinner?

–Me: If you're okay with a late dinner, I can wait and we can go out.

–Nicholas: I was going to ask the chef to fix something for you. She comes by every day during the week.

My shoulders droop. What's the point if he isn't going to be around anyway? I can just grab whatever. Maybe a taco or something.

–Nicholas: If you're not sure yet, you can text Cody later. He's my assistant, and he'll take care of everything.

Nicholas sends me his assistant's number.

I type, *That sounds great. Thanks,* then start to hit send, but stop. The message comes off as a little cold. But I don't know what else to add. He's being considerate, more so than any of my previous boyfriends, none of whom would've asked about a dinner they weren't joining. I could respond how a girlfriend in a situation like this might, but something holds me back.

I end up sending the text as is. Then at five, I drive to Nicholas's mansion.

The place is so big and empty. It wasn't like this when Nicholas was with me. I stand there for a minute, then cup my hands around my mouth and say, "Hello?"

It echoes back, "Hello, hello, hello..." in the vast hall.

I texted Cody in the afternoon that I'd like some beef and cheese quesadillas with salsa and guacamole. I find them in the fridge, plus an array of cubed tropical fruits and cheese and other munchies.

After heating my dinner, I pull up a stool, sit at the counter and eat. The silence is heavy, despite the hum of the appliances. The kitchen might as well be a giant cave. Or the deepest, most protected section of an Egyptian pyramid, where you stick the pharaoh's coffin.

I couldn't feel more like an intruder.

Dinner finished, I clean up and start to go upstairs. There's a huge, wall-mounted TV in front of a low coffee table, a sizable sofa and a couple of armchairs.

I wish Nicholas were here so we could curl up on the soft seat and watch something together. But that's just going to remain a wish—I can't expect him to change his routine just because of a houseguest.

I trudge up the stairs, checking my phone. No emails or texts from anybody wanting an interview. Damn it. The job market's tight, but is it supposed to be *this* tight?

Rob, the real estate agent I hired, hasn't texted with anything promising either. He only says the inventory is low unless I'm willing to up the rent I'm willing to pay. Apparently, an extra eight hundred bucks per month will do the trick.

I guess he hasn't heard of this thing called the need to eat. A roof over your head is nice, but so is having food in your belly.

Still, it's been less than forty-eight hours since I asked him to start looking. Something could pop up any time. And meanwhile, I'm not stuck at Owen's place! He would've kicked me out for sure by end of the month, which is this Friday, so his precious Dana can move in to take my place...

Which makes me and Dana sound like interchangeable widgets. Is Owen going to get himself a new and better girlfriend if his personal brand requires an upgrade?

Maybe he's having some kind of midlife crisis a dozen years early.

I open the door to my bedroom, then stop short, step back into the hall and look around. *No, wait. It is my room.*

But I didn't make the bed this morning. And now it's impeccable, with the pillows arranged perfectly. It could be proudly featured on a luxury hotel website. And on the table near the reading nook is a vase full of fresh pink roses and lavender, which emit a wonderful, soothing fragrance.

In the en suite bathroom, everything's been wiped clean. A couple bottles of lotion I left on the counter are lined up neatly along the shiny mirror. The bathrobe I used last night is gone, having been replaced by a fresh one on a hanger. The towels have been swapped out as well. The floor is spotless, and the shower stall sparkles.

I open the cabinet underneath the double vanity. The laundry hamper is there, but empty. I go to the closet and find my clothes neatly laundered, pressed and hanging. Inside the drawer, my underwear has been folded and put away. It smells faintly of the same laundry detergent that's on Nicholas's clothes.

Our clothes smelling the same isn't a big deal, but seems inexplicably intimate. I didn't feel this way when Owen and I were sharing the same detergent.

Maybe because we didn't share the same toiletries. Owen wanted a masculine scent. He orders his soap and shampoo specially from an online store in Rome, while I just use whatever's on sale at Target.

Then I realize a complete stranger has touched my underwear, and debate how I should feel about that. It wasn't like Nicholas's people were sniffing them or anything... So I should be happy...right?

In any case, it's neat that chores I normally spend hours on every week were completed while I was at work. On the other hand, this is above and beyond what I expected when Nicholas offered me a place to stay. I thought I was just getting a bed, not housekeeping, laundry service and a private chef.

Steady footsteps click softly on the hardwood floor on the other side of the door. *Nicholas.*

I open the door and stick my head out. He looks *delicious.* That's the only way to describe his impact in a suit, striding like he's master of the universe. There's something singularly sexy about stubble shading a man's jaw after a long, productive day at work. His cool gray eyes warm as they zero in on me, making me feel special. And I hold on to the fluttery sensation carefully, like it's a delicate dandelion puff.

"Evening! How was your day?" he asks with a smile.

"It was good," I say. It really wasn't, but I shouldn't unload all that on him. Why would he want to know about the awful texts from my dad or my unsuccessful attempts to get an apartment and a new job? "How was yours?"

"Pretty good. So. Everything's okay here?"

"More than okay. I didn't expect your people to clean my room or do my laundry."

"That's their job. Don't worry about it." His lips are pressed like he wants to add something, but is restraining himself.

"Right." Maybe Nicholas is waiting for me to offer, unlike Owen, who made the demand as soon as I moved in. I try to feign nonchalance, like it's every day I crash with a guy who has staff taking care of everything. "So how much am I supposed to chip in?"

Nicholas's eyebrows rise. "Chip in?"

"Yeah, you know—for utilities and stuff."

"Utilities?" He looks like I just said *roach kebab*.

"Shared expenses?" I suddenly feel like I'm doing something wrong. His reaction is incredulous and vaguely insulted.

"I didn't offer you my place so that you could 'chip in.'" He scowls. "I'm not Owen."

"I know. I didn't think you were." Nobody with functioning eyes would confuse him with my ex.

"Good. So, do you have any plans for this weekend?"

I guess that's the end of the utilities discussion. "I'll probably go apartment hunting, but other than that..." I shrug. Normally, I'd say something along the lines of grocery shopping, doing my laundry and cleaning the house. But obviously I don't need to do any of those things. Not that I'm complaining. It just feels oddly awkward to be this pampered when I'm not on vacation. "Are you doing anything special? Do you need me out of your hair?" After all, it's his place. He might be hosting some exclusive party with his fancy billionaire friends.

"No. I don't need you out of my hair." He mutters what sounds like, "I want you in my hair like shampoo."

Except I couldn't have heard that right.

He takes a step closer, and my heart starts pounding. I look up at him, mesmerized by his presence. The air in my lungs grows syrup-thick and starts to still.

He tucks my hair back, brushing his warm fingers over the shell of my ear and sending little shivers through me. My heart pounds louder.

His lips brush my forehead lightly, like a butterfly alighting. The spot tingles, and warmth coils in my belly.

"Good night," he says softly.

"Good night." Despite my best attempt, I sound breathless and slightly raspy.

He gives me a little smile, and looks like he might do—or say—something else, but then vanishes into his room. I close the door and lean against it, a necessary action, since my knees seem to have suddenly lost all their strength.

Maybe this is how our routine's going to be. He comes home a little bit after I'm done with dinner and we chat a bit. We won't be in each other's way too much.

But that isn't what happens. He begins coming home after midnight. I know because I stay in bed reading until at least eleven, when I can't keep my eyes open anymore. He must be extremely busy at work.

Still, he always makes sure we have breakfast together, asking me about my plans and how my week is going. The kiss he brushed on my forehead slowly migrates south until he's kissing my cheek before we leave for work. Part of me wonders if I should kiss him back on his cheek —or chin, since I'm so much shorter—but I can't seem to muster the courage. The only reason I kissed him at the pool was because Joey's accusation pissed me off.

Nicholas texts me at four to let me know he's going to be late. It's so...domestic. Like we are dating for real. Actually, it feels more than that. Owen never texted me when he was going to be out late, except when he felt obligated to ask if I wanted to join him at a club or something.

Stop being silly. There's no way Nicholas is feeling anything even remotely domestic. He's just being his usual considerate self. I should quit trying to associate domesticity—or anything relationship-esque—with Nicholas before I start acting like the offensive romance-reader stereotype Owen says I am.

19

MOLLY

FRIDAY MORNING, I still don't have an apartment. I can't believe Rob can't find anything. I thought real estate agents had secret handshakes, back-alley deals, hidden networks of contacts. He claims everything is getting taken off the market as soon as it pops up, which, honestly, sounds pretty flimsy. I'm beginning to wonder if all those positive reviews for his service are fake and he's really just some lazy bum who's going to end up wasting my time.

Maybe ask Dad for help?

No. No way. He might find me a place, but it'll be one *he* likes, not one that suits me. And he'll send me a list of properties I should buy because he's convinced I should buy rather than "waste my money paying somebody else's mortgage," as he likes to put it.

"Good morning, Molly!" Jack says to my chest as I walk into the gym.

"Hi." *My chest is doing great this morning, no thanks to you, and it really doesn't want to be stared at so closely.*

"In case you didn't know, your father bought some personal training sessions."

Oh *shit*. Did Dad tell him who they were for? "Ah, yeah, he said something about that."

"I gave him a special discount, being family and all." Jack beams at my cleavage. I wouldn't be shocked if he starts discussing a bosom discount.

"Great. Thanks."

"But my offer to train you for free still stands!"

So you can put your hands all over my body? Ha! I don't think so. "Thank you. You'll be the first to know when I decide I need to start exercising! Anyway, gotta get going here. Those accounts aren't going to reconcile themselves!"

"Hey, no reason to work so hard."

I wag a finger at him. "Oh no, there *is*. You're *paying* me to work hard. But I'm gonna work just as hard, considering your offer!"

I give him a little wave, slip into my tiny office and lock the door. Although Jack would love it if I let him be gross with my chest to his heart's content, I'm not going to waste my time that way. Besides, as long as I draw a salary here, I plan to do my job. If he needs a chest to flirt with, he can buy himself a bust.

A little before noon, there are knocks at my door. "Yo, Molly. It's Arturo."

I get up to answer him. "Hi." *Wonder what he wants.* Most trainers don't have any reason to visit accounting, unless there's a problem with their pay. But there's no payday this week, so...

Arturo is looking fresh and massive, as usual, and has gotten a new haircut. "You ready for lunch?"

"Lunch...?" *Shoot.* I totally forgot. I brought some lasagna that I could microwave, but I can't possibly say that to Arturo's hopeful, smiling face. "Yes, of course. Lemme just grab my purse." An *oh shit* sensation congeals in my belly. "So where are we going?"

"You like Italian?"

"I love Italian." *I was about to have lasagna.*

"Awesome. I know a place not too far from here."

Arturo drives us to a fairly upscale bistro about fifteen minutes away. I've seen it a few times, but never eaten inside. The dark wood and ivory exterior are elegant, and some cheerful classical music I've heard before floats in the air like lovely little petals. Already I can smell bread, butter, garlic, olive oil and tomato sauce. The bar to our right is packed with the lunch crowd. A huge TV is tuned to a muted sports channel. A waitress carrying a gigantic tray laden with plates crosses the packed dining area, quick and sure as a ballerina.

A hostess in a black-and-white uniform eyes Arturo like he's six foot, two inches of cheesecake, then sobers when he frowns at her. But he must be used to female attention. Just on a physical basis he beats Owen handily, and my ex isn't too bad himself. Women often ran their eyes all over him when we were out, which never failed to make him preen and laugh with good humor.

Arturo and I bypass the long line of people and get a secluded table by the window.

"Already scored a reservation," he explains.

"Smart move, with all the people here. But what if I was in the mood for something else?"

He grins. "Nah. Everyone loves Italian."

Laughing, I pick up the faux-leather-bound menu, then purse my lips with surprise and slight dismay. A lot of items are kind of expensive for just a friendly lunch out with a coworker. I'd expect this kind of splurge from a guy I'd dated for several months—or maybe earlier in a relationship if he was trying to impress me.

"Anybody else coming to this belated birthday celebration?"

"Nope. Just the two of us."

A server comes over. Arturo orders chicken parmesan, and I get clam pasta lightly tossed with basil olive oil. When the waiter's gone, I sip my water and look at Arturo over my glass. Is he trying to get something romantic going?

But if that's the case, wouldn't he have asked if I was in a relationship first? I have to be overthinking the situation. It's possible he didn't know how expensive the place was either. Or maybe this just isn't that much money for him.

"You okay?" Arturo asks.

"Huh? Yeah, why?"

"You were frowning."

"Oh. You know, just...stuff at work."

He nods. "Jack bothering you?"

I hesitate. The answer is a big fat yes, but how does Arturo know?

Although he was in the breakroom while Jack kept trying to have a conversation with my breasts, he couldn't possibly have seen enough already to get the full picture...

Could he?

Or maybe he's some kind of secret agent for Jack. That would explain the nice restaurant and rather private lunch. He could be gathering information so my boss can use it against me and my boobs.

"Jack's...Jack," I say finally.

Arturo's brows pinch together. "I don't know what that means."

"You will once you get to know him better." *I'm not saying anything that could come back and bite me in the butt.*

Arturo mulls that over while I munch on the garlic bread. It's excellent, with a crispy crust and soft, buttery inside. Fresh herbs add to the taste. And when the pasta comes, it's just as good, with fresh clams perfectly cooked so that they're flavorful and tender. The lack of tomato sauce enhances the overall dish, and I dig in, realizing I'm starving.

"I saw you broke up with your boyfriend," Arturo says.

"Yeah." It comes out a little stiff.

"I wasn't stalking you or anything. It was on Instagram."

"No, of course not." *Thanks, Owen, for wasting no time in sharing our private lives with everyone on the Internet.* I shrug. "It's practically public knowledge at this point."

Arturo regards me. "You don't seem too upset about it."

I blink, realizing that he's partly right. I'm not upset about losing Owen. I was already beginning to have some misgivings about our compatibility. My anger and dismay came from the fact that what our relationship represented, its potential, never meant enough to him that he wanted to fight for it. Every promise made was an empty platitude that led to nothing, and the loving partnership that could've been in our future wasn't meant to be.

Arturo looks like he's waiting for an explanation, but I don't want to bare that much of myself to a guy I barely know. So I just say, "Things were sort of fizzling out anyway. I'm not surprised it ended. The timing could've been better, though. There's something about a birthday breakup that makes the situation appear pathetic."

As I add the last part, I wonder if that's why Nicholas went along with my charade at Dolce. It might've been a type of birthday present—a way for him to take care of me. Georgia told me he was the one who took me home and made sure I was all right the night I turned twenty-one. Nicholas has done things for me without my recognizing the gesture, and I feel a little guilty. For someone like him, time is extra valuable because it's the one thing he can't buy more of. I'm a big believer in not taking more than I can give back, but right now, the balance between us seems heavily skewed.

"Cool that you aren't all upset about it, but you kinda seem distracted," Arturo says.

"Do I? Sorry." Embarrassment heats my face. "I don't mean to be rude. I was just thinking..." I trail off, since I don't want to tell him I was thinking about fake-dating my bestie's older brother. It's none of his business. Plus, if he saw the breakup post on Instagram, he might've seen Nicholas's comment, too. "Thinking that it's hard to find an apartment."

"You looking to move?"

"I was living with Owen, so..." I shrug, hoping that explains my distraction. I'm feeling a little guilty about the fact that I haven't been a very good lunch companion when he brought me here to wish me belated birthday.

"Totally awkward."

"Right? But it's okay—I'm crashing at a friend's."

"Couch surfing. Can't be that great." He shakes his head. I don't bother to correct his assumption, since it isn't important.

"If you want," he says, "there's an empty condo. Lemme send you some pics so you can see if you like it." He hands me his phone. "Gimme your digits."

If this is a ploy to get my number, it's an admirably smooth one. But at the same time, he *is* trying to help. And if he really wanted, he could get it from one of the other trainers at the gym. So I dutifully enter my info with a small smile.

"Cool." He grins and pokes his phone a few times. Mine pings and photos appear. I expected a modest place, but this one looks huge, with lots of gloss—spotless veined tiles and a vaulted ceiling with gold-edged fans and flower-shaped chandeliers. The kitchen looks modern, with stainless-steel appliances and lots of marble, and a balcony overlooks the city from on high.

This can't possibly be the right place. "Seriously? This is the empty condo you're talking about?"

He takes my hand and twists it around to see my phone screen. "Yeah. Why?"

"It's too nice! I can't afford something like this."

"You can't afford free?"

"It's *free*?" Hold on. When something's too good to be true... "How?"

"I own it."

"You're...looking for a housemate?"

"Nah, nothing like that. It's all paid for, just sitting empty 'cause I'm living in another place. I'm just offering. You know. It's not a terrible place to crash."

"I see. Well, thanks, but my realtor's going to send me a list tomorrow." It's not true, but his offer is a bit over-the-top, and I'm not comfortable accepting it. I might as well stay at Nicholas's place. "So how come you work at the gym if you own such nice places?" I try to sound casually curious.

"Ah, my old man's upset with me right now. So he told me to go get a job that requires me to be on my feet. But it's no big deal. He'll get over it soon enough, and then I'll be able to get you something nicer."

"Great." I have no idea what else to say. It sounds like he gets money from his father, and that makes me wonder if he's younger than I thought, and what his father does. Regardless, it must be nice to be able to depend on your dad, I think wistfully. I feel like at some point way back in the past, Dad was somebody who could laugh openly with me. I've seen photos of us—when there were still three in the family. The fact that he doesn't have the same open expression anymore claws into me.

Arturo and I get back to the gym a little after one. I clear my throat as he parks in the lot. "Thanks for the lunch, Arturo."

"My pleasure. We should do it again." He smiles.

I give him a neutral smile of my own. He wants more than just friendship, and I'm Nicholas's girlfriend, albeit a fake one. Even if I weren't in a pretend relationship, I'm not sure about Arturo. He's certainly handsome, and seems nice enough, but something about him is a little unsettling. I can't see myself dating him.

I start to go into the gym. As I walk across the free weight area to reach the back office, Dana and her friends start jumping up and down and screaming. What are they so excited about? Did Dana get another sponsorship deal?

As the girls circle and surge around her like fish eager to be fed, she raises her left hand, fingers spread. Something glints on her ring finger. The women shriek so loud my eardrums almost pop.

It's a diamond. A large one.

Oh my God. Is she engaged?

Did Owen propose?

It's been barely a week since he dumped me. This can't be happening.

But wait. Maybe Dana dumped Owen for being not good enough for *her* personal brand and got herself a rich fiancé. Unlikely, but it would serve my shitty ex right.

I pull my phone out and head to my office. After locking the door, I tap on the screen and bring up Owen's Instagram account.

A shot of a stunning ring on Dana's finger is the latest update. They're at Éternité—I can see a menu, and the sign in the background. Owen staged the photo so it would be obvious where they are.

According to him, the place has a long waiting list. He complained about it incessantly while telling me how upset he was that he wouldn't be able to take me there to celebrate our anniversary. According to him, the day he asked for my phone number was the one we should celebrate every year. "That's the day I met the love of my life," he'd say, and hold me like I meant the world to him.

Either he lied about the waiting list or he's been planning to propose to Dana for a while now—maybe even before he told me he loved me. He might've called me "the love of his life," but I never was.

It brings a fresh wave of pain and fury. *Why wasn't I good enough?*

The love of my life. She deserves the best. This is just the beginning—of us.

Every word on Owen's post drives a nail into my heart. This was supposed to be *my* future, but instead I was thoughtlessly discarded by the guy who professed his love for me only three months ago. Although I don't want him anymore, the feeling of inadequacy lingers, like the stench of cigarettes after somebody's smoked.

If Nicholas hadn't asked me to move in, I would've been stuck at Owen's place, witnessing the spectacle as it unfolded. But that doesn't lessen my humiliation.

The worst of it is how public my embarrassment has become.

Congrats. Your fiancée is hot.

Love at first sight.

It's so romantic how you just knew she was the one.

Some of the people wishing them the best are Owen's and my mutual friends. None of them questions the timing of the proposal or wonders about me. Actually, that isn't true. Stephanie does via private message, but her mouth is bigger than the state of Texas. She's fishing for something to gossip about.

I start to text Georgia with shaky fingers, then realize it's too early in Europe. She's probably asleep. Otherwise, she would've already texted me. She hate-stalks the people on her shit list, Owen included. Apparently, every time something bad happens to one of them, it reaffirms her belief that life isn't too awful because karma is still alive and well.

I leave the gym at four, which is a first. I make it a habit to stay until five because those are my hours. But nobody seems to notice. Then again, most people in the back office pack up by four on Fridays. Jack doesn't care because we don't sell memberships. We're just overhead.

I stop by the grocery store and pick up a few cases of cheap wine coolers. Nicholas told me I should text Cody for anything I need so he can have the staff restock it, but this isn't the kind of thing you can tell your fake boyfriend's assistant to handle.

Hi, I need some stuff to make myself feel better. Oh no, I'm fine. It's just that my shitty ex proposed to another girl within a week of dumping me. You know how that is, right? No? Well, I guess it's never happened to you. Haha. Lucky you. Hope it stays that way.

Back at the mansion, I place my coolers in front of the sofa and bring out a tub of chocolate ice cream from the freezer. Then I click around on the remote until I get a streaming service and start watching one of my favorite K-dramas. It's that or eat my ice cream in silence. And I don't think I can do silence right now, not when it will just amplify all the doubts and deficiencies in my head. Hopefully, the TV will drown out the cruel thoughts.

I dig into the ice cream and wash it down with the wine coolers, praying the sugar, fat and alcohol will make me feel better, even as part of me says they're not the solution I need.

But if I can't let go on a day like this, I don't know when I can.

20

NICHOLAS

For the first time in a while, I leave work at six o'clock. I feel terrible about having neglected Molly recently, but my agenda for the week has been packed tight, none of it pleasant. There's something particularly depressing and uncomfortable about having to let go of staff, but our newly acquired company had people whose duties not even the workers themselves could explain. The previous CEO apparently had a fetish for gift-employing people related to him or his friends.

I exhale and roll the muscles in my neck and shoulders. Hopefully the flowers cheered Molly up. I select each bouquet and have it in her room every night so she can see it when she walks in.

I've finished all my tasks, including those allocated for Saturday, to devote the weekend to her. There's a romance book signing in Vegas tomorrow, and I want to take her there tonight and return late Sunday. A surprise trip to an event that's going to have some of Molly's favorite authors, ones whose entire backlist she owns in paperback. She constantly gushes about them on her book account, too.

She's going to be so happy. I'll hand her my credit card and tell her to buy everything she wants. And there won't be any ridiculous hundred-dollar limit on her book money like before I was her boyfriend.

Her fake boyfriend.

Whatever. The key word is "boyfriend," not "fake." Besides, faking it is the first step. Fake it till you make it, and all that.

Molly's car is parked in the driveway. It's a cheap sedan that's probably seven or eight years old. I wish I could upgrade it to something nicer and safer. Maybe a Mercedes. That'd be modest enough that she wouldn't feel too uncomfortable accepting it, provided I work up to it gradually. I still can't believe she offered to "chip in" to help pay for some of the expenses.

Owen must've charged her. Since she didn't get to live at his place for the full thirty days this month, she should claw a prorated portion back for unjust enrichment. Maybe I'll call my lawyer and see what options are available.

I park the Spectre in the garage and get out, happily anticipating Molly's smile when she hears about the surprise getaway.

But the anticipation dies as soon as I step inside the house.

The TV's blaring, male voices shouting in a language I don't understand. Loud sobs accompany the noise, but they don't sound like they're coming from the TV.

I stride into the living room. Molly's sitting on the sofa, legs crossed yoga style. Her face is buried in her hands, and a spoon is held loosely between her fingers. A half-eaten carton of mostly melted ice cream sweats forlornly on the table. At least ten wine cooler bottles sit empty, making a protective half-circle around the ice cream. I wince. If she wanted to drink, I have something better than *wine coolers*.

I glance at the TV. Three men are arguing about something, but Molly still has her face buried and is making the saddest sound in her throat.

Is she one of those people who cries when they get drunk? Or is she crying because something sad is happening on the foreign drama she's watching?

Georgia cries when she watches dramas, saying it's "cathartic" even though ninety percent of her face is covered with tears and snot. I'll never understand it. But my understanding isn't important here.

My sympathy is.

I sit next to Molly and put a hand on her back.

"Hey. It's okay." It's the most neutral and empathetic thing I can think of, given my lack of information about the situation.

She finally lifts her face and looks at me. Her eyes are swollen and red, and her face is blotchy. Tears stream down in rivulets.

Even if she's just crying over a TV show, seeing her like this sticks a knife in my belly. "What's wrong?"

She points at the TV. The spoon slips from between her fingers, but she doesn't seem to notice.

"The girl in the story... She lost her mom when she was *just a child*." Her words are slurred, and her breath smells like cheap alcohol and chocolate.

Goddamn scriptwriters, going for the cheapest sympathy point. Of course Molly's upset—she also lost her mother early on. It's something I can never fix for her, and I hate feeling so helpless.

Molly says, "And her aunt took her in, but the aunt's family only wanted her because they thought that her mom left her a huge life insurance payout. Which, of course she did."

"What a bunch of assholes." I hope my words make her feel better. With any luck the show's writers will get struck by lightning—or some fertilizer company's semi packed with horseshit.

"I know, right? And they always *bullied her*, and called her *horrible things*, and even *hit* her, and made her do all the *housework*!"

So they ripped off Cinderella. Figures. They better have her best friend's older brother, who happens to be Prince Charming, suddenly appear to rescue her from her shitty aunt. "That's terrible."

Molly raises a finger. "But she stays true to herself! She's always trying to do the right thing—to be a *good person*. The only thing she wants is to be accepted and loved. For. Who. She. Is." The finger pokes my thigh with each word. "But nobody does, except for the ghosts around her."

Ghosts? "You're crying over a horror show—?" Actually, never mind. That isn't the point. "But she's going to meet somebody amazing, right? Who treats her well?" Georgia said a lot of these dramas end happily.

Molly nods.

"And...who isn't a ghost?"

She nods again and sniffs.

There we go. "Okay! So they'll get married and live happily ever after." Now she's going to smile and let out a soft, satisfied sigh...

Molly's face crumples, and a new wave of tears starts. "No!" she wails. "She does the right thing again and *dies*. All *alone*!"

Sons of bitches. Why the fuck does the drama have to end like that? Maybe I should buy the studio and fire all the writers. If Molly wanted to be depressed, she could've just watched the news. The economic indicators alone can make you want to jump off a cliff. "I'm so sorry."

"It's like...there's *no reward*. The world doesn't appreciate you if you're a nice person. Good things just randomly happen!" She flings a hand out, narrowly missing my nose. "To *anyone*! Trying to be good is such a wasted effort. If my mom's ghost is watching me, I doubt she's like, 'Yay, Molly, I love you. You're so good and sweet.' She's more like dying of embarrassment. 'What's wrong with you that nobody likes you?'"

I don't know anything about Molly's mother—she passed away so long ago. But I doubt that's the kind of thing she'd say. Now, my dad? Oh yeah.

Of course, Molly's mom could've been like that, but I prefer not to think ill of the dead. "I'm sure your mother wouldn't say that if she could see you now. She'd more likely worry about you with all this crying."

"You know what? You're right. It's more like something my dad would say. He's sooo disappointed in me." She lets out another heartbreaking sob.

Georgia once mentioned that Molly's dad is a dick. Back then I didn't know exactly what she meant, but if that man is responsible for Molly thinking so poorly of herself, he isn't just a dick. He's a prime reason humanity is so terrible.

Wishing I could undo all the hurt from her past and feeling helpless because I can't, I give her a gentle hug. "You're a wonderful person, Molly."

"Then how come nobody loves me? I try *really hard* to do the right thing and be, you know, worthy, but nobody loves me."

I love you.

I catch the words before they spill out. I don't want to tell her when she's drunk or high on sugar and misery. She might not even remember I said it, just like before.

I want to tell her when we're both sober, so she knows I mean it and will remember it. I want her to carry the knowledge that I love her above everything else, so none of the crap the world unloads on her can ever hurt her like this again.

"I have nothing," she says, then reaches for another wine cooler. She struggles to open it, then gives up with a sigh, her shoulders so low they almost touch her knees.

What happened? It can't be just a foreign soap opera making her lose control like this.

"What does she have that I don't?" Molly murmurs.

Who is *she?* "No idea. You have everything," I respond with full honesty. No woman in the world is worthier than Molly.

"Then how come he proposed to her, but not me?"

"Who?"

"Owen. He proposed to Dana."

Son of a bitch. What an asshole. How does Molly know this, anyway? Is she still pining over him? Stalking him on social media like Emmett used to with Amy?

I want to kick Owen's balls. Kicking him in the ass wouldn't hurt enough to satisfy me. "Molly, he's an idiot for not seeing how wonderful you are. You deserve the absolute best—everything you want."

"Owen said he loved me, like, *three months ago.* I guess he lied." She sighs. "I should've known. People don't love me."

My veins pulse with rage. *I'm going to destroy that son of a bitch.*

"And my dad said I'm nothing. Maybe I *am* nothing." She looks at me. "Do you know that the only people who are nice to her are the ghosts?"

"Yes," I say patiently. Her drunk talk would be cute, but right now it's just sad because she's suffering so much.

I swipe my thumbs over her tear-stained cheeks to dry them. I wish I could wipe away her pain as easily.

"Let's get you to bed." It's late and she needs to sleep off the alcohol. Also, a restful night should improve her mood.

"Don't leave me." She tightens her hand on my shirt.

"I would never leave you."

I turn off the TV and help her up. She sways a little, and I pull her close. She feels really good, but I remind myself this is about soothing her pain.

I lead her up the stairs. Her feet are unsteady, but I hold her protectively.

"Feels like I'm gonna fall," she murmurs. "Steps are so slippery."

The steps are carpeted. "I'm not letting you fall."

"I know." Her whisper is low, but I hear it.

My pulse accelerates. The alcohol has removed her filter, and I love knowing that she trusts me to take care of her and keep her safe.

I open the door to her room, help her inside and turn on the small nightstand lamp. She lands on the bed, but before I can step back, she reaches out and grasps my belt.

I freeze. The move would normally be a prelude to sex, but the way she is now... And no matter how long I've wanted her, we can't do anything when she's too drunk to give consent. "Molly..." I search for words to turn her down without making her feel even more rejected and unwanted. This is a delicate time.

"Don't go," she says, looking up at me with glazed eyes. In the soft golden light, she seems ethereal, like a forest nymph.

"But—"

"Please. I just need somebody to hold me for a bit."

I close my eyes briefly. "Okay."

She lets go of my belt, but holds on to my suit jacket. I shrug out of it, then, before she can worry that I'm leaving her, lie next to her in the bed in my dress shirt and slacks. She lays her head on my shoulder, then places her hand over my heart and loops a leg around one of mine, as though she's scared I'll disappear. She feels so soft against me, smells so sweet. It's all I can do to lie absolutely still.

Do not do anything stupid, like give in to the urge to kiss her.

I stroke her back, hoping to lull her into slumber, while my blood runs hot and fast in my veins. I stare at the ceiling. She shifts, shifts again, and then a third time. A vague sound comes out, like an annoyed kitten.

"What's wrong?" I ask.

"My bra. Can't get comfortable." She then contorts her arms, but huffs. "Still can't get the hooks off." Then she turns to me. "Hey, can you do it? The underwire is digging into my chest."

A fireball seems to explode in my heart. I try to swallow, despite my parched mouth. Alcohol has made her not only uninhibited, but sadistic. But when she looks at me with eyes that shine with trust, I go ahead and reach under her shirt. My body grows hot and tight at the feel of her smooth skin against my tingling fingertips. If only she weren't drunk...

If she were sober, she wouldn't have asked...

I unhook her bra and immediately pull my hand back so avoid temptation. She sighs as she wriggles and drops the bra on the floor, then presses tighter against my side. Her breasts feel as soft as marshmallow, and my blood flows to my cock despite all my honorable intentions.

She shifts, and her hair falls over my hand, which is currently stroking her back. I clench my teeth and try to think of leading economic indicators and what I suspect will happen with the labor market in the next two quarters.

It's not enough. My blood flows south and a sharp prickling spreads all over my body. My cock's impossibly swollen, but I move slightly to ensure she won't feel it.

This isn't the moment.

Her breathing begins to grow slower and deeper. Suddenly, she whispers, "My mom's ghost could be watching me right now."

I pat her comfortingly. "Yeah... She could."

"Do you think she's wondering why I'm not cool like her?"

"Half of you is her, Molly. You're more alike than you think."

"No. She was beautiful and smart and popular. She was everything I could never be. Not even my grandfather likes me, you know. He was devastated when Mom died, and never got in touch with me or Dad."

I put a finger underneath her chin and lift her head. Look into her alcohol-blurred eyes. She might not remember this—but I need to tell her.

"Molly, you don't have to be like your mom. You don't need your father or anybody else's approval. You're perfect just the way you are. I'd give up everything I have if I could make you see yourself the way I see you."

She blinks a few times. "Nicholas?" Her breath fans over my lips, and she's now half over me.

My mouth dries. "Yes?"

"You're the nicest fake boyfriend in the world. I wish you were within my reach so I could hold you and know you were mine forever."

A sense of triumph fills me—she doesn't just see me as that nice brother of her friend! But it's followed by a grim letdown—she also doesn't think I can be hers. Even through her drunk rambling, it's obvious that people have done incalculable damage to her tender heart. I wish I'd met her earlier, when it wasn't so bruised and hurting, so I could've protected her—and made her believe I'd be hers forever.

But it's never too late. I'm going to have to prove to her that everyone else is wrong about her. She deserves respect, kindness and love.

"I am within reach, Molly. I'm right here, and you are holding me."

"Yeah," she sighs, and her eyelids droop closed.

She's worthy of a happy ending. With me.

21

MOLLY

IF YOU GATHERED a bunch of five-year-olds and set them loose in a drum factory, the ruckus they'd make would be something like what's going on in my head. The last thing I remember is having a ton of ice cream and wine coolers, then being unable to stop crying over the K-drama.

I squint. The room is dark from the blackout curtains. That's nice...

Wait. This is *my room*. On the second floor.

How did I get up here? I don't remember...

Something pulses underneath my palm. I shift my hand and realize I'm not touching a cotton sheet. The fabric is different.

And the mattress underneath me is too hard. And lumpy.

And *warm*.

Oh shit.

I'm lying on someone. And not just anyone...

Nicholas.

The sleep haze vanishes instantly, and I freeze. Every vein in my head throbs, and I struggle to think through my hangover.

What happened last night?

I'm still in the clothes I wore to work, so...maybe nothing happened...

Hold on, *where's my bra?* Did I take it off in front of Nicholas? I concentrate, but...nothing. Did I take it off before he showed up? I hate wearing a bra when I'm trying to relax.

But why is Nicholas in my bed? He would never do anything to take advantage of a drunk woman. He's too honorable for that. So... Did *I* force myself on *him?*

I'm wearing my panties...and he's dressed...but that doesn't prove anything.

If you want to be sure, check and see if his pants are undone and he's sans underwear.

No. Absolutely not. I'm not going to feel him up like a pervert. Not when I'm beginning to think I had a lot to do with the way we're entangled here in bed.

What time is it? Maybe he's going to get up soon. I should keep my eyes closed and pretend to be asleep until he leaves to avoid any awkwardness—

No, stupid idea. *We live together.* There's no way to avoid seeing him.

Maybe I can delay the inevitable and buy some time to gather myself. But it's impossible to think when my head hurts and my body's half on top of the hottest and most wonderful man I know.

My breasts are crushed against his thick bicep, and my traitorous nipples bead like he's licking them. The achy sensation that's started at the tips of my boobs begins to pulse lazily through me until it ends between my legs. I want to squirm, find some way to ease the uncomfortable emptiness, except then he'll know I'm awake. Heat throbs through me, and everywhere I'm connected to Nicholas starts to prickle.

I don't understand how I can be so turned on. I've never responded like this to any guy. But with Nicholas, it's as though his mere presence is an aphrodisiac.

Suddenly he lays his hand on my back. Air whooshes out of my lungs, and I reflexively hold him tighter.

"Good morning." His voice is gravelly and rusty. I've never heard it like this, and it's super sexy and intimate to realize this is what he's like in the morning.

"Hi," I squeak.

"How are you feeling?"

Hot and horny all over, thanks. How about you? "Hungover, but much better. Thank you."

"I'm glad," he says softly. "Let me turn on the light." He reaches over with his free arm and flicks the switch, and the lamp by the bed emits a very low glow that doesn't hurt much.

He looks so good in the dim light. A day's growth of beard covers his strong jaw and his hair is slightly mussed from sleep. There's a hint of vulnerability and openness to him in the early morning, and a nearly irresistible urge to kiss the tip of his chin sweeps through me.

"I didn't, um, *do* anything yesterday...did I?"

"Other than ask me to unhook your bra?"

My cheeks flame and I bury my face in his shoulder, just to hide from shame.

He laughs softly. "You didn't do anything inappropriate."

I relax a fraction. He's in a good mood. I probably just got funny. Georgia says I'm hilarious when I get drunk.

"Let me..." He stretches, reaching for something on the nightstand. "Aspirin," he says, putting a couple of pills into my mouth. The pad of his thumb brushes innocently over my lips, but unholy shivers slither down my back.

He then puts a bottle of water to my mouth, and I swallow. The gesture isn't grandiose in any way, but very thoughtful. I can't remember a time somebody took care of me like this.

"I should shower and change," I say with a shy smile.

"Sure. I'll meet you in the kitchen afterward. Want some coffee?"

"Yes, please." Then I add, "You're the best."

"Only the best for my girl." He winks before gently slipping out from under me and leaving.

Somehow the air feels empty and off. A charge that's been crackling quietly in the background vanishes. Suddenly bereft, I hug myself, then go to the bathroom. A hot shower is just what the doctor ordered.

I flip the light switch, then put a hand over my eyes as the satanically bright bulbs come on. *Ugh.* I'm never drinking like that again! What did it solve, anyway? Owen and Dana are still looking forward to their disgustingly happy future together, and I'm the only one suffering.

My vision gradually adjusts, and I slowly lower my hand...then soundlessly scream at my reflection. My eyes are so swollen, they look like bread dough left out on the kitchen counter for too long. Mascara streaks line my cheeks. Is that a *chocolate stain* on my tunic? I sniff it. *Yep.* And my hair's sticking out in all directions like I've been run through a tumble dryer.

How could Nicholas not laugh seeing me like this? I would've never suspected I looked such a mess from the way he interacted with me.

All right. First step is a shower. When I come out my eyes are still swollen, but they look slightly better. Or maybe that's just futile optimism. I consider hiding in my room until I look more human, but no. Nicholas has made coffee and is waiting.

He didn't laugh before, so he probably won't laugh now.

Inhaling deeply, I go down to the kitchen. Nicholas is at the counter, tapping away on his phone. He's showered too—he smells like soap and aftershave. Underneath the scent is him—something warm and masculine that never fails to bring my nerve endings to life. A gray T-shirt and black shorts hug the thick muscles I clung to all night.

He places his phone on the counter. "How's your head? Aspirin kicking in?"

"Yes. Coffee will be perfect to get rid of what little achiness is left." I pour two cups and hand him one. The oven clock says it's one twenty-five. I can't believe he stayed in bed with me so long. He must've been awake for a while. "Thanks for taking care of me last night."

As he opens his mouth to say something, the doorbell rings. Another gaggle of women from Nikki and Ted?

He checks the intercom.

I brace for another tsunami of tall women pretty enough to be pageant queens. Instead, Nicholas murmurs something and the door shuts, plunging us into silence.

He reappears carrying a huge bouquet of yellow and orange daisies, cheery enough to make even the most morose person smile. There are some sunflowers in it as well.

"These came for you," he says, handing me the flowers.

"Me?" I take them, holding them close. Their lovely scent tickles my nose as confusion spirals through me. "From who?" Nobody knows I'm staying with Nicholas. Well, except Georgia, but she never sends flowers.

"From me." He retakes his stool at the counter.

"You?" I say stupidly. I *feel* stupid, since it's still an effort to think. I really need to finish my coffee. "For what?"

"Does a man need a reason to give his girl flowers?"

Ah. He must be worried about another Joey ambush. The flowers are beautiful. The misery from yesterday slowly ebbs, and warmth fills my heart. "Thank you. I can't remember the last time I got flowers."

Nicholas cocks a disapproving eyebrow. "Owen didn't give you any?"

"He has a pollen allergy."

He shakes his head and mutters something. Based on his tone, it's nothing flattering.

I pluck a note from the midst of the flowers. I open it, expecting a short but thoughtful message, like *I hope you're doing well* or something similar.

But instead, there is a line of beautiful foreign calligraphy in the center of the card. Below is Nicholas's name. "What does it say?" I ask, showing him the note.

He smiles. "I'll tell you later."

"When?"

"On the hundredth day we've been together."

"That's a long time."

"Only about three months."

Hmm. He might not even want to wait that long. Just look how quickly things fell apart with Owen in spite of the number of times he said he loved me.

I decide not to take the timeline too seriously. "So it's a secret?" I look down at the paper. What did Nicholas write? I'm dying of curiosity.

"No. You can use Google translate if you like. I just want to tell you later."

I didn't expect him to suggest that I try Google, but then, it makes sense for him to know that's what I could do if I don't feel like waiting.

He is looking at me with warmth in his eyes. It's so sweet, it makes me believe he holds something more than affection for me, too. So instead of pulling up Google on my phone, I smile at him playfully. "Then I'll wait. Hope you're worth it, mister."

22

NICHOLAS

MOLLY'S EYES shine as she tilts her face up and looks at me. A lovely rose colors her cheeks, and she is smiling like she's happy—as though last night she didn't cry like her world was falling apart.

Then I'll wait. Hope you're worth it, mister.

She doesn't ask for explanations. Now that I know more of the damage done to her fragile heart, I understand how precious the trust she places in me is. It makes me feel like a giant of a man—and at the same time, it's humbling.

I'd rather die than do anything to hurt her.

"What do you want to do today?" It's too late to go to the Vegas event, but we can do something else she'll enjoy.

"I was going to go apartment hunting, but my real estate agent hasn't contacted me with anything."

I try to look innocent. "That's too bad, but like I said, you can stay here as long as you need." *If things go the way I plan, he'll never find an apartment for you.* Cody should've signed a lease with every single place that fit her criteria.

"Thanks."

She didn't say anything about really *needing* a place of her own, like she did before, much to my pleasure. Maybe she's getting used to the idea of our sharing a home—even thinking of this place as hers.

"Maybe I'll bake some cookies." She smiles over the rim of her mug. "I promised I'd make some for you, and I want do something nice for both of us. My cookies are pretty awesome, you know."

Her good humor warms my heart. And I smile at her choice of phrase—*something nice for both of us*. It sounds like she's looking for things to do that we'll both enjoy, like a real couple in a committed relationship.

She finishes her coffee.

"Do we have everything you need?" I ask, since her desire to bake seems spontaneous.

"Cody should've taken care of it."

She goes to the pantry. I amble in behind her, in case she needs some help. She pulls out a few bags, then turns abruptly. "Oh! You scared me."

"Just here to assist." I flex my biceps, half playful, half showing off.

"You can bring those bags of white chocolate chips and the chopped macadamia nuts."

I reach around her and grab the ones she pointed out. My arm brushes against hers, and the hair on my forearm rises as a *zing* sizzles along my skin. Her swift intake of breath seems loud in the pantry, and the sound tugs at my dick, but she's already out and into the kitchen.

After placing the items on the counter, I pull out appliances for her —I don't cook, but I know where things are. The kitchen is sizeable and sterile, but it doesn't feel that way with her in it. She has a way of making the place feel homey. And I love having her do things with me on a lazy Saturday.

Mainly, though, I'm relieved that the pain from yesterday is nowhere to be found in her bright eyes.

Molly tosses everything into the machine. She's generous with butter, sugar and chocolate chips. A streak of flour cuts across one pink cheek like a sliver of cloud. In a simple shirt and shorts with her feet bare and her hair pulled back into a high ponytail, she looks adorable as she moves around with ease and confidence.

I'd give up everything if I could have her happy and at home with me like this forever.

I preheat the oven to her specifications, then bring out baking sheets and grease them for her. She puts dollops of dough on them until there's barely any left in the bowl, then puts them in the oven and sets the timer on her phone. She offers the wooden spoon with some dough on it. "Want some?"

I eye the mixture skeptically. "Is it safe to eat raw dough?"

"Of course."

"Wouldn't it be better cooked?"

"Think of it like cookie sushi."

"Oh, *that* sounds authentic."

"Don't be scared." She scoops a bit with one finger and puts it in her mouth. "See? Yummy."

There's a bit of dough on the center of her mouth. Before she can wipe it off, I dip my head, kissing her and licking the dough off. Her breath catches and she stills, her body taut. She tastes amazing, all beautiful fantasy and a sweetness that is uniquely Molly. Heat rises until I feel like I'm one of the cookies in the oven.

Part of me wants to be greedy and push her, but the tension vibrating through her makes me pull back. I smile.

She flushes, pulls her lips in.

"You're right. It's delicious." I wink.

She giggles. "You didn't really get a taste of the dough." She raises the spoon.

"I got something better."

Her cheeks grow rosier. Shyness and pleasure war on her face, but she isn't retreating. My affection for her swells over her ability to shake off the sadness from last night and enjoy what life has to offer.

Her phone vibrates on the counter.

"Is that the timer?" I ask.

"No. It's an alert from some of my friends on Instagram." She taps the screen. A wistful sigh escapes her parted lips. "Look at these photos! Everyone's having such a great time in Las Vegas."

Vegas. "Yeah?"

She leans against the counter. "Yeah… There's a book signing. A bunch of my favorite authors are there."

"Why didn't you go?"

"Didn't have the money." She frowns. "It's sad because some of my favorite authors are coming, and it would've been amazing to stop by to meet them and tell them how much I love their work. I'm sure they hear that from hundreds of readers all the time, but I want to tell them myself. And the photos would've been great for my Bookstagram features." She sighs again. "It would've been incredible to get autographed books, too. A couple of my favorites said they'll have special editions of their latest releases in Vegas."

"I see what you mean. Sorry you couldn't go."

"It doesn't matter. I'm having fun here with you instead." She smiles, standing next to the sunflowers I bought. Her expression is sunnier than the bright yellow blooms, and I can't tear my gaze from her.

It's disappointing that the trip to Vegas didn't work out, because we would've had fun there, too. But I appreciate her trying to look at things from a half-full perspective. Life might throw some nasty punches, and she might cry when they connect, but she's not the type to stay down.

My girl is a fighter.

The smell of fresh cookies starts to fill the kitchen. My place begins to feel like a home and hearth rather than a really expensive piece of real estate. I've never experienced hominess in all the years I've lived here, not even when my brothers are over for one of our brunches.

The alarm on her phone goes off, and Molly puts on a mitten and takes the cookies out. I reach for one.

"No, no!" She shoos me away. "You'll burn yourself. Give them some time to cool off."

I pull my hand back. "You mean I have to wait *more*?"

"Yeah." She laughs. "Good things happen to those who exercise patience. Didn't anybody tell you that?"

"Nope. My brothers told me I need to seize the day."

"You can seize all you want later."

That sounds suggestive, but before I can respond, the doorbell chimes. Molly frowns and looks at me. "Did somebody just bypass the intercom?"

"Yes." I stride to the foyer. Molly follows.

"Do you think it's Joey?"

"Better not be." I'll definitely dunk him in the pool. Maybe I should just get a couple of Uzis for home defense.

I open the door. Cody stands before us in a white *I Heart Vegas* T-shirt and denim shorts. His black hair is limp without any styling products—he's overly fond of gel—and his clothes accentuate the lankiness of his frame. His pale face looks so young it's like somebody put a high school kid's head on the body of a thirty-year-old. Next to him are seven neatly stacked cardboard boxes.

"Hey, boss," he says cheerily. "Hello, Molly." He turns back to me. "Got everything you asked for." He starts to carry the boxes in. His movements are measured and precise, and he doesn't appear to hurry. But he's so efficient that he moves more quickly than most people.

I help him bring the stuff inside. Molly makes as if to lift one, but I shake my head at her. "Leave them."

"I can help."

"I know, but you're supposed to let me carry the heavy things and admire me while I flex my arms manfully."

Cody makes a sound that sounds suspiciously like a snort.

"I already admire your body plenty," she says lightly.

"How can it be 'plenty' when you've never swooned?"

She laughs, then puts the back of her hand to her forehead and lets out a long, soft sigh. "Oh my..." she says in a faux-Southern accent. "Is it hot in heah? Ah feel so *dizzy*..." She collapses bit by bit into a chair, then squints at me through her fingers. "Satisfied?"

"Don't forget to say which of my body parts is making you swoon."

"All right. If Ah can mustah the energy while fanning mahself."

Once all the boxes are in the living room, I turn to Cody. "Thanks."

"Thank *you*. I'll make good use for your jet for our honeymoon."

Cody isn't somebody I can force to work overtime without an outrageous bribe.

"And do I smell cookies?" He shoots me a wicked smile. "Can I get one?"

I roll my eyes. "Not unless you want to die. Leave."

"We could give him some. I made plenty," Molly says.

"Just joking," Cody says. "I'm on a diet."

I wave him away, and he leaves with a soft chuckle.

"That's too bad about the diet."

I shake my head. Cody isn't dieting. He doesn't eat anything with more than a teaspoonful of sugar in any case. He was just messing with me because he knows I like Molly. I wish Molly could accept how I feel about her as easily as Cody does.

"He can get a little silly. But he's a great assistant." I gesture at the boxes. "Anyway, these're for you."

"For me? What's the occasion?" She walks toward the boxes, her eyes on mine.

"Open one. You'll see." Vegas didn't work out the way I wanted, but I'm dying to see her reaction to my alternate plan.

She pulls the tape off one of the boxes, then gasps when she sees books inside. She pulls one out, flips the cover open and puts a hand over her mouth. "Oh my God! This is the special edition I was talking about! And it's *autographed*. And *personalized*!" She takes out another and checks it, then picks up a third. "Are they all autographed?"

I nod. "I was actually going to take you to that event in Vegas, but things, ah, didn't exactly work out the way I had planned last night. So I sent Cody to grab them for you."

She takes a step back, looking at the boxes. Then she turns and jumps on me with a cry of excitement, looping her limbs around my neck and waist.

I hug her back, wrapping my arms around her and holding her tight. She feels like sweet dreams and heaven. But the bright light in her eyes is the greatest reward.

"Happy belated birthday," I say, my heart pounding.

"But you already gave me a present."

"That was for Pre-Girlfriend Molly. These are for Girlfriend Molly."

She pulls back to look at me. Her lips tremble. Happiness, trepidation and something else I can't put my finger on fleet over her beautiful face. I made such a tiny gesture, and she's already overwhelmed.

It's an inflection point in our relationship, one I need to take care with. When people are too overcome, they start to retreat. Like a computer shutting down when it overheats.

"If you keep doing things like this, I might not want to stay fake." She attempts a joke in a shaky voice.

Oh, baby, that's the plan. "You better get used to it, Molly. You're *my* girlfriend now."

23

MOLLY

MANIFESTATION WORKS, Georgia said. *You focus on what you want and wish for it and it's yours.*

I've given it a week, but it doesn't work. It's like the universe is punishing me for saying out loud what I wanted in my new apartment.

I do another search online early Saturday morning, hoping that the realtors and apartment management companies updated their listings. After all, aren't weekends the prime time to show vacant units?

But everything that pops up is out of my price range, too far from work or in areas I wouldn't feel comfortable driving through, much less living in. I haven't looked for a place to rent in a couple of years, but I don't remember my last search being this difficult.

I pick up my phone to whine to my bestie.

–Me: Argh! It's so frustrating! I can't find a new apartment! It's like this city doesn't have anywhere for a young woman to live!

–Georgia: Sorry to hear that. But it's not life or death. Just crash at Nicholas's place a little longer.

–Me: But I feel so wrong here.

Nicholas keeps doing things that confuse me. I keep feeling like I could be his *real* girlfriend. And I'm afraid I'm alone in this delusion. A little distance between us might clarify things, but it's impossible when we're living together.

–Georgia: Why? Does Nicholas walk around naked or something?

My face heats. If he did, I'd just turn into a puddle of hot need and die. There's only so much sensory overload my body can process...

–Me: No. He's a total gentleman. You know that.

Which is a problem. For me. Living with Nicholas makes me realize I'm a closet pervert...probably. There's an awful, naughty side of me that wishes he would be a little *less* gentlemanly. I wouldn't mind it if he pushed me against the wall like in that hot scene from *Wrong Jersey Right Guy.*

He wouldn't even have to be *actively* less gentlemanly. Like he could be so bad at tying a towel around his hips that it slipped off every now and again...

But no. He's annoyingly great at tying towels, and he's always courteous and considerate. He even helped me find a few books that were missing from the boxes from Owen's place. I don't remember taking them out, but I must've done so. Some of my favorites—ones with lots of highlighted passages—turned up in the library and the living room.

At the same time, he keeps sending me flowers at Get Jacked. They all come with notes in a foreign language. Each day there's a new language—I can tell because the writing is different. Then in the afternoon he'll send me the cutest cupcakes or truffles, also with mysterious messages. I keep them all to read on our one hundredth day together.

The little gestures make me feel cherished and important—because he is thinking of me, even when he's busy at work. If I didn't know better, I'd say he likes me, but I just can't believe it.

He must be acting in case we ever run into someone one us of knows —or Joey invades his home again. It's just that Nicholas is so convincing that I keep forgetting he doesn't mean any of it.

–Georgia: You're right. He's always really proper. I've occasionally wondered what kind of woman could shake that composure.

Yeah, you and me both. Maybe one of those hot actresses or models could shake him up. I can totally picture it. They're glamorous enough to match his effortless magnetism and panache.

Speaking of which... I need to figure out what I'm going to wear to the gala. I don't have anything sleek like what his other dates have worn to similar events. My closet consists of clothes I picked up from thrift stores and clearance racks. They're nice, but not good enough for the kind of functions Nicholas goes to. Well, there's what Dad bought for me, but those dresses are too small—and not very flattering because of that.

I don't want to embarrass Nicholas by underdressing. I need something spectacular, something that will wow. My gaze drops to my hands. At least my nails are nice. But that's not much of a consolation at the moment.

Definitely time to go emergency shopping. It's too bad Georgia's out of the country. She loves shopping almost as much as chocolate and reading. And she'd know the kind of high-end stuff I need.

Argh. I dig my fingers into my hair. I shouldn't have been procrastinating out of fear and uncertainty, but what do I know about high fashion or fancy clothes? I've glanced at *Vogue*, but the stuff the magazine features isn't anything I'm ever going to be able to wear and feel comfortable in. Besides, do I want to spend twenty-six thousand dollars I don't have on a dress that looks like malformed cotton candy?

I could ask Cody for help, but that seems wrong. He's Nicholas's assistant, not mine. And even if he gave me some suggestions, being able to afford the items is another matter.

I'm just putting my phone down when Georgia sends me a photo. It's a screencap of Owen's latest post.

Getting ready to take my girl to the charity gala tonight. They're going to auction off a date with my fiancée—which normally I wouldn't allow, lol, but it's all for a good cause.

Is he coming to the gala Nicholas and I are attending? *Probably,* I decide with a sinking feeling. How many charity galas are happening tonight?

And he's going to bring Dana.

Dad's disapproving voice rings in my head. *You had your chance to be better, Molly.*

How long does it take to develop food poisoning? I could eat an iffy egg in the next hour...

Wait. Would that give Nicholas enough time to find an alternate date for the gala? He won't want to show up solo.

–Georgia: His smug-ass posts are pissing me off. "My fiancée" this, "my fiancée" that. :puke-emoji: I can't believe he got invited to the Pryce Foundation gala. I thought that family had better taste.

–Me: They probably just want his money.

Maybe this is why he felt the need to dump me so abruptly. He didn't want to take me as his plus-one and ruin his "personal brand" in front of all the rich and important people.

–Georgia: Ha, he wishes! They laugh at his kind of money. He isn't rich or important enough to be invited. Nikki told me everyone wants to be on their good side.

–Me: What's so special about them?

And what do I need to do to make sure I get on their good side? Or at least their neutral side. I don't want to do anything to embarrass Nicholas or jeopardize his relationship with them.

–Georgia: They're old money. Not like Hollywood, even though Ryder Reed is some kind of cousin. And they married into other important and rich families. Like the Sterlings of the Sterling & Wilson fortune. They're somehow connected to the Lloyds too, I think.

I don't know anything about those people—other than Ryder Reed, of course, since he's a huge movie star—but I understand they're influential. The kind of people Nicholas would like to be friendly with.

My anxiety about the evening shoots up high enough to go into orbit. But being cooped up in my room solves nothing. I need to get a caffeine boost and figure out what I'm going to do. The iffy eggs option is sounding really good about now. Maybe Joey or Cody can find Nicholas an emergency fake date.

When I get downstairs, Nicholas is making coffee. He and I both prefer to have a slower start on weekends.

Several sips of the fresh brew later, my brain is functioning better. And with better brain function comes a better mood. I can probably splurge quite a bit on the dress I need. Look at all the money I'm saving on rent and utilities.

I put bagel slices for us in the toaster. It can brown four at once.

Nicholas puts a black AmEx on the counter and slides it over to me. "Get what you need for tonight—dress, shoes, jewelry, purse. The works." He waves negligently. "Whatever you like."

I stare at the card while my accountant brain redoes the math to factor in shoes, accessories and a purse into my budget. *Is there anything okay in my accessory collection? Do I need to get diamonds? Can anybody tell if I get cubic zirconia instead?* "But you're already doing so much."

He frowns. "My dates don't spend their own money to go out with me."

"They don't?" Does this mean I have to wear the kind of thing his previous dates wore?

"It isn't that much money, Molly."

That jerks me back to the conversation—and the list of things he asked me to buy. "Jewelry isn't that much money?" I don't know what kind of stuff his previous women splurged on, but he's got to be joking here.

Or they took advantage of him, which I have trouble believing. He's too sharp and capable. He probably looked the other way.

He shrugs. "Maybe they didn't buy jewelry with my money. Some of them."

"That's what I thought." Nicholas is too perfect to be somebody's sucker. "So what's the real budget?"

"The budget is: you buy whatever you want for the gala. And if you still haven't hit the credit limit, treat yourself to some books or whatever else you feel like grabbing." He smiles.

I pick up the card and consider its cool surface. The centurion in the middle gazes off into the distance. "*Is* there any limit on one of these?"

"Not that I've found."

"So..."

"So I guess you can buy all the books and chocolate you want."

He's joking... Right? Except his expression is dead serious. Like a doctor informing you you're having a heart attack.

Maybe his calm steadiness hides how frivolous he is with money. On the other hand, he's *really* rich. So it honestly might not matter if he gets a brand-new truck or offers to buy me whatever I want. Actually, considering the relative levels of our wealth, his spending five or six figures like this is like my cheering myself up by picking up a pretty lipstick from Walmart.

And he's probably worried that I won't be able to afford something nice enough to match up to the rest of the gala's guests. The family hosting the event might be more important to him than I thought.

But the thing that really decides me is—I'd rather choke on cat vomit than look shabby next to Dana. She has the better body and face, but I want to do what I can to close the gap. I don't want Nicholas to look at her and begin to wonder what the heck he's doing with me.

"Is there any particular store you want me to hit?" I have no idea where to get something suitable. The kind of place you'd take your fake boyfriend's black AmEx to, so you can shine like proper arm candy.

He looks at me blankly, then picks up his phone. He starts tapping the screen. "Let's find you a consultant."

He keeps tapping and tapping, then mutters, "That cocksucker." Finally he stops and smiles.

"Okay, so I couldn't find a personal shopper on this short notice, but one of my sisters-in-law is going to go with you. Lucie is nice, so hopefully you'll hit it off."

WHEN I REACH the exclusive boutique Nicholas told me about, I suddenly realize that his "sister-in-law Lucie" is actually Lucienne Peery of Peery Diamonds. It seems impossible, but the towering height, the gorgeous face with cool blue eyes...

It's her.

Although I don't follow celebrity news closely, everyone has heard of her and seen her photos. She's infamous in some ways. The woman has graced more gossip sites than anybody I can think of.

Plus, a few months ago the Internet was crazy with the news that her father had been convicted of a bunch of financial crimes, and her ex-boyfriend had stolen from her company. Her life is like a soap opera you can't tear your eyes from. It was plastered all over the TVs in the gym, and I saw a few segments. Plus, Georgia followed it religiously, saying she always knew Lucienne Peery was a good woman.

"Nobody's as one-dimensional as the media makes it sound," Georgia said.

If Dad were here, he'd fall to his knees. Lucienne is exactly the kind of daughter he wishes I could be. Tall, fashionable, accomplished and brimming with unshakable confidence.

A royal-purple dress and nude stilettos look incredible on her. Discreet rubies and diamonds glitter on her ears and throat. A string of rubies around one slim ankle glints as she struts toward me like the world's hottest model. On her finger is a stunning sapphire and diamond ring and a white gold wedding band with diamonds encrusted on it.

I feel *grossly* underdressed by comparison. I should've selected something better than a pink cotton baby tee, denim skirt and black sandals. At least my toenails are pretty...

"So you're Molly!" Lucienne says cheerfully.

I manage to smile. "Hello, Lucienne. So nice to meet you."

"Please, call me Lucie. Nicholas told me everything. So you're together." Her eyes sparkle.

Does she know I'm just a fake girlfriend? "Seems that way."

"How exciting. Let's get you dressed for the gala. I'm so sad I'm going to miss it. If I'd known Nicholas would be attending with his girlfriend, I would've never agreed to a dinner date with my husband." She might not want to have a date night with her husband tonight, but the flush in her cheeks betrays how much she loves him.

"I don't think hanging out at a gala is worth forgoing a romantic time with your husband." I'm not worth giving up a couple's night out.

"Yes, but Sebastian said it's a big deal that Nicholas is bringing a girlfriend. He doesn't really date."

We aren't really dating, either, but I keep that to myself. The first rule of fake dating is you don't let others know you're fake-dating.

She leads me into the store, her stilettos clacking quietly on the pale golden tiles. Fancy chandeliers glow over us. A few clerks nod in greeting.

Finally, she waves at a slim Asian woman in an ivory scoop-neck tunic and black pencil skirt. "Julie, can you please show us something suitable? My friend Molly here is going to the Pryce Foundation charity gala tonight. I want her to outshine everyone at the event."

The woman smiles. "Of course. This way. Would you like some refreshments?"

"A mimosa for me. How about you?"

"Um... I'll have the same." It's probably safe to follow Lucie's lead.

I expect to try on multiple dresses until I'm exhausted from taking things on and off. But it doesn't work that way. Lucie and I sit on a loveseat with glossy catalogues spread out in front of us. Two racks with dresses stand to our left, and I look at the photos, wondering if I'm supposed to select a few. After a couple of mimosas, a lot of things seem fantastic.

Julie says, "Given her curves and coloring—it's probably best if we stick to bold shades and simple cuts."

"The fabric has to be right, though," Lucie murmurs. "Something silk... Maybe chiffon...?"

"Of course."

Julie picks out six photos. Lucie taps her chin with a well-manicured index finger then looks at me. "What do you think?"

I think I'm overwhelmed. I smile. "They all look great."

"But I think maybe these two would be the best." She points to a super-slinky blue dress and a red one with a fitted top and a side slit.

I don't have what it takes to pull off the blue one, but maybe the other will be okay. "Let's try the red."

"Fantastic choice." Lucie nods.

Julie leads me to the dressing room, where the red dress is already hanging inside. I change into it. The dress has a built-in bra with surprisingly good support. The fabric on this dress isn't so thin that it shows panty lines, so that's good, too.

I study myself in the mirror. The outfit's glamorous and fits well, but I feel kind of awkward. Like a little girl dressing up with adult clothes. I've never tried on a dress this beautiful, and I don't know if I can do it justice.

When I come out, Lucie nods approvingly. "That looks *really* good on you, Molly."

"You think?"

"Yes. It's perfect. I love it."

Her smile is so genuine, my anxiety starts to ease.

She says, "But you need shoes—something that will add at least three inches to your height. And jewelry. This look won't be complete without a necklace."

"And chandelier earrings," Julie adds.

"Correct. Diamonds and platinum. I can arrange for those, of course." Lucie grins at me. "Aren't we awesome to pick out the best dress so fast?"

Her good humor is contagious, and my mood lightens. "We *are*."

Lucie's grin gets wider. "Julie, can you select proper lingerie to go with the dress and shoes? She's going to need a clutch as well. Something classy and timeless."

"Of course." Julie turns to instruct her staff.

I take my seat next to Lucie. "Wow. That was...fast."

"I don't believe in wasting time shopping. It should be as efficient as possible. After all, shopping is the least important aspect of our prep."

"There's more?" I ask in shock. What else did Nicholas's previous dates spend money on?

"Uh-huh. A spa. Get a nice massage and pamper yourself. A facial should help, too."

"Nicholas didn't mention any of that." He said "dress, shoes, jewelry and purse," although later he said the jewelry was a joke. Sort of.

Lucie scoffs. "Just because a man forgets something, doesn't mean we don't deserve it. He gave you a credit card, right?"

I nod.

"Well, then. It's all good."

And she drags me to a spa. I mean, it's called a "spa," but it's more like a place to do everything you could possibly need to get ready for an evening out. I probably shouldn't spend Nicholas's money like this, even though he said I could charge whatever I wanted.

But when Lucie told me what a facial can do—make me glow—I couldn't resist. I really want to be pretty for the event. I don't want people to think Owen did the right thing on my birthday. And I don't need people to look at me and Nicholas and conclude that he totally could've done better.

After a warm soak and massage, I come out of the treatment room to take a tea break. My skin feels softer, and I already feel more relaxed. I spot Lucie in her robe drinking herbal tea at a small, round table. She's chatting with a black-haired woman in a robe, then notices me and waves.

"There you are. How was it?"

"Great." I smile, taking an empty seat.

"Let me introduce you. Ceinlys, this is Molly. Molly, Ceinlys."

The other woman extends her hand, lifting intense blue-green eyes to regard me. "How do you do?" Her voice is soft and cultured. She's free of makeup, fancy clothes and jewelry, but her presence speaks of quiet confidence and glamor. If she were a perfume, she'd be one of those ultra-expensive and feminine scents nobody can resist.

I shake her hand. "Nice to meet you."

"So you're Nicholas's girlfriend."

I flush. "You know him?"

"We socialize from time to time. Lucie mentioned that the two of you will be making a public appearance together for the first time."

"Ah, yeah." The spa staff comes over with a menu, and I ask for hot ginger tea, which arrives promptly. I take a small, careful sip. It's sweet and delicious. "That's why I'm here." I take another sip. "To get ready."

Ceinlys's eyebrows rise. "You're nervous."

"A little, yeah."

"Why?"

Why? "Because he's just...perfect. I'm..." I take a third sip. "I'm just me." My face grows warm.

Ceinlys smiles. She can probably tell I'm not the kind of woman who frequents places like this. I've never even been to a spa before. Or had an "exfoliating and rejuvenating" soak.

I resist the urge to fidget. My sympathy for the animals at Furry Haven triples. This must be how they feel when somebody walks in to adopt—the desperate need to be deemed good enough to be accepted the way they are.

"You remind me of myself," Ceinlys finally says. "From a long time ago, of course."

I stare at her, not believing my ears. How could I have anything in common with this ultra-glamorous woman?

"Don't look so shocked, my dear. Not all of us are born into wealth. Some marry into it." She smiles. "If Nicholas loves you and wants you to be by his side, then that's all that matters. Provided, naturally, that you adore him in return."

Of course I adore him. But the problem is I'm not sure how *he* feels —or if it's going to last for more than a few weeks. Owen dumping me hurt. Nicholas dumping me would be devastating.

Come on, girl. It's fake dating, fake dumping and fake devastating.

Except an odd stutter in my heart says nothing feels fake with Nicholas.

24

NICHOLAS

THE LIMO MOVES in a stately manner through the L.A. traffic. More accurately, the chauffeur is trying for stately, but the pace is more suited to a snail.

Lucie texted and asked me to pick Molly up from a spa for the gala. She said Molly would be fully massaged, made up and ready for the evening. So I'm inside the vehicle, checking my texts, all casual and cool. But my heart is beating double time, and every cell in my body roils with restless energy.

This is going to be our first night out together.

I spent over an hour debating which tux to wear. What cologne to put on—or if I should bother with it at all. Which watch and cuff links to select.

I settled on Armani—because it's classic—and nothing for cologne because none of the scents seemed acceptable. A watch from Harry Winston, and cuff links from Sebastian Jewelry with emeralds in the center because the shade reminds me of Molly's eyes.

Then I picked out a bouquet with lisianthus and sweet pea—Molly's favorite flowers.

My phone buzzes with another text from Huxley.

—Huxley: I'd give a kidney to be going to the charity gala tonight with you.

—Me: Why? You don't like those things that much.

He goes to a select few high-society functions purely for networking. He doesn't care that much about schmoozing with the city's rich and powerful, since he is one.

—Huxley: Yeah, but my grandmother wants to see me. To discuss the "proper course" for my life.

That's Huxley's grandma-speak for "see the light and join the family law firm, my dear, ideally sooner rather than later." His mother's side of the family takes their legal dynasty seriously.

—Emmett: Guess you telling her, "I've already given my name to the firm. What more do you want?" didn't go over well?

—Huxley: You should've seen her face. She would've shot me if she'd had a gun. I apologized before she could get up to grab one.

—Noah: I didn't know she owned a gun.

—Huxley: She has an impressive collection. A crack shot, too. If life were a western, she'd be the bad-ass gunslinger everyone cowered around.

—Noah: If you send a hefty check to the foundation, your accountant will thank you for another tax deduction. Then you can tell her you're practicing tax law, LOL.

—Huxley: Yeah, that'd go over well. Asshole. You're just laughing because your family doesn't try to tell you what to do.

Herding feral cats would be easier than trying to get Noah to do something he didn't want to. Hell, half the time, you can't even get him to do what he does want. Like finishing the novel he started back in... I can't even remember when.

—Emmett: I sent some money, too, since I can't go. Monique needs me, and Amy apparently has to work late. I don't know why, but I'm sure Grant does.

Little Monique is their daughter. Amy works at GrantEm, a venture capital firm founded by Emmett and Grant. She used to report to Emmett, but after marrying him, she switched bosses to avoid any appearance of favoritism. But anybody who knows how smart and hardworking she is recognizes she's legitimately earned every promotion and bonus.

–Grant: It has nothing to do with me. I told her she didn't have to, but she said she wanted to get the project done today. She probably doesn't trust Larry. He fucked up once before, and she had to come in and fix it.

–Emmett: Can we fire him?

–Grant: You'll have to take it up with her, since he started to report to her.

Grant isn't getting himself stuck between Emmett and Amy. He isn't stupid.

–Sebastian: Don't be so sad about missing it. I can't go either. Got a hot date with Luce.

I can just hear Seb's laughter.

–Emmett: Stop rubbing it in.

–Sebastian: I wasn't rubbing. Just pouring the salt, but not rubbing it in. Speaking of dates, she told me Nicholas's girl is a babe.

Not just a babe. A goddess. *My* goddess.

–Noah: So you finally went for it. Good for you.

–Me: She's divine.

–Griffin: So what changed?

–Me: She's not with that guy anymore.

Who didn't deserve her in the first place. What an asshole. Not good in bed—yeah, right. Bet his dick is too soft to do the job.

Actually, no. I'm not going to think about her and her ex in bed. It's nauseating.

–Noah: I don't know why you let something like another guy get in your way for so long. Boyfriends can be disposed of. Which you apparently did, because she's with you, not him.

–Me: She was also too young.

–Sebastian: How young?

–Griffin: Jail bait?

–Me: Eight years younger.

–Emmett: WTF? You serious?

–Sebastian: I think I just peed my pants laughing.

–Me: Shut up.

—Grant: You're sad, bro.

—Griffin: It's only eight years.

—Me: That's almost a decade.

—Sebastian: So? She's legal.

—Me: You don't understand. I met her at her high school graduation. She still had some baby fat, for God's sake! I was in my mid-twenties!

AND MY ATTRACTION *to her felt criminal.*

—Sebastian: Again, so? Luce is nine years younger.

—Me: Congratulations, cradle robber.

—Noah: Gotta up your game, Nicholas. Need some tips?

—Me: The day I seek relationship advice from you is the day my doctor takes me off life support. How many croissants did you get from Bobbi's Sweet Things, slick?

For some reason, Bobbi has decided she doesn't like Noah and refuses to let him buy croissants from her bakery. It's been an ongoing battle for him because he's become even more determined to get them.

—Noah: Three! Ha!

—Grant: Only because Aspen bought them for him.

—Noah: Traitor!

—Grant: Hey, she deserves the credit.

—Me: I knew it! Tell Aspen to quit buying them for him, because when Bobbi finds out, she might quit selling them to her. Dough before bros.

The limo pulls up in front of the spa Lucie mentioned.

—Me: I'm about to pick my girl up now. You all behave.

—Noah: Make an impression she'll never forget! I have some suggestions if you need help.

Shaking my head, I put the phone away as the chauffeur opens the door. Noah's "suggestions" are bound to get me into trouble.

I step out with the bouquet and shoot my cuffs. I walk into the lobby, which is its own world of crystal, marble and soothing music. Although Lucie called it a spa, it also offers services like hair, facials and makeup to get a woman ready for a fancy night out. I wouldn't have thought of something like this. I make a mental note to send something nice to Lucie to thank her. Molly deserves to be pampered in every way.

Just as I'm about to speak to the receptionist, Molly appears. I turn, then stare, feeling like somebody's blowing millions of bubbles into my heart.

She glows like the sun. The brilliant smile on her beautiful face makes me grin in return. A long scarlet dress with a sexy side slit that climbs to mid-thigh wraps around her curves like a dream, and her wide eyes shine like the finest emeralds. The stylist curled her hair, which now bounces around her shoulders. A stunning set of diamonds hangs from her ears and neck—probably Lucie's selection.

I'm losing my heart to Molly...all over again.

"How do I look?" She spreads her arms, the gesture full of shy expectation.

You look so good I want to hold you and dance under the moon. Then I want to kiss you and peel you out of that dress. Love you until you come over and over again, your body quivering under mine. "Perfect."

She presses her lips together for a moment, like she can't believe it, then smiles like she's trying to power the entire city.

I remember the bouquet. "Here. For you."

Her eyes widen in delight. "Thank you!"

She looks at me like I've given her the world. For another such expression, I would lay it at her feet.

"Can we swap out your jewelry?" I ask.

Her smile loses some wattage as she runs her fingers over the stones around her neck. "You don't like it?"

"Lucie has excellent taste, but I actually brought something for the evening."

I signal one of the receptionists, and she takes us to an airy resting room with a huge lounger and an armchair. Golden tiles and satiny ivory wallpaper enhance the feminine feel of the chamber, and a huge vanity with a spotless mirror sits against the wall to our left.

I have her sit in the lounger as I pull out boxes with the pastel-blue Sebastian Jewelry logo on the lids. These are the pieces I've commissioned over the years.

Molly looks at them curiously, and I smile. "They're one-of-a-kind pieces for a one-of-a-kind girl."

The loveliest shade of rose colors her cheeks. I gently pull off the chandelier earrings, then replace them with drop earrings made with strings of diamonds that end with single teardrop-shaped rubies. She tilts her head to study them better, then smiles up at me. "They're gorgeous. Thank you."

"We're not done yet."

My fingers brush against her as I undo the necklace clasp. The pulse on the side of her neck flutters under the delicate skin. I lay Lucie's diamonds on the cushion next to her and pick up a diamond and ruby necklace that looks like a veil made with bursting stars. I wrap it around her throat. She looks at her reflection, then meets my eyes in the mirror. Holding them, I kiss the little bumps of bone on the back of her neck. Desire pours through me at the heated honey taste of her, and I can't help breathing a little harder. I nip the tender skin with the edge of my teeth. The air fans over her neck, sending a shiver through her entire body. She shifts her legs.

She feels something for me, even if it's something as simple and basic as lust.

I want to thread my fingers into her hair and kiss her hard. I wish we didn't have to go to the damn auction, but I said I'd take her, and I don't want to break a promise to her, no matter how small. Nothing she expects from me is inconsequential.

"You're perfect." I press a last kiss on her neck before tossing the diamonds into the jewelry boxes and offering her my arm. She lays her hand there. It feels right to have it in the crook of my elbow, to have her walk out with me like she belongs by my side.

I plan to keep her there.

25

NICHOLAS

The Aylster Hotel's Grand Ballroom is a great venue for a charity auction. The Pryce Family Foundation's head, Elizabeth Pryce-King, champions all types of worthy causes, and the woman has an incredible talent for squeezing funds from the wealthy with the right words and a smile.

The theme of tonight's event is Better Local. Elizabeth has raised hundreds of millions of dollars to build schools in Lebanon and Egypt, to bring critical care to parts of the world without sufficient medical infrastructure. But now she's focusing on improving Los Angeles. Tonight's bachelorette auction will be unique. Instead of one or two causes that the foundation chose, the bachelorettes can direct the proceeds from their winning bids to a charity of their choice. The new system has created more enthusiasm and excitement from the participants.

Thankfully, Molly won't be part of the auction. I checked. Furry Haven already has a bachelorette—Dana Mincer.

I just want to give Molly a chance to dress fancy, sip expensive champagne and have fun. She highlighted passages from some of her books about lavish social functions, so she must be particularly interested in them.

She highlighted a lot of sex scenes, too. I've committed those to memory as well. If she's interested, so am I.

The moment Molly and I enter the ballroom, many sets of male eyes swing toward her. They openly trace her curves.

One by one, I catch their eyes and hold contact until they look away. It generally doesn't take long. I have a reputation for being steady and even-tempered. But that makes my confrontational body language that much scarier.

"Do you know these people?" Molly whispers. "Should we go say hello?"

"I do, but we're going to ignore them."

A beat. "You aren't going to introduce me?"

"Why would I do that?" An introduction would result in their checking her out at close range, and I might end up poking their lecherous eyeballs right back into their brains.

A shadow fleets across her face. She drops her eyes, then looks around distractedly. "Right. We're not, like...really dating. It'd be kinda awkward."

Shit. She took it the wrong way. "That's not the reason. Those men are wolves in tuxedos. Cavemen with clubs. Except that cavemen are honest. They just grunt and beat each other up. But these guys fake it all the time. They aren't good for you."

She finally looks at me again, and the eye contact loosens the knot in my belly. "Aren't they your friends?"

"Not when they're looking at you like they'd like to screw you right here on the hotel floor."

She gasps and slaps my arm. "They are *not!*"

I shake my head. "If only you could read men's minds..."

"The only one I want to read is yours."

"Me? I'm an open book."

She laughs. But before I can enjoy her good humor, a large guy in a tux opens his arms to hug her. "Oh, hey! I didn't know you were going to be here."

I narrow my eyes. He seems familiar.

She gazes up at him in amazement. "Arturo?"

The name jogs my memory. Arturo Morales. The youngest son of

Esteban Morales, a popular movie star who owes his career to Dad. Esteban is a womanizer—just like Dad—and his sons seem to be competing to see who can screw more women than their father.

Arturo moves closer. Before he can hug her, I draw Molly toward me and wrap a possessive arm around her shoulders. *No way you're touching my girl.* Arturo probably breathes STDs. I'm not letting him put his filthy, diseased hands on my Molly.

She gives me a curious look, but remains flush by my side. The feel of her soft body pressed against me is soothing. But if I were a wolf, I'd be baring my teeth at Arturo.

"What are you doing here?" she asks, looking him up and down.

I resist the urge to put a hand over her eyes. "You know this guy?" Esteban and his boys hang out with certain types, which Molly—thankfully—doesn't fit.

"Sure. He's the new personal trainer I told you about. You know, the one who took me to lunch?"

This is the asshole? He got cookies out of her for it, too. She told me she took some to work to share with him, although I bet they weren't what he really wanted to eat. "What are you doing working at a gym? Don't you have money from your father?" My tone might be smooth, but my eyes are mocking.

Arturo's face twists with disgust. "Nah, bro. He cut me off for six months."

"Get your dick stuck in a goat's ass?" Arturo's older brother supposedly had that happen. A few badly focused pictures went viral a couple of years ago, and Esteban wasn't amused. Noah, who brought it to all of our attention at a brunch, wanted to know why people didn't buy phones with better cameras.

Molly gapes, while Arturo turns red. He gives me a why-you-gotta-bring-that-up? glare. "I totaled a brand-new Lambo."

"Too bad it didn't total your dick," I mutter.

"It wasn't a big deal, bro. The cops didn't say anything." His eyes are on Molly, gauging her reaction. He must not like what he's seeing. "Anyway, it was good seeing you, Molly. We'll catch up later."

"Yeah, sure." She waves.

He struts away like he owns the hotel. He probably doesn't feel particularly ashamed of his behavior—or his family's. Money and fame tend to put a thick coat of Teflon over you.

I grab a couple of flutes from a server and hand one to Molly. "Just how closely do you work with him?"

"Not very. I'm an accountant, and he's a trainer. I spend most of my time in my little office." She sips her champagne. "Did he do something to you?"

"Yes." *He breathes near you.*

"Oh. But you aren't, like, enemies or anything...?"

"No." If I considered him my enemy, he'd be dead...at least figuratively. Hopefully he's at the tail end of the six months of punishment, so he'll quit his gig at the gym soon. "Let's introduce you to the hostess, by the way. She should be around. She likes to personally say hello to everyone who attends."

We wander around a bit and soon find Elizabeth Pryce-King talking to a small group of businessmen. She's a pretty blonde with sleet-colored eyes and an angelic smile that never fails to put you at ease. When she speaks to you, it's as though you're the absolute center of her universe. It's a trick Mom can do when she puts her mind to it, but with Elizabeth there's no whimsy or over-the-top drama. She's in a modestly cut white dress that still manages to show off the lean lines of her body. She excels at navigating the line between classy and sexy.

Given the enormous charitable projects she's spearheaded, some believe she's a saint walking among us, but I don't buy that. She runs her foundation with an iron fist—a charitable iron fist, but an iron fist nonetheless. A woman who was merely nice wouldn't be able to manage it. Her family's foundation is one of a few charities I don't mind giving money to because most of the funds actually go toward helping the needy, rather than paying for overhead and cushy salaries.

She excuses herself and turns to us. "Nicholas! So nice to see you. And who is this lovely woman?" She turns to Molly. "I'm Elizabeth Pryce-King. Nice to meet you."

"Molly Greene. A pleasure."

They shake hands.

"Oh yes, I heard about you from Aunt Ceinlys. She's around here somewhere. She'd probably like to say hello again."

Molly flushes. "She was very kind to me earlier."

"You didn't tell me you met her." I'm relieved that Molly had a good interaction with Ceinlys, who wields enormous influence. If she deems you boorish, social life in the upper crust can be difficult. I make a mental note to thank her for being nice to my Molly.

"You didn't ask." She gives me a sly grin.

Elizabeth smiles. "If she liked you, so will my uncle."

I'd be on the alert if I'd heard this a few years back. But Salazar Pryce has reformed himself, so he no longer tries to screw every female he sees. Dad could benefit from spending some time with him.

"Sorry to greet and run," Elizabeth says. "But I need to go say hello to Ashley Aylster. She's here solo. So nice meeting you." She glides away.

"She's really sweet," Molly says. "Thank—"

"Nicholas! There he is!"

I stiffen. *Dad.* I can't even pretend I didn't hear him and walk away, since his hand is already slapping my shoulder.

I force a bland smile. "I didn't know this was your scene."

"Are you kidding? Everything is my scene."

A redhead with boobs too big for her skinny frame clings to his arm. She has an average facial bone structure that any wannabe starlet could beat. But her eyes are a stunning shade of blue. If it's their real color, I can see why Dad might find her interesting enough to hang out with, since it can't be her brilliant conversation. She looks like she's eighteen. Hell, I hope she *is* even eighteen. She gives Molly a stay-the-fuck-away-from-my-daddy look. Ugh. Like Molly would want to be with someone like my dad.

I pull Molly closer, giving the redhead a don't-fuck-with-my-girlfriend glare.

"Where are my other sons?" Dad asks.

"They aren't coming. Didn't Joey tell you?" Joey stalks us on social media and the news to find out what we're up to. That way, he can arrange things like a helicopter ride for Dad to crash Grant's wedding— while blaring "Ride of the Valkyries."

"He fell down some stairs." Dad shakes his head, ruefully annoyed. He isn't sad Joey got hurt. He's sad that he's being inconvenienced.

"Who pushed him?" I ask.

"No one. He just tripped."

"So God pushed him."

"If He did, He did a pretty shoddy job. Joey only broke his foot and sprained his wrist. He isn't as quick as he used to be, which is too bad." Dad finally zeroes in on Molly. "Who's this? Is this the same one from before? The one from our phone call?"

How much should I say? Actually, is it even wise to introduce him to Molly in person? He offered to put Aspen in a movie with lots of sex scenes. Then he told Lucie he'd pay for a boob job—like she needs the plastic surgery! I don't want him saying something to upset Molly. Like offering to pay for a nose job or something.

He squints as he studies her. "This one isn't the black-dress girl I saw with you last time. Her boobs weren't as perky. Unless she got a better bra."

Jesus.

Molly's mouth parts, and she blinks a couple of times.

"Don't be shy. I'm not weird. I make movies," Dad says. "I'm Ted Lasker."

Ted Lasker is a synonym for "weird."

"Hi. I'm Molly. I'm...not weird, either." Her eyes are wide with what-the-hell-do-I-do-now panic, while her mouth is desperately trying to maintain a friendly smile.

"What a lovely name."

"Thank you." Something beeps. She reaches into her clutch and fishes out her phone. "I need to take this." She can't hide her relief. "Excuse me."

God must love me to pull her away from this mess. But His love isn't big enough to save me as well.

"So, you makin' a baby with Bonnie?" Dad asks, leaning forward.

"*Molly* and I are not going to make a baby just to suit you."

He doesn't hear me. "Your mother wants one, too."

"The feeling will pass in a week or two." I'll buy her a new car. That should do the trick.

"No, it won't. She's hanging out with Rachel in Florence right now."

Fuck. Griffin has *triplets*. They're impossibly cute, and I can only imagine the kind of grandbaby envy Mom's experiencing right now. Maybe I should introduce Rachel to a barely legal boytoy who is hot and Instagrammable. That would distract her for sure. She can't stand being alone, and loathes dating men her age. Griffin would thank me for it, too. She calls him to complain about her horrible life every time she's between boyfriends.

"You knock that Zoey up, the kid should come out lookin' pretty good," Dad says, like he's talking about cake. "She's hot in that wholesome way. Like I could cast her as a Midwest virgin-next-door everyone wants to fuck."

I'm going to puke. Or punch Dad in the face. "Just stop—"

"You said you were going to cast *me*," the redhead interjects in an annoying nasal whine.

"Yeah, but not as a Midwest virgin. Nobody's going to buy that, cupcake," he says. "You gotta stick to what you can pull off, know what I'm sayin'?"

"Then what?"

He closes one eye and squints at her. "Hot strip-mall gas station attendant. Crack whore with a heart of gold. Like that."

"*Really?*" The woman starts hopping up and down, setting off seismic oscillations in her chest.

"Oh yeah. Straight to video and we'll sell a million copies, sweetheart."

Dad has no idea what her name is. That kind of detail is what Joey is for. The saddest thing is the girl has no idea Dad doesn't mean any of it. He only does blockbuster movies that get shown in theaters all over the world.

Molly returns all too soon. Damn it. I was hoping she'd text and say, *I want to go home. Meet me in the lobby.*

"Everything okay?" Maybe things aren't okay—nothing serious, but maybe she couldn't find anything she wanted to munch on—so we can leave.

"Yes." She smiles.

Dad brightens. "Glad you're back, Holly! I was just telling Nicholas that—"

"No," I say quickly, stepping between them.

Dad leans to the side. "I was just saying that—"

Owen and a blonde woman appear, disrupting my focus. Hands linked, they're homing in on us like a pair of ICBMs. They both have the desperately determined and hopeful look of someone who's just discovered a pot of gold at the end of a rainbow.

"Oh my gosh, Molly! I had no idea you were going to be here."

I might've thanked the man for interrupting my father if it weren't for his history with Molly.

Why does he act like he's still friendly with her? Isn't he really here for Dad? He's speaking to her, but his eyes keep straying to my father.

Owen looks outright ridiculous. He's in an ill-fitting Armani tuxedo. Probably grabbed whatever was left on sale because nobody would buy something that large across their shoulders—or he was deluded enough to believe he could grow into the jacket.

But what's even more absurd is that he thinks Molly's going to be civil to him after what he pulled on her birthday. In addition, he laid their entire relationship bare on social media and did his best to make her come across as pathetic and uncool. Dickhead.

Molly's mouth tightens. Finally, she looks at Owen like he's a fly on her sushi. "Hello, Owen."

"You really cleaned up nice. Gotta say I'm surprised."

Son of a bitch. The light in Molly's eyes dims for a moment. I'm itching to shove a few teeth down Owen's throat. But she lifts her chin. "Thank you. That tux looks amazing on you. I can just feel your 'personal brand' rising as we speak."

I swallow a laugh and draw her tighter to me. *That's my girl.*

The bottle blonde thrusts a hand out at Molly to get her attention. This is the woman Owen dumped Molly for? Her champagne-colored dress is so tight, it looks like somebody poured molten gold over her. She's pretty enough, but then, Los Angeles is full of "pretty enough" women who believe they have what it takes to be the next Elizabeth Taylor.

Her eyes are hard and cold, and there's a hint of brittle desperation that betrays a deep sense of insecurity and need for attention. Owen is an idiot. He threw away a diamond for a flake of quartzite.

"Hey, I'm Dana. You remember, right? We were friends in high school!" the blonde says with a blinding smile.

"We were? The clearest memory I have of you from high school is you calling me an ugly cow behind my back and laughing with your friends," Molly says.

I like this blonde even less. Dad raises an eyebrow and sniffs.

She doesn't seem to register what Molly's saying. "Can you introduce us to your group?" She gestures around, but ends up pointing at Dad.

Oh, for God's sake. Do these two have no shame?

"You've got some balls *interrupting my father* when he was speaking to me and my girlfriend." Dad hates being interrupted, and I want him to remember that Owen has committed the grave sin.

I also want to humiliate Owen and Dana for their horrible attempt to use Molly. I haven't forgiven him for throwing her away like trash, even though it gave me the opening I needed to make my move. She didn't deserve to have her heart trampled—much less publicly—on her birthday. She should've been made to feel like the most special person in the entire world.

"Right. The mother of your child," Dad puts in.

"We'll see. But if I have kids, it'll be with Molly," I say with a thin smile. "I only want one woman."

Molly's eyes bounce back and forth between me and Dad like ping-pong balls.

"Really sorry about your grandbaby-mama issues, but we were just so shocked at running into an artistic genius such as yourself," Owen gushes, oblivious to the coming storm. "I've always admired you."

The redhead glares at him like she'd love nothing more than to rip all the hair off his scalp. The only reason she isn't giving in to the impulse is that this is a classy kind of event, and Dad doesn't like it when the arm candy makes a scene.

"Who the *fuck* do you think you are?" Dad says slowly, looking the duo up and down.

Owen freezes, but manages to muster a syllable. "Huh?"

Dana doesn't bat an eye. But then, you have to be that shameless to demand an introduction to a Hollywood movie producer from your boyfriend's ex, much less one you apparently mocked and bullied in high school. "I'm Dana Mincer." She beams. "I've always admired your work." Apparently, she and Owen rehearsed the line.

Dad's expression is completely flat. "And?"

"I have about a million followers on Instagram. All the events I do are chosen with careful mindfulness to ensure I get maximum exposure. Like tonight. People will see me and know I'm all about bettering our community."

Dad's left eyebrow is twitching—an ominous sign. I wonder if there's a way to get some fresh popcorn?

"I think I'm ready to move on to bigger and better career opportunities." Dana sticks her tits out.

In response, the redhead rubs hers against Dad's arm. It's like the Battle of the Bulges.

"No." Dad looks at Owen, then at her. "Nobody butts into my inner circle."

"We didn't—" Owen says.

"Nobody contradicts me, either," Dad says.

That is true enough. He puts up with the attitude from me and my brothers because he knows we don't respect his fame or fortune. Plus we *are* family. But from anyone else...?

Owen might as well have plucked a lion's butt hair.

"Neither of you have star quality," Dad booms. His voice is so loud, it's drawing attention. People around us turn to watch. It's always luridly fascinating to see somebody get reamed. "My God. You'd have to pay *me* to use you in a movie."

"That can be arranged," Dana says hurriedly.

"But see, here's the problem. I don't want the humiliation of having the first flop of my long, illustrious career. If you're looking for bigger opportunities..." His contemptuous gaze rakes Owen and Dana. "I hear the Vegas whorehouses are hiring."

Gasps and titters rise from the crowd around us.

The duo turn bright red. Molly's jaw drops, and she covers her mouth with her hand. The redhead smiles smugly, apparently happy she managed to hang on to Dad.

Me? I'm impressed. Dad's always had a talent for invective, but this is better than I expected.

I squeeze Molly's shoulder. Owen and Dana shoot her dirty looks, like this is somehow her fault. And for that little bit of contumely, I'm going to make them pay.

26

MOLLY

—BRENDA: It's all set now. Thank you! You're an angel!

I smile at Brenda's text, then take a deep breath and pretend my palms aren't slick with sweat. I can't believe I agreed to auction myself off tonight. But when Brenda reached out during my chat with Nicholas's dad and begged me...

Just the thought of Cooper, Sam, Cutie Penny and the rest of the animals whose perfect forever families are somewhere out there, and any resistance to drawing attention to myself crumbled.

Plus, I refuse to let Dana deprive the shelter of the funds it's been counting on. She was going to allocate her proceeds to the shelter, but changed her mind earlier this morning. When Brenda told me Dana is going to direct the money toward a food bank, I knew exactly why she turned her back on the animal shelter.

Owen.

The local food bank is his pet charity. He donates there regularly and constantly posts about it on his social media accounts. Says it boosts his likability.

It's a worthy cause, but it's wrong for him to yank the funding Furry Haven was promised by using his relationship with Dana.

I look up and see a man in his late thirties bid half a million for a date with a gorgeous brunette on the stage. Nobody outbids him, and she steps down from the stage with a huge smile and hugs the man.

I lean over and whisper to Nicholas, "That's the biggest amount so far, isn't it?"

"Yes."

"Wow." I start to lick my lips, then stop, remembering I'm wearing makeup. I fidget and have another champagne instead.

"What are you nervous about? Furry Haven's going to get the funding it needs."

"Hopefully." I smile again. The thing is, I don't know who's going to bid on me. Nobody here really knows me. And I'm not even that pretty compared to the women who have already been on stage.

Maybe I should tell Brenda I can't do it. I can probably just give the shelter my savings and it'll be greater than what I can get from auctioning off an evening.

"Are you okay?" Nicholas says.

"Yeah." *Breathe, Molly, breathe.* "I'm fine."

The emcee announces the next bachelorette's love of feeding the hungry, and the crowd applauds to show its enthusiasm. But the cheers die abruptly when Dana stands up.

Um... What's that about?

Dana looks around, then shrugs with the smile of a woman who knows she's desirable. But then, she's been the most popular girl all her life. Ted might've cut her down a bit, but it wouldn't counteract a lifetime of male interest.

She gracefully mounts the stage as the emcee lists her accomplishments. Oh...*crap.* I didn't give the organizers any information about myself.

Is it too late to jot something down? Should I text Brenda and ask if she provided my bio?

Dana sounds impressive. All those followers on Instagram. Her brand sponsorship deals. She poses well, too, just like she does at Get Jacked. And her makeup is perfect, bringing out her eyes and highlighting her cheekbones. Her lips are pink and bee-stung, and the skintight golden dress shows off her perfect body. For all I know, her friends could be here, taking photos for her account.

But nobody makes an opening bid.

What's going on? I look around. The attendees didn't become suddenly shy. They didn't hold back earlier.

Dana's smile falters. The emcee leans into her mike. "All right, people, let's *get it going*! What am I bid for this lovely young woman?"

Whispers ripple through the crowd. A few men look around. Nicholas's dad chats animatedly with his date, who smirks. He bid two hundred thousand for her and won half an hour ago.

Nicholas looks bored with the silence. When he notices me scanning the crowd, he smiles. "More champagne?"

"No, thanks." I can just see myself stumbling up the stairs to the stage.

"Two thousand!" Owen calls out.

It's easily the lowest bid of the evening. The others have generally started out with at least ten thousand. But two thousand is pushing it for Owen. He still has that Ferrari to pay off.

Dana turns as red as Owen's car. She starts to shake. It might've been better if he hadn't made his bid.

"We have two thousand." The emcee pauses. She isn't showing an overt sign of embarrassment, but her tight and lackluster tone betrays her discomfiture. "Do I hear three?"

The loudest sound in the hall is glasses clinking as the waiters remove them.

"Come on, people, let's hear it. Anyone...?"

Still nothing.

"Um. Going once... Going twice... Sold!" She says the last part with more relief than excitement.

Dana gets off the stage, her face scarlet and her eyes brimming with unshed tears. Owen stands up to hug her, but she pushes him away and stalks off.

"So much for love," Nicholas mutters.

"I can't believe she didn't get more bids. What happened?" I whisper.

"She probably pissed off the wrong people."

I remember how annoyed Ted was with Owen and Dana. And he insulted them so loudly that everyone heard him. But that can't possibly be the reason people decided to sit this one out...can it?

"I still wish the winning bid was higher than two thousand dollars," I say. "Not that I expected Owen to manage more than that, but it's terrible that the food bank isn't going to get much."

"Food bank? I thought she was doing it for the animal shelter."

"No. Brenda said she changed her mind earlier today."

"What a shitty thing to do." Nicholas brushes the spot between my eyebrows. "Stop worrying. I'll send the food bank a big check in your name. Will a hundred thousand do?"

"You don't have to." The casual way he throws that kind of money around is stunning. It's flattering, of course, but also unsettling to hear him offer to do something that grandiose for me. I just...don't know how to deal with it.

"I insist. Besides, it'll make you feel better, right?"

"Well...yes."

"Okay. Settled." He smiles and takes my hand. As he does, his fingertips run along the inside of my wrist, where my pulse leaps at the electric touch. "That's all that matters."

I search his face. See the sincerity in his eyes. My heart skitters. When he looks at me and speaks like this, I feel like I'm the most important person in the universe. It's such a special gift, elevating and humbling at the same time. I don't feel like I deserve it—

"...big round of applause for *Molly Greene*!"

I flinch. I didn't expect the emcee to be so exuberant when she announced my name. Nicholas's head whips toward the stage, then back at me. "You're getting auctioned?"

I nod. "Brenda asked me."

"When?"

"I don't know. An hour ago?"

Realization dawns in his eyes. "Why didn't you tell me before agreeing to fill in for Dana?"

"I don't know...I—"

"Is Molly Greene here?" The emcee's tone says, *Please, please, please*. She probably doesn't want to deal with another awkward moment.

I stand up and give a small wave. "Sorry." People's heads swing in my direction.

"There she is!" the emcee says. "Come on up!"

Everyone seems to be staring. My lungs constrict under the weight of their gaze. The air feels thin.

Do not *pass out!*

It would simply be too humiliating to faint. Besides, this isn't a romance novel scenario when a hot hero catches the fainting heroine! Not even historical romance novels do that cliché anymore.

I walk to the stage, trying to hide the way my legs are shaking. I'll be happy if I get at least two thousand dollars for the shelter. I'd prefer to get more, of course, but if Dana only got two...

Finally, I stand on the stage. The light's bright, and blood roars in my ears. I try to smile—I think I manage it. The ballroom seems to grow in size, then shrink abruptly. Is it me, or is everyone staring and whispering?

My gaze roams everywhere. I don't know exactly what I'm searching for. But then I see Nicholas in the crowd.

He's looking at me with a small, concerned frown. My whole body stills at the sight of him. He mouths something as he holds my gaze calmly.

Breathe. He gives me a slow nod. It means *everything's going to be okay.*

His soundless reassurance wraps around me like a shield. My attention focuses on his self-possessed and confident presence. Suddenly, the tightness around my chest eases. The air trapped inside whooshes out. I inhale and my head starts to clear. The emcee is done with my intro. I'm pretty sure she made up something that sounded good to get the auction going, since I'm a last-minute substitute.

"Ten thousand," a familiar voice calls out before the emcee gets to ask for the first bid.

Jack?

Oh, no. Praying it's just a guy who sounds like my boss, I scan the crowd—and spot Jack in the back. I didn't see him earlier, but then, there are more than enough people to fill the huge ballroom.

Ah, crap. I'm glad the shelter will get at least ten thousand, but *Jack?*

Really? He's going to try to get ten thousand dollars' worth of touching.

My skin crawls. The champagne in my belly churns like an agitated sea.

"Five hundred thousand," another voice calls out.

That's Elizabeth's uncle Salazar I met after Nicholas whisked me away from Ted. Salazar says something to Ceinlys, who's sitting next to him, and she slaps his shoulder with a smile. I let out a relieved breath.

"One million," Nicholas says flatly.

Murmurs go up in the air.

I cover my cheeks and mouth with my hands. *Unbelievable.* My head is ringing, and I stare at him, trying to process what's going on.

"Oh my goodness! One million dollars for dinner with the lovely Molly," the emcee says breathlessly. This is the biggest bid so far.

"One point one," Jack shoots back.

What? He can't possibly have that kind of money.

The emcee starts to fan herself.

I begin to feel faint. Trembling starts in my hands and legs. Men simply...don't fight like this over me.

"One point two." Arturo gives a loud, derisive snort directed at the other bidders.

Didn't he say his father cut him off? Where is he going to get that kind of money?

"One point three," Salazar counters, unfazed by Arturo's attitude.

My time isn't worth that kind of money, even if it's for Furry Haven. Did somebody fill the air with hallucinogens or something?

Ceinlys waves at me, mouthing, *It's all good.*

It...is?

"Two million," Nicholas says, his eyes flashing with a hint of impatience.

My head spins. I must be more drunk than I thought.

"Oh my! Two—million—dollars!" the emcee squeals.

So I didn't mishear. What is Nicholas doing? There are a lot of increments between one-point-three and two! My heart races so hard and fast, my ribs feel bruised. A mixture of excitement and trepidation beat in my head. This doesn't feel like reality.

"Two point five," Arturo shouts. "Time's valuable, ol' man! Let's get it going!"

Nicholas shoots a contemptuous look in Arturo's direction. "Five."

The smile on Arturo's face falters.

The emcee scents blood in the water. She's shouting something, and I can't make it out. My entire focus is on Nicholas and his coolly determined expression.

Keeping my gaze on him, I shake my head. Can he take back the final bid?

"Five million bid, do I hear five-point-one? Now five-point-one. Will you give me five-point-one?"

NO!

Please...?

Thankfully, nobody says five point one, despite the emcee's excited encouragement.

"Going once... Going twice...! Sold! A dinner with the lovely and talented Molly Greene for five—million—*dollars*!"

Even as she smiles, what just happened doesn't sink in. I feel like I'm having an out-of-body experience. This sort of thing simply *does not happen to me*. I'm never the center of something this lavish and incredible. I watch others star in those movies.

I manage to step down from the stage without stumbling. Nicholas gets up and hugs me. "Hey, hot date." His voice is teasing, like he knows I'm overwhelmed and need to reorient myself.

His arms stay wrapped around me as he helps me take my seat. I search his face. He doesn't look dazed. No, his eyes are absolutely clear. And glimmering with satisfaction.

"You didn't really bid five million, did you?" I ask faintly.

He gives a short laugh. "Of course I did."

"A dinner with me isn't worth that kind of money, Nicholas! I eat dinner with you for free all the time!"

"Not the point. The point is, nobody *else* gets to eat with you."

He sounds possessive. *But we're fake-dating.* I feel weirdly guilty about his spending so much money on me. "You should've bid on somebody who's more..."

"More what?"

"You know... The kind of woman you're used to being seen with."

The good humor on his face fades. "You don't care if I go out with another woman?"

Hot acidic sensations stir in my belly, but I pretend otherwise. If this were a novel, I might think he wants me to act possessive, but this is reality. "Well..."

"You don't care if I give another woman flowers, treat her to a gorgeous meal, hold her hand? Dance with her on a beach under the stars?" he demands, his eyes intense.

Images of him and the mystery woman unfold like a movie in my mind. Instead of the woman, I'm focused on him. How he'd smile. How he'd press an affectionate kiss on her cheek as he picked her up. How attentive he'd be—oh God, do I know how he is. How he'd hold her under the night sky, warm, silky sand underneath their feet, their bodies pressed together and swaying to the sound of waves...

Jealousy rakes its claws down my insides, from my heart all the way to my gut, leaving behind bloody, burning gashes. The intensity of pain knocks the breath out of me. It's such an unfamiliar emotion. Even when Owen dumped me for Dana, I was hurt and sad—felt inferior, even—but I didn't feel *jealous*. Not like this.

But with Nicholas, it's as though somebody stuck her hand into my chest and ripped out my heart. Like somebody just stole something fundamental and critical to my existence.

Cheers go up around us, and someone walking by pats Nicholas on the back, congratulating him on his winning bid. Nicholas gives a curt thanks, then curses under his breath. He takes my hand, tugging.

"Let's talk someplace quieter."

I nod and stand. This isn't the kind of conversation we can have surrounded by all these guests.

He holds me tightly, like he's afraid I'll vanish, and leads me out of the ballroom. He pulls me into a small prep room and sticks a chair underneath the knob to prevent the door from being opened from the outside.

The room is dimly lit. There's one long table in the center and towers of stacked chairs in two corners.

I lick my lips, this time not caring if I smudge my makeup. My mouth is too dry, and my fingertips are tingling.

"Now. Can I have my answer?" he says.

I open my mouth, but can't articulate a response in a way that's honest, but not overly clingy or possessive.

Because I am totally both.

"Well?" he says.

I look at him. I can either lie and tell him I feel nothing at the thought of him with another woman or be honest and tell him I'm jealous. Neither seems like a good option. But given how sweet he's been, he deserves my honesty, even if it makes me squirmy.

"I don't like it," I say. "I hate it. I feel jealous, which makes me an awful person because I don't think I should—"

He puts a finger over my lips. "Stop there before you say anything you don't mean. Just so you know, I'd never spend that kind of money on you if you weren't worth it. You're worth everything, Molly. And what you felt when you imagined me with another woman—I felt that when I thought about you out on a date with another man."

The tingling that was in my fingers spreads to the rest of my body. Hearing him admit he feels the same way I do makes my heart thunder.

I suddenly realize that he's standing *really* close, only a hairsbreadth away from me. Goosebumps spread over my skin, and my lips soften against his index finger.

Heat flares in his gray eyes. Wrapping his arms around me and pulling me close, he slants his mouth over mine, sucking my lower lip, then running his tongue over the tender flesh.

My jaw loosens, and I open up for a deeper kiss. I stroke his tongue with mine, then suck it. He tastes like the wine we shared earlier and something darkly addictive I've never had before.

He devours my mouth like he's been starved. Then he thrusts his tongue in, like he's fucking it. The sweet achiness spreads, pooling between my thighs. My clit throbs, and I squirm with emptiness.

I've never had a man kiss me with such raw need. He doesn't try to hide how much he wants me. What he'd like to do to me.

The blood in my vein boils, and I fist the lapels of his tux, clinging. I press myself against the length of him. His huge erection pushes against my belly. He rocks against me, wanting me to feel every steely inch. My God. The emptiness between my legs grows unbearable.

My senses spin out of control despite my best efforts. How is it possible for Nicholas to make me this crazy with a kiss? It's like the romance novels I've been devouring. The unrealistic "drivel" that Owen and others would mock for giving me unrealistic expectations.

With Nicholas, the freaky-hot sex I've read about seems not only possible, but *assured*. His warm large hands glide over my curves. I tense a little. I don't have the kind of lean, taut body that his exes had, and...

"You're so soft and pretty," he whispers, his voice raw. He cups my ass and squeezes.

I feel the tight, possessive pressure all the way to my clit and shudder. His mouth runs over my shoulder and collarbone. He tugs at the zipper on the side of my bodice until the strapless top slumps to my waist. Millions of hot kisses land around my breasts. Every time his breath fans over the pointed tips, my toes curl.

A moan—I think it's mine. It's too high-pitched and desperate.

"Nicholas. Please," I beg.

"Patience."

"Somebody might come." The door's secured, but...

"You want to stop?" he says, his eyes hot on mine.

"No. I want you to hurry up!"

Laughing softly, he lays a kiss on my nipple, then pulls it into his mouth. *Oh my God.* My back arches as pleasure streaks through me, then winds tight in my belly. His mouth sears my sensitive flesh, and every inch of my skin seems to come alive. He sucks hard, and the bliss pooling inside me is more intense than some orgasms I've had. But instead of letting the sexual tension pop, the pleasure tightens its grip on me until I feel like I'm going to die. I rock against him, desperate for a release—and scared at what sort of heights I'll find myself at.

His fingers slip under the side slit and stroke my thigh. My legs quiver. I can only stay upright because I'm holding on to his shoulders, digging my nails into his jacket.

He runs his index finger over my folds through the thin fabric of my panties. I cry out softly before remembering we're in a room by the ballroom where the charity auction is going on. The emcee should keep the crowd occupied, but that doesn't mean the hotel staff or guests wandering around outside won't hear us.

His thumb brushes over the other nipple as he sucks harder, this time using his teeth. The tiny sting only sharpens my appetite, makes me more desperate for him.

He pushes the fabric out of the way and probes my slickness with his fingers. I squeeze my eyes as lust burns through me, fight to breathe through tight anticipation.

I know in my heart he's not going to let me down.

He sticks a finger inside, almost experimentally. I grip it, but it isn't nearly enough. "Oh my God, Nicholas. Please. I need more." My face is hot. I've never begged like this before.

He places another finger... *Ah...*

Then a third... *Yes, please...*

"Ride my fingers, baby," he whispers, letting go of my nipple. "Make yourself feel good."

He shifts his weight, and I'm pressed against a wall for better balance. I go crazy and rock against his hand, moving my hips. I can feel his gaze on my face. He's studying me like I'm the most important discovery of the century. Then suddenly, as I plunge down, he curls his fingers, and the tips graze a spot that—

A bolt of sheer pleasure cuts through me. My spine stiffens, and I bury my face in his shoulder as I shake with an orgasm that robs me of everything except ecstasy.

He holds me, keeping his fingers buried deep inside my spasming pussy. When my breathing settles a bit, he pulls them out. I shudder at the stimulating sensation, and heat rekindles. I squeeze my muscles, trying to will myself to stop being so greedy.

His eyes on my flushed face, he slowly licks the juices off his hand like they're the sweetest chocolate syrup. My cheeks burn. It's hot how he enjoys everything about me—how honest and open he is about it.

"This isn't enough," he says.

My gaze drops to the huge bulge. I should do something about that—

Suddenly, he moves, dragging my underwear down my legs and letting it drop to the floor. The silk of my dress brushes my heated butt, and I feel barer than if I were standing here naked.

He props me on the table. "Grip the edge," he orders.

I obey without thinking. What is he planning? Delicious anticipation crackles through me. Whatever he's about to do is going to be oh-so good.

He drops to his knees in front of me, then throws my thighs over his shoulders, spreading me. I can feel myself quivering down there, already expectant. He seems to sense it too, because a deep groan tears from his chest.

Pushing my knees apart farther, he buries his face between my legs. Hot breaths blow over my ultrasensitive clit, making me shiver. He runs his tongue over my slick flesh and laps me up like he's starved. Every stroke of his tongue is different somehow, but also more pleasurable.

It's as though he's learning my reaction to each stimulation and improving his technique as he goes on.

My grip on the edge of the table tightens as another orgasm swells. Then I let one hand go and tunnel my fingers into his hair, holding his head tightly against me. He grows more frenzied, pulling my clit into his mouth and sucking, while pushing his fingers back into me. I writhe against him as I come, teeth clenched so I don't scream.

He felt me orgasm, but he doesn't let up. He becomes greedier. More controlling. He runs his hand down the curves of my thigh and calf, then shoves his tongue into me, fucking the opening shallowly.

The stimulation is different, but potent. Another climax breaks over me, but he isn't finished.

He rubs two fingers against my mouth. I pull them in eagerly.

He fucks my mouth with his fingers. I imagine it's his cock in my mouth, and I'm going wild. My pussy's impossibly wet now, and I groan against his fingers, wishing it was his cock gliding against my tongue right now.

He continues to devour me until I feel wrung out. Sweat mists over my skin. The air is replete with sex, and every cell in my body is loose and languid.

He rains kisses all over my body. "Don't ever doubt that I want you."

I don't think I can after this. The dress is bunched around my hips; I feel completely debauched but at the same time so, *so* good.

I raise my torso until I can face him. His lips are flushed and wet, and lust burns in his gaze. He hasn't come yet.

"I want to suck you off." My own words stun me. I've never been so bold with my boyfriends before, but it feels right to tell Nicholas exactly what I want.

He curses under his breath. "You know what happens to good girls when they say things like that?"

I shoot him a mischievous smile. "Generally speaking, yeah. They get to suck their guy off."

I slide down from the table and push him in a half-circle until we've switched positions. The tent over his crotch is huge. Grinning, I run my hand along it lightly, just giving him a tease.

His hips instantly jerk forward, bolstering my confidence. I try to pull my dress back up before I get down to business, but he stops me. "I want to see your tits."

There's naked admiration in his gaze, and I adore how much he loves what he sees.

I reach for his belt. A few tugs, clicks of metal and the hiss of a zipper later, I have his pants undone. I push them down along with his boxers. His cock springs out. I expel a stunned breath.

He's *huge*. The hard thing I felt in the library—that I thought was his phone or something... *This was it.* I can't even close my hand all the way around the impressive girth. And it'll take more than two hands to cover the entire veined and pulsing length. The tip drips with clear liquid.

A tinge of trepidation skitters along my spine at his size. On the other hand, he made me feel so good, and I want him to feel just as good.

"Come here," he says as though he's sensed my uncertainty. Without waiting for a response, he wraps my hair in his hand and pulls me up, then reclaims my mouth. He kisses me, not with the out-of-control desire of a man dying for an orgasm, but with the tender care of a man who is kissing the only woman he loves.

Heat blossoms within me, and along with it, undeniable affection for him. This kind side is why I've been crushing on him all these years.

I kiss him back, then run my hand along his body, feeling the tautness in his muscles. He's tight with lust, but holding back for me.

I don't want him to.

I drop my hand lower until I can take his shaft. It throbs in my grip like a separate being. He moans, and I feel the vibration from his chest against mine. I pump my hand slowly up and down, run my thumb over the slick tip.

"I'm going to make you feel good." I glide down his big, strong body. Then pull him into my mouth.

I barely take in more than the cockhead, and my mouth already feels full. The saltiness from his precum coats my tongue, and I relax my jaw and try to pull him in deeper.

Air shudders out of him. He watches me intensely, the tendon in his neck sticking out. The muscles in his jaw bunch and flex as I attempt to adjust to him. His cock twitches in my mouth as I move my head carefully, giving me time to figure out a way to take more each time and get used to his size.

His whole body quivers. I run my hand over one thigh in a soothing gesture, then bob my head. He's hitting the back of my throat each time, but I don't even have half of him in my mouth.

I tighten my lips around him, hollowing my cheeks.

"Fuck!" he says, tightening his grip on my hair until my scalp feels a slight sting.

His hips move. But he doesn't try to shove his cock down my throat. He's careful, thrusting shallowly, no farther than I've been able to take so far. I cup his balls, stroking them tenderly. I can't believe how *good* this feels to me. How much it turns me on to feel him lose himself in the ecstasy I'm giving him.

Now he's laboring for air. His chest rises and falls hard and fast. His abs tighten. The rhythm of his thrusts is faster and a bit rougher.

But I love it. I adore watching him barrel toward the peak.

"Molly. Oh, Molly." My name falls from his lips like a prayer.

I suck harder, run my tongue over his length with more enthusiasm.

His cockhead presses against the back of throat. He makes an incoherent sound as an orgasm breaks over him and he empties himself in my mouth. And I swallow every drop—another thing I've never done before.

When he's finally done, I let him go, then kiss his belly.

He pulls me up and kisses me. "That was amazing. *You* are amazing."

I smile. "So are you."

"Just to be clear, we're dating-dating."

I blink at him over the silly fluttering of my heart. He's just saying things, swept up in the moment. Men say all kinds of happy crap after sex.

He continues, "I figured I should clarify that before you get any weird ideas."

"Why would I get weird ideas?"

"Because you keep expecting me to act like your shitty ex."

I shake my head. "I don't think you're anything like him."

"Really? You thought that I should let other men bid on you and win. And that I should bid on other women. That's exactly what Owen would've done."

I go still and process what he just said. I never thought my expectations had anything to do with Owen—or any other guy—in my past, but maybe they are colored by my experience. I would totally expect Owen to do exactly that. He wouldn't want to waste money on me when he could have dinner with me for free anytime.

"You're right," I say. "That wasn't fair."

"I want you, Molly. Just you. Only you. And I want you to want me in the same way. Exclusive. Unshared. The two of us together against the world." He runs his fingers through my hair gently, but his tone is anything but.

I struggle to understand what he's telling me, as my whole body is still buzzing from the orgasms. I can't believe that Nicholas Lasker, my longtime crush of eight years and model gentleman, has such raw proprietorial feelings about me.

It's clear that, to him, there's nothing I'm not worthy of. And the knowledge is so potent and delicious, I can't do anything but shiver with happiness and nod. Especially when I can feel he's hard again.

For whatever reason, he's really into my body, and I'm *totally* into his. I'm already dripping.

Maybe his lust is in charge, and I should be more cautious. But I don't care. I've never felt this desired. And for once, I'm fine with living dangerously.

27

NICHOLAS

Since I've fulfilled my duties at the charity event, I send instructions to Cody to handle the payment for the auction and head out with Molly.

It's a good thing we got a limo, because the taste of her is still in my mouth, leaving me high and intoxicated. My dick's impossibly hard and tingling. I can't get the sensation of her tongue against it out of my mind. Her mouth was shockingly hot. When she tightened her lips around me, I almost lost it and just drove into her mouth.

Except that would've hurt her.

I'm larger than average. And Molly is much smaller and softer. I wouldn't want to do anything that could cause her pain. I don't give a damn how shitty her exes were, or, given Owen's attempt to denigrate her bedroom performance, how acclimated she is to subpar sex. She's going to experience nothing but pleasure when she's with me.

The limo ride should take about an hour. She's properly covered, her dress smoothed out and zipped. The fabric lies properly over her lush body. But in my head, all I see is her lying on the table, breasts out and nipples hard. The goosebumps over her flesh, and the slickness dripping between her sweet, plump thighs.

Her pussy gripped my fingers hard when she came. I wish we'd had a condom so it'd have been my dick she spasmed around. But sex wasn't something I'd planned on. I just lost it when she acted like I should've let her go out with some other asshole.

Like Jack Peterson.

He might be a sought-after personal trainer, but he's not my favorite person. He slept with my mom before she married Paul. That wouldn't generally be a problem if he hadn't been dating somebody else at the time. I'm a firm believer that "once a cheater, always a cheater."

Then there's Arturo Morales. I trust that guy as much as I'd trust a starving cat with a piece of tuna. If even half the stories I heard about him are true, he's almost as bad as Dad. And he's only twenty-seven.

Molly reaches over and holds my hand. I squeeze, feel her rest her head against my shoulder. A small gesture, but intimate and satisfying. I want her to lean on me and let me be her shield against the world.

She places her free hand oh-so casually on my thigh. The touch burns through my pants. Then she moves it up and down along my quad, gradually working it closer to my dick.

Vixen.

She tilts her head and smiles. Mischief and desire glitter in her eyes, and I kiss her. If she wants more sex, I will *happily* oblige.

Not in the limo, though. I want to take her in my bed, have her drip all over it until her scent mingles with mine.

But that doesn't mean we can't play around a little right now. I pull her onto my lap and touch her, running my callused hands along her sides, kneading the sweet curve of her ass. It's round and soft and fills my hand just right. When I strip her out of the dress, I'm going to kiss it.

She squirms, her breathing shallower. "Nicholas..."

"Settle down. We're only about half an hour away."

"Stop teasing..." She trails off when I slip my thumb under the side strings of her panties. Whoever picked these out should get an A for taste. "Are you going to snap them off?" Her voice shakes with excitement.

"Beg me."

She makes doe eyes at me. "Oh please oh please oh please."

I rip the strings, then pull the panties off. I make sure to stuff them into my pocket—I'm not letting some asshole chauffer take them as a souvenir. "Better?"

"I might want more." She dips her hand between my thighs.

Blood instantly pools in my crotch. "I have no idea what you're talking about," I deadpan. "I'm an innocent man who—"

"You could stroke me."

That sounds more appealing than innocent. "Like this?" I run my fingers through her silky hair. "Or this?" I graze my knuckles along her collarbone.

"A little lower." She pulls my arm down until my hand is at her breast, then moves languidly, making her nipple bump and catch on the small hills of my knuckles, making herself feel good. I wish we had better light so I could see the flush I know is spreading over her cheeks.

It's time for more.

I run my hands along her legs. Brush the pads of my thumbs over her knees. My fingertips stroke her inner thighs. Her muscles begin to quiver and her breathing grows uneven. She tenses with anticipation as I move up and up until I'm less than an inch from her hot core. She's so wet I can feel the moisture in the air around my fingers, but I hang on to my control.

"Stop teasing," she whispers. Her heated breaths tickle my ear.

Hot goosebumps break along my spine. "I'm not touching you there until we're in my bed."

She pulls back a little. "Don't tell me you're traditional about sex."

"I'm very traditional about it." *Just you and me, committed.*

"What we did back in the hotel wasn't exactly out of the Miss Manners handbook," she says, then kisses me.

I fuse my mouth with hers and enjoy the closeness and intimacy I've always dreamed of. I used to regard kissing as a pleasant enough prelude to sex, but with Molly it's more. Like our souls are calling to each other across a void.

The limo pulls into my driveway. I pull the dress down and help her look presentable before the chauffeur opens the door. I hand him a fistful of bills and take her into the mansion...

...where I immediately push her against the wall and reclaim her mouth. She laughs, the sound breathless, then kisses me hard. I try to slip my hand through the side slit of her dress, but she moves away.

"This isn't your bed," she teases, laughing.

"Oh, that's how it is?"

She bats her eyes innocently. "You said it, not me."

I reach for her, but she spins away with another laugh. I love this playful side of her, but absolutely do *not* want to wait. I lunge forward, then pick her up like a princess. Gasping, she loops her arms around my neck, then squirms.

"Wait, wait. Put me down!" She kicks, which only makes her lose her shoes.

"Nope. Faster this way." I start toward my bedroom as blood roars in my head.

"I can walk! I'm too heavy. You'll throw your back out."

What kind of pussy does she think I am? "If I threw my back out carrying you, I wouldn't deserve you."

I kick the door to my room open, then flip the light switch and take her inside. We fall on the bed together.

Finally.

She stares up at me, hair fanned around her beautiful face, eyes wide with excitement. I've fantasized for so long about her lying on my bed. But nothing could prepare me for the reality of her spread out like a feast before me.

I grip the bustline of the dress and pull. The silk rips away, splitting in half. She gasps in horror.

"Oh my God! *The dress!*"

"I'll buy you another one." I push the tattered fabric out of the way like unwanted wrapping paper on Christmas.

She's stunning, all feminine curves and sweet softness. Her breasts are generous and pert, and the round line of her belly shivers as I gaze at her with admiration. I want to devour her, defile her and worship her, all at the same time.

Molly starts to raise her arms to cover herself, but then changes her mind and keeps them by her side, and her cheeks grow red. I smile tenderly and kiss her, not holding back. I kiss her like I'm opening my soul to her, and run my hands over her body like I'm ready to give her the world.

When I cup her breast and knead, she arches into my palm. Little whimpers fall from her plump lips, and I swear I could do this for hours on end. When I pinch a nipple, she twists like an electric jolt is crackling through her, pressing her legs together. I spread her thighs and pull her close, until her pelvis is on my thighs and her clit presses against my crotch through the pants.

She rocks against me shamelessly, clutching my shoulders. She's spreading her juices all over my tux pants, making a mess, and I love the sign of how much she wants me.

She moans against my mouth. I clench her ass, then slip my fingers below, easing her open.

"Oh my God, Nicholas, just a little more," she begs, muscles as taut as piano wire. "Please."

I curve my fingers and push them in, making sure to hit her most sensitive spot. She tightens her hold on me and shudders, dripping over my hand. I hold her as she trembles, enjoying her orgasm. She's adorable when she climaxes. All tense and shivery and clingy. Like she can't bear to let me go.

I run my free hand along her supple back, then lay her supine on the bed. Her pink flesh glistens, impossibly wet. Inviting.

I kiss her down there, holding her legs open and lapping her up. The sweet scent of her is driving me crazy. It's even better than at the hotel, because here I can see her better. Spread her wider.

"Nicholas, I can't," she pleads, even as she pants and her pelvis moves to the rhythm of my tongue.

"Yes, you can. And you will."

She squirms out of my grip and turns, getting on her knees and trying to crawl away.

"Oh no, you don't." I grab her ankle and pull her back to me.

She half laughs.

I rip my tie off and bind her wrists to the headboard. Her eyes go wide with shock and excitement. She licks her lips.

"If you really can't stand it, just say 'sunshine' and I'll stop."

Shock flares in her gaze. "Oh my God. Did you read one of my books?" "Sunshine" is the safe word used in one of the sex scenes.

"More than one, and I remember everything." She highlighted this particular one with lots and lots of notations. Most of them, *OMG. Holy shit. Is this really possible? Only in fiction!*

It's sad she thought multiple vaginal orgasms are something made up by romance authors to show off the hero's prowess in bed. Fortunately, I'm here to show her different.

I flick my tongue over her nipples. She writhes against the teasing motion, but can't break away from the tie. She wants more, but I withhold it from her.

There's no sucking. Just lots of light stimulation to drive her crazy with my tongue and teeth.

Her nipples are overly sensitive. She struggles, striving for a firmer touch. Anything to push herself over the edge. Her scent is growing stronger, and sweat mists over her. She tastes like salt, sugar and need.

"Oh my God. Please."

I pull her nipple into my mouth, feel her muscles quiver in anticipation, but after rolling it between my tongue and the roof of my mouth, I let it go and leave a long, hot trail of kisses down her soft belly...until...

I exhale over her dripping pussy. She jumps like my breath has a physical form. She rocks her hips shamelessly, and I lick her once, and then again, enjoying the sweet taste of her. She's so wet, it makes my blood boil. But this isn't a scenario that involves penetration.

Throwing her legs over my shoulders, I lap her up, then cup her breasts in my hands and lightly stroke them, paying particular attention to her tight nipples. Moans tear from her taut throat, then soft sobs, as though she's being pushed too far.

But she doesn't say "sunshine." And I want to reward my good girl.

I use every trick I know to bring her to a peak with just my tongue. The sound she makes is more animal than human. Heat burns through me, and my cock is so hard, it feels like it's about to burst.

But I rein myself in. She deserves another orgasm. And so finally, at long last, I give it to her.

She screams her pleasure. The cry is the best aphrodisiac. She shivers uncontrollably against my mouth, and even as she's coming down from the high, she continues to sob a little, her face flushed.

"Good girl," I praise her.

"Are you always this relentless?" She can barely get the words out.

"No. Just with you. I've been fantasizing for years about debauching you." I tenderly push the hair away from her cheeks, which are slick with a thin film of sweat. "This, and *lots* of other things."

"If this was any indication," she says, "I want you to do *all* of them to me." Her eyes shine with trust. "All you've done is make me feel good."

I'm at my limit now. I strip out of my clothes and shoes, eager to be as close to her as possible. She stares at my cock, slightly apprehensive but licking her lips. It reminds of the way she sucked me off at the hotel. And it's all I can do to maintain a slippery grip on my control.

I roll a condom down my dick, then press it against her dripping folds. I kiss her again, wanting to taste her. She strokes my tongue with hers, sucks it like it were my cock. I break the kiss and push in slowly, watching the emotions play on her face.

"Tell me how you feel." I can tell if it's pleasurable for her from her reaction, but I want to hear it.

Mouth slightly open and eyes wide, she says, "You're...*really* big."

"And you're unbelievably tight." I push a little deeper, resisting the urge to just drive into her in one stroke. She's so tight it might hurt her, even if she is already dripping.

"I feel stretched...in a good way." She squirms, then moves her pelvis to encourage me.

Sweat beads on my skin, and I fist the sheets hard. I don't want to grab her and bruise her. Well, I *do* want to, but—

"Sunshine," she says.

I freeze, even as my most basic instinct screams to keep going. "Are you okay?" I start to pull back, reaching for the knot at the headrest.

She wraps her legs around me. "I'm fine. Just want you to untie me so I can hold you." She slips her wrists free then grips my shoulders. "You could never hurt me, Nicholas."

Relieved, elated, I thread my fingers through her hair and kiss her hard, while I push the rest of the way in. She lets out a soft sigh and clings to me.

This was the angle that was best for her—I tilt my hips to hit just the right spot, and her back jerks off the bed. I start to go harder and faster, hear her low, rough breathing as she struggles for air. Her pussy tightens, then spasms, gripping my dick. It's like a drug, but I yank myself back from the edge. *Not yet.*

I let her come down a bit before driving her relentlessly toward another peak, higher than the one before. Then a moment to catch her breath before pushing her up again.

She shakes uncontrollably, screams until her voice changes. She begs me to stop, then pleads with me to continue. I grant the wishes that suit me. And adore her for being so openly greedy for me and the pleasure I'm giving her.

A fifth orgasm breaks over her, and she trembles, then goes limp. "Baby?"

Nothing. I look down at her closed eyes. Lax face. I might've thought she'd fallen asleep if it weren't for the shallow, rapid breathing.

I press a kiss on her mouth, run my hands along her sweet body until she stirs.

She blinks, slight confusion clouding her not-yet-fully-focused eyes.

"My Molly." I smile. "Ready now?"

She squirms, then lets out a gasp as she feels the hard length of my dick still inside her. "Yes," she whispers, then lays her hands on my cheeks tenderly and kisses me.

That's all it takes. I pound into her hard and fast until she hits another peak with a soft cry, and a monstrous orgasm barrels through me. She cradles me between her thighs, her arms around my neck. Groaning, I hold her tightly, like she's the greatest treasure of my life.

28

MOLLY

WHEN I WALK into Get Jacked on Monday, several trainers give me weird sideways glances. I surreptitiously check my clothes, but don't seem to have spilled anything. Skirt's not tucked into my underwear by mistake. Nothing on my teeth either, since I brushed my teeth after breakfast. Plus, I didn't give them a toothy smile, so they wouldn't be able to see anything even if I had something stuck between my teeth.

Well, whatever. Right now, I feel too good to be bothered by some odd looks. Spending the weekend in bed with Nicholas was ah-*may*-zing. Romance novel sex isn't just possible, but can be had for *hours on end* with the right man.

On top of that, he said we aren't fake-dating! I feel like I just won the lottery of life.

"What did you do? Jack's in a really bad mood," Petra says. Young, toned and with perfect platinum hair, she's one of our most popular female trainers. Every woman wants to look like her, and men want to train with her simply to spend time in her presence.

I give her a look. "I literally *just* walked in."

"Come on, Molly. It's got something to do with you."

"Kinda hard to see how. All I've done is arrive."

Plus, the man's too oblivious to let anybody influence his emotional state. If he were more observant, he wouldn't try to touch me all the time or stare at my boobs like they hold the answers to the existential questions of the universe.

"Oh, *there* she is! Ms. L.A. Bachelorette," comes Jack's voice. I've never heard him so sarcastic and rude before. He's more the I'm-playfully-gross type.

I swallow a sigh. Is he upset about losing out to Nicholas? "It was all for a good cause," I say with the fake smile I reserve just for him.

"Was it? You disappeared with the winner as soon as the auction ended. What could've been so urgent and important?" All he has to do is point a finger to complete the accusatory scene. Maybe I'll offer to introduce him to Ted Lasker as soon as I find a new job. Jack can have a long, storied career as an asshole in movies.

"He and I had things to do," I say.

"Like?"

"What I do with my boyfriend is none of your business."

He shakes his head. "You know, a guy like him isn't going to stick around."

Is *he* volunteering to stick around? If so, my response is an instant *no thank you.* "We can agree to disagree." I give him another insincere smile, then take a wide berth around him to get to my office. After locking the door to be doubly secure, I start my computer.

I *have* to find a new job!

After putting out some fires over a few thousand dollars nobody can seem to account for, I send out more résumés. *Please, oh please.*

A couple of knocks come from the door. I swivel around warily. It better not be Jack. "Yes?"

"It's me," says Petra. "Flowers came for you."

I unlock the door. She thrusts a huge flower basket full of purple and white tropical orchids through it, and I end up hugging them. They're gorgeous and smell like heaven.

"Somebody loves you." She leans forward. "Is it true Jack asked you out on your birthday, and you turned him down?"

"No. Who told you that?"

"James. He just came in."

"And where did he hear it?"

"Tim." She purses her lips in disapproval. Apparently, Tim didn't tell her first.

"Do you guys actually train people between gossip sessions?"

She shrugs. "Of course. But what are we supposed to do when we aren't training anybody or selling memberships?" She shoots me a sly look. "I think Jack likes you."

"What he likes are my boobs."

"Which are attached to you, so they're you."

"Not the same thing. Anyway, thanks for bringing the flowers. I gotta get back to work."

She looks around my small workspace, gives a conspicuous shudder and leaves. I shut the door and lock it again, then bury my nose in the blossoms. The silky petals tickle, and I smile.

I pluck the card. More writing in some new foreign language and Nicholas's signature at the end. I grin, then kiss his name. I don't generally like Mondays, but today's been amazing. I woke up in his bed, and we had quick morning sex and a shower, followed by a lovely breakfast. I sigh appreciatively, then laugh when I realize that every day can start like that.

I whip out my phone to share my happiness.

—Me: Thank you. The flowers are stunning and I love them. I want you to know that if every Monday starts like today, I could actually begin to like starting the workweek. You're the one who makes it special.

I hit send, then bite my lip, wondering if it was too soon or too clingy.

Nicholas and I have great chemistry. And he seems to like me, and I like him, too. But I know his dating history—I'd have to be uncaring and oblivious to be unaware when I've known him for eight years. He's a serial monogamist, but doesn't date the same woman for long.

Don't overthink it. I should just enjoy the moment. I can deal with the end of our relationship when Nicholas decides to move on.

My phone pings. Ooh, is it Nicholas? I pick it up with breathless anticipation...but it's Dad. Nothing pops my buoyant mood like seeing him on the screen.

—Dad: Is it true you were at a charity auction hosted by the Pryce Family Foundation and got the highest bid out of all the women there?

—Me: Yes. Why?

—Dad: I thought Renée was joking when she told me.

—Me: Well, she wasn't.

Will this make him happy for me? Maybe even a little proud that I'm fine the way I am?

—Dad: How can any man want to throw away money like that?

Slap, slap, slap. His words shatter my hope, claw at me with their casual cruelty.

—Me: Well, somebody "threw away" $5M. Why do you think that is?

—Dad: $5M? As in FIVE MILLION DOLLARS?

—Me: As in exactly that. Since most people don't "throw away" that much money for no reason, have you considered the possibility that maybe I'm fine the way I am? And maybe there are others who feel the same way?

I stare at the text. I've never spoken to my dad so bluntly, and my insides are shaky. But at the same time, it feels great to tell him what I think rather than demurring or just letting him bulldoze me to avoid an argument.

—Dad: There has to be something else involved. Money laundering, maybe.

His response leaves me speechless. He'd rather believe that a criminal is using me for some nefarious reason than acknowledge that maybe I'm lovable as is.

The fact that he'd go this far to insist that I'm not worth anything cuts deep, leaving a gash in my heart already battered from decades of abuse.

But I can't make myself quit hoping he'll change one day, so of course I keep opening his texts. I look at the flowers from Nicholas, but they aren't enough to cheer me up now. All I want is a family that supports and loves each other. But it feels like an impossible dream.

29

NICHOLAS

It isn't until after eleven that I get a chance to take a quick breather. Cody's compressed all my meetings into the morning and early afternoon to ensure I don't stay overtime.

During the last two weeks, I've cleared out my agenda as much as possible to make sure I get home early enough to have dinner with Molly every night. I'm not going to let her sit alone in the living room in drunken tears, sobbing about dying alone, even if it's over some fictional character.

Molly must've texted me when I was speaking with one of the investors, because I didn't notice her message until now. She's adorable when she's excited about something. I text back, *Every day is special if you're with me, my Molly.*

She doesn't read it immediately, though. That asshole Jack is probably keeping her busy. I tap my chin. Is he being petty to her because he didn't get to win the auction? He always gave off a bad vibe when he was cheating on his girlfriend with my mother. I should let Molly know she doesn't have to put up with her shitty boss.

–Me: If Jack is being difficult, let me know, and I'll deal with it.

I hit send, then remember Arturo works at Get Jacked, too.

–Me: Arturo as well.

Now... Let's see what else is on my phone. I've ignored everything since the auction to give Molly a hundred percent of my attention. Since my brothers have sent more than I could read in a day, I scroll to the recent ones.

—Noah: $5 million. I still can't wrap my mind around it.

—Griffin: True love. You'll understand if it ever hits you.

It's so weird to see those words from Griffin. He's such a numbers guy. I thought he'd marry a column of statistics because he used to hate women approaching him. He claimed they only wanted him for sex or his connection to Dad, both of which made him feel cheap. And when Griffin feels cheap, he gets extra grumpy.

—Grant: The only thing he wants to spend five million bucks on is croissants from Bobbi.

—Noah: Wrong! Her cupcakes are great, too.

—Huxley: I'm sure Bobbi's excited about that. Did you tell her you're as varied in bed, too?

—Noah: Hey, I got moves. Nobody's ever complained.

—Grant: Why isn't Nicholas responding to our texts?

—Emmett: LOL, yeah, what could possibly be keeping him occupied?

—Huxley: Most likely, his dick broke.

I snort.

—Noah: Huh?

—Huxley: If I were her, I would've ridden him until his dick broke.

—Noah: Meh, too vanilla. I'd expect something more exciting.

—Grant: Well, she isn't going to have sex with him while riding a zebra through the savannah.

—Noah: WHAT!

—Emmett: He read the first page of your book.

—Noah: That was like from ten months ago! I deleted that!

—Griffin: Did you know zebras can't be tamed? Why did you make the hero command zebras? Is he supposed to be some kind of zebra king?

—Sebastian: An alpha were-zebra!

I laugh. I love my brothers.

—Me: Sounds like a great romance novel hero, Seb. Just so you all know, my penis is fine, thank you very much. And no animals will ever be in my bedroom.

–Huxley: So you aren't dead.

–Me: Not even close.

–Griffin: If you're spending $5 million to have dinner with her, how much are you spending on the ring?

The idea of putting a ring on Molly's finger so everyone knows she's mine sends a pulse of warmth through me.

–Sebastian: Unless he asked Lucie, he hasn't made that decision.

–Me: I haven't ordered anything yet. Can't decide. Nothing looks good enough.

–Sebastian: Just give me $10 million, and I'll give you something perfect.

–Me: Ha! Are you not meeting your revenue goals for the quarter?

A text pops up. Mom.

–Mom: Paul just told me you won a girl for five million dollars! Good for you! So is this how we pay the surrogate?

–Me: You aren't paying anything. And she's not a surrogate.

–Mom: I suppose doing it publicly might be crass. What will the baby think? Assuming anybody tells the baby.

Ugh. I can feel a headache coming on.

She sends a picture of Griffin's triplets.

–Mom: See how efficient this is? Three at once! I feel like we're entitled to at least that many for $5M.

She's lost of her mind. Forget Europe. She should tour insane asylums so she can pick one she likes and stay there forever. Ideally, the facility won't have Wi-Fi or cell reception.

–Mom: If you want, I can wire you half the sum.

–Me: I don't want your money. And forget about triplets.

Triplets with Molly would be amazing, but I'm not planning our future based on what's going to make my mother happy. What matters is Molly's happiness.

–Mom: By the way, is the girl pretty? Smart?

I ignore her text.

Another group text arrives.

–Emmett: So are we going to meet this woman before you propose?

—Me: Lemme think about it. Mom's texting me about babies. Ideally, triplets.

—Griffin: Roughly one in ten thousand pregnancies result in triplets, so she should just give up. Also, sorry about the triplets thing. I can't control what my mother does with the baby photos.

Griffin's genuinely apologetic about the situation with our mothers. He knows his is egging mine on.

—Mom: Anyway, Georgia should be in Los Angeles by now to meet with your girl and work out the details. I'd do it myself, but Paul and I have decided to spend more time in Venice. It's such a lovely city.

Thank you, Paul. My mom's current husband knows how to rein her in so I don't end up committing matricide.

So Georgia's back in town. I don't want her offering to share her home with Molly. Although I've made it clear we're dating for real, she might still be hung up on having a place of her own. Georgia's apartment is tiny—she refused a trust fund I offered to set up for her because she said she wants to earn her own money, although she didn't refuse my paying her college tuition. But Molly might not consider the size of Georgia's apartment an issue.

Best to nip this in the bud. I send Georgia a text.

—Me: Where are you? Text me back as soon as you hit LAX.

—Georgia: Too late. I'm not in LAX. So does this mean I shouldn't text you back? :sticking-tongue-out-emoji:

Haha, very funny. Tears of mirth are streaming down my face.

—Me: Where are you?

—Georgia: Home, just got done unpacking. I landed at nine. Is it me or are you grouchy? Are you feeling buyer's remorse right now? Five million is a lot of money!

Buyer's remorse? Is this the kind of conversation she's going to have if she hangs out with my Molly?

—Me: Don't say anything weird to screw things up between me and Molly.

—Georgia: Ha! I knew it. So you bid $5M on her, right?

—Me: Yes. And don't tell Mom if you haven't.

Mom's terrible with Google, and her assistant isn't any better. I don't need her harassing and scaring Molly. I'm used to the way Mom get pushy, but Molly isn't.

—Georgia: I didn't and I won't. I'm not stupid. Nikki is amazing, but she can be single-minded.

—Me: Good.

—Georgia: But I have to warn Molly! She has no idea what she's getting into.

Oh no, you don't. I'm not letting my stepsister ruin the best thing that's ever happened to me.

—Me: Stay out of it. If you offer to let her crash at your place or say that I might be having buyer's remorse over the auction, I'll run you over with my car.

—Georgia: Ooooh. At least I'll be run over by a car worth over half a million dollars!

I generally enjoy her sarcastic humor, but not right now.

—Me: You wish. I'm going to buy a rusty Pinto just for you. You aren't worth a Bentley!

30

MOLLY

AFTER I SEND in my reports to Elaine, my phone pings and some texts from Nicholas pop up on the screen.

–Nicholas: Every day is special if you're with me.

Aww. I smile. All the stress from the day melts away.

Then I read the other ones about Jack and Arturo.

The former is always difficult... Oh...wait. Does Nicholas suspect that my boss could become vindictive after not winning me at the auction?

It's scary how accurate Nicholas is about Jack, but I haven't seen Arturo since Saturday at the ballroom. And he doesn't come in until midmorning anyway, according to his timesheets. I doubt he's going to bother me. He can be a bit intense, but he hasn't done anything to make me think he's a creep, even if he and Nicholas don't seem to get along.

I have a new email alert—it's from a small grocery store chain in the region. I applied to their accounting division a couple of weeks ago. But when they didn't respond, I crossed them off my list. Guess they were just taking their sweet time. But this is my first—potential—interview! Hopeful excitement twirls inside me like little ballerinas.

Dear Molly,

My name is Lilian Hampton and I'm the Personnel Manager at LocalGro. We are impressed with your qualifications and would like to meet for an in-person interview if you're still interested in pursuing an exciting career at our company. When would be good for you?

The email is short and to the point. I also appreciate that Lilian doesn't just assume I'm available.

Dear Lilian,

Yes, I am still very interested in a position with your company. I'm available any weekday between noon and two.

I can pretend I'm taking an extended lunch break when I interview, since I don't want Jack to know I'm planning to quit until I have a firm offer. Given how poorly he reacted to what happened on Saturday, I don't think anything good will come of his knowing about my intention to leave.

I should send more résumés out. I have a feeling today's going to be my lucky day. More companies might be interested in my skill set.

I pull up more listings from a bunch of job sites and submit my résumé. I have the right college degree and experience. Why *wouldn't* a company want me?

My phone pings. Maybe Lilian's getting back to me with possible dates?

–Georgia: Guess what? I'm back in town!

–Me: Hey! Welcome back!

–Georgia: We should do lunch! Are you available?

–Me: Now? Sure! What are you in the mood for?

–Georgia: Sushi! Please!

I laugh. I know just the place, and it's only a couple of blocks from the gym.

–Me: How about Zen Asia at noon?

–Georgia: Done!

–Me: I'll head over at five till so we can get a table.

Zen Asia is always busy, and it's impossible to get a table if you get there even a minute after twelve. I check my work emails to make sure Elaine hasn't dumped any last-minute items in my lap. She has a habit of doing that right before lunch, which can be irritating. But at least she doesn't do it often.

Around eleven thirty, I sling my purse over my shoulder and head out of the back office against a tide of people wanting to squeeze a quick workout in during their lunch break. Dana's on a treadmill, running steadily. If she's still upset about Saturday, you wouldn't know it. One of her friends is filming her from behind, so the viewer can only see her butt. Dana's Nike leggings are so tight, the fabric sticks to her glutes perfectly, molding even to her ass crack. I note James and Tim observing carefully from one of the power racks.

I walk across the gym, basically invisible. But then, I'm not in a skintight outfit, and I don't have a toned body like Dana's. My pink top and purple skirt are loose. My shoes are sensible mary janes in black.

"Hey."

I turn and see Arturo in his trainer's outfit. His mouth is smiling, but his eyes are tentatively searching mine. If I didn't know better, I'd say he's concerned about my reaction to him, except I have no plans to treat him any differently based on what happened on Saturday.

I give him a friendly smile, like always. "Hi."

The tension in his shoulders eases. "You heading out to lunch?"

"Yep."

"Wanna eat together?" He flashes a dimple.

"Sorry. Not possible today."

The skin around his eyes tightens, although he maintains his smile. "Is it because of Nicholas?"

"No. I'm meeting my best friend. Girls only."

Besides, although I don't plan to change my behavior around Arturo, that doesn't mean I'll spend more time than I have to with him. The fact that he's a famous movie star's son makes me wary. Like...why does he want to hang out with me when he could be with anybody? Petra for one would be totally interested, and they spend more time together on the floor than we ever could.

Despite the interruption, I reach Zen Asia before noon and snag the last table. The guy behind me groans in disappointment.

A plump, harried-looking Asian lady in a white-and-blue floral dress and tennis shoes takes me to a small booth. She's the owner's wife, and she's always here.

"Do you want something to drink? Hot tea?" she says, glancing at the big crowd milling in the entrance, then turning her attention back to me. "Sorry, we're short-staffed. A waitress is out sick today."

"That's okay. And some iced lemon tea would be great."

"Okay. You eating alone?"

"A friend is coming. Should be here soon."

She nods with a small smile on her face. "Enjoy your lunch." Then she turns around and bustles to the kitchen, saying something in Korean.

I thought she was Japanese for the longest time because she and her husband own a sushi restaurant. But she told me that she's actually Korean, from a city called Busan.

Sipping my tea, I watch the lady return to the entrance and start getting orders for takeout. If you can't get a table here, that's the only option left—unless you plan to take a *long* lunch break. Hopefully Georgia gets here soon, because the delicious aroma of rice, soy sauce and miso soup is making me hungry. The tea is tasty, but it isn't filling.

When my glass is half-empty, Georgia arrives. "Hey, did you wait long?"

"No. Just a few minutes."

"I need some genuine California rolls. Missed them *so* much in Europe. They can't do California rolls like we do."

"Probably not. Otherwise, they'd be called Tuscany rolls."

She laughs, pulling out an order sheet and marking the rolls she wants with a pencil. I do the same and hand our order sheets to the server.

Georgia produces a big bag. "For you."

"What is it?"

"A bottle of red and a white. I don't know the vintage or anything. Nikki helped pick them out, so I know they're good."

Georgia is a beer girl. I prefer cheap, fruity wine coolers, but they probably aren't available in Europe. Too déclassé.

"How was Europe?"

"Oh, incredible." Georgia sighs. "I just feel so enlightened, you know?"

"Why? Did you have a religious experience?" I say with a grin. "Perhaps with a smoldering Spaniard? Or a Greek tycoon?"

She giggles. "No! But I did meet someone truly aspirational." Her eyes grow dreamy, a look I've never seen on her face before.

"Who?"

"Rachel Griffin. She's Nicholas's half-brother's mom, and oh my God, she has the life I didn't know I wanted."

Two large platters of California rolls arrive with wasabi and soy sauce, and we dig in. I don't know what the chef does to them, but they should be named cocaine rolls for how addictive they are.

After a couple of happily satisfying bites, Georgia sighs. "God, I love California."

"Not the rolls?"

"These too." She grins.

"Anyway, tell me about Rachel and this life you didn't know you wanted." Whatever she's discovered is either really deep or really funny.

"Okay, so, number one, the woman's just gorgeous. I would've *never* known she has a son in his mid-thirties. And she had the cutest date. I think he's, like, twenty-six? Twenty-seven? He looked at her like she was the goddess of his world."

"Is she his sugar mama?"

"Probably."

"Well, there you go. That's why she's a goddess to him."

"Sure—but who cares? His tight ass would be worth it."

I laugh. "So that's your life goal. Be gorgeous and date a hot guy with a nice ass."

"Hey, it could be worse. And she's rich, too, which is important.

Having your own money like a boss is amazing, don't you think? But enough about *moi*, what about you and your hot guy?"

"Me?"

She leans closer. "Yes, you. You and *Nicholas*." Her eyes sparkle with conviction that there's something romantic and sexy going on between us.

"Don't you feel weird calling your brother 'hot'?"

She scoffs. "I didn't meet him until I was eighteen, so I don't get that ick feeling, if that's what you're worried about. Come on. Tell your bestie everything."

"Well... He won a date with me," I say, all casual and cool.

"But before that, you guys told Nikki and Ted you were dating!" Georgia says, her eyes sparkling. "I was listening!"

"You were?"

"Yes! And it *killed* me to keep my mouth shut that it was you on the phone! She couldn't stop speculating about Nicholas's *girlfriend* and asked me to help her figure out who it was."

"I was just helping Nicholas fake it because they were so insistent about wanting grandbabies. So it's good you didn't say anything."

"Oh my God, I know! She would've started calling you about making babies with her son." Georgia's eyes narrow. "But there's gotta be more. He spent *five million dollars*. Nobody spends that kind of money at a charity bachelorette auction."

"Apparently, they do it to launder money," I murmur darkly.

"Ah, shit." She knows what that means. "Your dad heard about it, too?"

"Oh, yes. And he wasted no time getting in touch."

"He's such a shitty human being. I can't believe you still talk to him."

"Well. He is my dad." The only family I have left—and I'm the only one he has left. Maybe that's why I find it so hard to turn away from him. And while I resent his hurtful comments, a tiny voice inside wonders if he's right—that his cruelty is really a desire for me to see the truth. Truth is supposed set you free, though, not make you want to crawl into bed and never come out.

"Forget your dad. No man spends that kind of money on a girl he isn't interested in. Trust me. Nicholas is totally into you!" She puts a hand over her mouth to contain her excitement. "I always knew there was something about the way he looked at you."

"What about the way he looked at me?"

"You never noticed? When I first introduced you to him, he was struck dumb. And he *always* has something to say. He looked at you like he'd discovered the eighth wonder of the world."

Georgia and her exaggerations. I laugh. "He was distracted."

"Yeah, by you. His eyes were super-glued to your face."

I flush at her insistence, especially since she's misremembering what happened. "He was staring at the grass in my hair."

She shakes her head. "You are so, *so* sad."

"No, seriously! Remember Jordi? He put that in my hair." He was in my U.S. government class, and liked to put stuff in my hair for some reason. Thank God it wasn't bugs or gum that day.

"That totally wasn't why," Georgia says. "But okay, fine, I'll give you some credit—I wasn't one hundred percent sure either, because he kept dating different women. But that was back then, and *this is now.* Why are you refusing to see what's so obvious?"

"Nicholas is bigger than life, so we're just attaching more meaning to this little situation than we should. I'm not going to delude myself simply because you think there's something more. I just want to enjoy what I have with Nicholas while it lasts."

"So you don't think it can go anywhere other than a lousy dinner date?"

"It's a five-million-dollar dinner, so probably not lousy," I correct her primly. "But expectations are not good for me, even if we are living together right now."

Every time I dream of something more, things end badly, and I'm left disappointed and upset. And I just don't want to open myself up to inevitable pain by thinking of what could be. Whatever I have with Nicholas could devastate me like nothing I've ever experienced, and I'm not brave enough to leave myself fully exposed.

31

NICHOLAS

"What time do we need to head to the shelter?" Molly asks over breakfast on Saturday.

"The shelter?" My plan is to spend the day rolling around in bed with her. I wish she could get a three-day weekend, but apparently Jack won't give her one.

Which is supremely dickish behavior. It isn't like he's running some vast financial empire that can't function without an accountant for a day. For a glorified personal trainer, he sure is difficult.

I should make a list of things we can do over two days. Molly was unusually down on Monday, and her less-than-stellar mood continued until Wednesday. I checked to see if she'd watched another girl-does-the-right-thing-only-to-die-alone-at-the-end kind of TV show, but she hadn't. She read a few books, but she only reads romance. As far as I know, they all end "happily ever after." I even scanned them after she was finished to be sure, and they just had a lot of creative sex scenes—most of which I intend to *re*-create—and happy endings.

When I asked her if anything was bothering her, she merely smiled and said she was having issues at work. I texted Georgia in case she'd said something stupid, but she said nothing happened. They just had lunch and got caught up.

Asking for more details would violate our privacy. We have the right to have a girly conversation without you wanting to know everything, she texted me.

Sisters are brutal. My brothers would've been on my side. Noah in particular would've told me everything in detail.

"Yes, the shelter," Molly says with a laugh. "Furry Haven. We volunteer there once a month? Remember?"

Oh, riiight. It's an effort not to sigh. I volunteered there to spend time with her. And now I've contributed five million dollars to their coffers, for which Brenda thanked me profusely. I was hoping to gracefully step back and give my allergies a rest.

But Molly's looking at me with excitement shining in her eyes. And I can deny her nothing. "Of course I *remember*." I try for an airy wave. "We can leave in half an hour if you want to be there by nine thirty. I'll drive."

"Great!" She beams.

I swear when she smiles like that, she can ask me for anything and I'll give it to her.

I look for my allergy meds in the bathroom cabinet. I get a special prescription because the OTC stuff doesn't work for me.

The ugly orange bottle is sitting there like some kind of petrified tangerine. The same shade as Joey's hair, now that I think about it. I pick it up, then curse.

I forgot to fill my prescription! Dr. Prescott can instruct the pharmacy, even though it's Saturday, but there won't be time to grab the pills before hitting the shelter.

Let's see... If I take dog-walking duty and avoid going inside the shelter, I'll probably be okay. And I don't have to be inside anyway. It isn't like I do anything on their computers. Brenda has never asked me to wash the animals, and I don't see her asking today.

I toss the empty bottle and head out. Molly's waiting, looking pretty and pleased. I select the Flying Spur for the drive because it just feels like the perfect car for the day—luxurious, classy and responsive. This is the first time we're going to the shelter together, and while spending the entire morning screwing would be better, I like how normal the shared activity feels. This might be why couples do volunteer work together. I should get my prescription refilled and continue, especially when she's so excited, humming along to the songs filling the car with a smile on her pink, kissable lips. She's impossibly cute when she's like this.

After I pull into the lot by the shelter, I kiss her, stealing a taste. *Yum.* She flushes.

"What was that about?"

"What, a man can't kiss his pretty girlfriend?"

Her flush deepens as her smile grows wider. She leans forward, her motion fast. Her mouth is aiming for my cheek, but I'm quicker. I tilt my head so she ends up kissing me on the mouth. I try to pull her closer and fuse our mouths tighter, but she retreats hastily.

"Later!" she says, bright laughter in her voice, then climbs out of the car.

I follow her out. "If you don't mind, let's walk the dogs," I call out to her back.

"Okay! I'll ask Brenda!"

I'm pretty sure she won't mind. I watch her hips swinging as she walks in, thinking about *later*, then lean on the car and check my email.

Molly comes out, but without any dogs. "Brenda wants to see you," she says.

"For what?"

"For *what*? To thank you for the donation!"

"Oh. She already said thanks, but you can tell her it was nothing. My pleasure."

Molly skips over, loops her arm around mine and tugs. "Come on. I want to see you get credit for your good deed."

"No, honestly, that isn't necessary."

But she pulls at me, drawing me closer to the building. Before I can protest, I'm already past the threshold.

Brenda puts down the cat she's been holding and bustles over, arms spread wide, then envelops me in a hug. The woman knows how to squeeze. "Nicholas! Once again, thank you so much! You have no idea what the funding means for Furry Haven!"

"It was nothing. Glad I was able to help. If you want, I'll see about setting something more regular up, so the shelter doesn't have to worry about steady cash flow." I manage to swallow a sneeze.

"My goodness." Her green eyes go wide, and she folds her hands over her chest. "That's a great idea! And so generous!"

Molly beams. My nose feels weird, but I can ignore that to see her happy.

"Yeah, I can have my assistant Cody get in touch." I sneeze. The skin around my eyes begins to feel tingly.

"Oh yes, he was very polite when we spoke on the phone. Such a nice man."

"Uh-huh." I sneeze again.

"Are you okay?" Molly asks.

"I'm—*achoo!*—fine." Another sneeze. Then another.

As Molly and Brenda watch, I let out six sneezes in a row, then sniffle and rub my eyes.

"Are you...allergic to something here?" Molly says, looking around uncertainly.

"I—" I sneeze.

"There's a CVS around the corner," Brenda says. "They should have something."

"No." I wave away her suggestion. "That won't work."

I need to get out of here.

I step outside. It doesn't help much. My body's already full of dog and cat dander that wants to torture me.

Molly follows me out. "Nicholas! Wait!"

I raise my hand and gesture reassuringly. It fails because I sneeze hard enough to crack a rib. "Just give me some time. I'll be fine."

She puts a hand on my arm and peers into my face. "Are you allergic to something in the shelter? If so, I'll ask Brenda and see if we can take it out."

When she looks at me with concern like this, I can't brush her off. "Won't work. I'm allergic to dogs and cats." I sneeze again, but thankfully not as hard.

Her face goes lax with shock. "You're allergic to *dogs and cats*?"

I nod, then clear my throat, feeling sheepish about admitting it.

"But...you come to the shelter..."

"My doctor prescribes me something, but I ran out today."

"It must be serious to need a prescription."

"It's no big deal."

"Of course it is! Are you okay when you take the medicine?"

She's doing that concerned peering again, which never fails to make me want to tell her everything. If she could bottle it the CIA wouldn't have to waterboard people. "Okay enough. It makes it bearable." I rub my itchy eyes.

"You must really love animals." Her voice brims with sympathy.

"No," I correct her. "I mean, yes, I do love animals. But I wasn't here for them. I was here for you. Volunteering here was the only way I could spend time with you." I lay my past actions bare so she can understand how special she is to me.

She looks at me like a bunny, mouth open and eyes glazed as she tries to process what I just said. Her reaction tightens a painful vise around my chest. Why can't she just believe it's possible for me to feel something deep for her?

"You came here to spend time with me. Even though you're *that* allergic to animals?"

I nod. Then I remember something else I should come clean about. "And since it's time for confessions, I'm just going to let you know I'm the reason you couldn't find an apartment."

She blinks up at me.

"I had Cody snap up every apartment that met your criteria. I didn't want you to leave."

"That's a lot of apartments. And money."

"There's nothing I wouldn't do for a chance with you."

Her lashes flutter as she digests what I'm telling her. "I wasn't worth it," she says finally, in a small voice.

"You're wrong." I look her in the eye. "You're worth everything."

The confession hangs in the air. She blinks, and something shutters in her eyes.

An invisible line forms between us, and she retreats behind it. She folds and unfolds her hands, dropping her gaze to the gray, cracked asphalt between us.

Somehow it's worse now that I've said what's in my heart, compared to before when I just showed her a good time in bed. It sends a painful pang through my chest until I almost wish I hadn't said anything.

Still, I wait. The ball's in her court.

Time passes, unbearably slowly.

Finally, she takes a deep breath, her eyes glinting like precious stones. She comes over and hugs me. My tension vanishes. I put my arms around her, holding her tightly, as she buries her face in my chest.

"Thank you. That's the nicest thing anybody's ever said to me." Her voice is muffled, but clear enough.

I hold her, grateful that she's erased the line she drew. It couldn't have been easy, giving up her mental and emotional shelter, and respect and admiration for her courage swell in my heart.

I kiss the crown of her head as I vow never to allow anything to hurt her.

32

MOLLY

Monday at the office, my hands pause on the keyboard as my mind wanders back. I still can't believe I hugged Nicholas like that outside Furry Haven. When he made himself vulnerable and told me why he came to the shelter even though he's allergic to dogs and cats, my first instinct was to pull back because I didn't feel like I deserved the kind of care he was giving me.

But then pain flashed in his eyes, and I realized I was hurting him with my reaction, and I had to give him a hug.

And it worked! The smile he gave me took my breath away with its beauty. But I was still slightly panicked, as though I'd peeled off a protective layer.

Nicholas will never purposely cause me pain. I know that much. But you don't have to mean it to wound someone. Even with the best intentions, sometimes it just happens.

Sighing, I save the work I've been doing and pull out my phone to take a break. *Let's see...what's on Instagram?* Lots of posts about upcoming books. Some talk about old favorites. I should do a monthly read update next week. Maybe I can make some cool visuals in Nicholas's library. I've already made three posts there, but it's just too gorgeous not to use again.

I notice a tag notification and frown. *Dana?* She and I have no reason to cross paths, even on Instagram. She does fitness; I do books. Our hashtags couldn't be more different.

The post she tagged me on is a video showing Dana in Owen's townhouse. The master bathroom is the same—except for tons of makeup strewn all over the vanity. Wait, does she have *three* tubes of mascara? I squint at the screen. *Oh yes she does.* Why the need for three? Even if she used one per eye, she'd only need two.

She twists around, showing off a dress.

"I know I mostly talk about achieving fitness and a healthy lifestyle through better eating and physical activity. But today, I want to touch on a different benefit of the lifestyle I'm promoting." Unlike most of her videos, this one has subtitles scrolling across the bottom of the screen as she talks. "My fiancé told me he's never been with anybody who can satisfy him like I do. I think that's one of the biggest reasons we hit it off so well—amazing sexual compatibility. It's so critical to your physical and emotional wellbeing. It's unfortunate we don't talk about the subject as much as we should because we're embarrassed or sex is taboo."

Well, good for her and Owen. I guess it's important for him to find somebody who's content with the little pops he hands out during sex. Even if he got on his knees and begged me to take him back, I wouldn't. Not after Nicholas and realizing how I've been getting cheated out of *real* orgasms, the kind that shake you up like a powerful earthquake. About all I can do when Nicholas makes me come is clutch him until the shock waves pass and I can come back down from the exhilarating height.

Dana drones on. "Over the last three weeks, I've started a new diet and exercise regimen, which I've shared with you already. And now that I've *lost a few extra pounds* and gained more flexibility and strength, our satisfaction in the bedroom—and the living room, and the kitchen"— she gives a saucy wink—"has increased even more. And when I say *more*, I know it's not just on my end. He says it's so much more satisfying to make love to a strong body, one that has the stamina to go for those marathon sessions, than one a more neglected one that's *carrying some extra baggage.* And as every girl knows, a satisfied man is a man who won't stray." She gives a little shrug.

"It's a bit of a challenge to maintain the lifestyle I've committed to, but I can do it for my fiancé. He deserves the effort—and all my love. Relationships are a two-way street. You have to get off your butt and do your half before you can expect your partner to *carry the weight* too and make the relationship better. I can't wait to see how much our lives improve once I hit the three-month mark with my new routine." She blows a kiss to the camera. "You gotta work for what's important! We're all on an individual journey of self-improvement, so that we can be loved and accepted for who we are."

She doesn't mention my name, but I know this post is all about me. Why else would she tag me? And those subtitles, with the italics!

Fuck her. Outrage starts to swell until my chest feels tight. She's basically blaming me for the relationship not working out, and hinting that I'm too lazy and unmotivated to "improve" myself. The parting remark about being loved and accepted for who we are digs in like an ice pick.

There are so many comments agreeing with her. Some even say a partner who doesn't try is a valid reason for breaking up.

Since Dana made sure to tag me, Owen and our mutual friends and acquaintances are going to know the video is about me. Actually, some of the people who follow my account are going to notice, too. Public humiliation sears my gut until I feel like curling up into a fetal position.

I reach for the home-baked cookie I brought with me and take a bite, then stop. Dana's words about self-improvement—especially the part about losing weight—boom in my head, full of judgment. And the fact that I might be giving up on better sex.

I'm not too worried about getting better orgasms, because the sex is already fantastic. *But would it make it better for Nicholas...?* He seems insatiable, but it's the beginning of the relationship. And he might get better orgasms if I did something about my body.

I touch my belly. It's soft. Squishy. And my thighs jiggle when I poke them.

Now my dad's voice joins Dana's. I'm pretty sure I'm never going to have a body like Mom, but...

It's possible I'm not doing my part. Viewed objectively, my relationship with Nicholas is pretty one-sided in my favor. He's letting me live with him for free, and I don't even have to do any chores or chip in with expenses. He's much wealthier than I am, of course, but maybe I'm taking advantage without meaning to. And maybe doing what Dana said could be my way of contributing. I'd hate to give the impression that I don't care about our relationship. I want Nicholas to know how special he is to me. I'd hate for him to think I take him for granted.

I dump the rest of the cookie in the trash can and text Georgia.

–Me: Did you see what Dana posted? She tagged me.

–Georgia: Gimme a sec.

A couple of moments later, I get another ping.

–Georgia: What a bitch! What the hell kind of passive-aggressive bullshit is that?

I smile a little at my bestie's outrage, but it isn't enough to silence Dana's words echoing in my head.

–Me: But maybe she's right about needing to self-improve.

Two beats pass.

–Georgia: Are you smoking something?

–Me: No! I'm talking about me and Nicholas.

–Georgia: Does he have trouble getting hard or maintaining an erection?

–Me: Seriously? You really want to know that about your brother?

–Georgia: Stepbrother. And this is so I can tell you whether he's worth keeping or not.

I sigh. *Georgia.*

–Me: No and no.

–Georgia: Okay. So why do you need to change anything? Men can't get hard if they aren't attracted to the body they're seeing.

And they certainly won't go down on you all weekend if they find you unappealing. You threw your cookie away for nothing! says a baleful voice in my head.

On the other hand, I *am* in one of the best-equipped gyms in the state, which I can use for free... And what Dana said keeps playing in my head in an infinite loop.

I sigh again and head out of the office to the gym floor. Dana and her friends are on the elliptical machines, their taut bodies bobbing at a steady pace. One of them says something, and they all burst out laughing.

Bitterness, envy and insecurity wind through me. I'm never going to look like them. And I hate how Dana has picked on me *again*—even now that we're done with high school—and I loathe how she was able to skewer me so easily. But just because I'm older now doesn't mean the old self-doubts are gone.

Jerking my eyes away, I go to the shop inside the gym and buy some exercise clothes and shoes. Employees get forty percent off, so it isn't that expensive to grab them all.

I hand the items I picked out to Petra to scan at the cash register. "Good choice. These are really stretchy and breathable," she says with a smile.

"Thanks."

A voice comes from behind me. "Those for you?"

Jack. What's he doing here? Isn't he supposed to be touching—er, spotting—his female clients? I paste on a smile. "Well, you know. Figured I'd take advantage of the free membership."

"Good for you." He turns to Petra. "You know what? Comp those. My treat."

No. Totally not necessary. He's going to want to get paid by a long, uninterrupted viewing of my boobs, and I'm not that desperate for free stuff.

Petra looks at him. "I already scanned them and rang them up."

Jack goes around the counter and inputs a code into the system. "There."

His smarmy smile makes my skin crawl. But just because he's a creep doesn't mean I should be rude when he's done something nice, even if it's something I never asked for. "Thanks," I say tightly.

"You know what? I have some free time around four, so why don't I show you some basic stuff?"

"Oh no, it's fine. You've already done enough with the free clothes and shoes."

"Ah, it won't be any trouble. And there's no sense spending time at a gym spinning your wheels. Results are what count!"

"I really can't afford personal training."

His laughter booms. "You're hilarious. I'd never charge you for something like that. Besides, you know your father got you some personal sessions."

Oh crap. I totally forgot about that!

"I should check how many, but I don't mind throwing in a couple freebies to help you meet your fitness goals."

Petra cocks an eyebrow at Jack. I want to bang my head against the counter. I should've gone to another gym—a Curves or something that only accepts women.

"I'm not done with work until five," I say. "And I really don't want to mess up your schedule. I'm sure it's full with—"

"It's fine. I'm free today, and I can wait until five." He smiles at my breasts.

So he's going to exercise patience in order to grope me. Gross.

I return to my office. Now I wish I could find a reason *not* to exercise, but at the same time, giving up before starting feels like letting Jack and Dana win. I'll just do some cardio. He can't really do much if I'm on a treadmill and trying to run, can he?

I check my phone, praying I have somebody else who wants to interview me in case LocalGro doesn't work out.

–Nicholas: What do you want for dinner? Go out? Eat in? Whatever you prefer.

I smile. He truly has a magical ability to make me happy. He could text, "Boo," and I'd still smile.

–Me: I'm going to be a little late. So maybe we can go out at around 7 or 8.

–Nicholas: What's going on? Jack making you work overtime?

–Me: No. I need to exercise.

33

NICHOLAS
I NEED TO EXERCISE...?

I STARE AT MY PHONE. Molly doesn't enjoy working out. She's never expressed any interest in the gym at the mansion, and Georgia mentioned once that the free Get Jacked membership is wasted on Molly.

So what's up with this sudden desire to work out? I have five minutes before the next meeting, so I call her.

"What's going on?" I say when she answers.

"Oh, hi. I didn't think you'd call. Um, it isn't a big deal." She laughs a little. "I just feel like I should. Something I just want to do. We're dating, and I just want to do my part and be, you know, better girlfriend material."

Better girlfriend material? Who filled her head with this garbage? "I don't need you to be 'better girlfriend material.' You're already a great girlfriend. Perfect."

"Thank you." The warmth in her voice overlays a sliver of skepticism running underneath. She either doesn't believe she's a great girlfriend or she thinks I'm just saying it. Neither of which is good. "Anyway, I'll be fine. I'm not going to hurt myself or anything. The gym's full of trainers."

And Jack Peterson. That cheating, opportunistic asshole. And Arturo.

"You don't have any clothes to exercise in," I say, hoping to talk to her in person about this later this evening. If she wants to exercise for herself, I'm in full support. But if she's doing this for me—God forbid— or because somebody told her some weird shit, I'm going to ask her to stop. It's only going to be torturous, and she'll end up resenting and dreading it.

"I got some from the store here. Jack gave them to me for free."

Oh, he did, huh? Wrong move. *I* pay for things for my girl. "I'll see you soon, sweetheart."

"See you soon." She hangs up.

I step outside the office. Cody stands from his desk, holding some notes and documents. Today his hair is gelled to the max, sticking up in angry black spikes. Dark circles around his hazel eyes make him look like he got into a bar fight last night, but they're from lack of sleep. I told him to hire an assistant, but he hasn't done it yet.

"Cancel all my meetings for the afternoon. I'm not available."

He places his notes neatly on the desk. "Reschedule or cancel the entire acquisition?"

I almost forgot. This afternoon's meetings are about a cement manufacturer acquisition. The company's been struggling under poor management, and I plan to fix it and turn it profitable. "Reschedule."

I drive to the original Get Jacked Gym. I know it well—Mom trained with Jack there before she decided to fall for his charms. Smarmy shit. He has a pattern. He flatters his female clients and constantly touches them to "spot" them and "prevent injuries." Once his clients become comfortable with his seemingly innocent touches, he escalates until he gets into their pants. What he didn't know was Mom wasn't his usual bimbo. She was quite annoyed when she found out he was seeing somebody else long-term, and also getting his rocks off on the side with an assortment of short-term flings. The dictionary has Mom's picture underneath "capricious," but there's one thing she absolutely insists on —faithfulness from her partner.

Molly isn't the type to fall for that sort of thing, either. She's too honest to betray me with Jack, no matter how charming he is. But that doesn't mean I'm okay with that piece of shit putting his hands on her.

I park my car and walk into the gym. A female trainer with a bright smile comes over. "Hi! Can I help you?"

"I'm here to see Molly. If you'll just point me to her office..."

She checks out my bespoke suit and hand-stitched leather shoes, then tilts her head. Naked curiosity blooms on her face. "What's this about?"

"I'm her boyfriend."

Her eyes grow wide. "Oh! I had no idea. Well. You can walk through there, and her office is the third door on your left. It says accounting. You can't miss it."

I nod my thanks and reach Molly's office. I knock and try to turn the knob, but it doesn't budge.

"Who is it?" comes her voice.

"It's me."

Something clatters inside. A moment later there's a click and the door opens.

Molly sticks her head out, surprise written all over her face. "Nicholas?" It's almost like she was masturbating or watching porn in there. Who locks their office door?

"Can I come in?" I ask.

"Yeah, sure." She pulls back and gestures for me to enter.

The office isn't anything special. It has no windows—which makes the space feel smaller than it is—and is crammed with two metal filing cabinets, a modestly sized desk with a faux-wood top and a wheeled chair that should've been replaced a decade ago. Jack apparently doesn't spend much money on the offices in the back, because the gym area has a lot of the shiny, modern machines that I have in my home gym. The bouquet I sent livens up the space a little. Otherwise, it's basically a jail cell.

She closes the door, then turns the knob until something clicks.

"Why are you locking the door?"

"Safety reasons."

Instant alarm blares through me. "What happened?" There could've been a stalker or some weirdo with anger management issues.

"Nothing. It just makes me feel more secure."

Is she downplaying a threat to her safety to make me feel better? But she doesn't seem scared or anything. Maybe the gym just has annoying people who don't knock. I had one too, until I fired him for barging into offices and conference rooms once too often. It almost cost us a lucrative buyout.

"Sorry there's no place for you to sit."

"It's fine." I like having her stand with me, especially in the small office. She's close enough that I can smell the shampoo in her hair.

"What are you doing here?" she asks.

"Did you really mean that about the exercise?"

Her gaze drops to her phone briefly, a frown pinching her eyebrows. It's more of an answer than anything she could say. "Yes. But seriously, I'll be fine. I'm not going to hurt myself lifting anything heavy, although Jack offered to wait until after work to train me."

Son of a bitch! "Tell him no."

"Uh. Now?" She blinks a couple of times.

"Yes. Now, Molly."

"I wasn't really going to let him train me," she says.

"Still. I want you to make your position clear."

She picks up her phone and texts. Then she shows me the screen. "Here."

–Me: Can't make it to the training session after all! Sorry!

"You're too nice," I mutter. But then, expecting her to flip the bird to her shitty boss is unrealistic. She's too sweet.

"Um, I'm planning to do mostly cardio, so..."

"You don't think you get enough cardio?" I place a hand at her waist and herd her toward her chair.

"Um..." She sits down. "I don't know...?"

I put a hand on each of the armrests and lean over. She looks up at me, her eyes growing wide. Does she have any idea how scrumptious she is? When she looks at me like that, I want to drag her into a dark corner and ravish her.

"I see. Well, that's entirely my fault," I say. "Let's go for twenty minutes of cardio at seventy percent max heart rate. We'll do it together."

Her gaze darts back and forth. "Here? There's no machine—"

"Oh, yes there is." I pull out my phone and set the timer for twenty-two minutes—I'm going to need two minutes to get us ready.

Then I drop to my knees and pull her forward until her butt's on the edge of the seat. I push her skirt up, then rip her thong.

She gasps.

"Don't worry. I'll buy you another." I shoulder between her legs, spreading her thighs.

"People could—"

I spread her flesh, then lick her.

Whatever protest welling in her throat dies. And I'm on her mercilessly. There's no teasing or taking time. If she wants her cardio, I'm more than happy to give it to her.

Her breathing quickens instantly. Soon her muscles tighten, then shake as an orgasm thrums through her body. She arches her back and digs her fingers into my hair, tugging as though to pull me away. But her pelvis is rocking against my mouth, and I let out a satisfied hum as I push her harder.

She twists, moaning and begging in a hoarse whisper. I hold her hips tightly while I position her legs over my shoulders to spread her wider, leave her more helpless and vulnerable. She's dripping, coating my lips and tongue with salty sweetness. I feel the racing pulsing in her pussy as I drive her even harder.

Her legs move restlessly. The need to debauch her in her office so everyone knows who she belongs to is pounding in my head, but I tamp down the desire. I don't want to scare her by revealing just how crazy I am for her.

"Oh my God, please," she sobs. "I want you inside me."

My dick grows impossibly hard. But I ignore her pleas and place my hand over her heart, which beats hard and fast against my palm. I plunge my tongue into her pussy, feel the tight trembling.

"I can't..." she whimpers, but she's rocking her slick flesh against my face, desperately seeking another high.

I suck on her clit, loving her wild response. Her whole body slowly grows taut, ready for another climax—

My phone alarm goes off, and I pull back from her.

"Wait, no," she says, reaching for me. Her face is flushed, and sweat mists her skin. A tremor runs through her. She was so, so close when my phone went off.

"Can you brace yourself?" I ask.

She shakes her head weakly. "But maybe I can if there's a reward." She gives me a playful grin.

"There'll be a reward." I tuck a wayward strand of hair behind her ear.

Knocks. She flinches, pulling away, while I glare at the door.

"Molly?" It's Jack. Her hand flies to her mouth, and she stares at the door, her eyes going round with shock. "I just saw your text and wanted to tell you my schedule's flexible, and I can show you anything you need."

I squint at the door, like I can see through the material. "She's busy!" I shoot back.

She bites back a laugh.

"What the hell? Who are you?" he shouts.

"Her man."

"What the fuck? You can't be there!" He adds more protests, but I'm not listening. I have something more important to do.

I push everything onto a corner of the desk and bend her over. Her chest is against the now-cleared surface. I push her skirt up to expose all of her gorgeous ass. I kiss it, then scrape the edge of my teeth along the curves while running a finger along her still-quivering folds. She tenses, then whimpers, squirming against my mouth. She's still on the edge, and the presence of Jack on the other side of the door isn't going to stop her from climaxing. "Please, Nicholas."

"Molly!" Jack shouts, like that's going to make her give a damn.

"Go away, Jack! I'm busy!" Molly says.

I press a quick kiss on the tip of her ear. "Good girl."

Ignoring Jack cursing from the other side of the door, I pull out my cock and quickly sheathe it with a condom. I drive into her, the motion raw and powerful. The old desk squeaks in protest. She presses a fist against her mouth to muffle a cry as she spams around me.

I can't get enough of her. I can't get enough of her losing herself in the pleasure I'm giving her.

I pound into her hard, savagely, over and over again so she comes apart in another climax. The desk screeches as it gets bumped across the cheap linoleum floor. Her pussy grips me greedily, and sweat beads along my spine and forehead. Heat pours through my veins. I drown in an orgasm as her vagina shudders around me.

To avoid crushing her, I brace my weight on my hands. I kiss the back of her neck. She reaches back and caresses my cheek.

"That was amazing," she murmurs after a moment, in the quiet afterglow.

"And great cardio. Accelerated heart rate. Prolonged period." I press another kiss on the delicate spot right below her ear. "You're already a great girlfriend, and I can't get enough of you. You have no idea how hard it is for me to resist the temptation to dissolve my company and spend my entire life eating your pussy and pounding into it."

A flush creeps up her neck.

I take the hand that's been caressing my cheek and kiss her empty ring finger. "I don't know what suddenly motivated you to work out. If you want to be healthier, I'm all for it. But just know that I've always wanted you the way you are." I kiss the finger again. One day, I'm going to put more than a kiss on it.

Molly shivers, then twists so she can look at me. "You knew the reason before I told you." She's quiet but also in awe, like she can't believe I was that keenly aware of her needs.

"Yes." I smile. "But if you're still determined to get in shape, we can do a harder session tonight when you get home."

34

NICHOLAS

I ROLL my shoulders after the rescheduled meeting the next day. The company's not as bad as I feared, but it's going to need some painful adjustments.

My phone buzzes. I look at it, wondering if it's Molly. But nope, it's Seb group-texting.

—Sebastian: Luce's new assistant went overboard with the tart order, so I sent some to your offices, enough to feed yourselves and your people.

I raise my eyebrows. The new assistant must've screwed up the order by a factor of about a hundred for Sebastian to want to send them our way.

—Noah: Are these tarts the naughty Ted Lasker kind, or are they actual food?

—Sebastian: Food, you idiot. Nicholas, I sent you some blueberry ones since they're your favorite.

—Me: Thanks, but I can't eat blueberries anymore.

—Grant: What? Since when?

—Me: Since Molly is allergic.

—Griffin: Eating a blueberry won't turn you into one.

–Me: I don't want anything that could make her uncomfortable near me. I don't know how severe her allergy is, and I'm not going to risk it.

–Noah: You're a better man than me. I'd miss them like crazy.

–Me: I do miss them, but Molly is more important.

–Huxley: And people say true love is dead.

–Me: It is dead to you since you only use it to sell things.

–Huxley: Not my fault people are so in love with love that they'll buy things they don't need with money they don't have!

–Noah: I'll take everyone's tarts. I'm not allergic to anything, and I don't have anyone to worry about.

I snort. Noah doesn't have an office to feed, but he can probably eat more than an office, especially if it's carbs.

–Noah: Also, you gotta do something about that girl, Nicholas.

–Me: What girl?

He attaches a screencap of Dana Mincer's Instagram account.

–Noah: The beer-swilling ass-thong chick!

–Noah: In case you didn't know, she tagged your girl in this video. I almost missed it, but you know me. I see everything.

–Emmett: The NSA should hire you.

–Noah: They can't afford me!

–Griffin: Even a donkey can set up a Google Alert.

Griffin's eye-roll comes through.

–Me: When do you have the time to photograph cheetahs and write your book?

–Noah: I multitask.

I open the link he sent. As I watch the video, I understand why Molly developed a sudden desire to exercise. And something else as well.

I've had enough of those two.

–Griffin: That's fucking nasty.

–Huxley: What a coward. If she has something to say, she should say it to Molly's face.

–Grant: You aren't going to let this go, are you?

–Me: No. I'll find some way to get them back, don't worry.

–Noah: Too late and no need! I already got the dirt on them.

–Me: What? When?

–Noah: Call me the Internet Ninja! Let me send you what I found.

You're welcome. You may kiss my beautifully formed ass when next you see me.

—Me: Show me what you dug up. We'll see about the ass kissing later.

—Noah: Oh, it's good. Something nasty enough to completely fuck him. He'll never be able to get a date after this. Or laid, unless he pays. Assuming hookers will want him.

I have no clue what Noah found, but if he's this confident, it's going to be good. Although Noah acts like he can't be bothered about most things, like most of us, he has a vindictive streak. If he decides he hates you, he'll devote himself to making your life hell.

—Me: What about Dana? What do you have on her?

I want her destroyed for what she's done to Molly. She's just as bad as Owen.

—Noah: Depending on what she does, I'm going to have something ready.

An email from Noah pops into my inbox. I click on it, then smile slowly.

This should set things in motion.

—Me: Thanks, Noah.

—Noah: My pleasure, bro. Nobody messes with the Lasker ladies and gets away with it.

—Me: Agreed.

And I'm going to make sure that Owen not only gets fired, but he never gets another writing gig again.

35

MOLLY

On Thursday, I leave Get Jacked at eleven and take an Uber to LocalGro's regional office, since my car refused to start this morning. I don't know what's wrong. Nicholas took a look, then instructed Cody to have it repaired.

"Take one of mine," he said, gesturing at rows of gleaming vehicles in his garage, including the brand-new truck he bought to help me move, but hasn't touched since.

"No, thank you." There was no way I'd take a car worth as much as a house. If anything happened to it, I didn't think selling my kidneys would be enough to compensate him.

So Nicolas drove me to the gym and said he'd come pick me up at five, even though I said not to bother. He seems to think that that's what boyfriends do. But I can't pull him out of his busy schedule just to ask him to take me to a job interview.

My phone pings again with another text from Owen. *What is* up *with him?* He's been calling and texting incessantly since yesterday. I block his number—no reason not to, and I don't want him bugging me while I'm at the interview.

The grocery chain's SoCal office is in a stout building with the first LocalGro to open in the state on the first floor. I sign in with security and head to the third floor. The HR person told me I'll be speaking with Sabrina Jefferson.

The interior is colorful, with lettuce-green carpeting and bright yellow and orange walls. Framed photos of fresh produce and fish dot the sunny corridor, and everyone seems to be busy.

Although Sabrina's the VP of accounting, her office isn't ostentatious. It has the same green carpet as everywhere else and sports a poster of the food pyramid on one wall. Her glass-top desk is functional, with a small metal cabinet. The printer on the stand next to her desk is a plain inkjet unit, nothing fancy.

Sabrina lifts her eyes from her laptop and stands. She's a statuesque woman with midnight skin and a welcoming smile, the kind that invites you to tell her all your secrets.

"Welcome to LocalGro! I'm so happy to finally meet you in person." Her voice is warm and resonant.

"And you as well. Thanks for inviting me." I smile.

We sit down and settle into the interview. "Mind if I ask why you're leaving Get Jacked Gym?" she asks. "I hear they pay very well."

The bluntness of the question throws me for a second, but I like it that she doesn't try to play games and gets to the point. If this is how she manages people, I'm going to love working for her. "They do, but I'm looking for different challenges and more responsibilities so I can grow in my career. I feel like LocalGro is the place for it. It's a bigger organization with more departments and a more complex financial structure."

She nods. "I see you've done your homework." She verifies some of the items on my résumé and asks the standard interview questions like "What are your biggest strengths and weaknesses?" and "What's the greatest challenge you've faced at Get Jacked and how did you resolve it?"

My biggest challenge is my boss's uncontrollable love for my breasts. But, of course, I can't say that, so I discuss some of the issues I've had with a couple of trainers wanting to be paid in advance.

"Finally, if you could be any animal in the world, what would you be and why?" Sabrina asks.

"A dolphin. They're intelligent, sociable and loyal. They never leave one of their pod members behind."

"That's a nice answer. Do you have any questions for me?"

"When will I hear from you about your decision?" *Please say, "You're hired!" right now!*

"In a week or two. There's one more candidate we're interviewing."

"Okay. Well, thanks again for seeing me." I stand, and we shake hands.

On my way back to the gym, my shoulders sag with disappointment that the company is interviewing other people for the position. But if I were them, I'd be doing the same thing. Hopefully, Sabrina picks me. If not... Well, I'll just keep on submitting résumés until I have a firm offer. *Gotta play the game to win the prize!*

One of our trainers, James, notices me walking back inside. "Did you Uber?" he asks, doing a slow air curl. Apparently it's something called "isotension," which Petra told me is a fancy word for flexing. He always flexes his arms when he speaks. It's like his vocal cords are attached to his humerus.

"Yeah. My car wouldn't start this morning."

"You should've asked me. I could've driven you."

"Oh, thanks. But I didn't want to bother anybody."

In addition to his incessant arm flexing, James loves to gossip about everything he hears to anybody who'll listen. I don't want him spreading the word that I'm looking for a new job.

"I don't mind," he says.

"Thanks." *But no.*

I'm just walking into my office when my phone pings. *Sabrina already?*

But it's Georgia.

–Georgia: OMG, Karma's a bitch! Did you see what happened?

–Me: No. What was it?

–Georgia: Owen's been canceled! He was fired yesterday. Or maybe the day before. Anyway, that isn't important. What's cool is that he's been—

She attaches a GIF of somebody dragging his finger across his neck.

I stare at her text for a long moment. Owen always said he was secure in his position because nobody else could do what he could. He also said he could bring in more clicks than any other food critic—which was apparently true. He has the biggest online following at the restaurant review site where he works.

—Me: What happened?

—Georgia: Somebody found some of his old Tweets and emails, disparaging big women for eating at restaurants when they "should be at home, dieting." Lemme send you the screencap.

The Tweet Georgia forwards me is much worse than she made it sound. Owen didn't just stop at telling big women to stay home and eat lettuce. He also attached a picture of an enormous pig covered with mud and captioned it, *What certain women look like when they're eating chocolate.*

Oh my God! How *awful.* What a jerk! It's so gross that I dated him! How did he really feel about me while we were together? Did he disparage me too? And why in the world did he say, "I love you," if he thinks this about women who aren't Dana-sized?

And Georgia said "Tweets." So there must be more. And emails too.

The Tweet Georgia sent is only four years old, so he can't blame youthful ignorance.

—Georgia: He issued a non-apology, which didn't work. Dana tried to defend him publicly, but made the post private when she got so many angry comments on it. Her entire Instagram account is private now.

—Me: OMG. That explains why she wasn't at the gym.

—Georgia: I doubt that beer brewery's going to keep her on. She literally blamed women for being humorless and taking themselves too seriously. And she also said the only people who'd be bothered by what Owen said are "fat people who have inferiority complexes." Apparently, "if you're proud and happy in the body you're in, you don't need anybody else's validation."

Wow. She really dug it deep. On the other hand, that type of attitude from her doesn't surprise me. I've never heard her say, "I'm sorry," to anybody. And it isn't because she's never done anything wrong.

Hmm. I wonder if Owen was contacting me to get me to defend him. He's delusional if he honestly believes I'll do anything of the sort.

—Georgia: Those two deserve each other. I'm so happy they're going to be miserable together.

I smile a little. I'm a bit surprised I'm not feeling anything strong for them one way or the other, unlike before, when I'd just been dumped. I'm not particularly thrilled about him losing his job or Dana going through whatever she's going through. But at the same time, I don't have much sympathy. They've been selfish and unkind. Not just with the social media posts, but with people in general.

But I'm not going to spend a lot of time on this. Owen and Dana are in my past. Nicholas is my present.

I wrap up the latest sales figures and projections and send them to Elaine to review. At five sharp I shut down my computer and head out so Nicholas won't have to wait.

The instant I step out of the air-conditioned gym's thumping music into the heat and street noises of Los Angeles, a rough hand grabs me and yanks me to the side. My heart starts racing. *Am I getting mugged?*

"What the *fuck*, Molly? I've been trying to reach you for over two days!"

"Owen? What are you doing here?"

My ex doesn't look so suave now. A baseball cap is low on his head, and dark Aviator glasses cover his eyes. Facial hair too long to be stubble and too short to be a beard covers his chin, and he smells faintly of vinegar.

There's a dark purplish and yellow stain on his blue T-shirt, which is a shock. The Owen I used to know would die rather than appear unkempt in public.

"I know you're upset about how we ended, but you didn't have to sic your boyfriend on me. Jesus, Molly! You had him buy the place where I work, dig up dirt about me and fire me? That's low. I never wished you ill."

Huh? "What are you talking about?"

"Drop the innocent act!" He points a finger at me. "We both know. Actually, Dana knows too. And digging up old Tweets? If you're that upset with me, fine, come yell at me all you like. But you don't get to destroy what I've built."

I yank my arm away from his grip. "I hate to shake you up, but I haven't really been thinking about you. You think I'd be obsessed enough with you to have Nicholas buy the place you write for and fire you? Or dig up your old Tweets? I don't care about you! I've *moved on*. I'm living my life. And it's a life that no longer includes you."

"Just change his mind."

Owen is only hearing what he wants to hear. And he's going to believe what he wants to believe.

"Owen, *listen*. I don't have that kind of influence over him."

"This is some kind of revenge for what I said, isn't it?" Owen slashes his arm up and down in frustration, like a guillotine. Maybe he's fantasizing about putting me and Nicholas on a chopping block.

"What in particular are you talking about?" He's said a lot of things in the past few weeks.

"About my personal brand! That's why you're destroying it! You're jealous because you don't have one of your own that's worth anything!"

"Oh, for— I don't care about your *brand*! I wasn't with you for a *brand*!"

"Of course you were! You must be a stupid bitch if you think I don't know."

"Molly, go to the car."

I squeeze my eyes shut. Nicholas didn't need to see this humiliating scene with my ex.

"Now, please." He pats my shoulder gently.

I start toward his Spectre. He doesn't follow, so I guess he wants to have a word with Owen.

Should I intervene? Stop things from escalating? Owen might provoke Nicholas. He's angry enough to do anything.

But if I butt in now, it might look like I don't trust Nicholas's judgment, which isn't true. He can handle himself. I have faith.

36

NICHOLAS

I CHECK to make sure Molly's in the car before I turn my focus on Owen. For a guy so concerned with "his personal brand," he looks like shit. And he smells like some kind of salad dressing.

"I'm going to sue your ass for wrongful termination!" he shouts, jabbing a finger repeatedly in my face. He's trying hard to look tough to compensate for his lack of height and muscle.

It doesn't work.

I step inside his personal space. "Feel free. Now, say what you just said earlier. To my face."

"Or, like...what?" he blusters, sticking his chest out. It isn't an impressive pose. "You think I can't tell you to your face I'm going to sue your ass?"

"You called my girlfriend a stupid bitch." My voice is terrible. "Say that to my face if you have the balls."

He licks his lips. Hesitation grips him for a fraction of a second, and he realizes he looks weak. "Bitch! She's a stupid bitch!" He hops a little and sticks his chest out further by arching his back. "So what?"

"Nobody disrespects my girl and gets away with it."

"Yeah? What you gonna do?"

He should just turn his cap backward and start waving his fists around. Except you can't project toughness when you're an overgrown man-child from suburbia who's worried about making the mortgage and car payments. Housing prices in Los Angeles are brutal, and Ferraris aren't cheap.

"You think you can kick my ass? Huh?" His shouting is as hollow and loud as an empty can.

"I know I can. And I would have if you'd touched her."

"You already fired me!"

"I can feed you your teeth, then make sure you never get a gig. Or get laid. Oh, and by the way, Molly is *great* in bed. It's just that your dick's so small she couldn't feel anything. Assuming you can get it up in the first place. And don't ejaculate too soon."

"I don't—"

"Might want to see a doctor about that. I hear these days they can cure almost anything. Even micro-penises."

Finally, it's too much for him. Owen takes a swing that looks like it's coming in slow motion. Obviously, he's never been in a fight.

I don't try to dodge it. He connects, hitting my jaw, then shakes his hand. He tries to grin triumphantly through the pain, but it looks more like a grimace. I suppress a sigh.

"Wow. That hurts," I say flatly. Then I smash his nose and mouth.

I don't do any special martial art like Griffin, but I can handle myself in a fight. It's the kind of thing you learn when you grow up with six brothers.

Blood spurts from Owen's nose, and he reels back. "Oh *fuck*! My teeth!"

"Told you I'd feed 'em to you," I say. "How do they taste?"

He's sobbing and yelling at the same time. I ignore him and go to my Spectre. Molly runs out of the car and rushes toward me.

"Oh my God. Are you okay?" She starts to touch my face, then drops her hand. She bites her lip. "It looks so bad."

Is she worried about that ridiculous tap to my jaw? I'm not even feeling it anymore.

She wrings her hands. "I'm so sorry I got you involved!"

I put an arm around her shoulders and escort her to the car, trying not to be irked that she tried to solve the Owen problem on her own.

That asshole wasn't going to quit until somebody bigger and stronger put him in his place.

"You got hurt because of me," she adds.

She worries about the most inconsequential things, but it's obvious she's never seen a real fight. I help her into the car, then get behind the wheel.

"Does it hurt when you try to talk?"

I start to tell her I'm not hurt, but the way she stares at me is so cute that I decide to tease her a little. "Mm-hmm. Throbs like hell." I purposely slur the words and faux-wince as I take the car on the road. "Ooh…"

"I knew it!" She stares at my cheek. "What if it bruises? Maybe I should get some eggs and roll them over the spot? I heard that helps."

"Got something that works better."

"What?" She looks at me earnestly.

"Sit on my face."

Three beats pass as her face slowly turns bright red. "*Nicholas!*"

"It cures every problem a man can have. Ask anyone." I try not to laugh, but my lips twitch.

"No, I'm not going to sit on your face! You'll suffocate and die."

"I'll die happy, you mean."

"You aren't taking this seriously—"

"I am. It's a time-honored remedy. The pussy poultice."

"Oh my God." She rolls her eyes, but there's a hint of amusement on her face. "I can't—"

"Cures everything."

"*Will* you shut up? Obviously, your jaw is fine."

"Just so you know, Owen's hurts more. And his bony fiancée sitting on his face won't fix it," I say with a superior smile.

"I am *sooo* proud of you," Molly says, batting her eyelashes. "But can we get serious? Is Owen going to try to sue? Make you look bad? I don't want anything to do with me to reflect badly on you and damage your reputation."

I stop the car for a red light. "Molly, listen. Nothing you do can make me look bad. Defending you against that asshole was my privilege, and you aren't going to take it away from me. I won't let you."

"But—"

I put a finger over her lips. She isn't going to give voice to the negative thoughts in her mind. That's giving them too much power. "I'm already angry with myself that I let you get hurt all those years. There's nothing I regret more than the unnecessary pain you've been carrying."

Her eyes glint with something that looks like unshed tears, and I kiss her.

"See? I'm not hurt. Not even a little."

"Okay," she says in a small voice. Her eyebrows pinch together, the tips low and her face scrunched.

I don't want to see her like this. I kiss her again. "You don't have to be so disappointed. Even if I'm not really hurt, you can still sit on my face tonight."

She bursts out laughing. The light changes, and I speed through the traffic.

We have a long night ahead.

37

MOLLY

WHEN WE ARRIVE HOME, Nicholas parks the car carelessly and hurries out to open the door for me. Stepping out of the Spectre, I regard him with amusement. "You're acting like somebody who forgot a cake in the oven," I tease, even though I know why. He's been hard since we left the gym.

"I have something better than cake in mind." He loops his arms around my waist and kisses me hard.

My response is immediate. I part my lips, letting him in. Our tongues tango. There's no coppery tang, and I'm relieved he really isn't injured.

Nicholas herds us inside in slow, wide circles, like we're dancing. Through the kiss and the pleasure stirring in my belly, I vaguely sense us moving past the foyer, and the living room...until we reach the staircase.

"Hold tight," he murmurs against my mouth.

I look up at him with trust and need, then wrap my arms around his strong neck. He puts his hands on my butt and pulls me closer. My thighs circle his pelvis.

He carries me up the stairs, his legs moving in a powerful rhythm, his mouth devouring mine. Lust starts to swell as anticipation builds.

My body has a visceral memory of the brutal intensity of pleasure he can give, and I crave it more than air.

He presses my back against the closed door to our bedroom, continuing to kiss me. I thread my fingers into his thick hair as my breath grows shorter and rougher and my heart races. I try to rock against him, but our position doesn't allow for much movement.

Frustration slices through the heated desire. I try again to ease the ache between my legs, and am thwarted again. Nicholas is lost in our kiss, even though I can feel how hard he is now, how feverish his skin feels against me. Maybe he wants me to make the move. He loves it when I demand—silently or loudly—what I want from him.

I yank my mouth from his. He makes a displeased noise.

"Into the bedroom," I say breathlessly, then lick my tingling lips. I swear I can taste him on my mouth.

His eyes flare. "Open the door," he orders, his voice low, then claims my mouth again.

I feel around behind me with my free hand until my fingers brush the cool knob, which I quickly turn.

The door opens silently, and we spill into the slightly darkened bedroom. I lower my legs, standing on my feet. He plunders my mouth like he owns it, and I do the same to him. It's liberating and sexy as hell to know this gorgeous man and the pleasure he can give belong to me.

Still kissing, we strip each other, our fingers hurried and clumsy. Garments fall from him, revealing more of the stunning, taut body. Lean, powerful muscles cover his tall and broad frame, exactly the kind of body that makes your knees weak with hunger.

I move toward the bed, then try to pull him on top of me as I fall back on the mattress. He puts a hand in the center of my back to stop me.

I look up at him in confusion.

"You're riding my face, remember?"

My cheeks heat with excitement, followed by trepidation. I meant what I said in the car. I don't think I'm the type of girl who can do that without hurting her partner. "I don't know... I've never..."

"That's precisely why you should."

The arousal from earlier cools a little as he sits against the headboard and brings me down, so I'm straddling him, with his cock between my thighs. It throbs against my slick core, and the proof that he wants me—and wants to do this for me—soothes my anxiety somewhat.

"Do you trust me to make it good for you?" he asks, placing a kiss on the corner of my mouth.

I'm still not one hundred percent sure about this, but if there's one thing I have, it's faith in him in bed. "Yes," I whisper.

"Good girl."

He kisses me again, his tongue stroking mine tenderly, like a reward. He strokes my back, his fingertips barely brushing my body. Delicious goosebumps break out everywhere he touches. I never realized my back could be so sensitive.

He drags his lips along my jaw, then drops kisses on my forehead, my eyes and cheeks. He wraps his hand around my long hair, tilting my chin so he can have better access to the fluttering pulse point on my vulnerable throat.

I whimper at the feel of his mouth on my neck. When he nips my skin with the edge of his teeth, just enough to send a little shock but not enough to hurt, the whimper turns into a moan. And I feel the flesh between my legs grow wetter and slicker. It's almost embarrassing how drenched I am. It's like somebody poured a large bottle of lube on my pussy.

I rock against his thick, hard length. I can feel the pulsing veins on his huge cock, each ridge providing a little wave of pleasure with each glide. His breathing is harsh now, but he still doesn't try to thrust into me. He just lets me use him to make myself feel good, then brings his mouth down until his breaths tickle my nipple.

I bite my lip, waiting for him to pull it into his mouth and suck. But he only uses his tongue, flicking it, teasing it, while his hands squeeze my ass and help me move against his cock better...

No. Not better. He's controlling how fast and hard I can rock against him. He's giving me just enough freedom to stay on the edge, an orgasm shimmering just out of reach, but not letting it shatter me.

My toes curl, and I twist, trying to push my breast into his mouth.

He switches to the other nipple—and sucks it, but the stimulation comes with slower gliding against his cock.

Oh my God. My head falls back as I struggle to breathe. He's going to kill me...

I tunnel my fingers into his hair. "Please," I beg.

He doesn't budge, but chuckles darkly.

He isn't going to let me climax until I agree to sit on his face. I'm still worried about being too heavy, but I can probably manage by holding on to the headboard and putting my weight on my knees.

"Show me what you want," he says, his eyes glittering with fire.

"On your back." I move to the side, so he can slide down until his head is on a pillow.

Excitement sparks in his eyes, but I can't decide if my own feeling is trepidation or eagerness. Maybe both as I place my knees on either side of his head and look down at him. Even though I'm on top, this position makes me feel inexplicably vulnerable.

I hesitate. He runs a warm hand along my thigh, the gesture soothing and intimate, and gazes at me with bright affection and admiration in his eyes.

"Come on, little goddess." His voice is soft with encouragement. His fingers stroke the sensitive skin on my inner thigh. "I can take it."

"Your body can, but your head isn't where your strongest muscles are." I try for a tart and snappy tone but just sound breathless instead.

I grip the headboard and slowly lower myself. Satisfaction flashes in his eyes before he runs his tongue over me. A breath rushes out of me, making me shudder. The muscles in my legs quiver as he licks me, just with the tip of his tongue, teasing me and keeping me squirming.

I make an impatient noise, but he doesn't give me more. I glance down, realize I'm a bit too far up and inch down a little. But the pressure still isn't enough.

He's not going to indulge me until I'm far down enough to suit him.

I'm closer to the edge than before, but I can't get there. I drop down more. His breaths fan my clit, and I whimper. He wraps his hands around my upper thighs and pulls me down, guiding me.

I'm so much lower than I ever thought I should be, and he licks me hard, running the flat of his tongue over my slickness. I grip the headboard with all my might, trying not to move too much. But when he's devouring me like he can't get enough, his lips and tongue drive me crazy. He groans like he's dying to get more of me. Sweat mists over my bare skin, and my back arches as I hit the peak I've never reached before, while my pelvis rocks against his face of its own volition.

I scream, shuddering, with Nicholas tonguing me slowly like a lazy, satisfied cat. I sit back on my heels, perching my butt on his thick chest. He grins, wiping the glistening layer with his fingers and licking them clean. "Told you nothing would break."

I laugh while struggling to draw in more air. "Did it cure your face injury?" I tease.

"Yup. One hundred percent."

"Mmm. But I think there's one more part of you that needs some TLC." I reach back and take his cock in my hand. It beats in my grip like a heart.

A raw hunger infuses the amusement on his face. I pump my hand a few times, hard enough to feel good.

He grows bigger and harder against my palm. I smile. "Let me make you feel good."

I start to slide down, but he puts a hand on my hip and stops me. "Uh-uh. Turn around."

My face heats with another wave of need at what he's about to do. "Sixty-nine?"

"Otherwise known as *soixante-neuf*."

"I've, um, never done that, either."

Raw possessiveness flares in his dark, gray eyes. "Good. We'll make your first time memorable."

I turn and position myself for him. The angle is different, but I'm eager to make him feel amazing. I hold him and run my tongue over the head like a lollipop, tasting salty male. He's incredibly large, and I can never get used to his size, how full he makes me feel. I pull him slowly into my mouth, relaxing my jaw. A low groan tears from him, then he places little kisses along my slit, kneading my ass.

Pleasure builds again, cresting higher. I suck him deeper into my mouth, using my tongue. His cock muffles my moan as he exerts more pressure against my clit.

A sharp sting on my ass almost makes me jump. The pain vanishes almost instantly, but I can tell he smacked me hard enough to redden my skin. The fact that he left his mark on my butt turns me on. It makes me feel naughty—*his naughty girl.*

I take him deeper into my mouth, then hollow my cheeks. As I move my head, he too is licking and sucking. Pleasure streaks through me, and as it builds, I bob with more frenzy and need, desperate to make him feel the same kind of delicious ecstasy building within me.

An orgasm swells faster, like I'm more pliant and ready after what I had earlier. Then, just as it's about to crest, he spanks me once again and my body seems to detonate with pleasure. I suck him in almost to the back of my throat. His entire being shakes as he fights the urge to thrust deeper, lest he hurt me, and he empties himself, filling my mouth with his hot fluid.

I swallow every drop, then hold him for a moment as he strokes my ass and the backs of my thighs tenderly. All the stress and tension from the day are gone, and my muscles feel like pliant clay.

Nicholas might be right about sitting on his face being a cure-all. Not only am I sexually satisfied, I feel emotionally happy and whole.

And I pray we can continue to enjoy what we have for as long as possible.

38

MOLLY

Nicholas makes a reservation at the Skyview—a brand-new steakhouse that opened on the top floor of the Aylster Hotel—for the dinner he won at the auction.

I go shopping with Georgia for a new dress. He hints that I could do the same thing I did to get ready for the auction, but I'm more comfortable with Georgia and a more normal pre-date prep.

"Holy shit," my bestie says when I tell her where Nicholas is taking me. "How did he manage to get a reservation? Dad was depressed that he couldn't get one for the opening weekend. He wanted to take Nikki."

"No idea. You'll have to ask Nicholas."

She looks over a few dresses on a rack, then shakes her head. We move on to the next set.

"He's really going all out with you," she says.

"Yeah..."

"Maybe it's true love." She grins.

"It's too early." It took Owen almost eight months to tell me he loved me, and not even three months after that before he decided he didn't. Thinking about my shitty ex when I'm considering my relationship with Nicholas is unfair, but life experience is life experience. It's one thing to believe in love—after all, romance is my favorite genre—but quite another to believe it will happen for *me*.

Right now, I prefer not to have any expectations. I don't want to be disappointed, especially when Nicholas has been so good to me. I want us to be able to break up amicably and remain friendly.

A nasty, burning sensation stirs in my chest... Probably just heartburn. I had Mexican for lunch, and the taco was too spicy.

She lowers her voice. "Tell me something, though. Is this a rebound for you?"

"What do you mean?"

"Do you like being with Nicholas because he gives you that nice feeling of *being in a relationship*?"

"That makes it sound like it didn't need to be him."

"Thank you. That's precisely my question." Georgia looks at me.

"I don't know if I would've moved in with another guy so easily. I knew him, you know? And I definitely wouldn't have agreed to a relationship so soon if it was somebody else." I'm generally cautious when it comes to dating. Until Owen, I'd never moved in with a boyfriend. I always tried to honor their boundaries and limits, doing my best to avoid pressuring anybody. I wanted to give them as much time as they needed to build up to wanting to be with me, even though I wanted to move to the next stage, closer to the lifelong commitment and love I longed to have.

"So it *is* Nicholas who's special," Georgia says.

"Yeah. You could say that." I've never been this excited shopping for a new dress to wear on a date.

And the anticipation only grows bigger as I do my hair and put on my makeup. Is it the going-out part that's exciting me? I stop in the middle of applying my lipstick and consider. No. It isn't just the fancy dinner out. I feel like this every time Nicholas and I are about to spend time together.

I wake up in the morning in his arms, and my heart tumbles and twists like a leaf in a gale. I could be curled up in any one of the cushy chairs with fresh coffee and a book, and every time I notice him, my insides flutter.

I know I'm falling for him, which is only natural. He's the kind of guy you can't help but love. I just want to be sure he feels the same way. It often seems like he does, but maybe it's just my being overwhelmed by the magnitude of his gestures. None of my exes could let me crash at their swanky mansion with full housekeeping, laundry and chef services. Much less just buy a truck over the phone to help me move. Or bid five million dollars for a dinner—or anything—with me. They couldn't offer to lend me a car that's worth half a million dollars because mine wasn't starting.

But all that could be nothing to Nicholas. He is extremely wealthy, after all, and he's probably used to spending whatever he wants on whatever his whims dictate.

Nicholas is waiting downstairs, giving me plenty of space and time to fuss over my appearance. He smiles when he sees me and produces a small bouquet of flowers from behind his back.

"Thank you." I flush. I don't think I'll ever get used to this kind of small, romantic gesture. Every time I get flowers from him, I'm reminded that he's thinking of me and that I matter to him.

The drive to the restaurant is lovely. A smooth jazz melody swirls like magic. I enjoy learning what he likes, and it's even more fun when I realize I like the same thing he does, like jazz.

"Thank you for the note, by the way," I say with a smile. "So it hasn't been a hundred days yet, has it?"

"Nope." He smiles, his eyes bright with mischief.

"You know it's driving me crazy, right?"

"I thought you were going to be patient."

"I know, but I am curious. Especially since they seem to be different languages each time."

"You'll find out what they say soon enough." He smiles. "But like I said, you can get somebody to read it for you, instead of waiting for me to tell you on the hundredth day. Whatever makes you happy." He isn't saying it to humor me. He means it.

"You're what makes me happy" is on the tip of my tongue, and I swallow the words. They seem...so vulnerable. Like saying them would strip me of every defense I have.

I don't want to leave myself that open. Nicholas would never hurt me on purpose, but I've always thought that about the men I've dated. And every time I let my guard down, they did end up hurting me. Even the most casual strike from Nicholas would hurt more than anybody else because he means more than anybody else.

The steakhouse is gorgeous—I can see why there's a huge waiting list to get in. The place doesn't have the stereotypical dark wood and brass feel. It's airy, with three floor-to-ceiling glass sides of the restaurant open to a stunning view of downtown Los Angeles. White and red dahlia blossoms are set in centerpieces on tables covered with thick white cloths that reach all the way to the floor. Next to them, small tea candles cast a soft glow. On a small stage is a live performance featuring a jazz singer in a glittering red dress.

The air is replete with the scent of sizzling meat and freshly baked bread. Wine flows freely. A crisply dressed maître d' checks our reservation, and we're shown to an intimate table by the window.

Nicholas and I walk to it together, our hands linked. I only let go when we're seated.

"This is gorgeous. Thank you." I smile.

"A gorgeous dinner for the most sought-after bachelorette."

I laugh. "Only because you were bidding so shamelessly. I still can't believe it." I remember what Dad texted, and my laughter dies.

"What?"

"Nothing, really. I think people noticed me a little too much when I got the crazy-high bid."

"They *should* notice the lady who was the biggest prize of the night —and who won her." His possessive tone says, *Mine*, which sends hot shivers through me.

Our waiter appears. Witty and energetic, he recommends all steaks equally, but suggests we also try their South African lobsters drizzled with herb and lemon butter. The sauteed mushrooms are "exceptional," the truffle mac and cheese "can't be beat" and their oysters on the half-shell are "extra fresh and succulent."

We order seafood bisque, a platter of oysters, steak, lobster, loaded baked potatoes and the truffle mac and cheese. Nicholas asks if I want champagne or red wine. I feel like a red, so he selects a bottle of Bordeaux. It's all smooth and easy, like we've been with each other forever and eaten out together millions of times.

While we wait for our food to arrive, I ask Nicholas exactly what he does, because it's not something I'm really familiar with.

"Initially, I invested my money in the market, and then with my brothers at GrantEm. They're really good at picking winners. And once I'd made more than I knew what to do with, I started to buy mid-sized companies that have growth potential but are somewhat mismanaged."

"Like...a corporate raider?"

He laughs. "No, not like that. I don't strip companies of their assets and sell them for a quick profit. The idea is to shake things up, improve the management and make the whole enterprise more profitable. Once that happens, I'll sell my stake. But then I got interested in private equity, so I started a PE fund on the side. I have a partner who helps with it, and I might get another manager, mainly to lighten my workload."

"I thought you liked working." Georgia told me Nicholas spends a ton of time in the office. Even blamed it for his short-lived relationships.

"It's fulfilling. But now I have something I like more." He gives me a gorgeous smile.

When he gazes into my eyes like this, I feel like we could be a forever kind of couple. The only question is...am I reading him correctly? I *sooo* wish I could see into his mind.

Our food starts to arrive. The bisque is exceptionally flavorful. The waiter wasn't kidding about the oysters, either. They're mildly salty, with a clean aftertaste and a hint of lemon.

As Nicholas and I have the last of the oysters, I wonder if he knows that they're considered an aphrodisiac. Not that he needs one. His problem—assuming it really can be considered a problem—is that he can't stop. He's absolutely relentless in bed. I actually looked around in the bathroom and cabinets to see if he's taking something special. But no. Just a bottle of plain multivitamins from Costco, and I'm sure his stamina in bed isn't coming from that. Otherwise, Costco would be making a fortune.

Am I going to have another hot, sleepless night?

Our waiter clears the table to bring out our steaks, lobsters and sides. Nicholas's mouth glistens in the candlelight. He licks his lips, then reaches for the wine. I take a quick sip of my red. The taste of dark berries, currants and smoky oak coats my tongue. It isn't overly dry, but not too sweet, either. He takes another slow swallow, and I can't tear my gaze from his mouth, the way a bit of wine lingers on his lips, making them look so wet.

It reminds me of how they looked after he went down on me. For some reason, he really enjoys the act, like he can't go a day without putting his face between my legs and devouring me until I'm a mess. My face heats for reasons that have nothing to do with the wine flowing warmly in my veins. I squirm.

"What?" he says.

"What what?"

"You're staring at me." His gaze drops to my mouth.

He knows. His playful smile eases something inside me. Suddenly, I feel like teasing. And being more honest than I might otherwise. "Your mouth makes me think of what you did to me last night."

"I did a lot of things to you last night."

"You know what I mean. I can't talk about it in public. I don't want to get arrested." As I speak, I pull my foot out of my stiletto and slide it under the table toward him...then along his calf.

His eyes change as he registers the touch. "Is that so?"

"Yes."

"If you get arrested, I'll bail you out."

I run my toes past his knee then slip them between his legs, along his inner thigh. "The police might not let me out on bail."

"Then I'll join you in your cell."

I grin, feeling breathless and naughty. I've never done this before. I move, a little bit bolder, inching closer. So much heat radiates from him—

"My God."

I flinch at my father's booming voice and immediately jerk my foot back and slip it into my shoe. Nicholas swivels his head, glaring at Dad.

In a nice suit, Dad looks lean and fit. He flicks his eyes at me, then at Nicholas, then at the food and wine on the table, then back at me. Judgment burns in their blue depths.

"Who are you?" Nicholas demands, bristling with annoyance.

"I'm Kevin Greene, Molly's dad."

The sharp edge in Nicholas's demeanor eases a little, even though the tight set of his mouth betrays some lingering irritation.

"And you are...Nicholas Lasker?" Dad adds, with anticipatory excitement at meeting somebody he deems *important*. He might think Nicholas can buy some expensive homes from him. Dad is all about making big sales and rubbing elbows with the right kind of people whose very presence makes him feel significant.

"Yes. Nice to meet you." Nicholas stands.

They shake hands amicably. Most wouldn't know Nicholas is displeased from the neutral mask on his face, but I note the slight tension in his brow, the set of his shoulders. Dad is playing it cool. Maybe too cool. If he were taller, he'd be doing his best to look down on Nicholas.

But then, he's tried that with all of my boyfriends. Apparently, the fact that they're dating his daughter means they're somehow beneath him. And they owe him a great deal of respect.

"So you're the guy who won my daughter in an auction." His tone is overly casual to hide the cautious skepticism—*I can't believe you bid so much for her. There has to be some nefarious reason.*

Nicholas's expression darkens as though he's caught the hint of Dad's unspoken disbelief.

"And this looks like a very nice and *massive* dinner." Dad shoots me a look. "You could feed a village."

I get the message loud and clear—*quit eating, Molly!* My mouth dries with humiliation, and I start to reach for my wine, my hand slightly shaky.

Dad clears his throat.

Since I don't feel like water, I just drop my hand and slide my gaze to the view of the city below.

"You can't afford your own entrées, is that it?" Nicholas says.

I jerk my chin up and stare at him.

Dad starts. "What?"

"It sounds like you want to take some of our food to your table for yourself and your dinner companion." Nicholas's tone is so charitable and conversational, it takes a second before the insult sinks in.

If Dad were a cat, all the hair on his back would be standing up. "How dare you talk to me like that?"

"I'm just wondering why you're here. You obviously aren't keen on merely saying hello, since you're lingering and eyeing our food." Nicholas picks up his fork and knife and cuts a small piece of the butter-laden lobster on his plate. He holds it across the table. "Here you go, Molly."

Dad glares at the lobster skewered at the end of Nicholas's fork, then at me. His blazing eyes challenge. *You wouldn't dare.*

Normally when he looks at me like that, I shrink a little inside, ashamed and sad that I'm a failure who can't measure up. But right now, rebellion churns in my heart. And I don't want to drink water instead of the delicious wine or worry about being a size zero and forgoing a wonderful dinner with Nicholas.

I lean forward and deliberately take the lobster into my mouth. My eyes on my father, I chew thoroughly and swallow, then take a generous sip of my wine.

A vein in Dad's forehead visibly pulses. He's probably imagining shoving his fingers down my throat and making me throw up what I just ate. Or he could be fantasizing about strangling me. I don't care at this point.

"Good girl." Nicholas smiles.

"It's delicious." I smile back at him. "Thank you."

Nicholas turns to my dad. "Was there anything else you wanted?"

Dad fists his hands. "No." Then he openly glares at me. "I can't believe you already forgot what I told you. Every time you try to reach for something you don't deserve, you're going to fall harder." *I'm so ashamed of you,* his expression screams.

He spins around and stalks off to a table where Renée is waiting. She looks at him curiously, but he shakes his head. I lift my wine glass in a silent greeting to her—she has no idea how my dad treats me—then turn to Nicholas. "Sorry about that." I force a smile as embarrassment and hurt burn my face. I don't want to ruin this time with Nicholas over what Dad did.

Nicholas reaches over and holds my hand, like nothing matters to him except being with me. "It's okay. Shall we continue with our dinner?"

"Yes." But no matter how hard I try, the light, teasing mood that my dad destroyed doesn't return.

39

NICHOLAS

I STAND IN THE KITCHEN, thinking. Molly's out shopping at a bookstore after our late brunch. I wanted to ask her to hang out with me, but she probably needs some retail therapy after that ridiculous incident with Kevin Greene last night.

What an asshole. My father is a dick, but he doesn't criticize us publicly like that. His problem is that he's too self-centered and oblivious to know he's being insulting and obnoxious. In his world, everything out of his mouth is golden and his every thought deserves to be immortalized.

But Molly's dad is an intentional asshole. He knows how his actions and words can damage her. And he enjoys hurting her for some reason.

She looked so pretty and playful as she teased me under the table. Her eyes darkened, and a flush cast a rosy glow to her beautiful face, as though stroking me was turning her on, too. I was this close to saying, "Screw dinner," and getting a suite at the hotel instead.

But after Kevin, that lightheartedness never came back. Sex that night was pleasurable, and I was extra attentive, but she didn't have her usual spark. Instead, she just clung to me like I was going to vanish.

Fucking asshole. I should've punched him. Couldn't, of course—he's Molly's dad. But I still want to throw him off a bridge.

That's the least he deserves.

I stare out the window, tapping a little ditty on the counter with my fingers, and then text Georgia.

—Me: What's the deal with Molly and her dad?

—Georgia: Why, what happened?

—Me: We ran into him last night.

—Georgia: Ugh. SUCH a dickhead. I feel bad about calling my best friend's dad a dickhead, but I can't think of anything kinder. Is Molly okay?

—Me: Hopefully. She's out buying books.

—Georgia: That should cheer her up. New books always make her happy.

—Me: Is he always so mean to her?

This sets off a stream of texts.

—Georgia: Yes. He belittles her in front of me, too.

—Georgia: So embarrassing for him, and makes me furious for Molly.

—Georgia: I can only imagine how he treats her when they're alone. And he's so controlling about her dating life!

—Georgia: He always talks crap about her boyfriends, but he also puts her down, like she doesn't deserve to be with them.

—Georgia: It's like, MAKE UP YOUR MIND, OLD MAN! Either they're unworthy of her or she doesn't deserve to be loved by them.

—Georgia: He constantly fat-shames her, too. I'm surprised she doesn't have an eating disorder.

Forget just punching him. I should've broken his jaw so he couldn't speak.

—Georgia: I honestly don't know how she puts up with it.

I do. It's easy for an outsider to say, "Cut your ties," or "Stand up for yourself," or "How can you let 'em talk to you like that?" But with parental figures, it's so much harder. Molly's mom died when she was just a child. Her dad is the only one left in her life.

But apparently he's abused his authority and her trust and love for him all these years. It explains so much about her feeling that she won't ever be loved. The way she cried, and spoke of her mom as a ghost who's ashamed of her.

I wish I could fix it for her. The fact that I can't makes my blood boil.

The door opens, and Molly walks in with a broad grin, carrying a tote bag full of books. It kills me to know that underneath her friendly, bright demeanor is a heart full of scars.

But I put on a smile to hide my inner turmoil. "Did you get everything you want?"

"Yup. And to make it even better, I spent Owen's money."

"*Owen's* money?"

"You know, the gift card he gave me on my birthday." She laughs, but the sound is a bit hollow. "I think I'm going to read for a bit."

"Okay. I'll be in the pool if you need me." I have to burn off this dangerous, churning energy. Otherwise I might just do or say something I shouldn't. I don't want her to think I pity her for what happened to her. She has too much pride to put up with that.

"Have fun." She goes upstairs, probably to make use of the library and its espresso machine.

I change into bathing trunks and do laps until my lungs burn. But my head is absolutely clear, and my heart is full of regret.

I shouldn't have thought she was too young for me and stayed away for so long. Then I would've been able to shield her from her abusive dad and all the shitty exes she's had. She wouldn't have to carry so much baggage from her past, and perhaps she'd see herself now the way I see her.

I swim for an hour, but it doesn't help much. Anger at myself, regret over what I didn't do and fury at her father still beat dangerously in my chest. I get out of the pool, stretch and grab a quick shower.

Even as I stand in my bathroom, freshly washed and in a clean T-shirt and shorts, I still feel like shit. And I need to see Molly. She clung to me last night like she was afraid of losing me, but I'm the one who's afraid of losing her. I do everything in my power to show her how wonderful and lovely she is. But if she has trouble believing it... Then it may all be in vain.

All my life, people have called me smart. Capable. Hardworking. I've always been able to do whatever I set my mind to. But I don't know how to heal her heart and repair the damage that's been done to her.

I walk to the library and stick my head around the doorframe. Molly is curled up in one of the armchairs under a throw blanket. Her flip-flops lie on the floor underneath the espresso machine stand. A book lies facedown on her stomach, her eyes are closed and she's breathing evenly.

Either the book's boring as hell or she's tired from last night. Probably the latter—we didn't sleep much.

I press a gentle kiss on her forehead. Then on her pretty cheeks.

She makes a soft noise in her throat. "Mmm." Her eyes still closed, she cups my cheek. Her small hand is warm and reassuring—*I'm here. I'm yours.*

I turn my face so I can kiss the center of the palm. A heartbreakingly beautiful smile slowly covers her face. I kiss her gently, just a brushing of lips. Then I lick her mouth.

She parts her lips and lets me in. I position myself between her thighs and deepen the kiss, tasting her. She's so warm and sweet, like heated honey. There's a languidness, too, like she wants to savor every second.

I oblige. Our tongues continue to tangle leisurely, like that's the only thing in the world that matters. She runs her hands along my shoulders, then drags them down until they're resting over my chest. She always positions her right palm so it's over my heart, which beats only for her.

She sighs softly, the same sound she lets out every time her need for me starts to fill her veins.

I push the blanket out of the way, then pull her shorts and underwear down. I dip my fingers between her legs and find her hot and slick. "What filthy things were you reading?" I whisper.

"I didn't even get to the good part," she answers in a low, dreamy tone. "It's your kiss that did it."

I run my finger over her clit, and she whimpers, then bites her lip.

"No lip biting," I say, then push the wet fingers into her mouth. She pulls them in and sucks them eagerly, like they're my cock. And I lower my face until I bury it between her soft, sweet thighs and lap her up.

She moans, long and low. The sound is muffled against my fingers, and I thrust them in and out of her mouth as I eat her out. She's so hot down there, so addictive. I can't get my fill.

The muscles in her legs quiver, then tighten. She arches her back as she comes against my mouth, sucking my fingers even harder in her climax, like she wants me to let go, too. I reach for the little cabinet behind her and pull out a condom. Ever since she moved in, I've stashed boxes of rubbers in every room in the house, just in case.

Once I'm covered, I pull her down from the armchair and onto a thick rug, then bury my face in the crook of her neck and glide into her searing depths. I whisper filthy words in French as I thrust into her.

She stills, then goes wild. I take her hips in my hands and angle her so she can get maximum pleasure out of each thrust.

"Oh my God!" she screams, but I continue to bang into her, showering her with more filthy phrases *en français*, just like that scene from *The Magic of You*, which she's read at least twice since she moved in.

When she sobs out again, I spurt into her, kissing her like the world is ending, and this is the only moment we're allowed.

She shudders for a long time. When her breathing finally settles, she threads gentle fingers through my hair. "What was that about?"

"Mmm?"

"All the French stuff."

"Just a fantasy I thought you might like. I saw you reading it a few times." I don't mention that I examined her notes and highlights. I don't want her to start hiding the books with her favorite sex scenes. "I wanted you to experience it."

She's quiet for a moment. "Well, thank you. But it's just a silly book." There's a tinge of resigned sadness in her voice that I hate.

"A book that says a woman deserves to be loved and worshiped the way she is." I kiss the spot on her chest, right where her heart beats. "Doesn't sound so silly to me."

"It isn't realistic."

I raise my head and look into her eyes. "If realistic is being treated like shit and feeling like you're going to die alone no matter what, Molly, *fuck reality*."

She gasps. I've never spoken to her like this before, but this is too important to sugarcoat. *She's* too important.

"Happily ever after, my Molly. We aren't settling for anything but happily ever after."

40

MOLLY

HAPPILY EVER AFTER.

Nicholas said we aren't settling for anything less, but I struggle to picture what that is. Maybe I'm weird, but I've never given really concrete thought to what the couples look like after I'm done with my books. I mean... The authors say they're going to be happy. They're probably going to get married and have babies and stuff.

Since I have a little downtime this morning, I send a quick text to Georgia.

—Me: Hey, what does HEA mean to you?

—Georgia: The couple gets together. Why?

—Me: That's it? The couple gets together, and...bam, HEA?

—Georgia: I mean, if you want to dig deeper, maybe all the bad guys go bald?

I snort. Owen and Dana going bald would be both comically and cosmetically just.

—Me: Never mind. Let me ask some other people, too.

I open my Instagram account and make a quick post about it, then tap my desk. I guess my personal happy ending would come with a new job. No callback from Sabrina yet, but I have two more interviews lined up. Thankfully, Jack's been busy with a new actress client who needs to get into shape for an action flick, and he's currently out of town for some fitness seminar in Vegas, so that gives me some time away from the boob talker. Hopefully he drunk-marries the love of his life there and never comes home. That'd be another form of happy ending —for me.

In reality, though, he's scheduled to be back this weekend. I wonder if I have enough vacation days to not come in for the next two weeks. I check my HR record, but nope. Just barely enough for four days off.

I could take them all off and go on a trip with Nicholas. Wouldn't that be nice?

I walk toward the breakroom. The free-weight area where Dana and her gang used to hang out is bereft of their pink presence. Dana quit coming to the gym since she made her account private. Her friends also started to skip their workout sessions. They're trying to distance themselves from Dana, lest they be found guilty by association.

Some friends.

It's sad and shocking how shallow some friendships can be. So many people are just worried about their "brand," like Owen. But then, a lot of people can't even work out without taking photos to show the world they're doing something good for themselves.

I step inside the breakroom and make coffee. I'm tired during the day—it's hard to sleep at night when Nicholas is an insatiable fiend and wants to play all sorts of sex scenes from my romance novels—but I can't complain too much. After all, he keeps me up in the most pleasurable ways. In addition, he doesn't try any scenarios from books that I don't feel comfortable with. Certain sex scenes are better left to fiction.

I add some sugar to my brew and turn around—and almost have a heart attack when I see Jack standing right behind me.

"Jesus, you scared me," I say, placing a hand over my chest.

He laughs. "Sorry, didn't mean to." He puts a hand on my shoulder... where it lingers.

I shrug a little bit, but he hangs on.

"I need to go back to my office. Excuse me."

"What's the matter? You can take a break," he says without letting go. "You did that before with your boyfriend."

I should've expected this. "Well, my boyfriend isn't here, is he?" I give him a pointed look that says, *You aren't my boyfriend.* "Can you please let go?"

"Why? I'm not hurting you, am I?" He rubs his hand against my shoulder.

"That isn't the point." I try to jerk away, but he merely tightens his hold. "I said let go, Jack."

"What's the matter? Why do you have to be so unfriendly?" he says to my breasts.

Ugh. "I said *no.*" I shove him.

He stumbles back—probably didn't expect me to push him away like that. His face turns red-purple, and thick veins stand up and pulse like worms around his forehead and temples. "Who the hell do you think you are?" he yells to my face for once. "You can't just smile and be friendly and nice?"

"I asked you to let go repeatedly. I don't owe you any 'friendliness' or my shoulder. And I certainly don't owe you a conversation with my breasts!"

"What's wrong with looking at them when they're hanging out?"

"*Hanging out?*" I look down at my shirt, which has a neckline higher than the Great Wall of China. I purposely wear tops that hide everything because of him! "Nothing's hanging out."

"Fine, *sticking* out! Same difference. And what's wrong with looking? You check me out, too."

"Oh my God, I so do *not* check you out! I look for you so I can *avoid* you."

Now tendons are standing out in his neck. "You're such a cold cunt! You think you're special because somebody paid five million for you? Have some respect for yourself, Molly! Only whores are proud of how much money they make for a date."

Rage swells. *Is this how he always saw me?* Something snaps in my chest. I pour my coffee into the sink. "You know what? I quit!"

"What? You can't quit! I'm not done talking to you!"

"Really? What are you going to do? Force me to talk to you? You can't pay me enough, you sexist, handsy, leering jerk!"

I try to storm out of the breakroom, but he catches my wrist.

"Ow, let me go!"

"I said I'm not done!"

There's a loud throat clearing from the doorway. Jack and I turn. Arturo rolls his weight on the balls of his feet, hands held loosely by his sides. Although Nicholas warned me about him, I'm relieved he's here.

He shoots Jack a steady look. "What's going on, bro?" And then to me, "Everything okay, Molly?"

Petra peeks out from behind Arturo's massive frame.

"It's none of your business," my former boss says, but his voice no longer has its earlier force. He's not an idiot. He doesn't want to act like a bully in front of witnesses.

I yank my arm away. Reddish marks cover my wrist. Crap. I hope they don't set into dark bruises. "Excuse me. I need to grab my things."

I walk past Jack stiffly. Arturo shifts out of the way, his eyes still on Jack, and Petra stares at me. I nod my thanks to both of them.

Trembling, I march to the office. I can't decide exactly what I'm feeling right now. Fury, yes, but also a bit of adrenaline and the shaky realization that I came pretty close to getting hurt. The wrist aches, and Jack is so much bigger and stronger than me. I was helpless in his grip, and he could have done whatever he wanted. I'm doing the right thing by quitting, even without another job lined up.

I grab my purse, tossing my phone into it. The laptop was issued by Get Jacked, so I leave that on my desk. It only has work stuff anyway. My résumé is backed up on my phone. I snatch the flowers Nicholas sent this morning. My wrist throbs, but I keep my chin up.

I stride past the door that separates the workout area from the back office. I want to raise my aching wrist and say something disparaging about Jack, to show these people what a terrible human being they're giving their money to. But if I do that, I'm not just hurting Jack. The other trainers, who really haven't done anything, might lose their jobs. Elaine, fine—she covers for Jack. But I don't want collateral damage.

My car's still getting repaired, and Nicholas won't be coming by for another three hours. I start to text him to see if he can pick me up early, but stop. He's working, and I don't want to disrupt his day.

Huffing, I stand on the sidewalk in front of the gym and tap on Uber. Petra comes out.

"Hey. Need a ride?"

I turn to face her. "Don't you have your shift?"

"No clients for the next two hours. So no prob."

"Yeah, but you'll lose out on your hourly pay," I say. Trainers are paid by the hour and get a cut of the fees their clients pay for their sessions.

She shrugs. "I'm better than Uber."

"I can't possibly impose. My friend's going to pick me up," I say, then text Georgia before Petra gets too insistent.

–Me: Can you pick me up from the gym right now?

–Georgia: Yeah. Are you okay?

–Me: Long story. I'll tell you when you get here.

I lower my phone, then look behind Petra at the gym. Jack's talking on the phone, his face scrunched in distaste and anger. He glances up and shoots me a dirty look, but he doesn't approach, since I'm not alone.

"You might want to put something on that." Petra gestures at my wrist.

"I will, thanks. Mind if I ask you to wait with me for my friend?"

"Yeah, that's fine." She shrugs. "So. You, uh, gonna sue or something?"

"Why? Did Jack ask you to find out?" Petra has always been nice to me, but that doesn't necessarily mean she'll side with me.

She snorts. "No. He's a dick. Do you know how many times he's tried to put his hands on me? It's just he can't really get a good chance because I'm always out on the floor with clients and the other trainers. But he's constantly looking for an angle, trying to 'innocently' brush against my butt."

My initial suspicion fades, replaced by shock and sympathy. "I had no idea. I thought it was just me. Elaine made it sound like I was being too sensitive."

Petra laughs humorlessly. "That basic bitch? Jack's banging her on the side, that's why."

"What? I thought she was married."

"You don't have to be single to screw a guy. And Elaine loves getting nailed by Jack. She thinks she's so discreet, but we all know."

Except me. "So if he has Elaine, why did he do that to me?"

"'Cause you got a vagina, honey. He can't help himself. And you aren't the first employee to quit over his behavior. Actually, you lasted longer than the others. The accounting girl before you quit within three, maybe four months, max. He tried so hard to *personally* train her, so he could touch her without getting sued. 'Oh, I was just correcting her form so she doesn't injure herself.'" Petra rolls her eyes.

"So why do you still work here?"

"Same reason anybody puts up with a shitty job—the money. He pays better than anybody else, and I need to cover my rent and eat. And I also have student loans. Now that I think about it, he probably has to pay that well to keep his employees, because who's going to stay without the extra?" She tosses her ponytail over her shoulder. "But you got yourself a rich boyfriend. I saw his car. A Spectre. It's supposed to be, like, $400k. And that isn't the only one—I saw him come pick you up in a friggin' Bentley a couple of days ago. Hell, I'm surprised you didn't quit sooner. I would if I had somebody who took care of me and paid all my bills."

"I don't want to use him like that."

"Oh, honey, it isn't a big deal if a man's loaded. Definitely let him buy you things and pamper you."

"But it sounds so one-sided. I don't have anything to give him in return."

"What are you talking about?" She laughs. "You have your body."

"How transactionally romantic."

"Fine. I'll put it another way. You have *yourself*. One of a kind, and irreplaceable." She gives me a wry smile. "Trust me, it's working fine for him."

Easy for her to say. She has the body of a goddess. The type that every woman at the gym dreams of.

Whereas I'm just...me. Molly Greene. Basic. No frills. Ordinary.

Suddenly, she pauses. "Hey, is Mr. Spectre the guy who bid that crazy money on you at the auction?"

I nod.

"*That* explains why Jack was bitching everywhere. He couldn't beat him on anything."

"What do you mean?"

"Jack has this crazy, like, rivalry against all men. No matter how wonderful and successful somebody is, he always finds some area where he can beat them. Like... He has better abs. Or he has more money. Or he has more employees. Or he's banged more chicks. Like that."

"Okay."

"But your man has everything. He's young, handsome and rich. Three things Jack can't beat him on. And based on the way his suit fits him, I bet his body's phenomenal, too."

"Well, yeah. It is."

"There you go." Petra smirks.

Georgia's white Miata pulls into the lot. "That's my ride."

"You let me know if you need anything. Like if you forgot something at the gym and don't feel comfortable coming to get it. Or if you ever want to sculpt your body and want a personal trainer, text me. I'll make a special trip for you. Away from Jack." She winks.

I laugh. "I'll let you know. Thanks, Petra." After waving at her, I climb into Georgia's car.

My best friend looks like she's about to keel over from curiosity. "What is going on, girl?"

"I quit my job."

"*What?* Since when?" she says as she pulls the car into the thick L.A. traffic. "Did you get an offer? We need to celebrate properly!"

"No." I tell her everything that happened since I nearly ran smack into Jack in the breakroom.

"Ugh, that's disgusting!" Georgia says. "What a creep! You should've kicked his ass! At least broken his hand! And fingers!"

"I wish, but I was intent on getting away first."

She stops at a light and looks at my wrist, which has red marks on it. "Holy shit, is that what he did to you?"

"Yeah."

She grabs her phone and snaps a few photos. "In case you want to call the police. I think at the very least you should sue."

"Yeah... Well, I'll think about it." I don't know what it takes to sue, or if I really even want to. There's the cost, time and public attention that are sure to follow. If it's going to be end in a slap on the wrist for Jack or some monetary settlement with the demand that I never talk about the incident again, it wouldn't be worth it. He can't use the "I only touched her to correct her form" defense with me, but he might have some other excuse ready. Why else would he corner me in the breakroom like that? My boobs aren't *that* nice. Besides, can I even afford the kind of lawyer who can beat him at his game? It just feels so daunting.

The light changes, and Georgia resumes driving. "Did you tell Nicholas?" she asks.

"I don't want to bother him when he's at work. I'll text him later so he doesn't go try to pick me up, and tell him what happened when he comes home."

She shoots me a look like I'm out of my mind. "Don't wait. Tell him now."

"Why? What would that accomplish?"

"He's your boyfriend."

"I know. I'm not going to hide it. I just don't want to interrupt his day with something like this." The incident with Jack wasn't life or death. I'm not even bleeding. And it isn't like Nicholas is a police officer who can go over and arrest Jack.

"Oh my God, you're in a relationship with him, Molly. If some guy grabbed me the way Jack did you, my boyfriend would be the first person I'd call."

"But..." I shrug to hide my discomfiture. A tiny part of me says maybe I should listen to Georgia, but another part—one that's terrified of being unlovable and bothersome—stops me.

You need to be less selfish. Consider that others have priorities that might be more important than you. What happened to my mother when I asked her to drop everything and buy me blueberries fleets through my mind. I don't think telling Nicholas now would end up in something that tragic, but...

"Has Nicholas ever made you feel like you aren't important to him?" Georgia asks.

"No, of course not. I just don't want to be, you know, burdensome. He's already done so much."

My best friend sighs. "This is going to hurt him."

I shake my head. "It's only a few hours. It isn't as dire as you think."

41

NICHOLAS

I WRAP up the final meeting of the day. Cody types furiously on his laptop to finish the minutes.

"I'll have your agenda organized and emailed to you by five."

"Thanks."

I start to gather my things and check my watch. Four thirty. I'll need to leave earlier than usual if I want to pick Molly up on time.

The mechanic texted and said he left the car in the garage. The parts finally came in, so he was able to complete the repairs. Although Molly said she'd handle the bill, I already paid it. I don't see why she should have to when I have more than enough money.

I'm just about to head out when my phone pings.

–Molly: You don't have to pick me up. I'm already home.

–Me: Really? What happened?

–Molly: I left early. I quit today.

Why did she quit all of a sudden? And why didn't she call me sooner? How did she get home? An Uber?

Annoyance starts to bubble up as I get into my car. I tell myself there has to be a good reason she didn't call earlier to go get her, but I can't think of one. *Does she not see me as somebody she can call when something happens?*

I make my way slowly through the congested traffic, and the annoyance begins to change into anger. And underneath is maybe a tinge of grim sadness and anxiety.

Just what does it take to be the person she can depend on? My brothers all say I'm like a tree—solid, reliable and unshakable. But what's the point of having those qualities if Molly doesn't see them? She said I was like my mom. Does she think I'm going to abandon her in her time of need because I have some more pressing whim to attend to?

Frustration and resentment twine around me until my lungs burn. I picture shoving them all into a box in my head, trapping them so they don't spill out and affect my mood or my interaction with Molly. She deserves a chance to speak without me making assumptions and getting upset.

She's thumbing through her phone in an armchair in the living room. She jumps out of the seat when I walk in.

"Hey," I say, not giving her my usual greeting of "How was your day?" It's obvious her day didn't go as planned.

"How was your day?" she asks, like today is like any other day.

"The same as usual. Lots of meetings." Dismissing her question and demanding she tell me everything that happened at work right now isn't going to help. I reach for her, then stop short when I see red marks all over her forearm. Four long, thick lines wrap around her, and I narrow my eyes. Are those *fingers*? Did someone dare lay their hands on her?

Murderous fury erupts. Blood roars in my head. My whole body shakes with the need to clench my hands around the neck of whoever bruised Molly. It's all I can do to rein myself back so I don't scare her. "What happened?" My voice rises despite my best intentions.

"Oh, it's nothing. Well, not *nothing*, but..."

My vision grows red. The blood in my veins run hot, cold, then searing. "*Who did this to you?*"

She shoots me a wary look. Like I'm the feral one for reacting like this, when she's been abused by some asshole! "Can we sit down?"

If that'll make you answer me faster. I park my ass on the sofa. "Give me the name."

"Don't do anything rash."

"The *name*, Molly."

She sighs. "It was Jack."

"Your boss?"

She nods. "Former boss."

"What did he do?" I need to know all the facts so I can decide how much pain to deliver.

"Just the usual jerk-off behavior. Staring and touching if he can. I've been avoiding him as much as possible—"

Something clicks in my head. "Is that why you keep your office door locked? To keep that piece of shit away from you?"

"Yes, but—"

"Why didn't you say something?" *Why didn't you let me help you?*

"I was trying to find a new job before I quit," she says defensively.

My frustration reaches a fever pitch. And the grim sadness I felt earlier slides deeper into my gut. "That doesn't answer my question."

"I don't know what purpose it would've served to tell you beforehand."

The knife's lodged so far down, I'm not sure if I can pull it out. "Did he grab you when you told him you got a new job?"

"No. He grabbed me, so I quit."

"And you came home."

"A coworker offered to give me a ride—"

"Arturo?" The idea of that derelict being there for Molly when I wasn't makes my belly burn.

"No," she says. "Arturo actually helped. It was Petra."

"Okay. So Petra gave you a ride home." I guess that makes a certain amount of sense, given that she was right there at the—

"Actually, I called Georgia. She came to get me."

My vision seems to go black for a moment. It's all I can do to get a sentence out. "You didn't think to call me?"

"I didn't want to bother you when you were busy at work. Georgia freelances, so she could take a little break to pick me up."

I jump to my feet, unable to sit like a housebroken dog. Bitter wrath surges, sloshing through me like a wave of acid. "You're *supposed* to bother me! *I* should've been the first person you thought to call!"

"But Nicholas, I *was* thinking of you. I just—"

"You thought I'd put my work before you."

"That isn't what I thought!"

"Isn't it?" I put my hands on my hips. Something unfamiliar and acrid pools in the back of my throat. It's the taste of *defeat*. I clench my teeth. I don't want to give up, but I don't know how to break down the wall she's erected. Bridge the distance she keeps placing between us.

I focus on breathing for a moment. I can't give in to my temper and shout at her. This is too important.

Finally, when I can control myself, I gentle my tone. "Molly. What am I to you?"

She looks at me like I just asked her to solve a multivariable equation using Roman numerals. Time stretches.

It shouldn't be this difficult. She just doesn't want to accept the most obvious—and correct—answer.

I take a step back. She doesn't take a step forward.

Of course she isn't going to stop me from leaving—nor is she going to follow me to close the gap between us. I should've realized that whatever I thought we had was all in my head.

"I see. Well, let me know when you decide." I steeple my fingers, trying to think clearly. "Cody will take care of everything, including the legal matter. And you can stay here as long as you need, since you don't have anywhere else to go."

I force myself to turn from her and walk out before I throw away my pride and beg her to take me.

If I go that far, I don't think I'll ever to able to forgive myself—or her for forcing me into a corner I never wanted to be in.

42

NICHOLAS

I DRIVE AIMLESSLY. My head is jumbled, and I can't organize my thoughts. Actually, forget thoughts. I don't even know what I'm feeling. I've never been this hollow. It's like somebody has reached inside my body—my soul—and ripped out everything that made me *me*.

Finally, I decide I need someplace to stay. It's just... I call Sebastian. "Hey, can I crash at your Residence? The Aylster, not your home." I don't want to deal with my brothers' concern, not right now.

"Yeah, sure. I'll let the concierge know. But what's going on? What happened to your house?"

"Can't stay there." Seeing Molly hurts too much.

"Need a general contractor? I know a couple of good ones."

I let out a hollow laugh. "I don't think he can fix what's broken. Thanks for the offer, though."

I hang up before he can probe, and head to the Aylster. The concierge greets me with an access card in the lobby. They know us well, and who's allowed to use the Residence.

"If there's anything we can do to make your stay more enjoyable, just let us know," the woman says with a hospitable smile as she hands me the card.

I nod and take the private elevator to the Residence unit. Despite its name, it's a sterile hotel with nothing but furniture, basic bedding, towels and silence. I realize I didn't bring anything with me.

I should probably ask the concierge to get me some clothes—something fresh for tomorrow. But I can't bring myself to bother. I throw myself on the couch and place an arm over my eyes.

I should also check the email Cody sent, but I have no motivation. I don't want dinner, either. Drinking is an option, but that would involve getting up. Too much effort.

Where did I go wrong with Molly? Did I push too hard, or somehow behave in ways that undermined her faith in me? Did I ever appear to be unreliable? Did I not present myself as a dependable man?

I never make promises I can't keep. So many of my previous dates and girlfriends said in so many words that they counted on me. But the only woman I want to count on me refuses. My brothers call me solid, but any given woman might have a different perspective. I should think about what that difference is, but I'm too tired and my head hurts and my heart is raw.

I LIE on the couch for a while, and then suddenly the door opens. I scowl. *I didn't order room service.* Wait a minute... If I had, they would've knocked.

I lower my arm and lift my head, then drop it back at the sight of my brothers pouring into the room.

"What are you doing here?" I say to the ceiling.

"How could we not come over?" Sebastian says.

"Especially when you aren't answering our texts or calls." Grant grabs a dining chair, spins it around and straddles it.

"Didn't hear it ring," I mutter.

"Everything okay with you?" Emmett says.

"Yeah, what happened?" Griffin says.

"Could be Molly," Huxley says.

Noah gives him a skeptical look. "I can't imagine Nicholas doing anything that would upset her."

My brothers take seats and look at me. They clearly aren't going anywhere until I talk—undoubtedly to help me come up with a solution.

Don't they know that some problems simply can't be solved?

They need to go home. Return to their wives. I don't need the women yelling at me for keeping their husbands away. Actually, they're too nice to yell. But whatever. I don't need their pity.

Fine. I sit up and tell my brothers what happened.

"Wow," Noah says slowly.

"It's like..." I sigh heavily. "She didn't even understand why I needed her to call me. Why I wanted to be the first person she thought of."

"Damn." Sebastian breathes out. "Yeah. I would've been pissed if Luce said she'd rather wait than to call me, especially after something like that." He would've been furious at missing a chance to break Jack's face, too. I don't think Lucie's brother's face healed right after the beating from Sebastian.

"Exactly." Griffin scowls, probably unable to imagine Sierra not calling him if she had a traumatic experience. "Doesn't she know you'd want to be there for her? You'd want to be there to keep her safe and beat the shit out of the other guy."

"So what is this? A breakup?" Emmett asks.

Grant goes into the liquor cabinet and pulls out a bottle of whiskey. Noah and Huxley grab glasses.

"I don't know. I want her more than anything, but I can't pretend I'm fine when she doesn't trust me to be there for her. I can't even make sense of why she's with me when she won't depend on me—not even a little. I don't know what more I have to do to prove how much I love her."

"Did you tell her?" Huxley asks, as Grant offers me a glass he just poured. "Sit her down, look her in the eye and say, 'Molly, you're the only one for me. I love you.'"

"Tell her you'd give up both your kidneys for her. Women love that sort of stuff," Noah says.

My brothers roll their eyes. I would too if I didn't feel like shit.

"Yeah, how's that working for you and Bobbi?" Griffin says.

"Unfortunately, Bobbi doesn't want my kidneys," Noah says.

"Doesn't seem to want any of your other body parts, either."

Sebastian takes a swallow of his liquor. "Especially the ones around the pelvic region."

"Yeah, yeah, yeah. Don't worry. I have a new plan."

I knock the whiskey back. The fire burning down my throat and in my gut doesn't do anything to soothe the ragged pain. I wish I had Noah's boundlessly optimistic enthusiasm, but I'm too drained to muster much. "I couldn't tell her. Every time I do something nice for her, she's happy. But then she gets this look like she doesn't think it can last. Or that it isn't really real. I don't think I could deal with it if she looked at me like that after I told her I loved her."

Grant nurses his drink. "Maybe she needs some distance to process her feelings."

"And let some asshole snatch her away?" When she and Owen broke up, I wasted no time swooping in because I was tired of giving her "space" and "time"—only to have some other guy ask her out. I thought I had a solid plan to show her how we could be together. I don't want to regress in our relationship, so we're back to what we were before, sending gift cards on birthdays and saying polite hellos when we run into each other. Nor can I bring myself to beg her to come back. It isn't a matter of pride. I can't tolerate the idea of her being with me out of obligation or pity. That would eventually make me loathe myself and resent her, too.

"Nah. She won't let that happen." Grant ponders, swirling the amber liquid in his glass. "I'm sure you've treated her like a princess—and I don't mean just giving her stuff. I know how you are, Nicholas. You probably did things to make her feel special, and whether she told you overtly or not, she loved it. Right?"

I grunt morosely, since what I did wasn't enough.

"I don't know what her issues are, but she might need some time to sort things out and admit to herself how much you mean to her," Grant says.

"Giving her some space is good advice. Let her experience what life is like without you in it anymore. I learned very fast I'd rather jump off a bridge when Luce and I went through that rough patch." Sebastian shudders, then takes a large swallow of his drink.

"But you need to stay strong. Stay the course. She has to come to the conclusion she wants you, too. Otherwise, she'll end up feeling trapped," Griffin says.

I stare at my grumpy brother. When did he become the love expert?

"What?" he says. "I'm not stupid. No woman wants to feel manipulated or cornered. Besides, it isn't like you can serenade her to convince her. Your singing voice is terrible."

"I'm not that bad," I mutter, although...compared to Griffin, I sound like a tone-deaf frog. For some reason, God gave him the voice of an angel, probably to make up for the fact that he also received the disposition of a honey badger with an achy tooth.

I reach for the bottle of whiskey, but Huxley pours me another glass and keeps the bottle to himself. Bastard.

"Thanks for coming over, but I need you to go home now. Say hello to your wives and babies."

"Looks like you need a few other things, too," Noah says, glancing around. "Like a fresh change of clothes. You bring anything?"

"No, but I'll ask Cody," I say. "He'll have to cancel my meetings tomorrow anyway."

"I'll stop by your place," Noah says. "You just take care of the other stuff."

"Call if you need us. Twenty-four seven," Sebastian says.

I give my brothers a halfhearted grin. "I'm fine."

Nobody believes the lie. Not even me.

43

MOLLY

I STARE at the floor numbly, feeling like I've just come through a tornado and am sitting in the wreckage of my home.

Why was Nicholas so upset? I wanted to make things okay for him—erase the pain in his eyes like he's always done for me, but I didn't know how. I can't even figure out what I did wrong.

He was obviously angry that I didn't call, but... Why was that such a problem? I was being considerate. I didn't want to bother him when he had other things to do. It isn't like I was planning to hide what happened at the gym with Jack.

Where did Nicholas go, anyway? He didn't ask me to move out. On the contrary, he told me to stay here, so maybe that means he's coming back...?

I pick up my phone and start to text him. *Hey, I know you're upset, and I'm really sorry. Can we talk about this? I want to understand how I can make you feel better.*

I stare at what I've typed up. If he wanted me to console him, he would've stayed. Also... He might become more agitated if he realizes that I have no clue why he's unhappy.

An engine roars outside before cutting off. I jump to my feet. *Nicholas?*

My heart races as relief rushes through me. He probably feels better after a drive and a little time away. We can have a calm discussion and work things out. I'll start by apologizing, since I want him to know I never meant to make him feel bad, and—

The door opens, and a stranger walks in. I yelp, clutching my phone as a weapon against the intruder. Am I getting mugged inside Nicholas's home? Why didn't the household security go off?

"No need to look at me like I'm a serial killer," the man says. "I'm Noah. Nicholas's brother. I'm here to pick up some stuff for him."

"Oh, thank God." Now that he mentions it, there is a distinct family resemblance.

"Nicholas wanted Cody to handle it, but I figured I would so I could see you for myself." His cool eyes rake over me. He couldn't be more impersonal or assessing. It's disquieting after the warmth I experienced with Nicholas's sister-in-law. Noah's gaze brushes over the wrist Jack grabbed, and his eyebrows pinch in disapproval. Why does it feel like he's upset with me, rather than Jack?

Anxiety winds tightly around my chest. What did Nicholas say to him?

"You don't look like a typical man-eater," he says finally.

His judgmental tone cuts, but also stirs my anger. Who does he think he is to talk to me like this? Does he assume I'm with Nicholas to take advantage of him? I open my mouth to give him a piece of my mind—

"I thought you might be, for hurting my kindest and most dependable brother."

Hearing him speak of Nicholas in pain snuffs out my anger. Concern and guilt tug at me. Noah must've seen Nicholas after he walked out. I never wanted to make Nicholas suffer. "Is he okay?"

"Why do you care?" He doesn't bother to look at me as he answers. He starts to climb the stairs.

I follow him. "Is he staying with you?"

"No."

"Do you know where he's staying?"

"Yes."

"Can you tell me where? Or give me more than a one-word response?"

"No."

What a jerk. I take a deep breath. Yelling at him in frustration isn't going to get me any answers.

We reach the master bedroom. Noah obviously knows the layout of the mansion.

"Is he okay?" I try again, hoping he'll at least give me a yes-or-no answer like he did earlier.

His eyes slide in my direction, sharp as razor blades. "Again, why do you care?"

"I just want to know if he's *okay*! I'm *worried* about him. I feel awful about the way he left."

Noah steps into the bedroom, then to the walk-in closet. If he has anything to say about my stuff hanging in there, he keeps it to himself as he pulls out a carry-on suitcase and lays it on a luggage rack. "Do you pity him?"

I recoil. "*No.*"

"You sure?"

"Of course I'm sure! I don't pity him. How could I?" Nicholas is too brilliant and wonderful. He's like the shining sun, and nobody pities the sun.

"Interesting response coming from a woman who thinks she's too good for him." He tosses a few suits and shirts into the suitcase.

"*What?* I never said that."

"Maybe not. But your behavior shows it."

"You don't know anything about me and Nicholas."

"Don't I?" He finally turns and faces me. "He won't even eat his favorite blueberry tarts because of your allergy."

I blink with surprise. "I didn't know..."

"Or maybe you didn't care to know. I've never seen Nicholas this upset. Not even his mother forgetting to attend his graduation, or the birthday party he planned for her, bothered him like this. You act like you can't trouble yourself to treat him with the same kind of care he gives to you. To you, he's an afterthought."

Every statement hits like a sledgehammer, filling me with shock and dismay. I never meant any of that, much less make Nicholas think I had no feelings for him. "Look, is this about what happened this afternoon? I was trying to be thoughtful and considerate of his priorities and schedule."

His eyebrows jump a couple of inches. "He wants to be the first person you reach out to, no matter what. *That's* his priority. You didn't put him first."

"I *did*." Why is he being obtuse? Is it because he's decided he doesn't like me?

"If he was hurt and called Stella to sit with him and look after him, would you be okay?"

Jealousy and a sense of inadequacy rake hot claws over my belly. "Who's Stella?"

"Nobody you know." The corners of his mouth turn downward theatrically. "You seem upset. But why? He's being so thoughtful and considerate. After all, you have your priorities."

He turns and opens a few drawers to find underwear and socks, dumps a fistful into the suitcase and zips it up.

"If you don't reciprocate his feelings, just stay away. Nicholas is a great guy. He deserves better."

44

MOLLY

My eyes feel like they're full of grit and dust. I couldn't eat or sleep after Noah left. I feel like a complete villain. A ridiculous one at that. Obviously, I hurt Nicholas, and I need to apologize. I still don't know exactly how I'm supposed to promise I'm not going to do it again, though. He says not calling him means I didn't put him first. But it's precisely *because* I put him first that I didn't call.

People have their needs. Things they want to get done. Me asking for help when I can manage on my own is an imposition. It's always been that way all through my life. Nothing upset Dad more than getting a call from school telling him to come get me because I wasn't feeling well. And it was the same for a lot of my previous boyfriends. They said the most attractive thing about me was that I was independent. Not clingy. Unless I'm bleeding out or have a broken bone, I'm not going to demand someone's time and attention.

Why doesn't Nicholas appreciate that?

Then I spent hours obsessing about who Stella is and whether Nicholas is staying with her. I texted Georgia, but she said she didn't know anybody named Stella in their social circle. Google, too, failed me. How can there be so many Stellas?

I wanted to text Nicholas, to ask him where he is. If he's with this

Stella person. But everything I came up with seemed clingy and pathetic. So I ended up sending just one: *I'm worried about you. Can you call me when you get a chance? We need to talk.*

He doesn't answer, and he's *never* ignored my texts. He always replies within an hour—at the most—and I've gotten used to him being responsive.

Since sleep is impossible, I get out of the bed and shower. I used to like the housekeeping service, but now I kind of resent it—fresh sheets don't smell like Nicholas. Although the laundry detergent is the same, without his arms around me at night, things feel alien and cold.

I make myself some extra-strong coffee and sip it. Nicholas told me to stay in his home as long as I wanted, but I should move out. It doesn't feel right to stay here when he's living elsewhere.

I bury my face in my free hand. Who am I kidding? My desire to move out has nothing to do with his being elsewhere. It's him with another woman. *Stella.* I don't think Noah dropped that particular name just for the hell of it. He wants me to know Nicholas can have any woman he wants.

I pick up my phone. A text notification—and my mood deflates when I see it's from Cody. He probably wants to know when I can get out of Nicholas's hair.

—Cody: You have an appointment with Jeremiah Huxley at Huxley & Webber at eleven today. If it's inconvenient for you, please let me know and I'll reschedule.

He must've gotten confused. I have no idea who Jeremiah Huxley is.

—Me: You sent the text to me, not Nicholas—or whoever you were trying to reach.

—Cody: No mistake. It's for you.

—Me: I don't know who Jeremiah Huxley is or why I should see him?

—Cody: She's a lawyer. And she'll take care of you.

Trepidation presses an icy kiss on the base of my neck. I'm not sure what Cody means by "take care of me." But it can't be anything good if Nicholas wants me to see an attorney.

—Me: What is this about?

—Cody: A possible lawsuit.

—Me: What lawsuit?

—Cody: Nicholas didn't say. Jeremiah will tell you.

An acidic knot tightens in my belly.

—Me: Where's Nicholas?

—Cody: I'm not at liberty to say.

—Me: Is he okay?

Is everything okay? Do you think things are going to be fine?

—Cody: I'm also not at liberty to say.

—Me: Is there anything you're at liberty to say?

—Cody: Your car has been repaired. It's been delivered to the mansion already, so you can drive it to Huxley & Webber. If that's inconvenient, I can have a driver pick you up instead.

His texts couldn't be dryer. Or more impersonal. Noah's judgmental attitude coms back to mind, and I tighten my grip on the phone. Does Cody feel the same way as Noah?

—Me: Are you upset with me?

—Cody: No. That isn't part of my job.

Ugh. I exhale with frustration. He sounds like an accidental love child between Skynet and ChatGPT.

—Cody: Do you have any instructions?

—Me: Can you let Nicholas know I'd like to speak to him?

—Cody: Yes. If that's all, have a good day.

I have another coffee. Nicholas doesn't text. Or call. Actually, I realize he hasn't even read my text. His phone might be dead. He didn't take his charger two days ago when he walked out.

Once he charges his phone, he'll respond.

I TAKE MY CAR, which now purrs like a happy cat, to Huxley & Webber. It's housed in a huge, swanky building with shiny chrome and glass. From the chandeliers to the sand-blasted logo on frosted glass walls to the gleaming elevators, everything screams courtroom success and victory.

The receptionist is in a crimson suit and smiles professionally when she sees me. I give her my name, and her smile grows wider. "Jeremiah's waiting for you." She shows me to a meeting room with an amazing view of the city.

I sit at the long, rectangular table and tap on it in random rhythm. It isn't a minute before the door opens and a tall, slim woman in spike heels walks inside. She's in a teal silk jumpsuit and a jacket, and three strings of pearls circle her throat.

"Jeremiah Huxley." She extends her well-manicured hand. "A pleasure."

I stand and shake her hand, stunned she is the Jeremiah.

"Please. Take a seat. Let's go over your case against Jack Peterson."

"My what?"

"Your case. Obviously you're going to sue." Her cool silver eyes glance at my bruised wrist, which is now turning an awful shade of purple. "Jack's doing?"

"Yes, but..."

"Good." She hits a button on the control in front of her. "Bebe, I need a camera to photograph evidence."

I give her a long look. I feel like I should bring it up, but delicately, so I don't offend her. I've been so preoccupied with Nicholas that suing Jack is the last thing on my mind right now. "You don't look like the type to do it, but...this sort of feels like ambulance chasing."

Jeremiah gives me a stunned look, then presses her lips together. But she can't contain the laughter. It comes out in a short snort, then she throws her head back and really lets go. "Oh dear... I haven't heard one that good in *ages*." She dabs at her eyes. "Ambulance chasing." She fans her face. "Just wait until I tell Catalina and Andreas. Nicholas, too." She tries to set her face into a semblance of sober attention, but fails as she laughs again. "I heard Nicholas fell for an unusual girl, but this is hilarious. You must've shredded his heart to ribbons. That poor child. It would've been funnier if you'd done it to *my* son, but..." She sniffs.

I have no idea what to say or how to correct her. Nicholas hasn't fallen for anybody as far as I can tell, unless she's referring to one of his exes. *Maybe it's Stella...?* And I don't have the power to shred his heart.

A cute, black-haired woman walks in with a huge camera. She looks at my wrist and gives me instructions as she snaps multiple photos from different angles.

"Do you have any other bruises or marks on you? On your torso or back? Thighs or...?"

"No! Just my wrist," I tell her quickly, before Jeremiah can order me to strip down. I don't think I can say no if she issues a command.

"Okay." Bebe walks out as abruptly as she entered.

"So." Jeremiah steeples her hands. "Tell me what happened. How long has Mr. Peterson been harassing you?"

"Before we talk about all that, shouldn't we discuss your fees? I don't think I can afford you."

"It's immaterial. Nicholas is footing the bill."

"Why?"

"Male pride, I suppose?" She shrugs. "He could theoretically go over to Get Jacked Gym and punch Peterson out, but that would be inadvisable. It'd be classified as assault, which is a criminal matter. Even if the DA decided to not pursue it, Peterson could go after him in a civil suit. Nicholas is a man of considerable assets, so it'd be a lawsuit worth pursuing. If Peterson were my client, I'd advise him to do so.

"Of course, Nicholas could taunt Peterson into throwing the first punch, but that's unlikely. Peterson has a reputation for keeping his tail tucked between his legs when he deals with people of strength."

I nod. I've never seen Jack try anything with the male trainers. As a matter of fact, he goes out of his way to get along with them.

"However, if you're uncomfortable, you don't have to pursue the matter. Nicholas arranged for this because he thought you might want some legal retribution against your former boss."

He didn't find out about what Jack did until two days ago...when he walked out. Does this mean he's calmed down? Or... "Does he really want me to sue?" I'm willing to do anything if it'll help him feel better.

"That wasn't my impression. He wants you to do what feels right to you. If you want to let it go, you can."

"Then nothing will happen to Jack."

"Insofar as a lawsuit is concerned, correct."

Petra told me Jack is gross with all the female employees, and he tries to make it up by paying them well. I've read articles about how generous he is as an employer. They contributed to my decision to apply to the gym.

If I'd known what he was really like, I wouldn't have taken a job there. Dad's voice in my head says I should just let it go, because what happened isn't important enough to make a fuss about, especially when it's going to cost so much. But there's another voice, a more authentic one, that doesn't want to shut up about it. Why should I be silent and let Jack get away with his behavior? What's wrong with making a fuss over what actually happened? If Arturo and Petra hadn't interrupted, I might've ended up with something a lot worse than a bruised wrist.

Besides, wouldn't this be a public service announcement? Nobody deserves to be treated the way I was at the gym.

"Do you think it'll become drawn out and ugly?" I ask.

"Possibly prolonged. Could be ugly, depending on what Jack decides to use as a defense. Most likely he'll say you came on to him first, or some other ridiculous excuse along those lines."

"I never did that!"

"Obviously. But it's my job to warn you and insulate you as much as possible from defamation of that nature. So. What would you like to do? If you want to think on it for a few days, that will be fine as well."

My hands shake with trepidation. I've never done anything like this before. Normally I'd pretend it wasn't that important—and tell myself I'm not worth the trouble.

But I don't want to do that anymore. I clench my hands and look Jeremiah squarely in the eye. "I don't need to think. Let's do it."

45

MOLLY

—Me: I saw Jeremiah. She's very nice. And I decided to go after Jack. Thank you. I wouldn't even have thought of taking legal action.

I wait six hours, but Nicholas doesn't respond.

Should I call? But will he answer if he doesn't even want to exchange texts?

Anxiety winds tighter until breathing is a struggle. I munch on a few Saltines, then have more coffee. I thought the place seemed really big and empty when I ate dinner alone during the first week I lived here. But now I feel like I'm being buried alive in a pharaoh's tomb.

So I send him another text.

—Me: I'm sorry about what happened.

I wince at how hollow that sounds. I'm still unsure exactly what I did wrong. And Nicholas is smart enough to realize that from the text.

The intercom beeps, and I rush over. I know it isn't Nicholas, but I feel hopeful that maybe it's flowers or something that hints at how he's doing—what he's feeling.

Georgia is at the gate. I open it, and a few minutes later, she comes inside.

"Hey, I brought some chocolate." She comes in carrying three bags full of gourmet chocolates. She hugs me, then holds me at arm's length and gives me a critical once-over. "You look awful. You hanging in there?"

"Yeah. Thanks."

"Sorry I couldn't come by yesterday. I had to wrap up a last-minute project for a longtime client."

"It's okay."

"Let's get something to drink with this. Nicholas has to have some decent liquor."

"We shouldn't."

"What?" She gives me a curious look. "Of course we should. That's why it's here."

She goes to the cabinet and pulls out a bottle of whiskey.

"That looks expensive," I say, uncomfortable with raiding his home for stuff when he isn't around—and we aren't together anymore.

She grins. "I know. He doesn't do cheap liquor. This goes down smooth. Hangovers feel different when it's the good stuff. Trust me." She isn't going to accept a refusal. We settle down in the living room with the chocolate and whiskey. "So he hasn't been back since he had his man-tantrum?"

"It wasn't a tantrum. He was just...unhappy with me." My texts to her were sort of incoherent. Actually, now that I think back on it, I don't think some of them were comprehensible English. I take a tentative sip of the whiskey. A few drops, and the tip of my tongue tingles.

"I see." She looks at me like she has a lot to say, including "I told you so," but she keeps it to herself. "Anyway, I asked Nikki about this 'Stella.'"

I tense.

"She said the only Stella she could think of was Stella Lloyd."

"Who's that?"

"Barron Sterling's girlfriend, apparently."

The name is vaguely familiar... Oh wait. I know. He's the mega-billionaire who's in his seventies or something. The man's ancient.

But given his wealth, he probably has a hot young girlfriend. Some supermodel. Does Nicholas have feelings for her? Is it some kind of unrequited love?

"But she's old," Georgia says.

"Some men like older women," I say glumly.

Georgia shakes her head. "Uh-uh. Like she-gets-the-senior-discount old."

Okay, maybe not *that* old. "So Nicholas wouldn't have any feeling for her?"

She almost spews the whiskey. She chokes, then gasps. "No!" She shoves a piece of chocolate into her mouth. "Not the kind of feelings he has for you! He's crazy about you."

My shoulders sag with a sad, reluctant laugh over how unrealistic and dramatic she's being. It's that or cry, and tears won't fix anything or soothe the pain in my heart. "Then why did he get so angry with me?"

"Tell me what happened. Your texts, uh, kind of didn't make a lot of sense." She makes a gimme motion with her fingers.

So I tell her everything, including my interaction with Noah, so she can get the full picture.

When I'm done, she sighs. Then shakes her head and sighs again. "Molly, I love you, but you really screwed up."

I've never thought I was a particularly stupid person, but I feel stupid now. "But *how*? How did I screw up?"

"Didn't you hear what I told you when I dropped you off? Or what Nicholas said?"

"I didn't need him for the ride because I had you."

"Argh! *No!* He *wanted* to give you that ride. It's his *job as your boyfriend.*"

"But he could've been in a meeting he couldn't cancel."

"Pfft. *Any* meeting can be cancelled. And no business thing is more important than you."

I have my doubts, But Georgia's giving me that stubborn look, so I'd better just go along. "Okay...?"

She studies my face, then shakes her head. "You really don't get it, do you?" She breathes in and out slowly. "Look, here's the deal. Your exes were pretty shitty, okay? Not exactly shining examples of men in love. They were also stupid as hell because they didn't realize you're a diamond of a girl. But listen. When you're in love with someone, you always want to let them know—*first*—when something happens. *Always*. It could be something good or it could be something bad. But you always want to celebrate with them first if it's good, or have them comfort you before anybody else if it's bad."

"Okay, well… If it's something good, fine. I mean, maybe. Depending. But I just don't feel comfortable *bothering* him. What if he gets tired of me imposing? Or gets annoyed because he can't, like, do something he wants to do because of me? Or there's an accident on the way?"

She squints. "An accident on the way?"

"Yeah, on the way to get me. One that he wouldn't have been in if I hadn't asked him for a ride."

Georgia shakes her head slowly. "Do you want to be the last one to know if something happened to Nicholas? Let's say…he got hit by a car."

I wince inwardly. Just the idea sends cold shivers into my gut despite the whiskey.

"Which, by the way, has nothing to do with you! People get hit by cars all the time. Or maybe he fell into a ditch because he wasn't paying attention. Accidents happen. But let's just say something happens to him."

"Okay."

"Everyone hears about it and helps him out. Like driving him to the hospital or buying him groceries or whatever. But he makes sure you don't find out about it because he doesn't want to *trouble you*. He thinks you have *better things to* do than care for him. Is that how you want your relationship to be?"

"No…" I blink as a realization dawns on me. I've never thought it was a bother when people I cared about asked me for help. As a matter of fact, I appreciated that they reached out, so I could be there for them.

I cut Nicholas out by prioritizing everything but his need to be there for me. And ever since I moved in here, he's been nothing but patient, affectionate and caring…

"He doesn't want you to call him *later*, Molly. He wants to be your first dial—*always*. Trust me, if he gets hit by a car, the first thing going through his mind is going to be you, and the last thing going through his mind is going to be you." She presses her hands against my cheeks and holds my head. "Now do you get it?"

"Yes." And I do.

"I think that's what Noah was trying to say, except he used a terrible example. Another woman." She shakes her head in disgust. "No wonder you were too distracted to see the point!"

"So I really messed up, but Nicholas won't even talk to me now. Or respond to my texts. It's like he wants to break up."

Georgia snorts. "No, he doesn't. If he wanted to break up with you, he would've told you to grab your stuff and get out. I don't know where he's staying, and I doubt Nikki does either. He has six brothers in the city, not to mention his friends. And if all else fails, he can just stay at a hotel."

"But I don't want him to stay away. Should I go to his office?"

"I wouldn't. Not until you're sure about what you want."

"I am. I want to apologize."

"That won't be enough, Molly. If that's all he wanted, he wouldn't have left." Georgia pats my shoulder, half sympathetic and half encouraging. "He's handed you ultimate control over your future." She gives me a significant look. "*And his.* So give it some serious thought before trying to see him."

46

MOLLY

THE NEXT WEEK passes in a blur. I have a few interviews with other companies and text Nicholas every night to ask him how he's doing. But he doesn't respond.

However, flowers, cupcakes and chocolates continue to arrive as usual. And short notes come with them, still in languages I don't understand.

The people taking care of his home continue to come and stock the fridge with food I like. The huge mansion gets cleaned. It's like nothing's really changed except for Nicholas's absence.

But it's that lack that leaves me bereft at night. I should've asked the housekeeping staff to leave the sheets in his bedroom alone, because now I don't have anything that smells like him. The things in his closet have been freshly laundered and smell of soap as well.

"Is there anything of his that you haven't cleaned yet?" I ask Carla. Steely-haired and no-nonsense, she's the most senior member of the crew that handles Nicholas's household matters.

"No," she says. "Nicholas likes to keep his home tidy."

Of course. It'd be nice if his people were less efficient, but I try not to be too disappointed. It isn't her fault.

Her expression softens. "Would you like to try some new coffee? I can stock the library with a sampler of specialty coffees."

Her kindness only depresses me further. She must've sensed something wrong between me and Nicholas, but she's still doing her best to perk me up. Someone else might blame me for upsetting her boss.

And the library... It's still as beautiful as before, but it's the most painful room in the mansion. I've been avoiding it since Nicholas walked out. He said *fuck reality*—we weren't supposed to settle for anything less than a happily ever after. I feel like I've ruined our happy ending.

Carla is waiting expectantly. "Thank you," I say. "But whatever Nicholas drinks is fine."

She gives me an odd look. "He doesn't."

"Doesn't what?"

"Doesn't drink coffee."

"What?" *Everybody drinks coffee.* And he always had it with me in the morning.

"He prefers Earl Grey. The tea. He only has a coffeemaker in the kitchen for when his brothers come over."

"What about the one in the library?"

"He bought it a few months ago, but I've never seen him use it."

My eyes prickle as I realize he must've bought it for me. Georgia doesn't hang out with Nicholas much, and he said he doesn't have people over. The romance novels—which he wouldn't normally read—occupy a huge section of the library and living room. The truck he bought to help me move out of Owen's place is sitting in the garage. I haven't seen him drive it again.

Nicholas has quietly done things that he knows are going to make me happy. The cost and effort are immaterial to him.

Cold shivers run through me, like a wintry wind. Sniffling, I take my phone and crawl into the bed where we spent hours entwined. I bury my face in the pillows, wishing I could smell something of him, but no. All that's tickling my nose is fabric softener.

I start typing my daily text to Nicholas.

—Me: How are you? I had another job interview. Now that I'm not at

315

Get Jacked anymore, more companies seem interested. Funny, isn't it? I thought I should have a job offer in hand before quitting.

I wait. The text remains unopened for an interminable ten count, then is finally opened. I pray for three dots to show...but they don't. I should've given up by now, but I just can't believe he can shut me out so easily. And how much it *hurts*.

He's done so much for me, catered to my needs so well. I've received affection in far greater measure than I deserve. Maybe subconsciously I knew that, which is why I kept pulling back. I was too afraid to settle in and seize the happiness. I was afraid that if I showed I wanted it, it would be snatched away—that something bad would happen.

But nothing prepared me for the icy pain of his withholding himself. If it hurts this much just to have him retreat, how much will it hurt if he dumps me like my exes? Or looks at me with disappointed judgment like my dad? Or worse, disappears from my life entirely, like Mom because she was trying to give me what I asked for?

I bury myself deeper under the sheets. Shame flows over me at the realization I didn't even know that he didn't like coffee. I know almost nothing about him—what he likes, what he wants. I was terrified of the possibility that when he realized what he wanted, he'd also realize that it wasn't me.

He told you what he wanted over and over again. You just didn't listen.

Nobody else is going to eat with you... The words he said after he'd won the dinner with me at the auction.

He defended me against Owen. Spared me any possible embarrassment at the auction and ensured that no one else would be able to have my company. Gave a ridiculous amount of money to a cause that I care about. Came to the shelter to see me even when he was allergic to animals. Then said I didn't have to do anything I didn't want to. He only wants me to do what makes me happy.

That, and open up to him. Tell him what I want.

But that means letting my shields down. Trusting that it's okay to ask for things—and that it won't necessarily end badly, like it did with Mom and the blueberries.

I didn't want to do any of that because it was too scary. I didn't think my actions would hurt him enough to have him walk away.

Intellectually I can understand that my being honest about what I want isn't necessarily selfish or destined to end badly. It's just...something holds me back. And if I'm one hundred percent frank, I did want to call Nicholas first—without feeling guilty or anxious—when Jack hurt me. I just didn't want to admit it because I thought that would make me selfish and wrong.

I turn over, then punch the pillow in frustration and fear. Nicholas isn't going to be happy with a mere apology. He wants more.

He wants my acceptance. He wants me to embrace what he's offering and let him in, not just physically but emotionally as well.

Except that's...

My hands tremble. I clutch a pillow, clenching my fingers, hoping they will stop quivering. But the tremor spreads all over.

If I continue on my current path, Nicholas and I are both going to be miserable. But I'm so afraid to change course. What if I end up hurting us even worse?

But what if you don't...?

Regardless, I can't live in his house, forcing him to stay elsewhere. I have decisions to make about myself—and him.

I stay up all night thinking about them. The next morning, I text Georgia.

—Me: Do you know where Nicholas is staying? Or can you find out? Cody won't tell me, but he might tell you.

—Georgia: I'll see what I can do.

A few minutes later, I have a response.

—Georgia: Cody won't tell me where he's staying, but he said Nicholas might be able to spare a bit of time after his lunch meeting at Nieve.

—Me: Okay. Thanks, girl.

I put my phone down and inhale deeply. I'm not sure exactly what I'm going to say when I see him, but I can't let both of us down without a fight.

47

NICHOLAS

Today is the one hundredth day since Molly and I started dating. Spending it in a meeting with Tara isn't how I envisioned it would go. But at least our conversation is pleasant.

A stunning Asian with flawless, milky skin and full red lips, the woman's as sharp as the crisp edge of her asymmetrically cut jet-black hair. She doesn't become emotional during negotiations. She's one of those rare people who truly believes it's just business, nothing personal —which makes her an ideal business partner. Perhaps she believes that because she generally gets the best of everyone in deals. Her preferred outfit is a red dress with matching stilettos, probably to hide the blood of whoever's across the negotiating table. Today is no exception.

"If they become much more of a pain, we should dump them," she says over a mimosa. "They don't have enough cash to make the next bond payment. Time to show them they're nothing to us."

"Do you suggest we take them back if they show enough remorse?" I ask, although my mind is on Molly. Some part of me wants her to be nothing without me so she'll be forced to come back. Except... That isn't her. I love her because she shines so bright and beautiful. I love her because of her warmth—like a campfire on a chilly night that draws me in.

"Remorse?" Tara laughs. "Let them default. We can grab the profitable pieces for pennies. Sucks to be them, but sometimes you have to be cruel to command respect."

I nod. That's what I would've suggested, too—business is business. And let them see what they threw away in their arrogance. My train of thought derails for a second. *Is that what I'm doing to Molly by staying away?* If so, I'm doing a shitty job. She has my house and my staff and is under my care. She has everything but me.

That might be the way she wants it, I think glumly.

"Something wrong? You look terribly unhappy." Tara signals our waiter for another mimosa.

"Just thinking about the acquisition."

"Uh-huh. You can't fool me. This acquisition isn't worth losing weight over. And you're too experienced and calm to care that much about a deal this small." She props her chin on her hand. "As a matter of fact, I've never seen you at the negotiating table without a dealbreaker. You're always ready to walk if you don't get what you want."

"I don't *always* get what I want." If I did, I wouldn't be living alone at the Aylster.

She sits back, frowns and gives me an uncharacteristic sideways look. "What's going on? Did Carla forget to restock your favorite tea?"

"No, nothing like that."

"Wait..." Tara blinks. Finally, her smug I'm-on-the-top-of-the-world veneer cracks. "Does this have something to do with the cute brunette you won at Elizabeth's auction?" She straightens before I can answer. "Oh my God, it does! Just look at your face!"

"Am I really that transparent?"

"You are with this girl. I was wondering because it isn't like you to be so impulsive, although in a lot of ways you're just like your mother."

"Are you calling me fickle?" Molly said the same thing about me and Mom.

"No. You both know what you want very clearly and go after it. It's just that what Nikki wants changes all the time. What you want doesn't."

I sit and consider her words. I've never heard that explanation before, not even from my own brothers. The waiter brings Tara her new mimosa. I swallow my whiskey.

"I should've known something was up when you ordered whiskey with your lunch," Tara says with an amused smile. "So. Who's more in love in your situation?"

Me. "I don't know."

"Relationships are like poker," she says in a low voice, like she's imparting a great secret. "Whoever loves more loses because they can't remain cool-headed. And whoever says the L-word first? Toast."

I cock an eyebrow. "Speaking from experience?"

"Of course. Derek has no clue if I love him." She sounds like we're discussing bond market movements in London.

"And he still proposed and married you?" I've met Tara's husband. He doesn't come across as the type to put up with that kind of uncertainty.

"Yes. Because he loves me." The smile on Tara's face is genuine. Even affectionate. But it's impossible to tell if she reciprocates his feelings.

It's similar to the one Molly often wears around me, except her green eyes are always bright with unspoken secrets. Like she's holding back words she's afraid will change everything between us.

"He told me so, too," Tara adds.

"Do you love him?"

She laughs. "I'm not telling."

"Fine. Are you happy? Or is that a secret, too?"

She laughs harder. "No. But if you're curious, I'm quite satisfied with my life."

"How about Derek?"

"He hasn't complained." She shrugs. "It's a good marriage."

I'd know if she was lying. She's always certain of what she's worth and what she deserves. If she weren't pleased with her marriage, she would've left Derek, no matter what he told her.

It's tempting to give in and go back to Molly. Even as my heart hurts, I can point to Tara and her husband and console myself that if they're happy enough, surely Molly and I could be too. But part of me hates settling for "satisfied" and "hasn't complained."

It's tempting to throw away my pride and go back to her. Being away from Molly is even more painful than I imagined. It's like every hour without her slices away another piece of my soul. I'm also anxious and dreading the possibility that she might never love me back—and find herself another boyfriend.

But how long would the satisfaction last?

I want to be her number one. I want to monopolize her attention, affection and thoughts, just like she's monopolized mine. I can't settle for less. I won't be able to bear it if she doesn't love me enough to say the L-word. I don't want her to think like Tara—to look at our relationship as some kind of high-stakes poker game.

"I need to get going," Tara says, swallowing the last of her mimosa. "Otherwise I'll miss my flight." She gathers her purse and stands. Wrapping an arm around me, she presses a quick kiss to my cheek and then pats me on the back. "Good luck with the brunette. And if she doesn't respect you enough to want you, dump her. I'll introduce you to some of my single friends. They're *hot*."

I laugh. Tara can be a good friend when she's in the mood. "Thanks."

She wiggles her fingers in a little wave and walks off. I sign the bill, then head out for my afternoon meetings.

I step into the lobby and start across the vast stretch of spotless marble under the glittering chandeliers. A hot prickling of the skin in the back of my neck makes me slow down and scan the area.

My eyes collide with Molly's. She stands with her arms crossed, her face wan and dark circles under her eyes. Her hair's pulled into a topknot, revealing the scrumptious line of her neck and shoulders. The memory of how her breathing grew shallow when I rained kisses there rips through me.

She uncrosses her arms and starts toward me. She's in a pretty green dress that brings out her eyes and flatters her lush curves, and her feet are in the same hot stilettos she wore to the auction. Given she chooses her clothes more for comfort than looks, they're unusual choices. If I didn't know better, I'd think she dressed for me.

But why would she? A bitterness not even whiskey could burn off lingers in the back of my mouth. She couldn't have made it clearer where I rank in her world.

Tara's parting advice rings in my head, at war with my instinctive desire to run to Molly and hold her tight, swipe my thumbs over her pale cheeks and kiss her until she clings to me mindlessly.

Then I recall the state of Tara's marriage. I'd rather die than have that between me and Molly.

My legs feel like they're made of lead. I force myself to turn and drag myself toward the exit.

"Nicholas," Molly croaks. She clears her throat. "Wait." Her voice is firmer and steadier.

I stop instantly, like every cell in my body has been just dying for a reason to talk to her. "What are you doing here?"

Say you're here for me.

Uncertainty skitters over her beautiful face. "I want to talk to you."

"Okay. Speak." I check my watch, to hide my reaction to her nearness. To disguise my disappointment that she's still unsure about me—about us. "I have a couple of minutes before I need to leave for my next meeting."

48

MOLLY

I had my thoughts organized. I wrote out what I was going to say on a piece of paper and reviewed it in the car on the way to the hotel. But when Nicholas looks bored and can barely glance at me, my courage crumbles.

He taps his watch, and the corners of his lips turn down. Am I bothering him? Is the gorgeous Asian woman who kissed him and left the one he's interested in now? He laughed at something she said. She's more his type than I could ever be.

The possibility that I could have been replaced slams into my head like a wrecking ball, and the notes I memorized vanish from my mind. All I can think is that he was with *another woman*, and maybe I was never that special.

Nicholas drops his wrist and straightens. He's going to walk away.

"Who was she?" I blurt out.

He tilts his head, looking vaguely confused. "Who?"

"The woman who was having lunch with you." I cringe inwardly at how jealous I sound. The plan was to talk to him about how I feel and explain myself to him, not sound like a girl accusing her boyfriend of cheating.

"She's a business partner." His tone is cool and dismissive. It says I have no right to feel anything about what happened. "If that's all you have to say—"

"Do all your business partners kiss you like that?" I feel sick to my stomach. I need to know what I am to him—if anything's changed since the day he walked away—before I can decide exactly what I'm going to tell him next. There's no point in baring my soul if he doesn't care about me.

"Why not?" Bitterness crackles under his otherwise smooth tone. "I'm available."

The last two words are a punch in the gut. It's actually an effort to remain upright. I feel an overwhelming, self-preservational urge to flee before he says anything more to shred me. And normally that's exactly what I'd do, but then...

Pain flashes in his eyes. And somehow I can't just leave. Why does he look like *he's* the one who's getting his heart ripped out when he's saying things designed to make me bleed? "Are you doing this on purpose? Is this some kind of revenge because you're mad at me?"

He looks at me as though I just backhanded him. "Revenge? Don't be absurd. If I wanted revenge, this is what I would've done to her, while making sure you were watching."

He cups my face with his large hands, holding me so I can't pull away. His mouth fuses with mine, and we kiss. My lips part at the heady feel of him. His tongue invades my mouth, stroking me. I place my hands over his shoulders and rise on my toes to fuse my lips better with his. And he plunders me like he's taking me with his mouth. Shivers run through me. Tears spring to my eyes as air shudders in my chest. This feels like a homecoming. I can't believe we've been apart for over a week.

Suddenly, he pulls away, still cradling my face. He looks at me, his blazing eyes intense. "What's wrong? Why the tears?"

"It's just a little bit around my eyes." I dab at them, surprised he noticed. But then he notices so much about me. The tears aren't even running down my cheeks, but he's acting like I'm sobbing in unbearable pain, and he's at a loss as to how to make it better for me.

"I'm so sorry," I say shakily. "I don't know how to be the kind of girlfriend you need. You keep showing me I'm important to you, but I can't stop wondering what will happen if you change your mind about me—about us."

He regards me for a long moment. "Despite what you said before, I'm nothing like my mother."

"Of course you are. You're both so interesting and beautiful."

He gives me a hard look. Except he seems more relieved than disappointed. I don't understand why he's reacting this way, and suddenly, I'm uncertain.

"I'm scared that when I think you love me is when our relationship ends." The words tumble out in a trembling torrent. "My relationships always end just when I think they're going somewhere. And then, if you know how much I love you, you might jerk back, like I just threw a snake at you or something, because that isn't what you want. I was so happy being with you, in your house, living together and sharing—I don't want to rock anything." I can barely hold his eyes. "I'm so *afraid*, Nicholas."

Hot elation blazes in the gray depths of his gaze, but I don't know what part of my disorganized rambling could've put that look on his face.

"Say that again." When I blink up at him, unsure if I can repeat all of it, he clarifies, "The part about 'you love me.'"

I nod shakily. "Yes. I love you. I'm sorry; I didn't want to say it like this. Or too soon. I just—"

"Too soon?" He laughs. "I waited eight years. I fell in love when I met you. And that hasn't changed for even one day in all that time."

I stare at him as my brain tries to process what he just said. Slowly, as the meaning sinks in, my heart skips a beat. Exhilaration flows in my veins, and I feel like I could fly to the moon.

He wipes away the tears that now are running down my cheeks and rests his forehead on mine. "I'm still here. I'll always be here. And before you bring her up again, Tara—my business partner—is married. Satisfactorily so." He takes my hand, threading and linking our fingers. "Let's go home."

"What about your meetings?" I ask breathlessly as we dash across the lobby like a couple of teens on their way to do something naughty.

"They can wait. You're more important."

ALL THROUGH THE DRIVE, his hand is linked to mine. I squeeze like I'll never let go, although I manage to text Cody to let him know Nicholas might not be available for his meetings.

–Cody: Thanks for letting me know. I'll adjust his schedule accordingly.

"What are you doing?" Nicholas asks.

"Telling Cody you might not come in for your meetings." I glance at the gorgeous profile of his face—and the huge tent below his belt. I wish I could touch him, show him how much I miss him.

He follows my gaze. I don't look away. I don't want to hide how much I want him.

"I wish we could do something about that right now," I whisper.

"After we're home. I won't be able to drive if you touch me. Just being in the same car is making it difficult for me to concentrate on the road."

Nicholas violates more traffic rules than I can keep count of. I'm shocked, since he's generally a safe driver. But I'm also too impatient to care as long as we make it home safely.

The car finally screeches to a stop, and we hop out. I wrap my arms and legs around him as he grabs me and devours my mouth like a man who's been denied sustenance for far too long. He tastes like love and the beautiful future I dared not dream of, and my heart swells with longing.

The door crashes open behind me, and he carries me inside the cool foyer. Carla lets out a small yelp from the kitchen, and I pull back in surprise. But her footsteps fade away as she leaves.

Nicholas rests his forehead on mine and whispers something. It takes me a moment to realize in my dazed state that I can't process what he just said.

"What was that?" I whisper.

"That's what's on the first note I gave you," he explains with a smile. "I told you I'd tell you what they meant on the hundredth day we'd been together. And today's the day."

He's been counting all this time, even when we were apart. His love never wavered. Every time I think I can't love him more than I do, he does something to prove that oh yes, I *can*.

"What does it mean?" I ask shakily.

"I love you." He holds my gaze in his, adoration in his eyes. "The notes said, 'I love you,' in a hundred different languages."

Tears of joy and elation spring to my eyes. I can't believe he's been telling me every day already. I should've trusted the intent behind his gestures from the very beginning—to ensure I understood that I matter to him. Then we wouldn't have had to go through this pain, separated from each other for the last several days.

He brushes his lips against the corners of my teary eyes, my forehead, my cheeks, and between each pressing of lips, he whispers, "I love you," in yet another language. And I realize he has all the "I love you"s *memorized*, just for me.

Love and hope fill my fluttering heart. I cradle his gorgeous face and kiss him.

He was right when he said *fuck realistic*. I was holding my happily ever after back then, and I'm lucky to be holding him now.

"Make love to me," I say softly.

"Anything you want. It's yours." Then he carries me to our bedroom for our happy ending.

49

MOLLY

I PACE THROUGH THE KITCHEN, then into the living room. I should probably sit down or check on the food like a good hostess, but I can't concentrate. Calm is the last thing I'm feeling.

"Oh my *God*, I'm so nervous." I wipe my clammy hands on my dress, then cringe and look down. No wet spots on my thighs. Yay.

"Relax. It's fine." Nicholas comes over and puts his hands on my shoulders, stopping me from pacing some more. "It's just a casual dinner with some people. No big deal."

He tries to kiss me, but I put a hand over his mouth. "No. You're going to mess up my lipstick."

His eyes twinkling, he kisses the side of my neck.

I laugh breathlessly. "Stop distracting me."

"It's working, though. Now you aren't worrying yourself sick."

"I want your family to *like* me." I'm meeting Nicholas's brothers and sisters-in-law for the first time. Well, I've already met Lucie, who is absolutely charming in a slightly dominating way. You can't ignore the force of her personality or sheer physical presence. She towers over many men and make them shrink before her. The encounter with Noah was less than ideal, but I decide I'm not going to count that. He was angry and disapproving. Hopefully he won't be today.

"It's just a lousy dinner. If they do anything to upset you, we'll kick them out and enjoy all the roast beef. Yum yum. Mmm. Roast beef. Just the two of us." Nicholas runs his mouth along my neck.

I reach back and thread my fingers through his hair, appreciating his attempt to get me to stop thinking about all the things that can go wrong. Intellectually, I understand there's nothing wrong with the food —Carla took care of that—and that Nicholas's family is probably going to be polite, if for no other reason than because they like him. But I also want them to like *me*. I want to be able to fit in.

The door opens, and I pull back from Nicholas so I can say hello to the first of his family to arrive. It's a tall, handsome man with a warm smile that puts me at ease. He's holding a tiny girl, who looks like a little doll, in one arm, and has the other one around a pretty blonde.

"Emmett! And you brought Monique!"

"Of course," he says to Nicholas, who takes the girl and kisses her.

She giggles, then runs her little fingers along Nicholas's cheeks and nose.

"This is my brother, Emmett," Nicholas says. "And his wife, Amy. And this little angel is Monique."

We shake hands. "We're so happy to finally meet you," Amy says. "We would've found a way to do this earlier if we'd just been able to find a good time."

"Blame Grant," Emmett grouses. "He's the one giving you extra work."

The door opens again. "Somebody talking about me?"

"Speak of the devil..." Emmett mutters with a slow smile.

Nicholas's brothers are punctual and all arrive within a few minutes. Although Nicholas's place is huge, they seem to fill it up with their larger-than-life presence.

Despite my worries, Noah doesn't do anything to indicate he's still upset with me. But he also hasn't made a friendly overture like Nicholas's other brothers. He just gives me a vaguely perturbed look before turning away.

We move to the dining room, where the food is laid out. Four of the brothers are married, and two have babies. In addition to Emmett and Amy's little girl, Griffin and Sierra have triplets—Ellen, Ben and Jon—

and they're simply adorable. The little ones are passed around to be fussed and adored. I smile as I watch the scene unfold. This just feels so...unreal. I've only seen family interactions like this in movies or on TV. I never knew they could actually happen in real life—much less that I'd be part of it. The realization is poignant and gratifying.

"You need to tell your mom to stop showing the triplets to my mom," Nicholas says, loudly bussing the triplets and making them squeal delightedly. He's obviously great with babies, and I swear, I'm ovulating at the sight of him dealing with his nieces and nephews.

"Is that why Nikki wants you to give her a baby?" I ask.

"Probably," Sierra says with a small laugh. "She sees it, she wants it. She's *great* for business."

Nicholas winces and holds up a hand to stop further talk. "Please. I really just..." He trails off.

I look at him. Nicholas is *never* at a loss for words.

Sierra leans closer with a wicked grin. "I manage a sex toy company."

"She doesn't just manage it. She's the CEO," Aspen says. She's a beautiful redhead who's married to Grant and has the casual grace of a dancer.

"Anyway, stop showing her baby pics," Nicholas says, recovering. "Then she'll leave us alone."

"Ooh, I have just the thing. *Puppy* pictures!" Lucie says. "But is she going to get one and then change her mind about having a pet?"

"Nah, she'll hire somebody to take care of them. That's what she does when she gets pets," Nicholas says. "And a puppy would be perfect. I can see Mom going for that instead."

"Somebody pass me the bread," Noah announces. "I'm starving."

"You mean you haven't had anything in the last two hours." Huxley is an ad executive. A little intense, but he seems nice enough. At least, he's been kind to me so far.

"You're unnatural, which is why you don't need carbs. Probably because you feed on the blood of the innocent. I can't believe you aren't a lawyer."

Huxley snorts. "Neither can my grandmother."

Grant passes Noah the bread basket, and Noah gorges on two huge rolls after slathering them with room-temperature butter.

"I have no idea where you store all that," Lucie says in awe.

"Just burns off. Mad metabolism." He winks. "And lots of energy for when it comes time to love the ladies." He points both index fingers down at his lap. "The D needs its fuel."

"Do that in front of Bobbi," Griffin says. "I'd like to know how much supercharged D she's been getting."

Nicholas leans over and says, "Bobbi's a baker. Specializes in croissants and Noah has a thing for her."

"Really? I love croissants." I turn to Noah. "Not that I have a thing for Bobbi." I wait for his reaction. I'm not sure if he's trying to avoid me or can't decide if he should accept me or not.

"Better not. You have Nicholas." He gives me a quick wink, and I smile at him, relieved.

He thinks "the D" is what makes ladies happy, but what he doesn't seem to realize is that it's more oral action that can make women swoon. I didn't know how much I loved it until I met Nicholas. But then, it's difficult not to adore the act when he licks you like he can't get enough—that he's going crazy for the taste of you.

I serve myself some beef. "Lickolas, can you pass me the potato salad?"

Everyone goes still. Slowly, heads swivel in my direction. The wives are looking amused while the brothers are just...speechless. The silence is suffocating. Even Nicholas is staring at me oddly.

"What?" Is there some secondary meaning of potato salad I don't know about?

"You called him Lickolas," Sierra says finally.

"Huh?" I let out a no-way laugh. "I did not."

"You did. We all heard you," Griffin says. He doesn't strike me as the type to joke about something like this.

I turn to Nicholas, hoping he can rescue me. But he shrugs and nods.

Oh no. I bury my undoubtedly flaming face in my hands. *I was thinking about oral action earlier...*

Your mom would've never made this kind of mistake, a voice that sounds just like Dad thunders in my head. *Now what will they think? You're such an embarrassment.*

I shrink a little. I wanted so much to make a good impression, but now...all ruined. I bite my lip, my appetite gone.

"Well, don't keep us in suspense," Lucie says, her voice warm and titillated.

"Yeah," says Amy. She grins. "Do tell us how you came up with that particular nickname."

I jerk my head up. *What?*

"I want to know *exactly* what he does to get a nickname—or should I say *lick*name—like that," Sierra says. "I've been looking for new product ideas, and I can literally see the whole packaging." She sweeps an arm in front of her, painting a vista. "Nicholas...Lick-a-Lass!"

"Get a couple of spoons and show us," Amy says, teasing sparks in her eyes.

Huxley frowns. "A couple of spoons...?"

"If you put two together," Sierra says, "they sort of have the right size and shape."

"You ladies think he's got something because you've never seen me do it," Noah says. "Behold the *true* Lick-a-Lass action!" He raises two spoons.

"Hey, that's *my* spoon!" Sebastian says, plucking one out of Noah's grasp.

The men start to get loud and rowdy. Undeterred, Noah slowly licks his single spoon. "What do you think, Molly? Better than Nicholas?"

Nicholas scoffs. "You're an amateur!"

I laugh. "I'm not getting roped into judging something like this."

Noah turns to Sierra. "She's too overcome to say. I demand to be the model for Lick-a-Lass! Which, by the way, should have a different name to fit me better."

"Like...?" Sierra says.

"Hey, get your marketing team on it," Noah says. "Do I have to do everything?"

"The only thing that rhymes with Noah is *boa*. I don't think that's the image you're going for here," says Emmett.

Griffin looks up at the ceiling. "There's *protozoa*..."

"Ugh. No," Sierra says.

"*Lower* sort of rhymes, if you say it with a Southern accent. Like *lowah*," says Amy. "And *slowah*."

She and Lucie exchange a look, and Lucie nods. "Those could work."

As Nicholas's family has fun with my slip of the tongue, the awful voice in my head recedes. *It wasn't a big deal. I don't have to be perfect and proper to be included.*

Nicholas squeezes my hand. "See? Told you they'd love you."

He did. And he's giving me more than just himself by loving me. He's giving me a family I can belong to—people who'll always have my back.

My eyes prickle with happy tears. I don't know what I did to deserve him, but somewhere I must've done something right. "Marry me," I whisper.

Nicholas goes absolutely still.

"I know this isn't the most romantic place or moment, but I love you so much." Now the whole table has gone quiet. "And I can't believe all the love and acceptance here and... I just really, *really* want you to be mine." I take his hand. "I'll get you a ring later," I add in a tremulous voice.

Everyone holds their breath. Nicholas kisses me hard. "I was yours since the day I met you." Something warm slides along my finger. "I've been carrying this for a while now."

I look down. A huge solitaire winks in the light. I cover my mouth, then hug him as hard as I can.

"Welcome to the family!" someone shouts, and everyone starts clapping.

Life simply cannot get better than this.

50

MOLLY

THE HEADY AROMA OF FLOUR, sugar, lemon zest and bubbling fruit fills the kitchen. According to Cody's text, Nicholas should be getting home soon.

I feel like I'm on the top of the world. I have the most wonderful fiancé, and I received three job offers and accepted one from LocalGro earlier this week. The train of my life is finally on the right track.

My phone pings again, and I start to reach for it, pausing for a moment to admire the ring Nicholas gave me last weekend. It's the most beautiful thing ever—a symbol of our commitment.

I blink and turn my attention to the phone. *Dad.*

Dread starts to unfurl. I hesitate, then pick up the phone.

–Dad: Is it really true you're engaged?

–Me: How did you know?

I never bothered to tell him. He's the last person I wanted to get in touch with.

–Dad: I saw the announcement. It isn't April Fool's Day, so I had to check.

–Me: I guess Nicholas sent one out.

Three seconds later, the phone rings.

"Hello?"

"So this isn't a prank?" Dad says. "He actually wants to marry you?"

Does he have to sound so incredulous? Some old doubts stir, but the great time I had with Nicholas and his family fleets through my mind. The warmth, love and acceptance I felt...

Suddenly, my doubts dissipate. Dad's words don't hurt like they used to anymore.

"Yes," I say. "Somebody out there decided I'm worthy after all."

"Huh. Well, that's surprising."

"I'm sure it is to you. By the way, you know how you're always saying I don't measure up to Mom?"

"I wouldn't use those words. I just think that you could try a little harder to—"

"Yeah, yeah, yeah, fine. I just want you to think about something. Whatever has prevented me from being like Mom comes one hundred percent *from you*. Might want to think about that. Oh, and you aren't invited to the wedding."

"Not invited? You can't do that. I'm your father!"

Does he honestly think I want him to walk me down the aisle and give me away? When I know he doesn't really wish me the best? Or love me the way a father should love his child?

"No. You were my sperm donor. You've never been my father, not the way it truly matters. I know what *family* really means now. Please don't contact me again."

"Molly! What's gotten into you? Do you think you can talk to me like this just because you got yourself a rich boyfriend? Let me tell—"

I hang up and block his number, upset that he can't respect me and sad that I let him hold so much power over me for so long. Somehow, feeling guilty about Mom's death twisted into thinking I owed him something.

So many years wasted.

Well, no more. I'm done letting him damage me, especially when it has the potential to hurt others who love me as well. I don't ever want to put myself or Nicholas through anything like the horrible time apart we had. And when I looked at the comments people left on my Instagram post about what a *happily ever after* means, one of the answers really spoke to me.

Happily ever after is believing in your love for each other and working through the problems you'll face together. This is so you can stay together no matter what because you complete each other.

And that means I need to fully recognize—in fact, *embrace*—the idea that a life with Nicholas is what I want, and not let somebody like Dad shake that belief.

The door opens, and I turn around. Nicholas walks in with a broad grin. "How was your day?"

"Fabulous!" Then I remember the unpleasant exchange with Dad. Normally, I'd hold back, but I'm not hiding anymore. "Well, except for one thing. Dad called, and I told him he wasn't invited to our wedding. You don't mind, do you?"

He pours himself a glass of red. He offers me some, but I shake my head and take a seat next to him at the kitchen counter. "Not even a little. I don't plan to invite mine, either."

"How come?" Ted doesn't seem that terrible.

"Because I want our wedding to be about our future, not his ego."

I don't know much about Ted, but if Nicholas feels this way, I trust that he has good reason. "How about your mother?"

"She can come...now that she's given up on the whole baby thing."

"She has? Is she going to get a puppy instead?"

"No, but I told her *I'd* be getting something if she brought it up again."

"Like what?"

"A vasectomy."

I gasp. "Oh my God... Are you going to? For real?"

He laughs. "Of course not. But it should get her to stop asking. My family kind of has a history with vasectomies."

"It does?" That sounds sort of dire. "Do I even want to know about it?"

"I'll tell you sometime. But listen, I don't want you to feel pressured by Mom or anyone else. It's ridiculous. You have to tell me if she asks."

"I will. But you know what? It doesn't matter who gets invited to our wedding or if we get asked about baby plans, so long as we're happy." I hug Nicholas, then close my eyes and bury my face in that perfect spot between his shoulder and chest. "How was *your* day?"

"Most excellent. So what are you baking?"

"It's a secret." I grin, biting my lip.

He frowns. "It's not cookies..."

"Definitely not."

"Cobbler?"

"Closer." I lay a hand on his cheek. "It'll be worth the wait. I promise."

There's a buzzing from Nicholas's pocket, and he pulls out his phone and frowns.

"Something urgent form work?"

"No. A text from Noah." He turns the phone so we can both see.

–Noah: Check this out! Nicholas, show it to Molly, too!

He attached a video. Nicholas clicks on it, and it shows the sidewalk outside of Get Jacked Gym. A few female voices are screaming profanities.

Suddenly, the door opens and Jack comes out. More cuss words.

"You fucker, I hope you get what's coming to you!" a woman yells.

"Creep!"

"Hey, watch it!" Jack shouts back, his face red.

"*You* watch *this*!"

A white object flies into his face and erupts into a spectacular explosion of yellow and clear liquid. I cover my mouth with my hand. "Did somebody just throw an *egg* at him?"

Nicholas squints, and his lips curve into a satisfied smile. "Looks like it."

"I'm calling 911!" Jack yells.

"Do it, asshole! I'll tell them how you grabbed my ass when I was working for you!"

"Pervert!"

These must be the former employees who left in disgust after Jack's grotesque behavior. I never heard of this kind of incident happening at the gym, but maybe these women feel emboldened now that I filed a lawsuit against him.

"Guess they decided to confront him, since they realized there are others who got the same treatment," Nicholas says. "It'll be impossible for him to get away with anything now. Not when there are probably dozens of other women who can come out to discuss his sexual harassment. Hope he enjoys his jail cell." His phone buzzes again.

—Grant: I wish I'd known. I would've shown up with a truckload of eggs!

I grin. Nicholas's family's support is as unconditional and automatic as the sun rising in the morning, and I'm so grateful for it. I turn to him. "Do you think there's something we can do to help those women?"

"You mean like help them sue?"

I nod. "They probably want justice—like me—but maybe they can't afford lawyers good enough to go after Jack."

"I'll speak with Jeremiah and see," he says without hesitation. His generosity is always touching. It's just the way he is, but I don't think I'll ever get used to just how magnanimous he can be.

"Thank you."

The oven timer dings. I get up and open the oven, a blast of heat hitting me in the face. I pull the pan out with one mittened hand and place it on the kitchen counter, then pour carefully washed and dried blueberries on top of the bubbling purplish goo.

"What is that?" Nicholas comes over, then looks at me in alarm. "Are you okay?"

"Perfectly fine. Don't worry."

"But...aren't you allergic to blueberries?"

I shake my head. "I'm not allergic."

"What?" His eyebrows pinch in confusion.

"Blueberries used to be my favorite fruit, but..." I take a moment to order my thoughts. I don't want him to pity me or feel bad. "When I was six, I really wanted some blueberries, so I begged Mom to get some for me. And she died in a car accident on her way back from the store."

"Oh, no..." He runs a gentle hand along my back, soothing me.

I squeeze his arm to let him know I appreciate his sympathy. "After that, I wasn't able to look at them without thinking of her and feeling guilty, like somehow what happened was my fault. But I didn't want to tell people, so I just made up an allergy."

"I'm so sorry." He hugs me. "We don't have to have blueberries if they bother you."

I smile at his understanding. "Thanks, but they don't anymore. I went to the store today, and I saw this lady and her daughter shopping together in front of the blueberry section, and I was okay. And when I heard her joking and laughing with her girl, I suddenly realized that Mom wouldn't have wanted me to wallow in guilt. She would've wanted me to be happy." I blink away the slight prickling in my eyes. "And I wouldn't have been able to without your love and support, Nicholas. You've shown me it's okay to be happy. As a matter of fact, I deserve to be."

He kisses me on the forehead. "You are the most amazing person I know."

"And you're my miracle." I lean into him, reveling in the knowledge that he'll always lend me his strength. "I haven't had blueberries since I was six. Want to share some of this tart with me?"

"Of course."

He pulls out a plate and a couple of forks, and I put a large slice on the beautiful porcelain.

Then we sit at the counter, and I share the blueberry tart with the most miraculous love of my life, my heart full of certainty that our future is going to be brighter than the stars.

TITLES BY NADIA LEE

ABOUT NADIA LEE

New York Times and *USA Today* bestselling author Nadia Lee writes sexy contemporary romance. Born with a love for excellent food, travel and adventure, she has lived in four different countries, kissed stingrays, been bitten by a shark, fed an elephant and petted tigers.

Currently, she shares a condo overlooking a small river and sakura trees in Japan with her husband and son. When she's not writing, she can be found reading books by her favorite authors or planning another trip.

To learn more about Nadia and her projects, please visit http://www.nadialee.net. To receive updates about upcoming works, sneak peeks and bonus epilogues featuring some of your favorite couples from Nadia, please visit http://www.nadialee.net/vip to join her VIP List.

Made in the USA
Monee, IL
17 February 2024

53654497R10204